THE
WERE ON THEIR TRAIL

Two Birds came into view a few feet apart, rifles poised. Varlik watched them in his monitor, zooming the camera until he could see, besides lean limbs and loincloths, the pouches on their belts and harnesses, the bolos at their hips. A dozen feet behind the first two, two more appeared. Bin fired a long burst, and Varlik saw all four fall. Instantly Bin shoved back from the edge, rose to a crouch, and led him off again in a run, angling up the ridge in the direction of their first encounter.

"Are there more of them?" Varlik asked. He prayed there weren't; he could hardly hope to run much longer.

JOHN DALMAS

THE REGIMENT

BAEN BOOKS

THE REGIMENT

Copyright © 1987 by John Dalmas

A Baen Books Original

Baen Publishing Enterprises
260 Fifth Avenue
New York, N.Y. 10001

First Printing, March 1987
Second Printing, November 1987
Third Printing, May 1989

ISBN: 0-671-69849-4

Cover art by David Mattingly

Printed in the United States of America

Distributed by
SIMON & SCHUSTER
1230 Avenue of the Americas
New York, N.Y. 10020

To Gail,

wife,
coparent,
best friend

Prologue

. . . . So the woman Ka-Shok, who would become mother of the T'sel, sat in the shade of a fish-hook bush, looking out through the heat shimmers across the gravel pan where the only midday movement was a drill bird flying from thorn jug to thorn jug, to listen and peep, peck and swallow. And Ka-Shok wondered what the truth was of our origins. For to her, the old stories of gods and demons seemed unreal in the world of heat and drought, of hard labor beneath the stars, of bore-worms in the root crops.

It occurred to her then that one should be able to look at a place and see what had been there in its past, seeing things the way they had been instead of the way they were at present. If one knew how. It also seemed to her that she did know how, if she could only do it right.

Now to do something, one must first start. And she decided to start by closing her eyes to what was there at that time; perhaps then she could see the long before. So she closed them, but before long went to sleep and saw only dreams until a scorpion stung her.

That was but her first attempt, for its failure, and the

1

failures that followed, did not discourage her. Before the season of rains came two more times, she had begun to see the past; and not only the past of where she was, but the pasts of other places. And of living people—things that had happened to them before that lifetime, which she had not expected. And she spoke of these things to her husband, who thereupon beat her and called her crazy, and to her daughters and son who, in fear, began to keep her grandchildren away from her.

But she continued looking, seeing more and more, further and further back, only saying no more about it. And it was as if this activity, though pursued in silence, was like a signal fire in the night, attracting seekers. For a certain few people, both old and young, some of them strangers, sought her out, confiding in her their dreams and wonderings, seeking her advice. Until at length, she and some of those few went away, west into the Jubat Hills, where they lived on the sparse catch of snares and fish traps and the roots of certain plants, and together they sought back in time, with her as their guide.

Mostly they kept apart from any others. But this one and that would return to their homes from time to time. And when anyone asked them what they had been doing, they answered simply that they had been praying in the hills with an old woman. For what they had seen seemed at the time too strange to tell others, who might beat them for it or drive them away.

Nonetheless, bit by bit, others, not knowing why they did so, decided to go and pray with Ka-Shok, who by then had begun to be wizened and gray-headed. And they became too many to be fed from snares and fish traps. So one who owned land and water rights took Ka-Shok and the others home with him, to the dismay of his son there, and they dug many cells into a hill, that each could have his or her own. And this man declared rules of conduct, and rules of duties, that so far as possible they might continue to seek without the distractions of misconduct, for they did not yet know T'sel.

And not only did they see more and more of what had been in the past, but they began to glimpse behind the Here, and behind the There. And before Ka-Shok departed the ancient husk her body had become, more and more seekers had come to her, until the community moved again, occupying an entire valley and building irrigation works greater than had been seen before on Tyss.

For they had seen marvels in their past, not only of vessels going among the stars, but of the place they had come from. And from the seeing, learned much.

And of even greater import, they had begun to perceive the T'sel.

—From *A Child's First Book of T'sel*, by Brother Banh Dys-T'saben.

PART ONE

Introduction To Enigma

One

Feature Editor Gard Fendel's index finger, stout and hairy, touched *refile*, and the personnel summary for Varlik 681 Lormagen disappeared from the screen. Not that Fendel didn't know the young man personally and professionally, but it had seemed wise to examine the background data.

Lormagen had been in athletics as a boy and youth, and ran and used a health club as assignments permitted. At age thirty he looked physically rather fit. More important, and Fendel hadn't known this, he'd served a three-year enlistment in the military a decade earlier. No combat, but he'd know his way around. The question left was how much stomach young Lormagen had for discomfort and possible danger.

Fendel's finger moved to his intercom. "Derin," he said, "send Lormagen in."

"Yes, sir."

The voice quality of the intercom system was excellent. The slightly metallic timbre had been designed in deliberately, for warships and privateers. It enabled a crewman or officer, intent on something else, to know without looking that the speaker was not someone in the same compartment, and should be acknowledged at once if possible. It also made the words sharper and clearer, helping to ensure they'd be understood.

That had been very long ago, very long forgotten. Now an intercom was just an intercom, made the way intercoms had always been made. They worked very well.

Varlik 681 Lormagen came in, the door sliding smoothly shut behind him. Gard Fendel motioned him to a chair.

"Sit, please."

"Thank you, sir."

Leaning his forearms on the desk, Fendel waited until the younger man was seated.

"You did a very professional, may I say very *Standard*, job in covering the Carlad kidnapping."

Varlik darkened just slightly at the compliment. In the context of journalism, to have one's work called Standard was highly complimentary, if somewhat inappropriate. "Thank you, sir. You honor me."

"I'm considering giving you a new assignment that's even bigger. One that can make your byline one of the majors among our subscribers."

Varlik's alertness level rose. He nodded.

"You're aware of the insurrection on Kettle, of course," Fendel went on, "and that it's continuing. Beast of a place for a civilized man to fight a war, but there it is. Well, it seems now that T'swa mercenaries are being sent there to break its back. That tells me it's worth having someone there to cover it.

"*Two* regiments of T'swa, actually, which really catches my interest. I'll certainly want at least one feature on them."

T'swa mercenaries. Varlik had seen a T'swi once, up close: a heavyset elderly man with skin incredibly dark, the color of a blued gun barrel; straight, close-cropped hair gone white; nose bold, hawklike; wide, thin-lipped mouth; unnaturally large eyes shaded by bushy, jutting brows. Despite his white business suit he'd looked so different, so striking, that the image, long unlooked at, was easily recalled.

When Varlik had commented on the man's appearance, someone had told him he was the T'swa ambassador to the Confederation. Tyss was the only gook world allowed diplomatic representation. The ambassador had a staff of two or three, housed in a cubbyhole somewhere in one of the peripheral government complexes. It was doubtful that they did anything. The T'swa had been granted the privilege centuries earlier by one of the Consars, probably Consar XVII, "the Generous," acting as suzerain and administrator general for the Confederation.

"The Department of Armed Forces," Fendel was saying, "admits that this is only the second time in well over a century they've contracted for a T'swa regiment. The last time was in the Drezhtkom Uprising, some eighty years ago."

His eyes stayed on the younger man's face, watching for any sign of reluctance or even tentativeness. He didn't want to send a reporter who'd spend his time there in an air-conditioned, safe-area headquarters.

Lormagen's eyes were steady as he nodded.

"If you're interested," Fendel continued, still testing, "and if I decide to send you, I'll want you to leave day after tomorrow on a military supply ship. It's a twenty-six-day trip, and I'll want you there while the fighting's still going strong. Those T'swa are likely to finish off the local gooks pretty quickly when they arrive."

"Yes, sir. Day after tomorrow, no difficulty. I'd like very much to have the assignment."

Fendel sat back then, decision made. "Fine. It's yours. Call Captain Benglet at the Army's Media Liaison Office and find out the departure details. The supply ship leaves sometime in the afternoon. And while I'm not expecting full-length video features, of course, take plenty of cubes. This assignment has strong visual potential."

He dismissed the young man then and watched him leave. There'd been no trace of unwillingness. They'd said they wanted someone with energy and imagination; Lormagen definitely had the energy.

Imagination! Fendel returned to his screen. *An odd thing to want in a newsman, or in anyone for that matter*. But there were those whose position put them beyond argument, or nearly enough for any practical purpose.

Two

Excerpt from "The Story of the Confederation," by Brother Banh Dys-T'saben. IN, *The Young Person's Library of Knowing About.*

You have already heard, my friend, of the Confederation of Worlds. But as yet you do not know very much about it. The Confederation of Worlds is an organization of 27 planets on which human beings live. The primaries of some of the 27 can be seen from here on Tyss. Ask your master or your lector to go outside with you some night soon and point out to you those which are visible.

Those 27 are not all of the worlds on which people are known to live in our region of the galaxy. They are simply most of those which have spaceships, and with spaceships, the Confederation worlds can usually control the others and cause them to do certain things that they want them to do. Our own world of Tyss is not one of the 27, of course, and we do not have spaceships. We have the T'sel, and that which grows out of it. That is why the Confederation does not have power over us, although it is all right for them to think they do.

The story of the Confederation of Worlds is quite interesting, and only on Tyss is it known. The first part of it is also the story of how we came to live on Tyss. Very long ago, many thousands of our years ago, people came to this region of space from another region very far away. They came across space in eight very large ships, at a speed much swifter than light, and the distance was so great that it took years to cross it. If you decide to follow The Way of Wisdom and Knowledge, or possibly if you do not, you will be able to visit that time and see that long journey for yourself.

They left their homes to escape a great war. The people who began that war, and who commanded it, were willing to kill to force their own wishes on others. They were willing to kill great numbers of people for that, although few of those killed had chosen for themselves the Way of War.

It was not like any war ever fought in this region, for they used weapons so powerful that they could kill all of the people on a planet in one attack. And that is what they did—they killed all of the people on certain planets, as a warning and threat to others.

On one planet, the government on one great populous island nation bought eight ships, old but large, for they believed that their world would be chosen for destruction. And besides that, they were a people who despised and rejected war, because of the kind of war, called "megawar,"* which they had in that region.

Hurriedly they prepared the ships for a very long voyage. Each ship would take several thousand people, and also things they would need when they settled to live on some far world, including seeds and certain animals. For there would be no towns or manufactories* waiting, or even people, but only the native planet in its wild state. Then each sept on the island selected one in 200 of its people to go, and when all had boarded, the great ships left, never to return.

---

*Words marked with a star are defined and talked about in the glossary volume.

They traveled together on a set course, not stopping anywhere at all until they were far outside the region they knew about. They wanted to be very far away from the war before they chose a new home. After that they continued on the same general course, but deviated* to one side and another to inspect star systems along the way for a planet on which they could live.

In this way they discovered the garthid peoples, who look quite different from humans. The garthids live on planets mostly too hot, and with gravity mostly too strong, for humans. Indeed, our own world of Tyss would seem cold to the garthids, although most humans find Tyss much too hot. But nonetheless, the garthids did not want humans to settle in their sector. So the people of the ships got from them the boundary coordinates* of the garthid sector and went on, not visiting any more worlds until they were well away. Our ancestors did not want anything to do with wars, because the wars they knew had been so indiscriminate* and unethical.

At last the little fleet of ships came to systems far enough away that again they paused here and there to explore for a world they could live on. Soon they found one. It was our own Tyss.

But meanwhile, certain things had happened on the ships. By that time they had been gone from their home planet for more than four of our years. And what did they do, enclosed in a crowded ship for more than four years? The crews were busy, of course, operating the ships and taking care of them. The other people had certain things to do too, such as taking care of children and cleaning. But still, much of the time they had nothing needful to do, and they were quite crowded. So they sat about and talked a great deal. And having nothing like the T'sel, soon they were bickering.* Before long, some of them came to dislike others quite strongly.

Factions arose. A faction is a set of people who feel very strongly in favor of some one thing or set of things, or against some one thing or set of things. It is a group of people who disagree with others, and it exists only in reaction to its polar* opposites. Factions are a major cause of destructive war, which is to say, the kind of war that does not respect the different Ways.

So·before they had been very long on their journey, the rulers of the fleet recognized that they carried with them the seeds* of the very kind of war they had fled from! For given time, the factions would surely start to fight among themselves! Therefore the rulers began to counsel together about what they might do to avoid war. But they did not have the T'sel: They could not see how such wars could be avoided.

But they did know that the destructiveness of indiscriminate war is proportional* to the destructiveness of the weapons used. Also, the human mind is prone to explore the operating rules of the physical universe. You already know something about that. When done in a particular systematic* way, following certain rules and limitations, this exploration was known then by the names "science"* and "research."* Certain operating rules of the physical universe, or approximations* of them, which science discovered and described, could be used to do things with, or to make things with. And the doing and making were known as "technology."* The ·weapons of their huge destructive war had been crafted by technology, by using the knowledge from science.

The rulers recognized all that.

Now, on the ships, not all of the people together had the knowledge to make those hugely destructive weapons. For theirs had not been a world which emphasized science. And indeed, not even their ships' computers,* in which they stored their knowledge, had any great part of the knowledge needed to make those weapons. But the rulers believed that the human mind, free to do research, would in time redevelop that knowledge and once again make those weapons. And this worried them greatly.

Yet they did not want to give up the machines which enabled them to live the way they had been used to. And to continue to make those machines and keep them operating required technology. So they believed they could not do without the technology.

Thus they decided to abolish* research if they could. Without research, without science, they could not re-develop the knowledge with which to reinvent those great weapons. Reactive wars they still might have, but they would not be nearly as destructive as the war they had fled. They would still be able to kill large numbers of non-warriors—those who had not chosen the Way of War—but they would hardly be able to destroy whole populations.

To abolish science was the only thing they could think of to do about it, and they did not at first see how they could accomplish that. All they could do at once was to erase certain knowledge within their computers. So they erased all knowledge which they thought might be dangerous.

But they believed that that would not be enough, for it seemed to them that in time, the knowledge would be rediscovered.

Now, they knew that some of the people with them, called "mentechs," had worked in primitive technologies of the mind, which they regarded entirely as an electrochemical* system. So they sent to the mentechs and asked them if they could suggest anything.

And they could. They thought it might be possible to treat everyone who was on the ships, and their children forever, so that they would never follow the way of science. They could still follow freely the way of technology, but research—the activity of science, the exploration of the rules of the universe—would become impossible. Hope-fully, even the possibility of science—the thought that there could be such a thing—would no longer occur to them.

The rulers decided to try it.

But, you may be thinking to yourself, that is going about it in a strange and illogical way. Why not simply decide not to make such weapons? Why not simply respect the different Ways? But they did not have the T'sel. So they did the best they could think of.

Soon the mentechs had developed a sequence* of actions, a treatment. This treatment caused the person to not look for understanding beyond that which people already had. It would not even occur to them that there was any further understanding to be had, and they would dislike and fear and reject any idea of it.

And secret tests showed that it was successful. People treated and then tested thought exactly the way the mentechs had predicted.

Here is how the treatment worked. The person was given a certain special substance which, to put it briefly, made him very susceptible to obeying commands. Whatever the command might be. The commands given him were, in summation,* that the understanding of nature was already as complete as possible; nothing further was knowable. And these commands were enforced by brief shocks of great pain. It did not take long to do this, and numerous people could be treated each day on each ship.

Now, people of different septs had been put to live in different compartments, so far as possible. And when the mental treatment had been tested and proven, the rulers approached the sept leaders. They told them only that they had a mental treatment which would make it impossible to develop great weapons. They did not tell them how it was done, or what the commands were. And they asked them to prepare their people to accept treatment.

And because they feared and hated the great war so much, many agreed to accept the treatment. Some accepted because their leaders told them to; other septs voted, and accepted because a majority agreed. But five septs refused the treatment. They voted, and most of their members said they should not accept. They said that while they abhorred* the great weapons, they did not trust anything which tampered with the mind and would make them less able in any way.

The rulers then discussed whether they should force the treatment on those five septs. But they could not bring themselves to do that, because they had at least some respect for different ways. On the other hand, they could not make up their minds, at first, on what else to do. So for the time being, the five septs were kept locked up, totally apart from everyone else, and the rest of the people were treated—even the rulers. Even the mentechs. And by so doing they denied themselves the satisfactions of playing or working at science. In fact, there appears to have been some loss of the willingness to question authority on anything.

What that meant was that they became less willing to decide each for himself, and thus tended more than before to follow orders and usual ways in directing their lives.

Soon after that, something happened that helped the rulers make up their minds about the five septs. They were by then far outside the garthid sector, and they found a planet where people could live. It was not a planet where any of them would want to live, for it was too hot there for the people of that time, and the gravity* was stronger than they were used to. But people might survive there. And because the conditions seemed so severe, it was considered that anyone living there would never be able to make great weapons. So they put three of the five septs there, with certain animals and the seeds of certain plants, which they thought might also be able to live there.

That planet was Tyss, our home, and those three septs were our ancestors. And here we have lived for a very long time. Now we think the heat natural, and no more than proper, and the gravity seems just right.

Then the ships went on.

In far later times we learned what happened to the rest of the people. After Tyss, they found other planets on which people could live. Rather soon they found another that was too hot except in a northern region, and they put there the other two septs that had refused the treatment. And after looking at several more planets, they found one which they liked very much. They called it Iryala, and made it their home.

In time they became very numerous on Iryala, and sent ships out to select other planets where some of them could go to live. Some people on Iryala wanted to follow ways that were not welcome there, and some wanted to adventure, and some, wanting to acquire wealth* and power,* thought it would be easier to do so elsewhere. After thousands of years, they peopled many worlds in this region of space. But Iryala held to itself alone the right to have manufactories to make spaceships, so Iryala was predominant.

Now, when the people of the ships landed on Iryala, they still had the machines used to prevent people from doing basic research, and they could easily make more of them. So it was arranged that each child would also be treated when it was old enough to survive the treatment.

For thousands of years they have done this, and have never regained the concepts* of science or research. The most they could do was to recombine information they already knew into new configurations* and test them, which, of course, was very useful in colonizing Iryala and doing the many things needful to establish a self-sustaining* technology there.

But after several centuries, even making new configurations became disapproved of. So they created the concept of Standard Technology. This assumed that the existing technology was complete and perfect. Any changes in it, they believed, would degrade it from that perfection.

Meanwhile, because of the treatment, they could not know what the treatment was intended to suppress. Except of course at the deepest, least available subconscious level, the commands were no longer understood by the technicians who chanted them. The treatment, which they had named "the Sacrament," was thought of as simply a formula* which would protect the people from great wars.

And after 20,000 years, knowledge of their origins faded to legends among those people because of certain things that happened. . . .

Three

Mauen 685 Hothmar Lormagen had been home from the shop nearly half an hour. Small, cute, she looked as pretty as the girls in the ads for the beauty aids she sold. Varlik was usually home before her, but there was no sign of him, and no message.

She considered taking out her paints. She was working on a very famous and popular theme—the Coronation of Pertunis. Occasionally Varlik worked quite late, and when he did, might have no chance to call. She might have a long or a short wait, and didn't like to just get started at painting, then have to stop for supper. Intelligent and rational, she understood the demands of his job, and was ambitious for him, but it did have certain drawbacks.

The sun's rays, softened by lateness, came horizontally through open glass doors, tinging the room with gold. Mauen went out onto the west balcony. Spring was in full flush, the trees of the parklike grounds light green with new leaves. Partly screened by the half-woods, she could see the next apartment building, Media Apartments Four, a hundred yards distant. To her left, surrounded by its broad open ring of apartment buildings, stood the heart of Media Village, the towers of the Planetary Media Center. In that direction, her eyes turned four stories down to the sidewalk, on the chance that she would see Varlik just returning, but all she saw was a groundskeeper riding her sibilant lawn mower.

A flutebird sang nearby to the west, a song somehow nostalgic, though Mauen couldn't have said why. Then she heard the door open, and turning, saw her husband enter the apartment. She went in to meet his embrace and kiss. When they were through nuzzling, she stepped back.

"They gave you your new assignment," she said.

"Yes. How did you guess? Ah. Because I'm late."

She nodded. "What would you like me to key up for your supper?"

"I'll eat whatever you eat; I need some extra togetherness this evening." He moved toward the balcony, then looked back as she stepped to the services panel. "Just be sure there's brandy with it," he added.

Outside he leaned on the railing, inhaling deeply through his nose. For him, the smells of spring and autumn had special character, and of the two he liked spring best. He wondered what Kettle would smell like. Not like spring here in Landfall; not like anywhere on Iryala, he supposed.

Kettle, a world generally ignored. The public curriculum treated it—treated all the gook worlds—very slightly: a listing in a table, and perhaps a paragraph or two. Kettle was the Confederation's sole source of technite, and had been these past several centuries. And Kettle was hot, a jungle planet. That was almost all he knew about it, that and the fact of some crazy workers' revolt there. Neither the paper nor the video had much more than mentioned the insurrection, as if it were unimportant.

Mauen came out to stand beside him, her arm around his waist, her head against his shoulder. After a little she looked up at him. "I ordered a chicken casserole, with beng nuts and gondel pods. It will be a few minutes. Tell me about . . . Oh! I almost forgot! I have news, too!"

"News? What news?"

"Hmm. Maybe I ought to wait till later to tell you. You probably won't be interested anyway."

He turned and grabbed her, grinning. "You're teasing! And you know what I do to teases!"

"Um-hm. That's why I tease you." Mauen stepped back from him, smiling, eyes on his. "Tomorrow morning I go to the clinic. We've gotten approval from the genetics board—for three! They finally decided that because our C22.1734 match is so favorable, they can accept the possibility of the C.6.0023 recessives matching. They'll dissolve the Fallopian implants tomorrow morning."

Her happy expectancy faltered at his expression. "Is anything the matter?" she asked.

"How long after the removal before you're receptive?"

"I'm not sure. I'm pretty sure I can have intercourse practically right away, but I don't know when I'll be receptive. I can ask them, though. Varlik, what is it?"

"Come inside and let's sit down. I need to tell you about my new assignment. I'm going to be away from home for a while."

They went inside and sat—he on a fat, lightweight chair, she on the end of the matching couch—leaning toward each other, her knee almost touching his. With the partial setting of the sun, evening had taken the room, the remaining sunlight dusky rose and failing by the moment.

She said nothing, waiting.

"I've been given a great opportunity," Varlik began. His words sounded strange to him—forced, recited. And that seemed unreasonable, because they were patently true. "It's a chance to do a series that can establish me as a really prominent feature writer. Fendel knew that when he gave it to me; he likes my work. But it's going to be a bigger story than he realizes."

As he said it, he believed it. He hadn't thought of it that way before, but now it seemed true beyond doubt.

"Where?" she said.

"On Kettle."

"Kettle?" From her expression, he realized she hadn't heard of the trouble there; she'd probably forgotten the planet since school.

"A gook world, the planet Orlantha. Kettle is its nickname because it's so hot. There's an insurrection there, and I'm going to cover it."

"Is it going to be dangerous?"

"Not really. There's some danger in almost anything. Getting out of bed in the morning. What makes it interesting is that the government is sending in two regiments of T'swa mercenaries—the 'super soldiers' of adventure fiction. That's where the real story is. Usually they get hired into regional wars between governments on this and that trade world, and no one even hears about it until it's over with. Then these hearsay stories come seeping out, ninety-five percent fiction, mostly in the men's magazines. Remember the holo drama, *Memories of a Traitor?* The mercenaries in that were supposed to be T'swa. What I'm going to do is give people an eyewitness report—interviews with real T'swa and video clips—all on the jungle world of Kettle."

It made sense. It was the approach to take, and he could do it nicely. He pulled his attention into the present again. Mauen wasn't staring, just looking quietly at him in the dusk, her face a pale oval with dark eyes.

"How long?" she asked.

"I don't really know. It'll take twenty-six days to get there, and presumably twenty-six back. And I could be there for as long as a dek,* I suppose, although Fendel

---

*The Standard year is divided into ten decimi, or "deks."

is a little worried that the fighting will be over before I get there." Varlik paused. "Say three deks—four at the outside."

"When do you leave?"

He didn't answer for several seconds. "The day after tomorrow, at 13.20.* But I can take tomorrow afternoon off. I took care of most of the preparations today; there's really not that much more. And I can do my background study on the ship!"

He had planned to spend the next afternoon at his desk, calling up material from the archives bank and the Royal Library, but that was selfish thoughtlessness.

"You can get off work tomorrow, can't you?" he asked.

Her response was to get out of the chair and move to the couch beside him.

---

*The Standard clock is divided into twenty hours of one hundred minutes each. Thus 13.20 is midafternoon.

Four

"Reasons" as stated and believed are seldom true, and their seniority is illusory. Rather, intentions *and events,* in their order, precede the reasons perceived and give them birth. The most common order is intention, event, reason, but it may also be sometimes event, intention, reason. Be aware also that the operative intention may not be apparent, even to its originator, on this side of reality. On this side he may not be aware of his actual intention, which, of course, originates on the other side.

You may ask how an event can precede the reason. And this brings into question the nature of reasons. More instructive is the question of how the event can precede the intention, which brings into question the nature of time, and once more of reality. But the latter question could only be posed from a this-side viewpoint, which is, of course, very restricted.

—Master Fo, speaking to Barden Ostrak in the peanut field behind the Dys Hualuun Monastery (unedited from the original cube).

It would be Varlik Lormagen's first time off planet. Space travel was expensive, and why should an Iryalan leave the queen of worlds if he didn't need to?

He sat in the small observation lounge with the vessel's two other civilian passengers, watching a phlegmatic ground crew clear hoses and conveyors, then move aside on hover carts, away from the impending AG distortion that occurred when a large ship activated. The ship moved, almost imperceptibly, the ground crew pausing to watch. One tall heavy man, arms folded high on chest, left a brief image on Varlik's mind as the ship raised. Liftoff was gradual but acceleration constant. The ground fell away, the spaceport shrinking. The city spread its pattern, a grid of indistinct transitways with "villages"—function centers ringed by apartments—at intersects.

Smoothly, with increasing speed, surface features drew together, lost resolution, until the continent spread white and green and tan to a perceptibly curving horizon. Lake Kolmess was a cold-blue, two-hundred-mile pennant far to the south—poleward here, for Landfall was in the southern hemisphere. Then the cobalt ocean, marked with white, appeared over a horizon whose curvature grew as he watched.

He continued watching until their trajectory had left the planet out of sight of his large bulging window, then looked around him. The other two in the viewing compartment were a man and woman—a news team from Iryala Video. He knew who they were, had seen them occasionally but had never met them. There was no hurry to now; he had twenty-six days. He got up and left, not even nodding to them.

There were two men in the officer's lounge, an off-duty mate and a warrant officer. Varlik struck up a conversation. The ship was army, the mate a genial captain in rank who was happy to give him a brief tour. His name was Mikal 676 Brusin. And yes, it was perfectly all right to use any of the ship's library consoles. There would probably always be at least one available. Varlik got the feeling that Brusin was pleased to have him there, that he liked to have new people to talk with.

When they parted, Varlik went back to the library. The consoles were Standard, of course. The entire ship was the Standard military cargo design. He'd now be able to find his way around any H-class military cargo ship. These things never crossed his mind, though; he took them for granted.

Sitting down, he called up the file on Kettle by its official name, Orlantha. He'd given even less time than intended, the previous day and a half, to background study for the assignment. Mainly he'd reviewed the archives for the little that Central News had said about the war. Even less had been said about it on video, which was understandable. There were always wars of one sort or another on the trade worlds—presumably, it was even worse on the gook worlds—and only devotees paid much attention. But Kettle wasn't your ordinary gook world, sitting out there with no one caring much one way or another. Kettle was where technite was found, the source of the technetium used in steel manufacture throughout the Confederation. The amount used in making a pour of steel was tiny, but it was used in every batch of every alloy; that was Standard.

Kettle had been assigned as a fief to the Confederation planet Rombil, and Rombil had been mining technite there for 279 years—since the Year of Pertunis 432—apparently without earlier trouble with the natives. Now the Rombili had more trouble there than they could handle, and Iryala was bailing them out, obviously because of the importance of technite.

Varlik called up Kettle's planetological parameters and read over them. Most were meaningless or unimportant to him, but some stuck. Surface, 86 percent water. Surface gravity, 0.93—that sounded nice. Rotation period, 0.826 Iryalan Standard—pretty short days. Axial tilt only 2.01 degrees—no seasons, apparently. Briefly, a map appeared beside the text. The inhabited continent, which was the one with the mines, extended from the high middle latitudes in the north to the low middle latitudes in the south.

And hot! Representative daily high and low temperatures on land were, at the equator, 120°F and 105°F respectively; at 25° north latitude, 125°F and 105°F; and at 52° north latitude, 110°F and 90°F. And those temperatures were ordinary! Varlik could imagine what a hot spell would be like. In addition, with so much ocean, the humidity would generally be high; the place was virtually unlivable.

He scanned the summary on bioclimatic zones. The equatorial zone was defined by unbroken jungle, and extended north and south from the equator roughly fifteen degrees of latitude. "Jungle in the extreme," the summary called it, especially in the zone between 10° north and south. Rain was frequent and heavy all year.

As on most free-water planets, planetary circulation made even Kettle's subtropical latitudes relatively dry. The semiarid zones extended roughly between latitudes 20 and 30 in both northern and southern hemispheres. Some semiarid land was desert grassland and some was scrub woodland, grading into forest toward both equator and middle latitudes. Its higher mountains and plateaus were forested.

The middle latitudes lay above about forty degrees latitude, and much of it was jungle or other forest. Some, in the rainshadows of mountains, was savannah or prairie.

According to the summary, the only cool climates on the whole planet occurred on mountains and plateaus above about 12,000 feet. These areas were described as generally extremely wet and misty, an "incredible tangle of smallish trees, standing up at every conceivable angle or lying down, overgrown with vines and lianas and slippery with mosses and saprophytes."

That didn't sound very good either, he thought, then read on. "The exceptions are certain high mountains and plateaus in the arid zone, where the climate tends to be quite pleasant and the landscape ruggedly attractive."

He knew automatically where the Romblit planetary headquarters had to be. And probably the army's.

He skimmed down over material on the geology, flora, and fauna until he came to a summary of Orlantha's history. Very little was known of Orlantha until Y.P. 422, when a survey team found technite there. It wasn't even known from which Confederation world Kettle had been colonized, or at what remote date. The people had sunk into stone-age primitivism, and severe environmental selection, perhaps combined with genetic drift, had produced a very distinct species of *Homo*.

Varlik thought he knew what had happened. Most gook worlds had been settled by one Confederation world or another using them for human dumping grounds—cost-free prisons—long ago. Even several trade worlds had gotten started that way, though in cases where they'd been colonized before the Amberian Erasure, there was only folklore or learned supposition to tell of it. Ordinarily the exiles had been sufficiently equipped to maintain some technology, but Kettle's breeding stock seemed to have been cast away with very little.

Convict dumping had been outlawed when most of the habitable planets in the sector had been settled.

The rest of the historical material on Kettle dealt briefly and summarily with the subjugation of tribes and with mining, and he only skimmed it. He decided to give it a more thorough read tomorrow. Right now he wanted to look into the T'swa mercenaries, and their homeland, Tyss. It was beginning to seem to Varlik more and more that the T'swa were the element to stress in his articles. It was they who would capture reader interest.

Five

Excerpt from "The Confederation of Worlds," IN, *The Encyclopedia*. Lodge of Kootosh-Lan.

Pertunis. With the collapse of the brief Thomsid Empire, the Generals' Junta surveyed the merchant houses of Iryala and subsequently appointed Pertunis of Ordunak as King of Iryala and Emperor of the Worlds. Pertunis's first official act was to dissolve the empire formally. While this was no more than official recognition of the existing situation, it made of Pertunis a sectorwide hero. Indeed, the Confederation numbers the years of its calendar from Pertunis's coronation.

Within 34 years, Pertunis had reestablished the Confederation in much the same form as before the Charter of Halsterbors a millennium earlier. He based it, however, on a network of new trade agreements, the desire of certain rulers to safeguard or regain certain fiefs and other advantages, and, of course, on Iryala's shipbuilding monopoly and military fleet. He did this without any apparent desire for self-aggrandizement. And it served essentially to strengthen the unity, homogeneity, and central guidance—the "Standardness," if you will, of civilized humanity.

The 26 other member worlds were not without differences and ambitions of their own. And their ruling classes could see themselves becoming vassals of the Iryalan throne through the commercial network. But each world had a strong taste for off-planet goods. And each had evolved an economy and developed a standard of living that depended on exports and imports. One by one, Pertunis made them certain guarantees in exchange for their joining the commercial network or for certain modest fees in currency and services. They were also to acknowledge the Iryalan crown as the Administrator General of the network.

Each step into the net seemed the best alternative at the time, the decision to take it the most logical and favorable. And as one after another joined, the remainder began to see that, if they excluded themselves, they would end up in the "trade-world" category, along with the 14 old "junior autonomies," with minimal commercial rights and mostly unable to acquire ships or land those they had on Confederation member worlds. As trade worlds, they would be outside the Confederation but dependent on it, in positions of considerable economic disadvantage. Only Splenn and Carjath chose ideology over logic, and in their newly reduced positions as trade worlds, neither was long able to maintain a centralized planetary government, nor generally to develop a peaceful and stable alternative. Which of course suited the Confederation, whose merchants then played the various states against their rivals.

At this writing, life on Splenn and Carjath remains quite stimulating and interesting after nearly 500 standard years. Their mostly aged, though well-captained ships, keep reasonably busy. Some provide a service important in the farflung Confederation: smuggling.

All the 26 other ex-senior autonomies finally joined

Iryala in the network, which in the Year of Pertunis 37 was reproclaimed the Confederation of Worlds.

With the firm establishment of the new confederation, Pertunis was able to give more attention to a project he had worked on at intervals since he'd taken the throne: the development of a logical system of rules, guides, and procedures for the operation of organizations—any organizations—but with special reference to the Iryalan and Confederation bureaucracies. He worked on this, as opportunity allowed, into his final illness. It had begun as a means of rationalizing and lightening the labor of ruling as king and administrator general. In the later stages of the project he elaborated it in extreme detail, in a considerably successful effort to more fully circumvent the bureaucratic stupidities he observed around him. Despite certain weaknesses, it is a true masterwork, of major value to those who are polarized to any major degree. Even to those who are not polarized, it can be well worth contemplating.

After Pertunis's death, this work was declared by the new king, Wilman IX, to constitute "Standard Management." It has markedly reduced operational variation within the Confederation and occupies a place in Confederation life second only to the Standard Technology of "prehistoric" origin.

But while adding efficiency both to government and business, Standard Management further calcified the already rigid Confederation culture.

Six

Like every army messhall, the officers' mess was a study in stainless steel. Varlik paused as he entered, looking around. Its round tables, more numerous than necessary for the ship's officers, were segregated into a section for senior officers and a larger one for junior officers. Just now they were sparingly occupied.

The mate he'd talked with, Captain Mikal Brusin, looked up and beckoned, and Varlik walked over.

"Might as well eat here with me, Varl. And meet another guest on board, Colonel Carlis Voker." Brusin indicated an officer next to him who wore dress greens instead of the blue tanksuit of most of the working crew. "Colonel Voker's been on Kettle. Went back to Iryala to expedite getting some of the equipment they need, and now he's going back with it."

The mate turned to Voker. "Varlik's the man I mentioned, with Central News, going out to Kettle to report on the war. Served a hitch in the army a few years back; you don't find many media people that have done that, I'll bet at five on it."

Without standing, Colonel Carlis Voker looked Varlik over as if inspecting a not very bright recruit. After a few seconds Voker stood and put out his hand. Varlik met it and they shook.

"Served a hitch, eh? Well, at least we won't have to wipe your nose for you and explain the difference between a rocket launcher and a flare pistol. You might even be able to hike all day in a cool-suit without collapsing on your face. Possibly. If you decide to go into the bush."

Arrogant bastard, Varlik thought, sitting down with the two officers. Still, it had been a favorable evaluation, even put in rather derisive terms. A messman came over and took Varlik's order while Brusin and Voker continued their conversation, a discussion of stations they both knew. They finished their meal before Varlik was well started, and Voker got up.

"Colonel Voker?" said Varlik.

The officer paused, looking at him, his expression for some reason verging on a scowl. "Yes?"

"May I meet you after supper and ask you some questions? I know very little about the war on Kettle, or about its antecedents."

"Antecedents? You won't learn much about those from me. Or from anyone I know of. But the war I can tell you about. Meet me in the officer's dayroom in"—he looked at his watch—"fifty minutes."

Voker turned on his heel and walked away. Varlik watched him leave, then looked at his own watch.

Mike Brusin grinned at him. "He likes you."

"You could have fooled me."

"He's exasperated from dealing with civilian bureaucrats and army data shufflers for the past ten days—people who use Standard Management to slow things down instead of make them go smoothly. No, he likes you, about as much as he's apt to like any male civilian. He comes from one of those army families you run into—army for generations back.

"The colonel feels that most journalists are too ignorant to report on a military operation. They don't know what they're looking at, so they sort of dub in their own misconceptions. And he's got a low tolerance of anything he considers stupidity."

Brusin paused, grinning. "I confess, I set you up for this. I told Voker about you going to cover the war, and then I watched for you, to call you over. He's basically a combat man, though he's on General Lamons's staff now; I figured he could be valuable to you.

"But after he finished telling me what he thought of journalists in war areas, I decided not to mention *them*." Brusin indicated the video team seated with the junior officers. "They're too ignorant to know the difference between the two sides of the room, and the differences in service that go with them."

Brusin swigged down the last of his joma, wiped his mouth with the cloth napkin at his place, then stood up. "I figured he'd talk to you, though. Anyway, I've got to hit the rack now, Varl. I go on duty again at midnight. See you around."

Carlis Voker sat in the dayroom reading, and looked up. "You're right on time," he said. "What do you know about Kettle?"

"Not much. Too humid-hot for a real human, and a lot of it too overgrown for decent surface mobility. Even the gooks didn't live south of the middle latitudes."

Voker nodded, a jerky nod. " '*Didn't*' is the word. They do now. There's got to be thousands of them in the equatorial jungle and the subequatorial scrub. Lots of thousands."

He looked at Varlik, who sat waiting. Voker went on. "When technetium was discovered there, the initial intention was to mine and refine the ore ourselves. It would give Iryala added leverage, because no one could make steel without getting their technetium from us.

"But about then there was a big upset among member worlds over Iryalan domination. And the worked-out technite mines were on a planet in the Rombil sector; Rombil had been responsible for technite mining throughout recorded history. So Consar XV assigned Kettle to Rombil in fief, with the condition that a royal embassy and a royal military garrison would be kept at a place of the royal choosing and at Romblit expense.

"The Rombili run the place, though—mines, refineries, the whole works. Or they did. There were two technite operations, both in semiarid scrub country—one in the northern hemisphere, a place called Beregesh, and one in the southern.

"For more than two hundred and fifty years, occasional slaves and their women escaped from the compounds. Never any big breakouts, just three or four gooks at a time; no problem. They could easily be replaced and they weren't a danger. The country around the mines was unlivable—scrub woodland with almost no water. That was the key: water was scarce. And when a heat wave moves through, it can be 140° for three or four days at a time. The best thing fugitives could hope to do was work their way up-latitude and try to last twelve or fourteen hundred miles to where the climate eases up. Which of course they could never do. A hundred miles north of Beregesh the hills turned into desert grassland—no shade and no water—while in the southern hemisphere, the continent doesn't extend far enough.

"So went the theory."

Voker's lean face had been intense as he'd talked; now he paused for a moment, his eyes like drill bits, as if to evaluate what his listener was making of it all.

"Of course, a few gooks might find their way onto the plateau south of Beregesh, where it's cooler, and the Rombili considered that a potential problem. So every now and then they'd send floaters over the plateau for any signs of cook smoke or huts or garden patches. Whenever they'd see anything, they'd put down a couple of platoons to clean them out. Then they'd bring in any gook bodies and hang them on the fence of the slave compound as object lessons—just let them hang there and rot.

"But now it looks as if most of them headed for the equatorial jungles, the last thing anyone expected. On the face of it, it made no sense. And the ones that survived must have raised families there. Big families. Gradually they ended up with a whole equatorial population developing under cover of the jungle.

"Then, last year, a force of them attacked the Beregesh Compound, wiped out the garrison, took their weapons, and released the slaves. Not that they didn't already have weapons. They did: rifles, hoses, lobbers, shoulder-fired rockets . . . And no one knows where they got them. Now they've got more."

Voker sat quietly for a long moment, scowling at his thoughts. Varlik didn't speak; he sensed there was more to come.

"They had more than weapons," Voker went on. "They'd learned tactics and coordination somewhere, because about five minutes after the attack started at Beregesh, another force attacked the planetary headquarters on Wexafel Mountain, thirty miles southwest.

"The Rombili had a regular resort at Wexafel Mountain, well guarded but not fortified: a tall wire fence and sentries walking around inside it. Our own token 'garrison' was stationed there at the Royal Embassy—two platoons—and the Rombili had two ornamental marine companies. By Kettle standards it's up in the cool, at 10,800 feet. It's still fairly hot by Iryalan or Romblit standards, but decent—a compromise between heat and an atmospheric pressure acceptable to lard-ass executive types. Sea level pressure on Kettle is a little higher than on Iryala, but only about 85 percent of what they're used to on Rombil.

"Anyway, the gooks wiped them out, too—planetary director and all. I suppose the staff there was running around in circles yammering about what they'd just gotten on the radio from Beregesh and didn't even look out the frigging windows until the shooting started. Probably never even warned their sentries that there might be trouble. And you can guess what sentry discipline would have been like after 280 years without an alarm, unless they had a real ass-kicker C.O., which obviously they didn't."

He shook his head, gaze indrawn beneath a scowl.

"The stupidity didn't end there, though. Three days later another gook force attacked the guard detail at the southern hemisphere site, Kelikut. And the Rombili bungled there, too. They'd begun to build log and dirt fortifications and to patrol a perimeter around the site, but they hadn't sent in reinforcements. They said afterwards they hadn't thought they were needed. They hadn't even set out mine fields! They could enfilade the fields surrounding the compounds with automatic weapons fire, but only from the compound's watch towers, which were nothing more than little air-conditioned tin boxes on legs. They stood up there just inviting someone to hit them with rocket fire.

"Anyway, the patrols were pulled in when it got dark, if you can believe that. So about midnight the gooks hit the guard compound, a couple of hundred yards from the slave compound, and they hit the guard posts at the slave compound at the same time. Total surprise. The Rombili did get one of their patrol floaters up, but it didn't do any good. Another wipeout."

Voker's brooding eyes rested on Varlik's.

"The floater hung around a while, and they claim it attacked the guerrillas effectively. I don't know what they mean by effectively; they lost the place and all personnel, and all the slaves took off. And it was dark, with no one around to make a body count. The floater was lucky to make it up north on the charge it carried."

"Up north?" Varlik said.

"Yeah. The Rombili have a big agricultural operation at Aromanis, 52° north latitude—several thousand acres of grassland country converted to irrigated farmland—

and a lumbering operation a couple hundred miles north-west of there in the foothills, all using cheap native labor. This being in native territory, with free natives running around loose, the Rombili had a lot stronger military force there. Why they hadn't flown some of them south to the Kelikut site when they lost Beregesh, I'll never know. Maybe they were too used to getting their instructions from the big brass at Wexafel Mountain, and no one at Aromanis was willing to make a decision like that."

Voker leaned back in his chair now, resting his elbows on the table behind him. "Anyway, that's how it started, more than a year ago."

More than a year! That stunned Varlik, and Voker read his expression.

"That's right; more than a year. The landing control ship picked up the distress call during the Beregesh attack, of course, and again at the Wexafel Mountain attack, and sent a message pod to Rombil. Finally, after they lost Kelikut, they sent a request for reinforcements."

He looked at Varlik again, mouth a thin line, eyes smoldering. "And that's how it started. Except it really started a lot earlier. *Because someone had to gather the gooks together and organize them, which couldn't have been easy. And smuggle weapons to them, in quantity, and train them.* We have no idea who, and even less why, but it's got to have something to do with technite."

His demeanor changed then. He turned to his cup, found it empty, and stood up with a lopsided, humorless grin. "You've got twenty-five more days to Kettle," he said. He took his cup over to the stainless steel joma urn to refill it, talking without looking back. "That little mystery ought to give you something to chew on along the way. Solve it and you'll *really* have a story."

Voker wasn't interested in talking anymore that evening, so after a short cup of joma, Varlik went to his tiny cabin and lay down to think. What Voker had told him was shocking. Why hadn't any of it been mentioned in the media so far? It was easy to understand why so little attention would be given to an ordinary gook war, but this one wasn't ordinary at all. Kettle was the technite world, the only one known, and the gooks held the mines.

What the government had released to the media had mentioned none of what Voker had told him. The reader or viewer had been left to assume that it had just sort of grown out of native dissatisfactions, or minor incidents between the natives and the Rombili, the way you might expect an insurrection to start—especially when the natives were supposed to be stone-age primitives.

And Voker said it had been going on for more than a year! Something smelled rotten all right.

Varlik got up abruptly. It was pointless to think about it with no more data than he had. He left his cabin for the library again, to see what he could find to fill the holes.

Voker didn't stay in the officers' dayroom when Varlik left, opting instead to read in his cabin. But Varlik Lormagen stayed in the back of the colonel's mind. It seemed peculiar to give the time he had to the young newsman. But Voker wasn't a man to question his own actions, his own intuition. He'd go with it and see what, if anything, developed.

Seven

Finding technite deposits is facilitated by two observations. First, all past known technite planets, and now Orlantha, were found in the five-parsec Rombil Sector. And second, all known technite sites, including now the Orlanthan sites, are within some area of impact terrain very rich in radioactive elements. The apparency is that, a rather long time ago, each technite area was struck by a large, more or less coherent radioactive mass from space. What the origin of such masses might be is not known.

From: *Summary Report of the Orlanthan Survey*, Royal Library, Landfall, Iryala, Y.P. 423.

In the library, Varlik looked at what little the library had on the planet, this time scanning more closely the brief technical summary from the planetological survey. It still didn't do him much good. Then he called up *technetium*. A silvery-gray radioactive metal, said the summary, known only from a rare ore called *technite*. Atomic number 43, half lives up to 2.4×10^6 Standard years . . .

From the beginning of history, technite had been mined first on a planet called Technite 3, then Technite 4, Technite 5, and finally on Kettle, the first known technite planet to be human-habitable, if just barely. Like Kettle, Technite 3, 4, and 5 were all in the five-parsec Rombil Sector. Other planets in the same sector, with evidence of ancient mining, are assumed to have been Technite 1 and 2. Records of their exploitation do not exist, as the putative Technite 1 and 2 workings predate the organized historical record that began with the First Empire.*

Technite is sufficiently radioactive that miners as well as refinery crews had to wear heavy and cumbersome "hot-suits" and breathe bottled oxygen, as protection against radioactive dust. Exhaust fans ran constantly in the mines and refineries to minimize suspended dust in the air. The refined technite was shipped off-planet for extraction of its technetium, as the extraction process required considerable support technology.

It occurred to him to call back the information on Tyss, the homeworld of the T'swa mercenaries, but data on Tyss proved even skimpier than data on Orlantha, because there'd been only a cursory planetological sur-

---

*The first known emperor, Amberus, had had public and private libraries and collections destroyed wholesale. Government and other computer banks, archives, and paper files had been ruthlessly culled of everything earlier except Standard Technical material and very limited current administrative records, on the psychotic consideration that all events prior to his reign were not only irrelevant but an insult. Writing or telling about history became a capital crime, and historians were executed wholesale. While there were numerous efforts to secret historical materials, over the course of his twenty-seven-year reign, and with considerable use of bounties and informers, these were generally rooted out. Only fragmentary materials have been recovered.

vey. The T'swa sounded like naturals for fighting on
Orlantha, because if Orlantha was nicknamed "Kettle,"
Tyss was often referred to as "Oven." Temperatures
ran even hotter on Oven than on Kettle, though the
atmosphere was generally much drier; Tyss was a
world characterized by deserts, as Kettle was by
oceans and jungles. And if Kettle was unique among
gook worlds for its technite, Tyss was unique for its
exports of fighting men. It wasn't even usually referred to as a gook world like all the other "resource
worlds—worlds without significant statutory rights."

The entry listed a minimum of physical parameters
and no history at all. He could see nothing relevant that
he'd missed earlier. At the end it was cross-referenced
to *T'swa Mercenaries* and to *Philosophies: Exotic*. He'd
already read the entry on T'swa mercenaries, which in
two paragraphs only mentioned their exceptional skill
in individual and small-unit combat and barely named
some of their more significant military actions. It made
him wish he'd had a day or two more on Iryala, where
he'd had access to the most complete library bank in the
Confederation.

He decided to call up the cross-referenced entry on
philosophy, and found it obscure and uninformative.
The unifying element in human life on Tyss, it said, was
a philosophy, *T'sel*, the literal meaning of which was
"life on Tyss." It claimed to allow for and codify "every
human bent," whatever that meant, and classified the
various "Ways" of T'swa life, with a chart showing the
categories:

THE MATRIX OF T'SEL

	FUN	WISDOM/KNOWLEDGE	GAMES	JOBS	WAR
PLAY	Play just for fun	Study as play; learning unimportant	Games as play; winning unimportant	Job as play; reward unimportant	War as play; victory unimportant
STUDY	Study for fun; learning secondary	Study for wisdom &/or knowledge	Study for advantage	Study to enhance job accomplishment	Study for power
COMPETE	Compete for the fun of winning	Compete to be wisest or most learned	Compete to win	Job as a challenge	War as a contest
WORK	Work at playing	Work at learning	Work for advantage	Work for survival	Soldiering
FIGHT	Fight to control pleasure	Fight to control knowledge	Fight to subdue	Fight for monopoly	Fight to kill or destroy

It didn't mean much to Varlik. He read on:

Very briefly, at any time in a person's life, one is said to have a clear mindset for one or another attitude—the rows of the chart—and after childhood these tend to be more or less permanent, with changes toward the lower levels more likely than upward changes. Further, a person is said to be born with a proclivity for certain fields of activity—one will tend to put one's self or find one's self in situations that fall within the columns of the chart. And someone whose mindset is for Work will perform differently on a job from someone whose mindset is for Fight.

As for the terms, *Play* is a nonpolar activity—one without winning or losing positions from the standpoint of the player. The only function of Play is the pleasure of the player.

To *Compete* is to engage in a polar activity—one that has a winning position, a losing position, and partisan spectator positions. The intention is to win, with no intention to destroy or subdue. The primary rules governing Compete, which are universal laws, are generally inaccessible to the competitor. The secondary rules, however, which define and control the specific games, are known or readily knowable and are generally enforced.

Work is similarly polar, with success, failure, and partisan spectator positions. The primary rules are generally unknowable to the worker. Secondary rules are generally in place and knowable but in practice are more or less circumvented, ignored, or altered.

Fight has winning, losing, and partisan spectator positions, and differs from Compete in that the intention is to subdue and/or destroy, and in having secondary rules which are bypassed at the opportunity and convenience of the participants.

Study is also polar, with succeed, fail, and watch positions. (I have some difficulty understanding this level, which Master Gao says is because it is the level I am at, and said that from it I might well attain a great deal of knowledge but not much wisdom. I'm afraid that for me it will have to suffice.)

Levels below *Play* involve increasing amounts of seriousness. There is no seriousness in Play.

Master Gao also pointed out that the chart is a two-dimensional simplification with the sole purpose. . . .

*   *   *

Varlik shook his head impatiently and simply skimmed to the end of the article. He'd had the idea that he would arrive on Kettle armed with a mass of data, well digested, to serve as a framework for understanding, with pigeonholes to fit his observations into. Well, he'd have to do the best he could with what he had. Absently he called for a printout, then cleared the memory. He'd have to try Voker again the next day and see what he could learn about T'swa equipment, tactics, and strategy.

Meanwhile, it was too early to go to bed. He keyed the author index, then called *Hasniker, Gorth* to the screen. Hasniker was a popular adventure novelist who reputedly researched his story situations diligently. Varlik slowly strolled the annotated titles and, sure enough, there was one that dealt with T'swa mercenaries: *A Crown Prince on Ice*. Maybe, he thought sardonically, Hasniker had found something he hadn't.

The next morning, the female half of the video team came into the messhall while Varlik was eating breakfast. Mike Brusin's attention left his plate to pass Varlik's right ear, and Varlik rotated his head enough to see. She was walking over to them, a husky young woman looking like an ex-athlete who'd gained some weight.

"Mind if I sit here?" she asked.

"Be my guest," Brusin replied.

Varlik rose while Brusin was speaking. "I'm Varlik Lormagen, with Central News."

"Konni Wenter, Iryala Video," she answered, and sat down.

The messman arrived to take her order, then left.

"Where's your partner?" Brusin asked.

"Sleeping in, I suppose."

"I thought he might be." Brusin grinned. "He sure knows how to pour it down. Holds it well, but that much is bound to have aftereffects."

She avoided the invitation to talk about her partner.

"Who do we see to get video cubeage of the war equipment you're carrying to Kettle?"

"You talk to Major Athermon, the ship's executive officer. That's him over there, with the thinning blond hair. And he'll want you to clear it with Colonel Voker, sitting across from him, in green. Colonel Voker is in charge of the ordnance."

"What do you do?" Konni asked.

"I'm the watch officer in charge of the third watch, and I'm also the supercargo." Brusin paused to grin. "And the self-appointed, agreed-upon shepherd of guests. Which one of you is in charge—you or Mr. Bakkis?"

"Bertol's the boss, but he usually puts me in charge, except on a shoot, as long as everything's going all right. He's the creative genius and cameraman. I'm the expeditor; I arrange things and do interviews."

Bertol Bakkis, thought Varlik. That was the name. The man had won prizes for his coverage of—what was it? The Omsedris flood and—the big fire in the Kolmess Forest.

Varlik finished his chops and fries, then glanced toward Voker. He'd hoped to sit by the colonel again this morning, but the man had been sitting with others, with no available seat adjacent or across from him. Varlik held up his cup and received a nod from the messman, who headed for the joma urn. He'd wait and catch Voker before he left, or follow him, if necessary.

His attention went back to the conversation between Brusin and Konni Wenter. Apparently Brusin was proving uninformative, because Konni turned unexpectedly to Varlik. "What have you been able to learn about Kettle and this war?" she asked.

"Not much," Varlik answered. He'd keep what he knew to himself, although he felt uncomfortable about it. It was his professional edge. "How about you?"

She made a rude sound, not loudly. "I planned to spend a day or two in the royal library, but it only took me about an hour. There was a lot of planetological data, including the mineralogical survey and some old stuff on tribal customs. That's all."

He decided not to ask if she'd found anything on the T'swa mercenaries. Perhaps she didn't know they were involved. Then it struck him that he hadn't brought up the T'swa with Voker, either, and Voker hadn't mentioned them on his own.

Two of the men at Voker's table got up and left, leaving only the ship's executive officer still sitting with him. Meanwhile, Konni Wenter was just starting to eat. Varlik got up, excusing himself, and walked toward the E.O.'s table, joma cup in hand. Voker and the E.O., Major Athermon, had finished eating and were talking, not the most propitious situation to interrupt. Athermon looked up with a slight frown as Varlik arrived. Varlik bobbed a small head bow.

"Excuse me, Major Athermon, Colonel Voker. Major, my name is Varlik Lormagen, with Central News. I just want to ask Colonel Voker if I can meet with him sometime this morning." His eyes moved to the colonel. Surprisingly, Voker smiled.

"Sure, Lormagen. Major Athermon just said he needed to check the bridge." He turned to Athermon. "Lormagen served an enlistment in the army a while back. Made sergeant. Central News is sending him out to report on the Kettle war."

Athermon looked at Varlik and nodded, a nod that was curt without being rude. "Well," said Athermon, "it would be unreal to tell you to enjoy your assignment. Let me wish you long life." He turned to Voker. "Have a good day, colonel. It was nice talking with you."

"Thank you, major. Same to you." Voker and Varlik watched the executive officer out the door before talking further, then Voker spoke mockingly. "Did you have any inspirations after we talked?"

"No, sir. I made further use of a library console, and

found essentially nothing. Nothing of value on Kettle, and almost as little on Tyss."

The colonel's eyebrows raised fractionally and he looked around them. "Tell you what," Voker said, "why don't we talk in my cabin? It has the advantage of privacy."

Voker got up without waiting for a reply, and Varlik followed him out of the messroom, down a wide corridor and up a companionway, saying nothing, then down another corridor, narrower but nicely carpeted. Ranking officer country, Varlik thought to himself.

Voker's cabin, though small, was twice the size of the cubbyhole Varlik occupied. It even had its own computer terminal. Voker motioned him to a chair, opened a knee-high refrigerator, and took out a bottle.

"Whiskey do?" he asked, and held up a bottle of smooth Crodelan. "One of the little bargains available on out-worlds." He put ice in two glasses, poured a liberal shot in each, then handed one to Varlik and sat down. "I like this stuff too well, so I ration myself to two a day. Might as well have the first one now." He took a small, critical sip. "You mentioned Tyss. I take it you've heard the rumor about T'swa mercenaries. Where?"

A rumor! It could be false then. If it wasn't true, he needed to rethink some things. "From my boss," Varlik answered. "But he considered it fact. It's probably the reason he sent me to Kettle."

"Interesting. Do you know where he heard it?"

"No, but I could make an educated guess. Central News has close connections within His Majesty's administrative staff. We're often chosen to, uh, release selected 'rumors' or 'leaks' to test public reaction. Not that this was anything like that, but it could easily have come from the same kind of source."

Voker looked thoughtful. "I heard it suggested some four deks back, but General Lamons turned it down."

"Why is that?"

"First, he doesn't believe in elite units. They offend his sense of Standardness. Plus the T'swa are as non-Standard as you can get." The colonel's eyes met and held Varlik's as he said it. "Actually, neither Standard Management nor the army's supplemental policies say that elite units aren't all right. Or that non-Standard contractor forces aren't."

Voker slowed as if for effect. "Besides which, there are places for Standardness and there are places for innovation—creative imagination. Every damned thing man has or does was an innovation at some time or other, and imagination before that."

Varlik didn't flinch, but inwardly he squirmed at the concept. Voker saw it, and his slight smile came out awry. "Besides that, Lamons considers that to use mercenaries in a situation like this would be an affront to the Iryalan Army."

"The T'swa would seem to be almost perfect for Kettle, though," Varlik said.

"Exactly. They're adapted to the climate, they're specialists in wildland fighting, and they're more expendable than our own people. T'swa casualties are more acceptable to the public as well as the government. This was pointed out to Lamons, but he refused the logic."

Voker swirled the dark liquor in his glass, eyeing it thoughtfully. "I wouldn't be surprised if what you heard about bringing in T'swa is true, though. Not a bit. The suggestion seemed to have high-ranking interest back home. Someone may have bypassed Lamons and gotten the idea to the Royal Council."

"What, specifically, could the T'swa do that the army can't?" Varlik asked. "Besides stand the heat."

"Huh! What can the Royal Ballet do that the army can't? And a lot of things that the army can do, the T'swa can do quicker and more efficiently." He grimaced wryly at Varlik. "I regret to say."

"Have you ever worked with T'swa?" Varlik asked hopefully.

"No, but I've read a couple of contract monitor debriefs from trade worlds, and the War College study on the T'swa, such as it is. How much do *you* know about them?"

"Not much," Varlik admitted ruefully. "Only that they're supposed to be almost—super-soldiers. Most of what I've read is adventure fiction, I'm afraid. I haven't been able to find anything else."

Voker grunted. "And you checked the ship's library? I'd have expected better of it; any base library would have the War College study on them. Not that many read it; like I said, the T'swa aren't—Standard."

Again Varlik's stomach twisted: The colonel had said the word "Standard" in a tone bordering on condescension.

"You used the term 'super-soldiers,'" Voker went on. "As individuals, that's not an exaggeration. They start their training as little kids. The T'swa philosophy has it that a person is born imprinted with a preference for a particular kind of life, and they claim they can tell what it is when the kid is only five or six years old.

"I know that doesn't make any sense genetically, but it's the basis they operate on, so that's the age they start training them—five or six. From then on that's pretty much all they do—train as warriors and study T'swa philosophy.

"They have *discipline*, of the kind that works best: self-discipline. And maximum individual skills. And their small-unit performance is supposedly the best. Their drawback, such as it is, is that they won't operate as an integral part of large units—armies, corps, divisions. That's undoubtedly part of why Lamons doesn't want 'em: he doesn't know what to do with 'em. Their contracts specify that they operate on their own, subject only to agreed-upon objectives. And they don't hesitate to refuse assignments if they don't fit the contract terms.

"The thing to do with T'swa is, first you know the

contract thoroughly, then pick something you need done that no one else can do and that fits the contract terms, which are broad enough. Then you tell them to do it. Nothing hard about that. House-to-house combat, for example: they're great for cleaning out a town. Or fighting in wild country. But to use them, it helps to have a couple teaspoons of imagination."

"What would you tell the T'swa to do?" Varlik asked.

"Easy. I'd tell them to find and hit the guerrillas' main headquarters, capture as many top-ranking officers as they can, and bring them in. Take explosives and blow out a clearing big enough to come in with floaters, then lift out with their prisoners."

"That doesn't sound easy to me."

"I didn't mean it would be easy to do. The *decision* would be easy for me."

"Do you think they could pull off something like that?"

"I wouldn't be surprised. I wouldn't bet a dek's pay on it, but I'd go a week's. Or maybe I would go a dek's pay. Anyway, it'd be worth the try. The T'swa don't mind casualties; they just like to fight. And if they got some really high-ranking prisoners, we could probably find out who's behind the uprising—who provided the weapons, the training. Maybe even why. If we knew that, maybe we could end this war by hitting the source, whatever that is.

"One thing I do know for sure: I don't want to spend the rest of my career trying to root gooks out of the bush at a hundred and thirty degrees of heat."

"How does General Lamons intend to handle the situation?"

"Land heavy forces at Beregesh, take over the surrounding area, fortify the perimeter to keep out the gooks, then rebuild the refinery and reopen the mines."

"Is that practical?"

"If we're willing to commit, say, six divisions there. Lamons is assuming that the gooks have ten or fifteen thousand troops, and I wouldn't argue about that. There are two main problems: One, protecting the engineering and other units while they build an infiltration-proof defensive perimeter that's got to be—oh, maybe twenty miles long. And two, the steambath Beregesh environment. In the mining districts, the troops have to wear cool-suits to function, and they're uncomfortable and damned clumsy. The climate's bad enough up north at Aromanis, but that's a resort compared to Beregesh. At Aromanis we don't need cool-suits."

Voker stopped and regarded Varlik as if something was dawning on him. "Lormagen," he said, "do you have it in mind to feature the T'swa in your articles? Is that what you plan to do?"

"That's what I was thinking about."

"You don't know what you're letting yourself in for. They may be the most interesting thing to write about, or to read about, but frankly, you'll never keep up with them. I'm not sure any Iryalan would be able to, even if they'd have him."

Voker leaned forward, forearms on knees. "Tell you what. You forget about the T'swa and I'll feed you all the leads you can follow up on."

"I really appreciate the opportunity," Varlik answered slowly, "and I hate to turn it down. But what I really want to do is go with the T'swa and let people see them in action—in reality, not in fiction. At least I want to try. There'll be more public interest in them."

To his surprise, Voker grinned. "Got you," said the colonel. "And you'd make a bigger name for yourself. In your shoes I'd feel the same way." He stood, took a case from an open-front cupboard, put it on his bunk, and opened it. There were a number of cubes in it, and he took one out.

"Here," he said, holding it out. "Conversational Tyspi, self-taught. Maybe it didn't occur to you, but the T'swa have their own language; several gook worlds do, more or less. All T'swa mercenaries supposedly speak decent

Standard, but among themselves they'll probably talk their own lingo. You'll want to understand as much of it as you can." Varlik took the cube as Voker continued. "Although anyone who thinks as differently as they must . . . But if you can even sort of talk their language, they'll probably like you for it."

He didn't sit down again, but stood as if waiting for Varlik to get up. "And if you're going to tag along with them, you'll have to be in great physical condition. You've got twenty-five days!" He stepped to the door and held it open. Varlik arose, uncertain. "You don't think a man in a cool-suit can keep up with the T'swa, do you?" Voker asked. "You'll have to be in incredible condition and able to take the heat unprotected."

It hadn't occurred to Varlik, and his face showed it.

"Although it just might be possible," Voker said. "If you've got the guts for it. You don't look too bad physically. A prospector team was stranded on Furnace One for three weeks after their suits gave out, and three of them survived. Out of eight. And Furnace One is a lot hotter than Kettle. Like a sauna. Of course, they didn't have to exert themselves."

Voker's grin was wide now. "Come along, bucky boy. We'll get you fixed up with a firefighter's outfit and start you on a good tough stamina routine in the officers' gym. Sweat all the softness out of you and get you ready for the heat. Those firemen's suits can simulate Kettle's climate; with their cooling systems disconnected, they'll keep body heat in as well as they keep external heat out."

Eight

In Tyspi, besides the masculine and feminine personal pronouns *he* and *she*, *him* and *her*, and the impersonal pronoun *it*, there are neuter personal pronouns, which prove to be quite convenient where male or female identity is not relevant. And outside the military, the neuter personal pronoun is used more than the masculine and feminine pronouns, which in itself tells us something about the T'swa.

—Lecture by Barden Ostrak to the Philosophical Society.

During the 25 remaining days to Kettle, Varlik, enclosed in a fireman's suit, worked out every morning in a cycle of varied and almost nonstop strenuous exercises, mostly steady-paced but occasionally sprinted. Sweat ran down his body and squidged in his socks. He'd complained to Voker, his self-appointed and unwanted overseer, that it was better for the body to have alternate days off. But Voker had scorned the notion, said they weren't trying to build bigger muscles, just toughness, and bullied and browbeat a grim Varlik through it, skirting collapse.

In fact, every day during the first week, Varlik had

57

truthfully expected to collapse from heat prostration. And there'd have been some satisfaction to it; it would have made Voker wrong.

The colonel worked out too, mostly on gymnastics and hand-to-hand combat drills. He exercised strenuously enough, but without a fireman's suit and with numerous breaks to supervise Varlik. When Varlik pointed out the difference, Voker, leaner and harder than any colonel Varlik had ever imagined, pointed out that *he* wasn't going off to follow the T'swa.

Varlik's first two workouts had been an hour each, and left him utterly exhausted. By the fifteenth day, the workouts went on for three hours with a pair of five minute breaks, the soreness forgotten, and Varlik was pleased with his sinewy new physique.

After lunch and a short nap, he studied Tyspi till supper. His progress with the language cube was less satisfying than the physical training, partly because there was no one on board to test him. The colonel had never gotten around to learning it. Varlik could follow the conversation exercises on the recordings well enough, but that wasn't the kind of barracks talk he expected to hear. He couldn't imagine mercenaries speaking with the precise and deliberate diction of the lesson recordings.

After supper he studied Tyspi again, to crowd in as much competence as possible. Relaxation consisted of a drink and idle conversation with Mike Brusin before bedtime, sometimes with Voker sitting in. Occasionally Konni Wenter joined them, twice with a torpid, almost unspeaking Bertol Bakkis, his eyes opaque with seeming disinterest. When they appeared, Varlik kept his mouth shut, excusing himself as soon as he gracefully could.

Following his very first workout, Varlik had asked Colonel Voker if he would record for him a summary of the war to date, to go with his description of its start. Voker had answered that he might if he found time for it. Varlik hadn't pressed the matter. The colonel had already been more than generous with his help and confidences.

Occasionally Varlik had misgivings about attaching himself to the T'swa, and not just because of the Hasniker novel and other fiction depicting the T'swa as ruthless and cruel. Voker had said they began their military life at age five or six! What would men be like who'd spent their childhood in barracks, preparing for life as mercenary killers?

They weren't even *Homo sapiens;* they were *Homo tyssiensis.*

At last Varlik finished his final workout. Tomorrow before lunch they would arrive on Kettle. As he sat freshly showered, putting on his shoes, Voker turned to him. "Lormagen," he said, "I've got something for you in my quarters. I wrote it last night. It's handier than having it on a cube: You won't need a player when you want to refer to it."

Varlik followed him to his cabin, where the colonel gave him an envelope, not thick at all. When he got to his own cabin, he opened it to find a summary of the war indexed by year and dek.

Yr 710.1—Rebels capture mines, as already described.

710.3—Romblit reinforcements arrive Kettle—one division with support units. Brigade assault landing at Beregesh, mine and refinery area retaken and "secured" with no resistance or enemy presence. Found refinery demolished, ditto other structures and mine shafts. Then Kelikut retaken with no resistance; similar destruction found. Troops begin to construct temporary camp and defenses.

710.4—Construction crews arrive from Rombil, begin reconstruction of mines, refineries, etc. Guerrillas infiltrate both areas at night, in force, massacre Romblit construction crews, destroy equipment, pin down garrison remnants. Reserve regiments flown in, land under heavy small-arms fire. Eventually, troops and remaining civilian personnel evacuated under fire, as they cannot reconstruct and maintain air-cooled mines, refineries, camps, in combat situation. Enemy well trained, very effective. Enemy casualties believed substantial due to floater gunnery.

710.6—Rombil lands two additional divisions up north at Aromanis base, along with 1,000+ construction workers and heavy equipment, to establish major military base of operations. Also prefabricated cool-huts, etc., for transfer south to Beregesh. On Rombil, government calls up reserves, begins training. Iryalan government sends military "observer" team to Kettle, headed by General Lamons.

710.8—Full Romblit division lands at Beregesh with strong floater support, under heavy fire from log-and-earth bunkers, including lobbers and blast hoses not evidenced before. Casualties heavy, particularly due to destruction of unarmored troop landers in flight by M-3L rockets, also not used before. Area taken and secured.

710.8.10—Beregesh area fortified under frequent harassment. Casualties moderate, chiefly to patrols.

711.1—Construction crews begin 'round-the-clock work to rebuild refinery and reopen mines. Progress rapid. Considerable pressure from gov't. for technetium.

711.3—Refinery rebuilt to 0.4 of old capacity. First cars of ore from new shafts, using imported contract workers. Enemy floaters, previously unknown, make surprise attack. They bomb and demolish refinery, mine head, worker dormitories, barracks. Mine field breached by aerial bombing, enemy assault troops overrun part of area before withdrawing. Romblit troop casualties moderate; worker casualties heavy because of destruction of refinery and mine head. *This firmly demonstrates enemy policy of with-*

holding unexpected resources for surprise use later. How far resources will permit continued escalations is not known, but I suspect not much further.

711.5—Surveillance platforms (first direct Iryalan participation) parked on strategic Heaviside coordinates. General Lamons returns to Aromanis with Iryalan Royal Guards regiment and with orders from His Majesty. First Romblit reserve division arrives. More Romblit air attack squadrons begin to arrive.

711.6—Iryalan 12th Division arrives. General Lamons relieves Romblit General Grossel as planetary commander. Iryalan Army assumes direction of the military situation on Kettle, without however relieving Rombil of responsibility as fief holder. I get sent to Iryala to expedite shipping of needed ordnance.

711.9.14—We will arrive at Kettle, you and I. You're tougher than I thought, and you'll need it all. Good luck!

It wasn't all Varlik could have wished, but it was more that he'd thought he'd get. It was something to work from; he could fill it in later, on Kettle.

The last sentences had affected him emotionally, although he didn't examine the fact. Praise and respect were not freely given by an officer like Voker; to receive them could create a magnetic attachment, a sense of loyalty. The colonel knew the value of loyalty in a military organization, and that officers who enjoyed the greatest loyalty were hard taskmasters who demanded much. They drove their men hard, made them perform beyond their self-image, then gave the survivors their respect, at least, and privileges as possible. Their men, in turn, tried to live up to expectations.

Voker had just handled Varlik that way. And with that, Varlik Lormagen was fully committed to going with the T'swa. He didn't analyze it, but to do less would have seemed a retreat from a commitment that Voker respected or even admired.

Nine

On the approach to Kettle, there were again only three people in the small observation lounge—the same three. As he took a seat, Varlik nodded and murmured a quiet hello, actually to Konni. He was surprised that Bakkis was there. The evening before, the man had gotten visibly drunk for the first time on the trip, and it had taken a lot to do it. Drunk, Bakkis had had even less to say than usual.

From space, close on, Kettle was beautiful, showing a lot of blue and cloud white. Inside the atmosphere, the view was still magnificent. At first there was the impression of vast dark forest feathering into greenish tan grassland. Gradually the artificial rectangles of the agricultural district and nearby military base became prominent until, with the intervening prairie, they dominated the view.

On landing, they were called to the airlock—the three of them plus Colonel Voker and two ship's officers. When the door dilated, Varlik realized why they weren't using the ordinary personnel exit: The air temperature outside was somewhat hotter than normal for 52° north latitude on Kettle—115° F at midmorning,

63

nearly twenty degrees hotter than any air temperature he'd experienced before. While in the intense sun . . .

Still, he was encouraged. As they walked to the waiting personnel carrier, forty yards away, he did not find the heat oppressive, merely impressive. The air-conditioned vehicle lifted a foot or so on its AG pressors and sped off down the travelway as if there were some hurry. There didn't seem to be; the young private at the wheel just liked to drive fast. Varlik was glad his stomach didn't feel like Bakkis's must.

The Aromanis Agricultural District was almost three centuries old, and at the edge of his sight he could make out tall planted trees, undoubtedly irrigated, that seemed to line other travelways. The military base was on native prairie without a tree of any description, its grass flattened, beaten, and worn. The drilling troops they passed marched in a cloud of dust that rose tawny gray around them.

Long rows of tents extended from the road, mere roofs above raised floors of boards, their sides rolled open to the usual prairie breeze. At short intervals stood low, premolded buildings topped by air-coolers— the company orderly rooms, mess halls, dispensaries, and other accessory facilities of the units they passed. Quickly enough they approached a broadly rambling complex of connected modules with, in front, the twin-stars flag of Rombil beside and slightly below the Royal Starfield of the Confederation. There were numerous cooling units on the roofs, and a vehicle park spread before it. Their driver parked some seventy yards from the entrance.

"Soldier," Voker said quietly, "why aren't you parking near the entrance?" The question was like the purr of a jungle cat.

"Colonel, sir," the driver said, "that area is unofficially reserved for assigned vehicles, sir. And this is a pool vehicle."

"Fine. What is my rank again?"

Belatedly the driver sensed he was in trouble. "You are a colonel, *sir*."

"Again?"

"You are a colonel, *sir!*"

"Fine." The purr again. "What is your name and serial number, private?"

The young man answered like someone holding his breath. "Private Jaster Gorlip, 36 928 450, *sir*."

The response snapped like a whip. "I didn't ask for your rank, private. I can see your rank. I asked for your name and serial number." Then abruptly the soft purr. "Without any unasked-for additions now, what are they?"

"Jaster Gorlip, *sir;* 36 928 450, *sir*." The driver was answering now like a recruit to his drill sergeant.

Again the purr. "And what is your unit, private?"

"First Army Headquarters Battalion, *sir*."

Varlik found himself sweating despite the air-conditioned coolness.

"All right, Private Jaster Gorlip, 36 928 450. Let us out thirty feet from the entrance."

Carefully the private drove to a position thirty feet from the entrance, stopped, jumped out, and opened the doors for his passengers, holding Voker's open for him. When they were out, and before the driver closed the door, Voker said, "Thank you, private. Hmm. I seem to have forgotten your name." He turned on his heel then and led the three journalists to the entrance. "Reservist," he murmured to Varlik, and chuckled. "He assumed we were new here, and thought he'd play a little game with us; make us walk in the heat. Regular army would have known better."

He caught Varlik's eye and smiled amusedly. "You wouldn't have done that when you were in, would you?"

"No way. Not with a colonel, not with a sergeant. Maybe with a green junior lieutenant, but I doubt it."

Voker laughed, then held open the door of the headquarters building for them. Inside was not exactly cool, but relatively so by local standards: perhaps ninety, Varlik thought. There was the sound of coolers, communicators, voices. "The place has grown since I left," Voker muttered. "Let's see if they've left the Information Office where it was two deks ago." They had, and after knocking, Voker introduced them to a lieutenant, who looked surprised and pleased to have them.

Lieutenant Brek Trevelos was probably, Varlik decided, the source of the non-news that had been released to the public at home. But the policy would not have been his own; lieutenants didn't set policy, nor did colonels, for that matter. Cheerful and bright looking, Trevelos made sure they'd entered the planetary adjustment factor into their watches, correcting them to Kettle's day length. Then briefly he summarized the army's buildup and preparation here, not mentioning, however, any of the history that Colonel Voker had confided. After that, instead of using his desk comm, he opened the door into an adjacent, somewhat larger office, crowded with several desks.

"Sergeant Wagar!" Trevelos called, and a man came over. "These are newspeople visiting us from the capital." The lieutenant gave their names. "I want you to call the vehicle pool and have them send over an air-conditioned car and driver. When it gets here, I want you to take our guests over to QM and get them fitted with whatever field clothes they need; three sets each. After that, you'll give them a tour of the base. Show them everything. I expect you won't be done by lunch, so at noon, you'll take them to the officers' mess and pick them up there afterward to complete the tour." He turned brightly to the three. "How does that sound?"

Without waiting for their answer, the sergeant went out to make his call. "And now," Trevelos went on, closing the door, "perhaps you have some questions you'd like me to answer while we're waiting for your vehicle."

"Yes," Konni said. "Where will we be quartered?"

"Forgive me, Miss Wenter, I should have mentioned that. We have special air-conditioned quarters for journalists—six sleeping rooms and a large common room. They've never been used. I'll call and have three rooms made up and the coolers turned on so they'll be comfortable. Sergeant Wagar will take you there at the end of your tour, or sooner if you'd like. I suggest you wait an hour, though, for the rooms to be prepared.

"Now, if you'll excuse me for just a moment . . ." He murmured a call code into his communicator and waited for a brief moment. Then faintly they heard the tinny voice at the other end—a voice with no face, for there was no screen. "This is Lieutenant Trevelos, Information Officer," Trevelos said. "Three journalists just arrived from the capital. Their baggage needs to be picked up and delivered at media accommodations. Do you know where that is?"

The tinny voice said something back, about twenty words worth. Trevelos thanked him and hung up, then turned to the three. "A Captain Brusin on the IWS *Quaranth* has already had them sent. Now, is there anything else?"

"I presume we'll be able to stop along the way and ask questions," Varlik said. "Or shoot some video cubeage."

"If you'd like. But this tour is mainly for orientation. You'll be assigned a vehicle to yourselves tomorrow— more than one, if you'd like—and be able to go about more or less as you wish."

It occurred to Varlik to ask about the T'swa then, but he didn't. He still hoped to send home a feature on them before Bakkis and Wenter could, and it seemed possible that they hadn't heard about them.

Then Trevelos issued them media passes, which they signed. The passes would admit them to the officers' mess, commissary, and lounges, among other things. And sooner than they would have thought, their driver arrived.

* * *

When they'd had their tour and Bakkis and Wenter had gotten out at the media quarters, Varlik asked the driver to drop him off at headquarters. They left the video team, Konni looking questioningly after him. At headquarters, Varlik went straight to the Information Office and knocked. Trevelos answered him in.

"What can I do for you?"

"I wondered," Varlik said, "where I can find the T'swa mercenaries."

On Trevelos's face, a look of surprise was followed by one that might have been concern. "The T'swa mercenaries?"

"Right. My editor was told by a spokesman on His Majesty's staff that T'swa mercenaries were being contracted with for Kettle. Two regiments." Varlik was not given to lying, and he heard himself say this with some surprise. But it seemed to come out believably enough. "My instructions are to get interviews with them. Where will I find them?"

Trevelos looked clearly worried now, which immediately struck Varlik as odd. Captain Benglet, back on Iryala, had accepted his interest casually enough, and Voker. . . .

"Um. Well." Trevelos wasn't sure how to respond. "We don't have any T'swa on Kettle."

"When are they getting here?"

The lieutenant lagged for three or four seconds, then gave in. "They're supposed to land about midnight tonight, in two transports. But not here. They'll land at their bivouac area over east about thirty miles; a landing site has been marked out there for the ships."

"I see. I'll want a vehicle and driver then, at about 19.10 hours local.* I'd like to see them come in."

---

*The Standard twenty-hour day, with its hundred-minute hours, are used throughout the Confederation, the unit lengths varying according to the planetary diurnal cycles.

Trevelos nodded. "Of course," he said, and waited for Varlik to leave.

"I'd like you to make the arrangements now," Varlik said, "so I'll be here if there are any questions, or if there's anything I need to know."

Again Trevelos nodded, and murmured a code into his communicator. Again a tinny voice responded. Trevelos spoke.

"This is Lieutenant Trevelos, Information Officer. I want a field vehicle at media accommodations at 19.10 hours tonight. It will pick up a Mr. Varlik Lormagen, a newsman, and transport him to the mercenary bivouac site. The driver will have to know how to get there, and where media accommodations is."

The tinny voice spoke briefly.

"Good. That'll be fine. At 19.10." He hung up and looked at Varlik. "It's all arranged. You took me by surprise. We hadn't realized that anyone off command lines had been informed about this."

"And I hadn't realized you didn't know," Varlik replied. "I guess we surprised each other. Thank you very much for your help."

He started back to media accommodations on foot. Mercenary *bivouac* area. *Odd*, he thought, *how the command here seems to feel about the T'swa*. They hadn't wanted them in the first place, and getting them regardless, were putting them thirty miles away, apparently with no accommodations. Were the reasons Voker had given him all the reasons there were?

Probably, he decided. The military command mind didn't need good reasons. It could be arbitrary, it could be very spiteful, and it was in a position to exercise and enforce both, especially on a planet twenty-six days from home.

It was 120° in the nonexistent shade, a breath-stifling heat that had the sweat oozing again before he'd walked a fifth of the four hundred yards there. After supper he'd shower and lie down, he decided, sleep if he could. It promised to be a busy night, and there was the matter of adjusting to the short days here, and the short hours.

PART TWO

The T'swa

Ten

Arapping drew Varlik out of sleep, and he sat up abruptly. "Come in," he called. He got off the cot, wearing fatigues but barefoot. His alarm clock looked reproachfully at him. Apparently he'd forgotten to set it—a hell of a way to start. A corporal, husky and square-faced, stood in the short hallway looking in, and gestured at the rectangle of notepaper Varlik had taped to the door.

"Mr. Lormagen?"

"That's right. Come in. What's your name, corporal?"

"Duggan, sir."

"Sit down, Corporal Duggan." Varlik motioned to one of the two folding chairs. "What do your messmates call you?"

"Pat, sir. Short for Patros."

"Pat it is, then. Mine's Varlik."

Varlik pulled on his boots and pressed them snugly closed, snapped his recorder on his belt, slung his video camera under his left arm, slipped the band of his visor-like viewer over his head, then left with the corporal. The night felt strange to him, unreal, like one of the occasional dreams he had of being back in the army

73

in some impossible situation or other. Outside, the air reminded him of a hot pool—all right for sitting in. The vehicle was an uncooled hovercar with the top and windows retracted. The corporal held the door for him.

Aside from their headlamps, almost the only lights in camp were at the few locations where work went on at night—motor pools, the hospital, and, of course, Army Headquarters. The perimeter, about a mile outside the encampment itself, was a barbed wire fence, tall and silent; outside that, accordion wire; and beneath the ground, string mines, no doubt. String mines, at least. A concrete and earth blockhouse stood by the steel-bar gate, which a guard opened for them while others no doubt watched from the blockhouse. Presumably there were other blockhouses at intervals around the camp.

Then they were out, accelerating across the prairie, the treated travelway giving way to the prairie's loose dry soil. A trail of dust rose with their passage. Here the way was only barely marked, as if a reaction dozer had scraped a minimal scalp across the grassland, careful to displace as little soil as possible—almost as if it had backed, dragging its blade behind. At intervals stood marker rods, slender, chest high, catching the head-light beams on reflective surfaces.

The air was still hot, the temperature surely well over a hundred, Varlik decided, and he wondered if the nights here were long enough to allow much cooling. The air that swirled about them seemed hotter, in a way, than it had in stillness outside the hut. But it wasn't really oppressive, not with the sun's fierce rays departed. A person *could* adapt to Kettle, he thought, at least at 52° north latitude.

"What do you think of the camp's defensive perimeter, Pat?" he asked. "Is it adequate? Or is it even necessary?"

Duggan answered without taking his eyes off the cone of their headlights. "You'd need to ask the general about that, sir, or one of his staff. But one thing you ought to be warned about—don't go trompin' around outside the fence. You're likely to lose a leg, all the way to your windpipe. And that's if someone don't shoot you first. The gooks on this part of the planet have been pacified for three hundred years, damn near, and from what I've heard, they've never been known to join together in anything. But it looks to me like the brass isn't taking anything for granted."

He drove in silence for a minute or so before saying anything more. "And we may not see them, but there's security patrols flying around over the country in light scouts, with scanners and ultra-aud. There's probably one of 'em readin' us right now. We give off a radio signal they recognize. No signal means 'investigate possible hostile.'

"And besides that, there's heavily armed recon floaters that go back and forth over the whole damn region, watching for anything like a mobilization or large movement of gooks. Just in case."

They had left the near-flat vicinity of camp for broadly rolling country, and the camp's few lights had disappeared behind the first gentle hill. What he was seeing now, Varlik realized, was the raw, native planet, marked only by this meager track and the cone of their headlights. Here, low rounded ridges ran almost north and south, and on their east-facing slopes, prairie gave way to savannah, its widely scattered, globular trees lurking darker in the night. Varlik wondered if large animals roved here, and whether any were inclined to attack people. Probably none could catch a hovercar if they tried.

The sky was innocent of city glow, stars myriad against and around the Milky Way's white swath. The present human sector was farther in toward the hub than mankind's earlier home, and the star display a bit richer, although Varlik knew nothing of that. He only knew it was beautiful. Scanning it for a recognizable constellation, he found none, and wasn't sure whether that reflected his sketchy knowledge of constellations or his displacement in space, or possibly the fact that he was in the middle northern latitudes here while Landfall was in the southern hemisphere at home.

His misgivings about the T'swa returned again, to mind and gut. He was on his way to meet them, to arrange to live with them, share a squad tent with some of them. A picture flashed in his mind, not for the first time, of large, black, hardbitten men who held life cheap. They were gambling, a fight broke out, knives flashed . . .

Maybe he'd end up with Colonel Voker after all.

And the T'swa would arrive in the middle of night. Captain Trevelos had said they would bivouac, which implied an unimproved area. When they got off the ship, would they have to dig latrines in the darkness and set up kitchens before they retired, besides erecting tents? Welcome to Kettle! They'd be in a great mood!

Or maybe they preferred it that way. Outside the Confederation worlds, and maybe some of the trade worlds, attitudes deviated a bit from Standard. And the T'swa were gooks—barbarians in uniforms, more or less. You couldn't know what they'd consider satisfactory.

After a while the mild hills gave way to an area almost as level as the military camp they'd left, and the hovercar slowed. "It's right about in here, sir," said Duggan. It was the first either of them had spoken for quite a few miles. "Hard to locate exactly in the dark. What we did was, we brought a reaction dozer out, and it sort of scalped a perimeter line around a big square so the ships can find it on the scanners at night. Or they can hang around up there till it gets light, or just set down blind by gravitic coordinates, I suppose; but if they tried that, they might miss the place, depending on how good their coordinates are set."

The corporal's speech was Iryalan instead of Romblit,

his diction marking him back-country rural; a lot of soldiers were.

"Would it make any difference where they put down?" Varlik asked. "Couldn't they as well camp in one place as another, way out here?"

"Not very well. We drilled some water wells for 'em; they're going to need 'em when the sun gets up. They're really gonna need those water wells. I've heard their world is as hot as this one, but if they're human, they're gonna want lots of water."

He stopped, and they settled mentally to wait. "Pat," Varlik asked shortly, "what do you think of the Rombili?"

Duggan didn't answer at once, sitting back with one arm leaning on the top of the door. "The Rombili? They seem all right to me. They kind of screwed up the war, but it's easy to see how that would be; nobody had any idea that all those sweatbirds were running around loose down there, or that they had weapons or anything. I've talked to quite a few Rombili, and they're not much different from us."

"Sweatbirds. Is that what you call the gooks here?"

"Right. They got a funny build—long legs, big chest, and kind of skinny. All they need is a long neck and beak for catching fish, and they do have quite a nose. Longish necks, too."

"What do you think about T'swa mercenaries coming out here?"

"Seems good to me." He turned his face to Varlik, a brief reflection of starlight in one eye. "Let the T'swa fight the gooks. I hear they love wars; why not give 'em this one? I'd like to see two divisions of 'em, not just two regiments. Specially if they're as good as you hear."

Varlik watched the man remove something, a small package, from a pocket of his fatigue shirt, take something from it with his fingers, and put the something into his mouth. The spicy smell of nictos reached Varlik's nose. For a moment the corporal chewed, compacting the plug, then spat onto the prairie.

"Is that how most of the men feel about the T'swa? They wish there were two divisions?"

"Or a whole army." His eyes returned to Varlik. "We're not afraid of the gooks. Don't get me wrong. But they've got big jungles down south, hotter than a cookpot. I mean, it's bad up here, but it's supposed to be a lot worse at Beregesh. So there's this bunch of crazy sweatbirds down there, and it's gonna be bloody work doin' anything about 'em. If it wasn't for the technite, I'd say let 'em have the place. And we probably would, too."

He spat again and said nothing for half a minute. Then, "That's kind of what we're trying to do anyway, I guess. What General Lamons has in mind, accordin' to rumor. Just take back the country around the mines, fortify hell out of it, and let the gooks have the rest of the planet. Except for Aromanis.

"And stop usin' slaves. That's where the Rombili screwed up. If they'd have just started mining with mechanicals and contract workers, the gooks wouldn't have even known the Rombili were on the planet."

The corporal paused then, as if uncertain, and peered at Varlik in the starlight. "If I tell you somethin' private between the two of us, will you keep it that way?"

Lormagen extended his right hand. "I guarantee it." They gripped on the promise.

"My best buddy's a computerman, and he called up the staff briefing file on Kettle, to read it. The gooks never even lived where the mines are until the Rombili took slaves down there. And the first batch they took there, a lot of 'em died, because they made 'em work without cool suits. And the women they took down there, some of 'em died when they got pregnant. So the gooks that could take it lived, and the toughest got away to the jungles and had families there. And that's the strain we gotta fight."

He spat again, shrugging. "Not even a gook likes bein' a slave."

Varlik nodded, and the conversation died of conta-
gious introversion and the night. They watched the sky
and waited, and after a few minutes they didn't really
watch any more, only sat with their faces aimed upward
a little.

Then Varlik began to feel something, and his alertness sharpened. He became aware that his driver too
had taken life. Carefully they scanned the sky, and
realized that within the blackness was a different black,
an area poorly defined that showed no stars, moving
from what he thought was the east. As they strained to
see into it, it grew, encroaching upon the Milky Way,
slowly crossing it. Varlik didn't think to lower the visor-
like camera monitor. With it down he could have peered
beneath it to see normally or cast his glance upward a
little to watch through the eye of his camera, which
adjusted constantly to target illumination.

Abruptly the night was broken from above by a powerful beam of light that slid across the ground, passing
near them, then made an angle nearby.

"Consar's royal balls!" Duggan swore. "I parked in
their landing square! Must have missed the dozer scalp
somehow; maybe there was a gap in it at the travelway."
He laughed as he swung the car around and moved
away. "All this empty prairie out here and I parked
where they're supposed to put down." They hurried up
a mild slope, Varlik with camera busy, then stopped
again three hundred yards distant while the powerful
light continued to trace a rectangle on the ground.
Abruptly it went out, and gradually the vague blackness
became a ship settling groundward, no lights showing.

Brief minutes later it rested on the prairie, its powerful lights flooding the area on one side. A second ship
took shape above, and five minutes later it rested some
hundred yards from the first. More lights brightened
the area between the ships, while others flooded thinly
a larger area beyond them. Squares opened in the
hulls. Hundreds of uniformed men began to file from

some of the smaller openings, moving on the double. Some trotted into the thinly lit area, while most formed ranks near the hulls.

Cargo movers floated out with boxes and duffle bags stacked beneath them, setting down their burdens along a line midway between the ships. Then they floated back through the gangways and out of sight for more. A long low pile of material took shape quickly. At one end of it, men were calling and gesturing, and from the ranked troops, squads quick-timed over to pick up gear and trot away with it.

Suddenly, from the darkness to one side of Varlik and Duggan, a voice spoke, seeming not more than a dozen yards away. "Hoy!" it said, quietly but firmly, a neutral, nonthreatening, but attention-taking sound. Varlik's and Duggan's eyes snapped in that direction but saw nothing. Nothing but night.

"Who are you, and what are you doing here?" the voice asked. Its Standard was accented but easily understood.

Varlik's eyes checked the power light on the small recorder at his belt, then he answered in Tyspi. "I've come to speak with the T'swa. My name is Varlik Lormagen. I am from Iryala, and I am . . ." He had no word for journalist. "My job is to tell the people of the Confederation what T'swa warriors are like."

A ring of chuckles sounded softly all around them, and Varlik felt his hackles rise. Even on his bare forearms the hair stood up like tiny antennae. But there was no malice in the laughter. None whatever. Obviously he and Duggan had been spotted on scans from the ships, and a patrol had been sent to check them out.

"You are speaking with a T'swa warrior now," the voice said. "Our commanders are occupied. We will wait here."

This had been said in Tyspi also, and Varlik was surprised to find that the diction was as clear, the speech as easily understood, as the lesson recordings had been. He spoke now in Standard. "Is it all right to talk with you while we wait? If so, I would prefer to speak Standard just now. My driver doesn't know Tyspi, and it would be more courteous if we spoke so he can understand."

There were no more chucklings around them. "Standard will be satisfactory," the voice said in kind, and now, by starlight, Varlik could make out the T'swi as the man walked toward them, a little taller than himself, looking bulky and powerful. Holding the video camera in one hand, Varlik lowered the monitor with the other. In it he could see what the camera saw: dark face, large eyes, hawk nose, wide lipless mouth, and a helmet that seemed quite standard. About ten feet away the T'swi stopped. His sidearms were a holstered pistol and a short sword. He held a rifle ready in his hands.

The sword surprised Varlik. He'd assumed that the swords the T'swa carried in adventure stories had been the writers' creation. Swords were a primitive weapon, seen on gook worlds and perhaps on parts of some more primitive trade worlds. And while the T'swa *were* gooks, they were not supposed to be primitive in the military sense. Even Colonel Voker considered them superb troops.

Now that they were here, in front of him, Varlik had to grope for questions. "How many of you are there?" he asked.

"We are two regiments."

"About thirty-eight hundred men, then?"

"My regiment is the Red Scorpion Regiment. We recently finished a sporadically rather vicious war on Emor Gadny's World, and our numbers are reduced to 934 officers and men."

"In a regiment? You came straight here without refitting or replacing your casualties?"

"No. We refitted on Tyss, and spent two months

enjoying our world and our people, healing our wounds and replacing such weapons as were worn out or lost. We do not replace casualties."

Didn't replace casualties! Varlik wondered if somehow he had misunderstood the T'swi. "How many were in your regiment when you went to—what world was that?"

"Emor Gadny's World. An interesting place—beautiful but difficult. We went there four years ago with about twelve hundred. Before that we were on Gwalsey, a dull war, and before that, Splenn. We went to Splenn a virgin regiment, with a full complement of 1,720 officers and men. That was more than fourteen years ago, Standard."

"But . . ." Varlik could not comprehend. They didn't replace their casualties! "How can you call yourself a regiment, then? How many did you say you have now?"

"Nine hundred and thirty-four effectives." The T'swi chuckled. "Abundantly effective effectives. And we will be the Red Scorpion Regiment until there are none of us left."

Varlik pursed his lips and whistled silently. This was something the fictionists hadn't mentioned, probably didn't know about. He imagined for a moment three scarred and gray-haired veterans charging an enemy—or slipping up on them in the dark, more likely.

"How long do you think it will be before you'll be in action? Do you have any idea?"

"It depends on the urgency of the situation. Normally, after landfall we spend two weeks in reconditioning, per contract. The opportunities for exercise are somewhat limited on a troopship, and our manner of combat requires physical excellence."

This guy, thought Varlik, *talks like someone out of staff college, not like anyone who'd be sent out to lead a patrol.* "What rank are you?" he asked.

"I am Sergeant Kusu. This is my squad."

"What's your education?"

"We have been educated as warriors of Tyss, by the Lodge of Kootosh-Lan."

Varlik glanced down at the recorder and camera. The tiny red glints reassured him; he wouldn't want to lose any of this. "The Lodge of Kootosh-Lan. I know very little about the T'swa. Does the name Kootosh-Lan have some special significance?"

"Kootosh-Lan founded the lodge, in the year 8,107 of our calendar. That was more than 14,000 of your Standard years ago."

Varlik tried carefully to see the black face more exactly, to read character and mood. *If that is history instead of folklore, their recorded history is a lot older than ours.* He decided to approach the matter indirectly— see if the story had mythic elements. "Was Kootosh-Lan a great warrior?"

A couple of chuckles were audible behind him. "Kootosh-Lan was no warrior at all. She was a teacher, the most renowned master in the history of Tyss. It was she who traced out and codified the Way of the Warrior, then established the first warrior lodge, that those who chose the Way of the Warrior could be properly prepared."

This Kusu, Varlik told himself, *is a great interview. Answers everything directly with full pertinent details.*

The sergeant's gaze had moved to the ships; Varlik's attention and camera followed. No longer did the cargo movers float in and out of the freight doors. Troops still picked up gear and carried it away. In the diffusely lit area on the far side was a lot of activity now; they were setting up camp there.

"One ship will leave soon," said Kusu.

"How soon?"

"A few minutes."

Incredibly quick. They probably drill disembarking, Varlik decided. "Will the other ship stay?"

"Briefly. While camp is being set up."

"Did the troops unload their own materials, or was that done by crewmen?"

"The ship's crew operates the cargo movers. The ship is T'swa, a troop carrier leased from your own world, and its crew is trained and experienced at unloading military material. They are to their jobs what we are to warring—expert. The Way of Jobs is not less an art than the Way of war. Are you familiar at all with the Ways?"

Varlik recalled vaguely the chart in the *Exotic Philosophies* entry. "Very slightly. I recall seeing a chart showing Ways of, uh, Work, and Fighting, and . . . Study was one. There were others." He wished he could read the T'swi's reactions. Then a movement caught his attention; one of the ships was lifting, and he thumbed the camera's trigger again. In little more than a minute it was lost to darkness. The other ship showed no sign of leaving; its floodlights still illuminated the bivouac area.

Sergeant Kusu interrupted Varlik's watching. "Follow me; I will take you to our colonel now."

Somehow it sounded more an order than suggestion. Kusu had probably been told to bring in whoever was waiting out here. "Okay?" Duggan asked. Varlik nodded. As the corporal activated the AG unit, the burly T'swi turned and trotted off down the slight slope toward the landing site. The others waited behind and to the sides until the vehicle began to follow Kusu, then moved along in its wake.

They drove right through the mustering area. Considerable material remained on the unloading site, unattended now. Two cargo movers were parked there, waiting to transfer more of it, perhaps to the kitchens when they were ready. In about two minutes, Duggan drew the car up to the regimental headquarters site, where already a considerable tent had been erected. A miniature ditch was still being dug around it, to catch and carry off the water from its roof in case of rain.

There was a great deal of crisp and purposeful activity roundabout. Squad tents were being raised. These men knew what they were doing, and did it rapidly, with a modest amount of quiet, cheerful talk in Tyspi.

At the regimental headquarters Kusu reported, then introduced Varlik to Colonel Koda. Except for the patrol's black, the T'swa uniforms were a curiously, irregularly blotched green, Koda's included. In the monitor, the colonel looked no older than the sergeant and carried much the same belt gear. Only the shoulder insignia were different. They were standard—cloth wings versus the sergeant's sewn-on patch with the initial *T*.*
Colonel Koda examined the Iryalan for a brief moment, then spoke in Standard with a slight accent that was mostly a matter of precise diction.

"Varlik Lormagen." He said it as if tasting the name; his eyes were alert, direct but unthreatening. "And you want to tell your people about T'swa warriors. Very well, you can report to—Lieutenant Zimsu of the First Platoon, Company A, in the morning. He will expect you. You can accompany the platoon in its daily routine and observe T'swa warriors to your fill." Then he spoke briefly to his aide in Tyspi before turning again to Varlik.

"Thank you, colonel," Varlik said. To his surprise, the T'swa colonel flashed a quick grin.

"You are welcome," the colonel replied, then dismissed him unmistakably, simply by removing his attention totally.

Unaccompanied now, ignored, Varlik and Duggan climbed into their vehicle and drove away, picking a careful route through the encampment. Hovercars do not ride an air cushion; they operate on the same gravitic principle as floaters. But as hover vehicles are functionally limited to near contact with massive bodies, the

---

*For *torvard*, *sergeant* in Standard.

turbulence of rapid passage can raise dust. Duggan's caution among the tents avoided this. Even so, he cleared the area quickly enough, and swung around in an arc that would find the marker rods.

Once more on the track, they started back for the Confederation military base, not speaking till they topped the first low hill. Then Duggan swung the vehicle around and stopped for a last look. At almost the moment they stopped, the floodlamps of the ship flicked off, leaving the plain in darkness. There were not even the white sparks of handlamps.

"What do you think of them, Pat?" Varlik asked.

"The T'swa? First-rate soldiers. They set that place up quicker than I ever would have thought. And that patrol! Whoosh! They could have shot us before we ever knew they were around; could have slit our throats, as far as that's concerned." Duggan shook his head in wonder. "They're good, all right. Better'n good."

He paused. "You coming to see 'em again tomorrow?"

"Right."

"Going to stay with 'em while you're here?"

Varlik's misgivings were gone, leaving only a light unease in its stead. The T'swa had seemed both civilized and intriguing, unlike anything his imagination had conjured up.

"You can bet on it," he said.

Duggan nodded as if approving, then swung the car around and started back toward the base. They hardly said anything all the way there.

Eleven

Varlik arrived at officers' mess thick-headed and sluggish from the combination of the short Orlanthan diurnal cycle, the army's daybreak reveille, and having gone to bed so late the night before. Before hitting the sack, he'd copied and edited his cube, intercutting his narration, covering not only the T'swa but the Aromanis camp and the heat, with a brief statistical description of Kettle he'd excerpted in the ship's library. It was his first feature on Kettle and the T'swa.

Now, as he stepped into the relative coolness of the mess hall, the pungent smell of fresh-brewed joma met him, along with the different pungency of fried bacon. He'd have liked to take the empty seat at Colonel Voker's table, but the brisk and businesslike pace of eating there warned him away and, at any rate, the media people had their own table assigned here. It might be a breach of etiquette to sit elsewhere uninvited. So instead he crossed to where Konni Wenter and the typically withdrawn-looking Bertol Bakkis sat eating.

A messman in crisp white apron had seen Varlik enter and, tracking him with his eyes, slanted quickly over, stainless steel thermal pitcher in hand, to pour his joma and take his order. Varlik gave it, then unfolded the waiting white cloth napkin onto his lap as the messman left.

"I saw you leave last night," Konni said.

Varlik looked up, noticing Bakkis's opaque gaze on him.

"You did? I'm surprised," Varlik said. "It was close to 19.20 when we left."

"Nineteen-fifteen; I looked. I couldn't get to sleep, so I'd been out walking around to get tired. I saw a car pull up, and five minutes later you left in it."

"Right."

She said nothing then, as if waiting, and he ignored her, testing the scalding joma with a cautious upper lip, deciding that cream was in order, for cooling. If she wanted information, she'd have to be specific.

"Where did you go?" she asked finally as he put down the cream and reached for the sugar.

"Off base." Varlik's eyes moved to Bakkis for a moment; the heavyset cameraman had shifted his attention back to his plate, half cleaned of its eggs and bacon.

"I'd hoped," Konni said, "that we might cooperate here, to some degree at least. It's not as if we're rivals."

She'd hit close to home, and it annoyed Varlik. He finished sweetening his joma before turning his eyes to hers. "I'm afraid I tend to be a loner," he said stiffly.

The messman was approaching with Varlik's breakfast on a large plate, and Varlik gave his attention first to receiving the food, then to opening and buttering a hot roll.

"I suppose you've heard about the T'swa regiments."

The voice as well as the words startled Varlik, and butter knife poised, he turned abruptly to Bakkis. The man had never spoken to him before. "We plan to find out where they keep them," the cameraman went on, "and go out there today. You're welcome to ride with us if you want."

"That's where I was last night," Varlik found himself

answering. "I was there when they landed, about thirty miles from here."

"Two regiments, were there?" Bakkis asked.

"Right. Just the way I'd heard back in Landfall."

Bakkis nodded, face still inscrutable. "Do you plan to go back there today?"

"Yes. Matter of fact, I do."

"Be all right to go together, or do you want to go alone?"

Varlik was amazed. He'd thought of Bertol Bakkis as a lump of barely aware flesh, its intelligence pickled in ethanol, operating in some obscure, automatic way along a subconscious thread of journalistic intention. Now the man was talking as casually and intelligently as anyone might, and for the moment it was Konni who sat quietly.

Bakkis had been the icebreaker. While they finished their breakfasts, the three of them talked about the T'swa, about Varlik's brief talk with Colonel Koda, and the invitation to attach himself to Koda's regiment.

"I suppose you got some cubeage of the landing," Bakkis said.

"Some. If you'd like to copy the field cube with your equipment," Varlik found himself saying, "you're welcome to."

"Thanks. I will. And when we get back to our quarters, I'll have Konni interview you on camera. That will make the field shots more meaningful to viewers, and it'll set people up for the feature articles you send."

It made so much sense to Varlik that his earlier guardedness seemed incomprehensible and petty.

After Bakkis had copied parts of his T'swa cube—the landing and the bivouac—and shot Konni's skilled interview, they went to the communications center. On the way, Varlik apologized, not very articulately, for his boorishness, and Konni, for whatever reason, had stiffened at the apology. Bertol's reaction, somewhat amorphous, seemed to say that he hadn't felt aggrieved, but thanks anyway.

The temperature had soared, and sweat had soaked through Varlik's twill shirt; workouts aboard the *Quaranth* had developed his sweat gland function well beyond the ordinary. After filling out brief forms and labels, they left their packaged cubes with the sergeant there for dispatch to Iryala in the day's message pod. Even by message pod, the sergeant told them, it would take 9.83 standard days for reports to reach Iryala—11.90 Orlanthan days.

From the communications center, it was no more than an eighty-foot walk down a corridor to the information office. At their knock, Trevelos called out to enter, and they did, Varlik holding the door for the other two. Trevelos's almost boyish pleasure of the day before was gone. The expression that met them now was stiff and guarded.

"How can I help you?" he asked.

It was Varlik who answered. "We'd like a vehicle."

Trevelos's expression became stiffer, yet vaguely unhappy. "I'm afraid I can't do that."

Varlik was dumfounded. "Why? Yesterday you said we could have one or more if we wanted."

Trevelos's discomfort was tangible. "I'm afraid I overspoke myself. If you want to go somewhere, perhaps I can arrange a chauffeured vehicle."

"Okay. We'd like to be taken to the T'swa camp."

Trevelos didn't answer for several seconds. "I'm afraid that's impossible. The T'swa camp is off-limits."

"Off-limits? Why?"

"The T'swa's privacy is to be strictly respected."

"But lieutenant, I was there last night and had a direct invitation from Colonel Koda of the Red Scorpion Regiment to stay with them, to describe them and their training for the Iryalan public. He told me he'd expect me today."

Trevelos actually blushed. "I'm afraid I can't help you with that, Mr. Lormagen. Perhaps something else."

Hormones—something—surged through Varlik's body, with a feeling first of heat, then of internal numbness, incredulity, as he stared at the information officer. Then Bakkis spoke, his tone casual.

"What, specifically, did the general order, lieutenant?"

Varlik's eyes turned to Bakkis's sweaty, somewhat florid face, then to Trevelos again. Bakkis had put his finger on the problem, Varlik was sure: Lamons. But the only result was that Trevelos looked less uncomfortable, as if with a shifting of blame from himself to the general.

"I do not feel I should discuss my orders."

"Of course." Bakkis had taken over, and Varlik was willing, for now, that he should. "We can understand that," Bakkis went on. "In that case, we'd like to see the agricultural operation."

Trevelos brightened. "Certainly. When would you like your car?"

Bakkis looked at Varlik. "Varl?" he said.

"Uh—why not now?" At the moment he didn't care—he had no real interest in the Aromanis farms—but it was an answer.

Trevelos looked almost happily at Bakkis. "I can have a car and driver here in fifteen minutes. And I'll call the farm headquarters so you can have lunch there. Their executive dining room has a marvelous reputation among the general's staff; almost everything they serve is fresh, and the cooks are excellent."

Bakkis asked that they be picked up at their quarters in fifty minutes—half a local hour. After the lieutenant had made arrangements with the motor pool, the three journalists said goodbye and left. When the office door had closed behind them, Bakkis muttered an obscenity, but without heat, and started toward the communications center. "I'm going to dispatch my office and ask them to get this restriction lifted if they can. They were especially interested in the T'swa. Meanwhile, let's keep Trevelos happy and relaxed."

So Iryala Video had also been especially interested in the T'swa. "Messages will take ten days Standard each way," Varlik pointed out, "plus whatever time it takes at the other end to get an order issued—if it gets issued."

They had stopped outside the comm center door. "The next time we see Trevelos," Bakkis said quietly, "I'll tell him we've dispatched our offices for a reversal, and that we appreciate what he's done for us. He'll assume we're content to wait, that we're trusting our offices to take care of things for us. That's the way he'd do it. Maybe that will relax him about our wanting to get to the T'swa. Then, in three or four days, we'll try to get a car without a driver, to hop around and interview some Romblit troops. He's already feeling propitiative, and if he'll go for that, screw the restriction; we'll go see the T'swa."

Varlik wondered if that would work, and if Bakkis actually believed it might. One thing was certain: He'd drastically misjudged this man back on the *Quaranth*.

The trip to the farm had been more interesting than Varlik had anticipated. The travelways were lined with tall native trees. The headquarters buildings were comfortable, rambling, air-conditioned, and beautifully landscaped, with everything marvelously clean and well-tended. The cuisine was better than anything he'd experienced before. The Romblit personnel there seemed competent and friendly. Security personnel were numerous, well-armed, and relaxed—were paramilitary employees of Technite, Ltd., the firm that had long operated the Orlanthan fief for the Romblit government. The army apparently restricted itself to patrolling the surroundings, leaving the on-farm scene at something like prewar normal.

Remarkably little powered machinery was used in

the agricultural operations; hand labor was compellingly cheap, apparently, and probably more precise for many tasks. Even the removal of weeds in large rowcrop fields was done by a line of tall thin workers, the hoes in their hands rising and falling in unison.

The field workers and domestics had given Varlik his first look at sweatbirds. They were a brownish people, slender except for barrel chests, their coarse brown hair straight and almost crested, their flaring eyebrows like tufts of golden-brown feathers that presumably served to divert sweat. And even those who served in the dining room showed little sign of subcutaneous fat. They reminded Varlik of kerkas, the tall wading birds of Iryala; their noses really were relatively long and pointed, and their necks too long as human necks go. Their physical structure seemed designed to maximize the body's surface/mass ratio for dispersing body heat. They were quite different from the husky T'swa, whose phenotype had evolved under considerably heavier gravity.

Varlik had wondered what the local sweatbirds thought of the war; perhaps, he'd told himself, they didn't even know about it, although all the nearby military activity must have told them something was happening somewhere.

After the farm, Bertol and Konni had been ready for a shower, to be followed by editing their field cubes in air-conditioned comfort. Varlik, though, had decided to take care of one final job, and jogged through dusty 120° heat to headquarters. After the aesthetics of the farm, the drab and dusty military base seemed utterly graceless. He knocked at the information officer's door and identified himself, and Lieutenant Trevelos's voice bade him enter.

"How can I help you?" the lieutenant asked when Varlik had entered.

"I'd like to see the Orlanthan briefing. It will give me a much better sense of the overall situation here."

Immediately the lieutenant looked worried, then apologetic. "Mr. Lormagen, I really dislike telling you this . . ."

"But you can't let me see it."

"That's right. You're neither a staff officer nor a command officer."

Varlik nodded slowly. "Well . . . thank you, anyway."

He turned and left, jogging back to his quarters for the postponed shower. While showering, he rehearsed several scenes with General Lamons, none of which, he knew, would ever occur. A couple of them were probably physically impossible. Then he too sat down to play his field cube of the day and record his article. When he'd finished, he had to admit it was good, something that readers would appreciate. But it wasn't what he was here for.

After supper he found out where Colonel Voker was quartered—a one-room hut of poured concrete in officers' country. Varlik stood hesitantly, unsure he should be there, then knocked. The colonel opened the door and scowled out at him.

"What do you want?"

"I seem to be running into brick walls at the information office. I hoped you could advise me. Again."

Voker's surliness softened slightly, and he gestured Varlik in. His quarters, though military, managed, through the prerogatives and resources of a senior officer, to reflect his personality. The windows were curtained. A small and clearly expensive tapestry softened one wall; a burnished wood bookcase with expensively bound books stood against another. The air conditioner held down the interior temperature to a luxurious 85°. Next to a lightly upholstered chair, a book lay open, face down on a small stand, and a red light glowed in an expensive cube player beside it.

"Specifically?" Voker asked.

Varlik told him of the prohibition against being taken to the T'swa camp, and of Trevelos's refusal to let him see the briefing on Orlantha.

"And this Colonel Koda invited you to stay with them?"

Varlik nodded. "Right."

"Huh." Voker gazed reflectively at him, lips slightly pursed, then abruptly grinned—a grin of pleasure tinged with something else. Malice. "So you still want to live with the T'swa. Well, fine. Be at the headquarters entrance at 05.50 hours tomorrow morning. And carry everything you absolutely need on your person, in case you luck out and make it to the T'swa camp—recorder, camera, toothbrush. The minimum. Don't be obvious—no suitcase. From there it's up to you—your wits and your guts. And your luck.

"And as far as the briefing cube is concerned, you got the essential picture from me aboard the *Quaranth*."

He stepped back to the door and put his hand on the handle. "And I don't mind telling you, I'll be interested in seeing what happens in the morning."

At 16.00 hours, Lieutenant Trevelos, reading a novel on the computer screen in his office, was interrupted by a knock. Irritatedly he cleared the screen before saying, "come in." It was Colonel Voker who opened the door, and Trevelos got quickly to his feet.

"At ease, lieutenant. I just came by to ask a question or two."

Trevelos receded into his chair. "Of course, sir." He looked around. "Would the colonel care to sit?"

Voker waved it off. "The reporter, Varlik Lormagen, and I got to know one another on the *Quaranth*. I ran into him on my way over here, and asked how he's doing. He told me he's been refused access to the Orlantha briefing. Can you give me the background on that refusal?"

"Yes, sir. Last night Mr. Lormagen went out to the T'swa area, and somehow the general heard about it this morning. It made General Lamons very unhappy, and he made it extremely clear to me that under no conditions was I to allow the media to go there again. He was particularly unhappy about Lormagen, and told me—these are his exact words—'You are not to allow this young fart any special privileges.' " Trevelos shrugged, spreading his hands.

Voker nodded thoughtfully. "I get the picture. Thank you, lieutenant. And have a good evening."

In the corridor, Voker allowed himself a chuckle. The situation was exactly as he'd suspected. In fact, he'd have given odds on it, but it was nice to know with certainty. Tomorrow he'd see just how good, and how lucky, young Lormagen was.

Twelve

At the Aromanis Base of the Orlanthan Counterinsurgency Army, the working day began at 05.00. Varlik, Konni, and Bertol Bakkis were outside the headquarters building entrance a quarter-hour later, at 05.25, twenty-five minutes before the time Voker had told him. All three were in field uniform, each with a musette bag slung on one shoulder, video camera on the other. The sun was up, but by only a hand's breadth, and it was still "cool"—about ninety-five degrees.

Konni Wenter was thinking how hot it would be in another hour—worse, another two hours—and whether Lormagen had been truthful when he'd told them he didn't know what was supposed to happen, only that something was. And what his real reason might have been in suggesting they be here with him.

Varlik was glad they'd come. He had the definite idea that he was on somebody's shit list, and that he'd be much more subject to counteraction if he were there alone, perhaps being told he couldn't loiter outside the entrance. This way it wasn't Varlik Lormagen standing here, but a group of journalists.

Bakkis's mind was on idle, thinking nothing, an abil-

ity he'd always had when there was nothing requiring
his conscious attention. He'd been fifteen years old
before he'd realized that everyone didn't do that. Only
an occasional thought drifted unbidden through his mind.
Just now he was aware of moderate soreness in his
thighs and abdomen; the evening before he'd gone to
the officers' gym, a set of connected modules with
assorted equipment, and begun the distasteful task of
becoming physically less unfit.

At 05.45, a sergeant came out, followed by a captain,
and told them politely to move aside a few yards, which
they did. Moments later they could see a hovercar
approaching, open to the heat. They watched it come
up the surfaced travelway, through the vehicle park,
and pull up before the entrance. The occupants were
T'swa, their skin blue-black.

As the vehicle slowed, entering the vehicle park,
more men issued from the headquarters entrance. Varlik
glanced at them, relieved to find that none wore the
novaburst of a general. The time, Varlik realized, was
definitely at hand; what he didn't know was what to do
about it. Almost unaware of what he was doing, he
moved closer, out of the background, visor down, belt
recorder on, camera in his hands, its red light blinking.
Bakkis advanced beside him.

Varlik's eyes were on the T'swa as they dismounted
from the light field vehicle. One of them was Colonel
Koda, and one of the others also wore the stylized
wings of a full colonel. All wore garrison caps tilted to
the right, and by daylight their bristly, close-cropped
black hair, like their skin, had a distinct bluish tinge. It
was when Koda's feet were on the ground that Varlik
stepped forward. A subcolonel in charge of the reception group glanced at Varlik angrily, his mouth opening
to speak, but Colonel Koda, stopping to look at the
reporter, spoke first.

"Lormagen! My visitor at the landing! I had expected

you yesterday. Are you no longer interested in my invitation?"

"Very interested, sir. I was refused transportation to your camp; otherwise, I'd have been there."

The white subcolonel's brows had knotted, his mouth a rictus of consternation.

"Ah!" said Koda. "Are you a soldier? Or under military command?"

"No, sir. I'm a journalist. But I depend on the army for accommodations and assistance."

"Then it was only a matter of transportation?"

"That's right, sir."

"Are you available for additional employment, if it does not interfere with your existing assignment?"

This, Varlik realized, was the moment of decision. "Absolutely, colonel."

They stood there for just a moment while the subcolonel fidgeted inwardly.

"Well, then," Koda said casually, "perhaps you will consent to be my civilian aide—my press aide. I have never had a press aide before, but I imagine that your new duties will not interfere with those of your present employment. Perhaps they will even expedite and mutually strengthen each other."

Varlik felt a grin seep up from somewhere to spread over his face.

"I'd like that very much, sir."

"Good. You are now officially in the employ of the Red Scorpion Regiment, of the Lodge of Kootosh-Lan, of the United Lodges of Tyss, as the regimental press aide. You will accompany me until I instruct you otherwise." Koda turned to the other T'swa colonel and nodded. The other in turn spoke to the Iryalan subcolonel.

"Colonel, we are ready to be presented to your general."

The subcolonel was outranked. Stiff, expressionless now, he turned to the headquarters entrance and led the T'swa party—the two colonels, two majors who were their executive officers, and two captains who were their aides, plus Varlik Lormagen—in to meet General Lamons. A standard army headquarters had a briefing room, and it was there that the general awaited them with several other officers, including Colonel Voker and Lieutenant Trevelos. Lamons stared the T'swa coldly into the room, not noticing the uniformed Varlik behind them.

"Colonels," said the general, "I am General Lamons, commanding." He gestured to the officers on either side of him. "This is my executive officer, Brigadier Demler, and this is Major General Grossel, commanding Romblit forces on Orlantha. The other gentlemen are our immediate staff. Welcome."

He was reciting; there was no welcome at all in his words. Chairs stood around a long table, but they were neatly, uniformly shoved beneath it; General Lamons had no intention of inviting them to sit, let alone offering them the quasi-ceremonial courtesy of joma. As he'd spoken, the general's eyes had noticed Varlik, clearly no T'swi, and with his last words of welcome, he looked at the subcolonel who stood beside the T'swa.

"Colonel Fonvill, who is that white man with them?"

"He's their press aide, general."

"Press aide?!"

Trevelos elaborated in a tentative voice. "He's Varlik Lormagen, sir. The journalist from Iryala."

Lamon's face darkened, and he barked out a command as he speared Lormagen with his eyes. "Provost marshal, get that man out of here! Confine him!"

The provost marshal hadn't had time to move when the second T'swa colonel spoke, his voice a flat snap, his black eyes glittering not with rage but with intention.

"General, no one will touch that man!"

The general's head jerked as if slapped, his mouth slightly open, face darkening even more, his eyes narrowed. Then, in a calm voice, the T'swi continued. "I am Colonel Biltong, commanding officer of the Night Adder Regiment. More pertinent to the discussion of the moment, I am also the contract officer of the Lodge of Kootosh-Lan for this expedition. You received a copy of our contract, but perhaps you have not fully familiarized yourself with it. We are a military force of a foreign nation, contracted to Confederation service here. Journalist Lormagen is the civilian employee of one of our regiments. Our personnel are not subject to arrest on your order, except for proper, documented, and verified criminal cause, as expressly provided by contract. Any breach of that contract on your part is grounds for our departure."

Lamons's jaw tightened. "Colonel," he bit out, "I would be delighted to contribute to your departure. The sooner, the better. I did not ask for you, I do not want you here, and I will not brook insubordination."

"General, I appreciate your feelings," Biltong said mildly, "but let me point out that if we leave through a breach of contract on your part, the very large advance payment made to our government by your own, and your government's considerable expense in our transportation, are not reimbursible. Per contract. If you were held accountable for that sum, five million dronas on the advance alone, you would be a ruined man, financially and professionally."

The black eyes looked around the room, taking in the faces, shocked or deliberately expressionless, evaluating each in that one glance. The general was not an easy man to serve under; thus, amidst the embarrassment, there was a certain amount of concealed pleasure among his staff.

"Beyond that," Biltong continued, "insubordination is not an issue here. Neither I nor my troops are your subordinates; mine is a contracted independent force. It would be well to read the contract, general; I can recite it verbatim. Now, I believe we have business to discuss."

No one said anything for perhaps ten interminable seconds. Varlik was aware that his military-length hair, already more or less erect, had become almost rigidly so, as if the follicles had spasmed. When at last the general spoke, his voice was rough with emotion.

"Here!" he said, and thrust papers at Biltong. "Your orders."

Biltong took them casually, seemingly without any sense of upset at the hostility he'd met, or of pleasure at his victory thus far. He scanned the two sheets, then looked up at Lamons again. "According to these," he said, "we are ordered to fly to Beregesh in two days, take the area from insurgent forces, and hold it. General, are you familiar with our contract at all?"

"I obtained and read a copy of your standard contract as soon as I heard you might be coming."

"But apparently not thoroughly. And have you studied the specific contract for the employment of our two regiments on this particular planet?"

Lamons seemed to go mentally inert, as if afraid to know what lay behind the question. Biltong turned to his executive officer, who carried a time-worn attaché case.

"The contract, please." The man gave it to him.

"General, I understand your confusion. First, your experience has given you no reason to anticipate such a non-Standard situation, nor such non-Standard persons as ourselves. And secondly"—he paused, and held out the contract to Lamons—"in some respects, this is not the usual T'swa contract. Incidentally, I'm not giving you this copy; you've been sent one of your own, I'm sure, which you can study during the two weeks our regiments will spend reconditioning here. But just now I'd like you to look at the signature of the contracting party. It is not, as you will see, your Department of Armed Forces."

For a moment the general only stared at the proffered

sheaf of pages, then took them, turned quickly to the signatures page, and paled visibly.

"That's right, general," Biltong continued, quietly now. "Our contract is with the Crown, in the person of His Majesty, Marcus XXVII, King of Iryala and Administrator General of the Confederation of Worlds. That is his signature."

Every white man in the room stood stunned, even Varlik.

"For the benefit of the moment, I will point out that even the usual T'swa contract authorizes us two full weeks to recondition ourselves. Further, Section 3 of Clause IV.B deals with proper use of T'swa units, and Section 4 states that the T'swa commanders can refuse any assignment that does not meet contract specifications. Incidentally, that section is not often invoked; we are, after all, in the business. But to use special assault troops in routine holding actions is, in the language of the contract, 'a misuse of the contracted force.' It subjects our regiments to debilitating casualties in an action which could as well be carried out by Standard units, wasting our potential as a special force."

Biltong continued more briskly now. "Next, about facilities. To the best of my knowledge, T'swa contracts invariably, and this one definitely, specify that contract forces will have made available to them full and equitable support by the contracting entity *and its agents*— meaning you in this instance, general. And by established legal precedents, that means we are to be provided facilities and other resources equal in kind and quantity to those of the military forces of the contracting entity in comparable circumstances.

"That, of course, has been drastically omitted in this case. However, assuming the situation is corrected without delay, I am willing to register no complaint with His Majesty about the primitive bivouac conditions we've been provided, or their remoteness from base facilities such as hospital, supply depot, and communications center.

"Regarding the communications center, we will of course require unrestricted and uncensored use of message pods, to make regular and irregular reports to our contract control office, which is our embassy on Iryala, and to our lodge on Tyss. Both will be expecting them. Not that censorship would be practical in any event, since our reports are made in Tyspi."

Lamons's bristly stiffness was entirely gone; he stood a defeated man. Now Biltong proceeded to inject the seeds of a working relationship. "It is unusal, General Lamons, for there to be an initial misunderstanding when a T'swa regiment collaborates with Confederation forces. Confederation general officers are usually unprepared, initially, to assimilate the real meanings of T'swa contract terms, or to understand the uses of T'swa units. We are—too non-Standard for that. And I suppose that, as their adjustments offend the military sense of propriety, none of this is reported in print or taught in your Academy.

"Usually the commanding general of the contracting entity, considering his many and varied responsibilities, will avoid the distraction of working directly with us by assigning an officer of suitable rank to liaise with the T'swa force. And if the liaison officer is one with an interest in the use of small assault units, this will result in more effective planning and coordination.

"We realize that you face a difficult military situation here, and we wish to be of maximum value to you. And not only does the Iryalan Crown have an urgent interest in renewing and securing technite production; it is personally very concerned over the severe military environment on Orlantha. It believes that we, with our unusual experience in wildland conditions and our tolerance of high temperatures, will prove to be an important factor in avoiding a protracted struggle, which the Confederation cannot tolerate. His Majesty expects our ambassador at Landfall to provide him with weekly summaries and, of course, both you and I want the military situation to progress as smoothly and swiftly as possible."

Unexpectedly the T'swi thrust out a hand to the general, who received it with his own, unprepared. They shook hands then, the volition being the colonel's.

"My aide, Captain Dotu, will be here tomorrow to meet with your liaison officer," Biltong continued. "We will want them to begin at once to plan our combat utilization. I will send with Captain Dotu a communications sergeant, who will be in charge of our communications at your communications center. The contract calls for providing him a special office there.

"And general, I regret any trauma this meeting may have caused, and I am sure we will soon find ourselves working together very effectively." Biltong bowed slightly. "To His Majesty's pleasure and our joint success, which are one and the same."

Both Biltong and Koda came to sudden attention then and saluted sharply. The general, after momentary surprise, returned the salute, and the T'swa, including Varlik Lormagen, exited, leaving the general still in shock.

They walked briskly, never pausing, out of the building. Their driver was parked only a few yards away. They climbed in as he started the engine. A moment later they pivoted and left, cruising leisurely out of the vehicle park and down the main travelway. The gate guards, seeing their shoulder insignia, saluted, opened the gate, and let them pass.

Varlik stared back over his shoulder at the retreating base, with an unexpected sinking feeling. He was leaving behind him civilization as he knew it—air-conditioning, comfortable beds, showers, people whose ways he understood . . . and a very hostile general who'd never let him function there now except as the press aide of Colonel Koda.

He looked at the calm, cool colonel beside him.

"Colonel Koda?"

"Yes, Lormagen?"

"What are my duties as your press aide?"

"It is time for the T'swa to make use of something the Iryalan and most other armies have used for a long time—a publicist."

"But I don't know enough about Tyss to prepare publicity for your people. And besides . . ."

"Not for our people, Lormagen. We need you to publicize us on Iryala, to your own people. I suggest you use your usual resources for dissemination—the offices of Central News and any others available to you. Those were journalists outside headquarters with you, were they not? I presume they'll be happy to receive information from you, certainly until we can arrange for them to visit us."

Varlik was aware that the other colonel, Biltong, was looking on, listening.

"We can discuss it further later," Koda was saying, "but I believe I said it when I first proposed this to you: It seems to me that you can go about your journalistic duties for your regular employer quite largely as you'd intended in the first place. That may well be all the publicity we need.

"At least to begin with, you will live with the First Platoon, Company A, First Battalion, accompany them in their training, learn about them. It would be well also to train with them yourself, so far as you are able. Then you can truly tell the people of Iryala what the T'swa are like, and what kind of warriors we are. And when we go south to fight, you can come with us, unless it seems too dangerous, and tell your people what the T'swa are like in battle."

Koda looked away then, sitting calm and quiet, surveying the Orlanthan grassland, as if Varlik had been dismissed, and the rest of the way to the T'swa camp they said almost nothing to each other.

Thirteen

You ask how the newly entitled T'swa warrior, a youth barely full-grown who has lived from childhood in a warrior lodge, never been off his home world, never seen a city or a ship or a foreigner, seems so considerably educated in what you term "the liberal arts." The answer is that on Tyss, all learn the T'sel, which is translated as "the Ways of Life on Tyss." However, it might as accurately be translated simply "the Ways of Life," for it applies as well anywhere; it is universal. But only on Tyss is it recognized and practiced—thus the term *T'sel*. And it is useful to rational living, which is to say wisdom, for anyone—the follower of any Way—whether on our world or yours. It is not simply a subject for scholars. It is also a subject for warriors, for example—including the young men you have observed and spoken with.

As to how every T'swa warrior can speak your language fluently, be conversant with your history and culture as well as his own, and know more than a little of your technology—it is largely a matter of learning them, which is less difficult than you might suppose for one who knows the T'sel. When your children undertake to learn, they are beset by many hindrances, encounter many obstacles—those from without and, more importantly, those from within. But when our children are still small, they are early helped to ... let us say, dissolve the inner obstacles and hindrances, at which point those hindrances outside them, already at a practical minimum, become of much less effect and more easily deflected. With that, learning becomes swift and smooth.

And the use of knowledge far easier, which use is part of wisdom.

The Confederation, I must tell you, is fortunate that the T'swa do not lust for power, for we are the swiftest of learners, and the greatest at the exercise of knowledge. But we have looked far, and have seen that such a lust degrades the field for all—for the one who lusts as well as for all others. And indeed, when one knows T'sel, there is no lust. Nor can the T'sel be known while there is lust.

It is not the having of power which ruins; that belief is an error, though an understandable error. There is nothing wrong with having power. *Rather it is the lust itself that ruins, the scale of ruin increasing exponentially with the success of the lust.*

—*Lodge Master Gun-Dasaru to Barden Ostrak, following the graduation of the So Binko Regiment of the Lodge of Kootosh-Lan (unedited from the recorded comments).*

The day promised to be even hotter than the two before, and a line of towering thunderheads were visible along the southwest horizon when the T'swa officers, with Varlik, arrived at the bivouac. On the flat ground behind the encampment, Varlik could see hundreds of men in groups, doing what appeared to be choreographed tumbling in a thin haze of dust. Even at a distance it was a remarkable sight.

And they definitely were not the entire T'swa force; perhaps the rest were on a field march, he told himself.

The hovercar stopped outside the headquarters of the Red Scorpion Regiment, a largish tent that nonetheless seemed to Varlik too small for its function. Its sides were rolled up for maximum ventilation. There he, Colonel Koda, and the colonel's executive officer and aide got out, and the vehicle left to deliver Colonel Biltong and his own E.O. and aide. Inside the tent were only three men besides themselves. Koda, in

Tyspi, told the sergeant major to have Varlik put on the rolls as civilian aide in charge of publicity, on the usual warrior's allowances, and to assign him to Lieutenant Zimsu's platoon for purposes of quarters, supply, and mess. When he'd finished, he turned to Varlik, speaking again in Standard.

"Sergeant Kusu told me you spoke Tyspi with him. Did you understand what I just told the sergeant major?"

"Yes, sir," Varlik answered, and repeated it quite closely in Tyspi, without too much stumbling or hesitation. "I expect to do much better with experience," he added.

"Excellent." The colonel's eyes reexamined the Iryalan. "You are very unusual among your people."

Despite himself, Varlik was pleased and embarrassed at the comment. After a pause, Koda continued. "Lormagen, I feel very—optimistic over what we did this morning, you and I. Colonel Biltong and I have intended, since we received this assignment, that the people of Iryala should get a much improved understanding of the T'swa through our regiments, and I have no doubt that you will prove most helpful in this."

Again the colonel withdrew his attention, this time to his desk and in-basket. Varlik looked around, found a folding camp chair, and sat down. With nothing to do for the moment, he felt the heat as a heavy fluid settling around him. The sergeant major, a one-eyed man scarred from hairline to jaw, had used his field communicator, and in two or three minutes another enlisted man entered the tent. Speaking Standard, the sergeant major introduced the soldier as Bao-Raku, with no mention of rank, and told Varlik to follow the man. Then the sergeant major too withdrew his attention, definitely the T'swa form of dismissal, and Varlik left behind a quick-footed, if limping, Bao-Raku.

It took less than a minute to walk to the headquarters tent of Company A, First Battalion. It was not at all like any company orderly room or field headquarters that

Varlik had seen in the Iryalan army; it had three small folding tables and a small file cabinet, no computer, and five visible folding chairs. No one at all was there except he and Bao-Raku. The T'swi pulled out a file drawer, removed a chart, sat down, and looked up at Varlik who, after waiting a moment for an invitation, sat down himself, unbidden.

Bao-Raku also spoke in scarcely accented Standard. "I am to assign you to a squad in the First Platoon. Do you have a preference?"

"Not really, unless . . . Except for Colonel Koda, I'm acquainted with only one other man in this regiment, a Sergeant Kusu. I don't suppose he's in this company, though."

"Sergeant Kusu is the leader of the Second Squad, First Platoon. Is that the squad you prefer?"

"Yes."

Coincidence? Or had Koda sent him to this platoon because Kusu was here? That didn't make any sense, but it occurred to him nonetheless.

The company clerk, Varlik supposed the man was, got up. "Have you any clothes besides those you are wearing? Supply will have difficulty providing you with uniforms that fit, until we've had a chance to procure some from the Iryalan Quartermaster."

"I have some on base. I can get them when I go there next."

The man nodded. "Good. And you have eaten today?"

"Yes, I have."

"Then I will take you to your squad."

Without saying anything further, the T'swi went out the door and, despite his limp, broke into a lope, Varlik hurrying behind him through the encampment over trampled bunchgrass clumps. By the time they'd run the quarter mile to the drill ground, sweat was running from Varlik's every pore.

The T'swa troops were in separate groups of ten, squads apparently, each with its own drill square defined and separated from its neighbors by harness belts, with knives and canteens attached, which had been removed for the drill. Each squad trained independently; in a sense, each individual or pair seemed to work independently, for there was no apparent leader. Yet their movements were integrated, whether by long practice or some nonevident communication, Varlik couldn't tell.

"That is the Second Squad of the First Platoon," Bao-Raku said pointing. "They will take a break soon, and you can talk to Kusu then."

Varlik nodded, and the clerk turned and loped away in the direction of the company area. Varlik returned his attention to the drilling troops, recording with his camera.

In part the drill resembled tumbling, in part some strange and acrobatic ritual dance, but withal, it was clearly training for some art of combat. Some of the movements were broad and flowing, others abrupt and accompanied by audible, forceful expulsions of breath. There were gliding movements, striking movements with hands and feet, some independently by an individual trooper, some with two interacting. Or a man might grasp another and throw him to the ground with a quick sweeping movement or a short choppy one, perhaps to be followed without pause by another, somehow all synchronized with the movements of every other. Men rolled smoothly, swiftly, leaped high, bodies amazingly flexible despite their physical bulk. Varlik watched entranced, even as he recorded the scene.

Then, without command, the entire drill stopped, and each T'swi went to his belt and drank from one of his two canteens, synchronization suddenly replaced by individuality. After drinking, men sat on the ground or stood around, most talking or laughing quietly together, while others lay quietly, perhaps with a forearm shielding their eyes from the sun.

Varlik walked over to Kusu, who looked up and rose

at his approach. The T'swa face was gray and grinning,
greased with muddy sweat.

"So you came," Kusu said in Tyspi, and reached out a
hand. "I am glad to see you."

Varlik took it and was startled. He'd expected its hard,
beefy strength; what surprised him was its hardness of
palm and the inner surface of the fingers, as if they'd
been armored with tempered leather. He didn't have
callus like that even on his feet! It seemed impossible
that it resulted from training—it almost had to be in-
herent, he thought, inborn—and for a moment his surprise impeded answering.

"Yes," he answered, also in Tyspi. "With the help of
your colonels. I'll tell you about it when we have time.
I came to report to you; I've been assigned to live with
your squad. How long is your break?"

"We still have two or three minutes. But we have
only one more drill cycle, of about ten minutes. Then
we break for lunch. Wait and watch if you wish."

Varlik retreated outside the square and waited in the
intensifying heat. Someone whistled shrilly, a quick
piercing pattern, its instrument human lips, and those
who'd lain down or sat got up at once, all moving into a
pattern of positions. When the drill began again, Varlik
once more recorded with his camera until they were
done. When it was over and the T'swa formed ranks,
Varlik, on his own volition, fell in with them at the end
of Kusu's squad, feeling awkward and out of place but
doing it nonetheless, then semi-sprinted with them to
the encampment's edge, where they halted and were
dismissed.

He was enormously pleased that he'd done it, grinning through his sweat as they walked among the tents
to that of Kusu's squad, rubbernecking now as he walked.
T'swa grinned back at him as they went, the grins
friendly, and a few thumbs were raised in his direction,
a salute of friendship common enough at home among
friends, but surprising him here.

The tent was floored with dirt, and had five cots along each side, with a duffel bag at the foot of each and a barracks bag beneath. From the roof pole hung an insect repeller. On each of the cots sat a field pack attached to a harness, the harness also holding assorted pouches and pockets. A rifle lay beside it.

An eleventh cot stood in the middle of the tent, like the others complete with pad, pad cover, and thin pillow. "That must be yours," Kusu said pointing. There was even a towel, wash cloth, belt with canteens and knife, a potlike helmet with liner, and a small block of what he surmised was a cleaning agent.

Bao-Raku must have brought the things, Varlik told himself. And he'd been half afraid—more than half— that these would be cruel and vicious men! Instead, this. And no one had sneered or needled or even been condescending.

Meanwhile, one of the T'swa had taken a plastic jerry can of water and poured some into each of a row of the potlike helmets outside. There was no rack for the helmets; there'd been nothing to build one with. They'd simply been set into shallow holes dug for them. Borrowing a trenching tool from the nearest T'swi, Varlik quickly gouged out a place and put his own helmet into it, then poured in water and, on his knees, joined in the pre-meal washup—face, hands, wrists.

The T'swa had stripped to their waists, and he was deeply impressed by the massive yet sinewy torsos and arms he saw, muscles sliding and bunching as they washed. Varlik was muscular by Iryalan standards, sinewy now as well, and as tall as most of the T'swa, but almost any of them would outweigh him by more than twenty pounds, all of it muscle.

He wondered what they'd do at day's end in lieu of a shower. In novels, gooks were usually filthy, but clearly not the T'swa, not where there was any choice.

When they'd washed, he followed the casual train of still shirtless black men to the A Company mess tent.

Apparently they ate without shirts if they wished! Such a thing was unthinkable in any Standard army. Varlik felt ill at ease now in his shirt, and moved quickly through the mess line. The food seemed of low quality, though doubtlessly nourishing. It consisted of a single, to him unidentifiable, mixture from a pot. Each man scooped his own serving into a broad bowl. In place of joma was some unfamiliar drink, tepid and sweet. Each squad had its own table with a bench on either side— long enough, with a little crowding, for an extra man. Following the example of the T'swa, Varlik poured a sauce onto his food, fortunately with caution, for the sauce was hot, currylike.

There was not much conversation at the meal, and what he heard seemed small talk, although some of it he couldn't follow. Most of the words he knew, but the referents weren't always familiar; he lacked the contexts necessary to give parts of it meaning. An uneasy feeling touched him, not for the last time, a certain sense of unreality that he could not dispel. These T'swa were so *non-Standard!*

Men began to leave, and he left too, his food unfinished, like them scraping his bowl into a garbage can before stacking it. Then he returned to his tent. He too was sweaty, and somewhat dusty. To avoid getting dirt on his bed he lay down on the ground outside, in the shade of the tent. It wasn't as if he was tired. He wasn't, despite the heat, and the humidity which seemed to be increasing. But the others were resting and there wasn't much else for him to do.

Minutes later Kusu arrived, strolled over to him and squatted down on heavy haunches as Varlik sat up. "We are going on a field march this afternoon," Kusu said, in Tyspi again. "But not a very hard one; we're too soon off shipboard. You are welcome to come if you'd like."

"Of course I'll come," Varlik replied. "It's the sort of thing I expected to do. In fact, I trained for it on shipboard, doing heavy workouts in a firefighter's suit, every day coming out from Iryala. If the march is too much for me, I'll find out soon enough by trying."

Kusu nodded. "You have almost an hour then to rest before we fall in. I suggest you sleep; I intend to. And if you are coming with us, you'll need to bring your canteens."

Varlik got up, filled his canteens from a jerry can, then lay back down again, draping the harness belt over his body. He closed his eyes and put his field cap over them, not anticipating sleep, but intending at least to rest. Sleep came nonetheless, to be broken by another shrill pattern of human whistling that brought him awkwardly to his feet, sluggishly aware of hustling bodies. He fastened the belt around his waist, then trotted after them, the dopiness dissipating with exertion, to where the T'swa were forming ranks on the mustering ground.

In ranks, he became aware that the others carried rifles and wore field packs, with magazine and other pouches clipped to their harnesses in front and assorted smaller pouches secured to their belts. Then, without verbal command, another quick whistle pattern started the column in motion at a brisk swinging stride, a column of fours broken into platoons.

He looked around him more alertly now as they moved away from the bivouac area. Rolling hills lay ahead, and in moments they were running through belly-deep prairie grass, where somehow the air seemed hotter, as if the mass of plant stems had trapped or perhaps exuded heat. At about sixty degrees from their line of march and a half-mile distant, he saw a vehicle coming along the track from the Aromanis base. Even from there he recognized it as a staff car, not open like the T'swa field vehicle but enclosed and undoubtedly cooled. Apparently the general wasn't waiting till tomorrow, but had sent someone to meet again with the T'swa. Probably to determine what was needed and wanted in the way of proper facilities for the regiments. For a brief few seconds he played with the fancy that they had come here to claim him back, and began to imagine the T'swa refusing to give him up. Then a single whistle shrilled, breaking his fantasy, and the column began to jog through the tall grass. In half a hundred yards the ground began to slope upward. The column alternately ran and walked, roughly in quarter-mile installments, the sun beating down on them, the ground heat stirring into sullen life with their passage. At the end of a local hour, another whistle stopped them. After drinking, and licking the salt that a T'swa trooper had offered him, he lay down like the others on the lumpy ground for a break. There was no shade, and the heat was suffocating near the ground. Varlik began to realize what kind of campaign environment this planet was—even here, more than halfway to the pole.

Silently he thanked Colonel Voker for ramrodding him through the twenty-six days of fire-suit workouts on the *Quaranth*.

Then, in about ten minutes, whistling got them up again. They formed ranks, there was another whistling command, and once more the column moved out, walking the first quarter mile, then running again, then walking, and the air he sucked into his lungs seemed stifling hot. After a bit, his legs began to go wooden on him, and he began to worry, wondering if he'd make it. The last thing he wanted to do was fall out, perhaps collapse, so he gathered himself, willing energy to his muscles, strength to his knees. He realized that his eyes had been directed at the ground and the boots of the man in front of him, and raised his face to look ahead.

The long row of thunderheads, though still distant, was nearer now, billows towering to form a single anvil top, an opaque veil of rain slanting from its blue-gray base as it marched on legs of lightning, too far away for thunder to be heard. It seemed to Varlik that if he could hang on till it reached them, he'd be all right.

His eyes soon turned back to the ground without his realizing it, but he persisted, running slack-mouthed, sucking the hot air, his right hand at frequent intervals wiping sweat to keep it from his eyes as much as possible. Then there was whistling again, another break, and somehow he was still with them. Again he drank, the water hot as soup, gratefully licked offered salt, and flopped on the ground, closing his eyes, his face turned away from the sun.

Behind the lids was red, with idly floating spots like tiny oil globules. Then a voice called his name—Sergeant Kusu's voice—and Varlik first sat up, then with an effort stood. A hovercar was coming up from behind— seemingly a T'swa vehicle—and they watched its approach until it drew up a dozen yards to the side.

"Get in," Kusu said gesturing, and despite himself, Varlik started to object. "No, get in," Kusu repeated firmly. "You'll do no one a service collapsed in the base hospital, or maybe dead. It's been standing by, waiting for a call, and I've been watching you. You've done extremely well, but it's time for you to ride."

Varlik found his legs taking him to the vehicle, and he got in, feeling not so weak after all. The sides were open, but the vehicle's top was up to keep the sun off. The steady-eyed driver handed him a vacuum flask— surely a luxury among the T'swa!—with some cool liquid that seemed to be fruit juice.

"Steady there," the driver said, "don't make yourself sick," and Varlik paused in his drinking. Then, after a pause and one more swig, he handed it back, and the T'swi capped it and put it in a bag without taking any himself. In another minute there was whistling again, the ranks reformed, and the battalion moved out, jogging through the grass, the hovercar keeping pace to one side.

Varlik started to take off his shirt to let the hot air flow over his body, the better to cool himself, then became aware of the forgotten camera he'd carried inside it, and raised it to record a few minutes of the march, enough to include one of the run segments, while murmuring comment for its sound pickup. When he felt he'd recorded enough of that, he tucked the camera away again, wondering if any of the T'swa felt resentment at his riding. Somehow, he didn't think so.

He was surprised at how far they went in the hour before the next break, over the rolling hills, curving around to head eastward again in the direction of the bivouac. He licked salt again, drank more of his hot water, then more from the vacuum flask, and all in all felt much recovered. After they stopped, he got out and walked over to Kusu. They shared salt, and he drank again.

"I feel a lot better now," said Varlik. "I'd like to finish this on foot with the rest of you."

Kusu looked him over, smiling a little, and nodded. "Fine," he said, "if you want to. But the last will be the hardest, and there will be no disgrace in riding again if the need arises."

Varlik nodded back, then took out his camera and recorded the resting T'swa, their shirts sweat-soaked, rings of whitish salts marking where it was most concentrated. *And they look as content as anyone I've ever seen*, he thought. The T'swa in Gorth Hasniker's novel couldn't touch the reality, at least in character. Briefly, he wondered what these men would be like in combat; he couldn't picture them cruel.

Then the command came whistling and he put the camera back inside his shirt as they formed ranks. Another whistle and they started off. They walked twice, then the second run continued until he realized they were to trot the rest of the way, and his heart sank. This was what Kusu meant by the last hour being the hardest. Only once more did they slow to a walk, just long enough to drink and let the water settle in their bellies before the whistle brought them to a trot again.

Just once he looked back over his shoulder, praying

that the rain would arrive. It was nearer, in fact not terribly far, and he let that hearten him. Rain! Cooling rain! Thunder rolled. Then his attention was trapped again by the travail of running.

Topping a long low ridge, he saw the encampment ahead, no farther than half a mile, and for just a moment his heart leaped with exultation. Then a whistle shrilled, once and long, and the battalion broke into a gallop, almost a headlong run, so that he veered off to the side to keep from being trampled, speeding up as best he could, seeing black men in sweat-soaked mottled green run past him. He sucked wind into tortured lungs, felt his legs flagging, staggering, slowing to an unsteady shuffling jog. He was unaware of Kusu running backwards to keep watch on him, of the hovercar close behind, but kept doggedly on, gasping, half-blinded by stinging sweat, until he stumbled onto the mustering ground. The nearing thunder hadn't registered on him, nor had the puffs of cooling breeze. The T'swa had already been dismissed but had not dispersed. They were waiting more or less in ranks, grinning, all eyes on him, and somehow, as he staggered up, he did not collapse. And when he stopped before them, they applauded, big hard hands clapping, throats cheering. Those nearest stepped up to him, clapped his back, shook his hand.

And when they stopped, Varlik became aware of another sound, behind him, a soft murmur. He turned, stared, fumbled at his shirt. A wall of rain was sweeping from the southwest across the steppe, its murmur gaining force. Sudden wind whipped. A hammer of thunder smote the earth so that even the T'swa flinched, and the first fat drops splatted around them, the T'swa's white teeth flashing a choir of grins, then rain swept over them, a body of it, an assault of it, and instantly they were drenched, water streaming over black faces that beamed and gloried—desert people receiving the gift of storm. And Varlik's camera, in his right hand, sheltered by his field cap, was registering all of it on the molecules of its cube.

Fourteen

Excerpts from *The Concise Pocket Guide to Land Warfare Weapons*; Evening Books, Ltd; Landfall, Iryala. 78 pp, Ð1.89.

Model 1 Rifle

The .24 caliber M-1 rifle can be used with solid steel bullets as well as with rifled explosive bullets, known as "blast slugs," that burst on impact. The barrel is 21.8 inches long, and the weapon weighs 7.32 lbs. without clip.

The M-1 rifle fires a blast slug with a muzzle velocity of 3,750 fps (feet per second) or a 90-grain steel slug with a muzzle velocity of 3,480 fps. The cyclic rate on automatic fire is 4 rounds per sec. The slender cartridges are two inches long and slightly stepped down for the bullet. The M-1 is very accurate. Firing an eight-round marksmanship trial with it from a prone position, free-hand and with open sights, the best marksmen can lay down a 16-inch pattern inside a two-foot bull's-eye at 500 yards, singleshot and without appreciable crosswind.

Clips come in two sizes: 25 and 40 rounds. Customary combat practice is to fire bursts of 3 to 6 rounds.

Blast slugs are usually used in combat, steel bullets in training.

Model 2 Rifle, "Blast Hose"

The blast hose has a bore of .28 caliber, and almost invariably, rifled blast slugs are used in combat. The blast hose weighs 20 lbs. without the 5-lb. box magazine, and is customarily fired from a barrel bipod for reasons of controlling the recoiling weapon and better supporting the weapon's weight. The rate of fire is 8 rounds per sec, and the blast slug weighs 148 grains. An eight-round burst from this weapon can fell a fourteen-inch hardwood tree. Each infantry squad carries a blasthose.

Model 1 Sidearm

The M-1 sidearm is a quick, emergency-response weapon carried by officers and certain auxiliary personnel. It is 8 inches long and used for close fire. The bore is .16 caliber, and while solid bullets are used in training, the blast slug is always used in combat. Like the rifle, it can be fired on automatic or semiautomatic. A clip holds 18 rounds, and the rate of automatic fire is five rounds per second.

Model 3L Rocket Launcher

The M-3L Rocket Launcher is 40 inches long, has a bore diameter of 1.23 inches, and is fired from the shoulder using a simple, side-mounted optical sight. It weighs 5.31 lbs. exclusive of clip. The spin-stabilized rockets are 8.17 inches long. They are fed from a top-loading clip of eight and are fired semiautomatically.

Rockets for the M-3L are of three main kinds—armor piercing, penetrating, and impact rockets. They vary in both propulsion explosive and strike explosive, and of course the casing. Often a rocket man will carry clips of each of the three kinds of rockets.

Model 4 Rocket, "Floaters' Bane"

The floaters' bane rocket is similar to the M-3H rocket. It is 55 inches long, has an inside diameter of 1.23 inches, and is fired from the shoulder. It is aimed, however, simply by pointing, depending on the target-seeking capacity of the rockets to hit the target.

The spin-stabilized rocket is 17.81 inches long, including the target seeker. The target seeker homes on all models of standard floaters and hover vehicles, via their electrogravitic fields. Targets can, in turn, cause rockets to explode prematurely by emitting directed electrogravitic counterpulses.

Model 1 Lobber

The M-1 Lobber has a length of 26 inches, a bore of 2.87 inches, and weighs 19.83 lbs., complete with base plate and bipod, which provide support and aim the weapon. The lobber is used to fire rockets over intervening barriers. The computerized bipod sets the tube at appropriate horizontal and vertical angles using range, azimuth, barrier, and wind data.

The rockets themselves are programmed by a separate charging computer, using similar data to those used in aiming the tube. The firing sequences vary in both outward burn and downward burn, to help deliver the rockets at appropriate angles and velocities of impact. Rockets are of three kinds: impact (exploding on impact), penetrating, and armor-piercing.

Grenades

Grenades are of several kinds, ranging from 2.17 inches to 2.68 inches in diameter, and weigh between 4.83 and 7.17 oz. They include antipersonnel grenades with fragmentation casings; blast grenades, with a much more powerful explosive; incendiary grenades; and several kinds of chemical grenades. Grenades are armed by twisting the two polar hemispheres into a reversible locked position—the reversible "readiness" step—then pressing a triggering socket firmly with a finger. Once triggered, the grenade will explode either on impact (blast grenades, for example) or after five seconds.

Model 1 Light Combat Sphere, "Killer Ball"

The Killer Ball is a highly mobile, normal-terrain, self-aiming, remote-controlled surface weapon. Control is usually from the heavily armored Model 7 floater. Diameter of the cleated track is 47.91 inches. Lightly armored and weighing 4,264 lbs., exclusive of drive charge, it depends on nimbleness and speed to avoid fire from, for example, the Model 3-H rocket launcher.

Driven by the 450 kw, DW-3C solid-fuel engine, the Killer Ball is immune to target-seeking rockets. It is armed with a single 65 kw pulse burner capable of the lethal penetration of ordinary concrete walls and all but the heaviest concrete and earth bunkers.

The Killer Ball will climb slopes as steep as 25-35 pct., depending on the surface. (A 35 pct. slope is equivalent to a 35-ft. climb over a horizontal distance of 100 ft.) It will also cross marshes if they overlay firm substrates at depths not more than 20-25 inches. It is particularly useful in supporting infantry attacks on towns that do not have sophisticated fortifications.

Fifteen

The rain would have been considered warm on Iryala, but on Kettle it cooled. They walked to their tents in it and stripped off their wet uniforms, draping them over the guy ropes where the rain continued to soak them. The T'swa had no body hair, not even pubic hair. Then Varlik followed the naked T'swa through the thunderstorm again, each carrying his soap and helmet, to the nearest hydrant. There they lathered themselves—Varlik had the advantage, his moderately hairy skin lathering more readily—then drew water and poured it over one another. Cleaned, they returned to their tents through the slackening rain, where they sat on the edges of their cots and used dirty undershirts to wipe the mud from their feet before putting on dry trousers and wet boots.

The slimmest T'swa in the squad loaned Varlik dry trousers which were only a little too large. Meanwhile, Varlik felt considerably recovered—tired, but not exhausted—again thanks to Voker's hard training, he told himself.

By the time they went to supper, the rain had stopped, and steam rose from the hot earth. The air was like a

Turkish bath. Supper was another mixture, not very different from what he'd eaten at midday, but nonetheless more appetizing to Varlik now. The evening was growing dark when he strolled back to the tent with Kusu, his belt recorder operating as it generally was among the T'swa.

"What do you do when it gets dark here?" asked Varlik. "Go to bed?"

"That is a matter of individual preference. Some will reread favorite books. Others will talk with their friends, or do certain things—personal things we learn as children. They are not known to the Confederation Worlds; when you see someone kneeling quietly, perhaps on a small pad, he is doing one of those things. And some will no doubt wander out into the grassland—to the east, away from camp and our disturbances—to sense the life there." He looked at Varlik. "What will you do?"

"I need to go somewhere where I won't disturb anyone, and narrate on cube my impressions of today and the T'swa."

"Ah. Of course."

"You said some of you will read. Where do you have lights?" He gestured about him. "The only lights I've seen are in the mess tent."

"That is where they will read."

The mess tent as a place to read! It didn't really surprise Varlik. The T'swa were different in so many things, and he was getting used to them. "How much can they see of the local lifeforms at night? At least now, with no moonlight."

"It is more than seeing, although we T'swa see considerably better at night than you do."

"Really?"

"Yes. In the early generations on Tyss—for many generations, actually—our ancestors worked their fields by night. In fact, they lived much of their active lives at night, when it was not so hot. So far as possible, they spent the daytimes in holes dug into the north slopes of hills, to escape the worst of the heat. It is even hotter on Tyss than here, you know, and it was hotter then than now.

"Those were very hard years. Many died of heat and hunger—especially babies and pregnant women. In time, those genetic lines that continued saw better at night than their ancestors had, and tolerated greater heat. Even today, some field labor and other strenuous outdoor activities on Tyss are done at night, although the climate no longer seems cruel to us."

The two men, one black, one white, went into the tent. Only two other men were there, lying silent on their cots. Kusu lay down on his, and Varlik also. "Is it all right to talk here," Varlik asked softly, "or will it disturb the others?"

"They will not be disturbed."

"How do you know about those early times? I've assumed that Tyss was settled before the historical era."

The T'swa sergeant nodded. "It was. Our knowledge of history reaches further back than your own."

"By how much?"

"By rather a long time."

Varlik wasn't sure he should ask his next question, but so far the T'swi had seemed very open, and he was curious. "We've assumed that the resource worlds, and probably some of the trade worlds, were colonized by dumping convicts there in early times. Was that how Tyss was settled, do you know?"

The T'swi smiled. "One could say so."

For a moment Varlik was silent. Then he asked, "Did I offend you with that question?"

Kusu chuckled softly, a sound which Varlik thought might have been echoed by the other two at the edge of audibility.

"No, Varlik Lormagen, you have not offended. You are a considerate and courteous man. I am glad to answer your questions, so far as I can; I consider you my friend."

Then Kusu stretched out on his cot, and Varlik sensed the withdrawal that meant their conversation was ended. Quietly he took his recorder and wandered out to the tiny vehicle park, to sit in the unmuddy privacy of a T'swa hovercar and record his still-fresh thoughts and impressions. Briefly, when he had finished, he watched the moon Gamma, barely large enough to show a demi-disk, like an overlarge star low in the east, then started back to his tent in the steamy, star-vivid night. Tomorrow, if he could find a ride, he would go to the base camp, pick up his other things, share his audio and video recordings with Bertol and Konni, and send off a report to Iryala via the message pod. And a letter cube to Mauen.

Sixteen

Excerpts from *Briefing on T'swa Mercenary Forces*, Department of Armed Forces; Document 711.5 290 196.

Introduction

All T'swa military units are light infantry.

The T'swa rarely, perhaps never, fight with war machines. This is practical because they do not accept assignments where they anticipate facing war machines or needing them. To date, at least during recorded history, they have been employed only on trade worlds and resource worlds, where the multiplicity of national states and the frequency of foreign rule and Confederation trade prerogatives bring about wars and revolts.

Occasionally, regionally entrenched revolutionary movements on trade worlds have been able to hire T'swa. Only the wealthiest revolutionaries are able to afford them, however.

T'swa mercenaries are very highly regarded as units and as individual soldiers by those who have employed them. They are especially valued in wildland fighting and for clearing hostile towns, actions in which superlative individual and small-unit skills are most advantageous.

T'swa Military Organization

The foundation of T'swa military organization is the "lodge," of which there are five, each located in a different region of Tyss. Physically, each lodge is said to consist of a ring of barracks and training facilities around a central administrative installation and school.

The regiment is the largest military unit used, supposedly without exception. The lodges form, recruit, and train the regiments. The lodges are also the contracting agents with whom prospective employers must deal. (There is no planetary government nor any national governments on Tyss. Trade and transportation remain primitive enough and the population orderly enough that local governments, trade associations, lodge councils, etc., suffice.)

The lodges select and recruit children, reputedly of ages five and six, and their training begins at that age. At age 11–12, the trainees are formed into proto-regiments, and from that point, regimental personnel continue to serve together as a unit. After seven years, the proto-regiment graduates as a combat regiment, at which time it becomes available for service, and usually will go into combat within the year. The first contract of a virgin regiment is often part of a multi-regimental operation, in partnership with a seasoned unit, but this is by no means always the case.

One of the advantages of the long T'swa training is the degree of cross-training possible. Every man is able to function in every post with every weapon used by the T'swa. The officers are of the same age and experience as the enlisted ranks, apparently being selected on the basis of demonstrated superior ability during the training years. But every man is supposedly capable of leading his platoon or company, or even regiment.

As in standard armies, the basic T'swa unit is the *squad;* however, the T'swa squad contains only 10 men. The *platoon* is made up of four squads, a platoon leader (lieutenant), a platoon sergeant, and two medical specialists, or 44 men. The *company* consists of four platoons and a command staff of eight: the company commander (captain), an executive officer (senior lieutenant), first sergeant, two communications specialists, and a three-man medical team, or 184 personnel. The *battalion* consists of 560 personnel; the *regiment* 1,720, all ranks. That does not include a variable number of *base personnel* who do not accompany the regiment into the field. Except in virgin regiments, where kitchen and clerical duties rotate among the ranks, base personnel are men with physical impairments, apparently resulting from combat or training injuries.

You will have noticed several peculiarities which will be gone into later. First, however, we will look at what we will term the "shrinking regiment."

The strength cited above—1,720 effectives, all ranks— is the *initial* strength. As casualties reduce squads to six men or fewer, decimated squads are consolidated within the platoon or company. As platoons lose personnel below some variable level, usually about 30, platoons are consolidated within the company. Higher level units are also consolidated as necessary.

The process of consolidation may, for example, result in platoons with only three short squads, a company with only three short platoons, and a battalion with only two short companies.

Of course, none of that is unusual in combat. What is unusual is that afterward, *the units are not brought back to their full complements. Casualties are never replaced.*

All of the consolidations described above will be made before the regiment is reduced below three battalions, but in time the regiment will inevitably be reduced to two battalions. As time passes and the attrition of per-

sonnel continues further, the regiment will be trans-
formed to a single battalion, redistributing remaining
personnel within it. However, the regiment still carries
its original designation—the Blue Tiger Regiment, for
example—even though it operates only as a battalion. If
a contract continues long enough, casualties may reduce
a regiment to company size or smaller.

The unit of hire is always the regiment, but the fee
charged varies with the regiment's effective strength.
Not infrequently, two or three battalion-strength "regiments" may be sent. They will function as a single
regiment under a senior colonel, but will continue to
carry their separate "regimental" identities.

Apparently there have never been T'swa units larger
than regiments, and they never function as ordinary
regiments belonging to a division. They operate simply
as assault forces or hunter-killer groups. This is written
into their contracts. They will refuse to fight on any other
basis, standing on their contractual prerogatives. . . .

T'swa Relations With Employers

T'swa mercenaries are invariably loyal. We have been
unable to find any verifiable report of T'swa mercenaries having broken a contract. But if a contract with
them is broken by their employer, they will invariably
extricate themselves from the fighting as promptly as
practical, and will usually depart the planet. They have
been known, however, to take punitive action against
the contract breaker on the authority of the regimental
commander. The T'swa mercenary lodges, which commonly operate their own (leased) troopships (!), have
even been known to make a punitive strike against
particularly treacherous contract breakers, at a time and
place of particular inconvenience to the contract breaker.
This attitude of the T'swa has become especially well
known among the governments of trade worlds, from
whom come most of their employment, and a contract-

ing authority seldom breaks a contract with T'swa mercenaries.

The T'swa warrior lodges never contract to undertake punitive expeditions against populations. They will, however, put down uprisings, and they are in fact most renowned for their exceptional value in breaking guerrilla insurgencies. Their approach to this kind of action, interestingly enough, is restricted to recognized guerrillas. They claim the ability to identify combatants through the recognition of what they term "auras." An aura (if it actually exists) is presumably an electromagnetic field around the individual human being.

Weapons

Procurement

With one exception, all T'swa weapons are standard, and since Y.P. 461, the T'swa have purchased their weapons from the Royal Armory on Iryala. (Previously they had been purchased from various worlds, based on the most favorable delivery price available.) The single nonstandard weapon is the *bayonet,* also produced by the Royal Armory, exclusively for the T'swa. The routine *issue* of standard weapons within a T'swa regiment is nonstandard, however. And as they commonly operate without the service of major ordnance depots, the weapons they take with them on a contract substantially exceed the standard complement. Those carried in any particular action vary depending on the nature of the action.

Bayonet

The bayonet is a form of short sword, appropriate to personnel from primitive worlds. The blade length is 18 inches. It can also be attached to a rifle barrel for use as a clumsy thrusting weapon. Apparently the bayonet is routine issue for all T'swa ranks, including officers, whether or not they carry rifles. The T'swa are said to be well drilled in their use. Bayonets are reputed to be effective psychological weapons when used by well-drilled troops against irregular forces.

Individual Firearms

Enlisted ranks normally carry the M-1 rifle, and by all reports, every T'swa is military personnel trained to a high level of skill in its use. Commissioned ranks normally carry the M-1 sidearm, but reportedly, platoon leaders may also carry the M-1 rifle in combat situations. . . .

Seventeen

The air-cooled staff car was approaching the T'swa encampment in the second hour of daylight when it passed the open-topped T'swa vehicle. Voker saw young Lormagen riding with two T'swa, and wondered how the journalist's first day had been.

The young man was naive, but he had persistence and at least a modicum of guts. And more importantly, he had luck. He'd need it, Voker told himself, he'd need it.

A few minutes later Voker's car crossed a low ridge, from which he could see the T'swa camp. When he'd first visited it, the day before, Voker had been astonished. It seemed impossible that Lamons could have read the briefing and a T'swa contract—any T'swa contract—and then tried to palm off a place like that on them, especially with a lumbering operation and cement plant in the Aromanis District, and a supply depot set up for major base expansion.

Standardness, with a large S or a small one, is a two-edged knife, he told himself, *and we keep cutting ourselves with it.* There were too many minds that couldn't function in the face of something nonstandard.

They went idiot. Not that he'd voice that observation out loud.

At least the rain had settled the dust here, he told himself as they pulled up outside the headquarters tent of the Night Adder Regiment, and the soil wasn't a kind that made problem mud. As he stepped out of the staff car, the morning heat blanketed him. The waiting captain offered a handshake; the T'swa didn't seem to salute except ceremonially. The captain's hard palm didn't startle Voker. He'd gotten over that the day before, had concluded that the thick calluses protected the hand from hot surfaces, which on Tyss was probably almost any surface. It might be a genetic adaptation or simply have developed in childhood and youth in connection with some aspect of training.

Colonel Biltong and Colonel Koda were waiting in the tent for him; they stood up and shook his hand perfunctorily with hands as hard as the captain's, then invited him to sit. He did.

"Gentlemen," said Voker, "I gave our rough plans and specifications to the base engineer, Major Krinder. He and his staff worked up a materials list last night and they'll start work on your new camp today, two miles southeast of the army's base camp."

The T'swa nodded almost in unison. There'd been room for them inside the base perimeter, with the security and convenience that would provide, but they'd insisted on being outside, as if they felt no concern about possible Bird attacks. Voker had found it hard to believe they'd be careless after all their years of war. Perhaps they'd welcome an attack.

"Today," he said, "it's time to look at possible actions for your regiments. What kind of briefing have you had on the situation and combat environment here?"

"We received copies of your army's Orlanthan briefing cube before we left Tyss," Biltong said. "And we have an action to suggest. We generally prefer to engage a new opponent briefly, and so far as possible on our own terms, before any major campaign. To learn what he is like, and what the field of operation is like. Therefore, we would like to stage a raid in force on the two mining sites, simultaneously. My regiment will hit the Kelikut site, and Colonel Koda's the Beregesh site, by night."

"You'll find both sites strongly defended," Voker replied. "How do you propose to go about it? How much preparatory aerial bombardment will you want?"

"None. No aerial bombardment of any kind. We propose an attack by stealth. Marauder squads will parachute in from 30,000 feet, from several miles away, and strike enemy installations by surprise. We will want to examine aerial holos of the sites in detail, to help in planning."

Voker was staring, incredulous. "From—30,000 feet? They'll be scattered all over the district!"

"Not at all. It is a technique we T'swa are trained in, and use rather frequently. We will choose a night when the greater moon is large. We see almost like cats at night. Our marauders will freefall to within a few hundred feet, each squad body-planing to remain in contact and reach the drop site.

"While the insurgents are being distracted by the marauder squads, the regiments proper will put down by armored troop carriers, different companies at different points, and attack enemy fortifications in force, doing as much damage as possible. We will then disengage, leaving the marauder squads behind briefly as a rear guard to provide covering fire and confusion while the major part of the assault force withdraws to pickup areas."

"How will you get your rear guard out?"

"Once evacuation of the main forces is well underway, the rear guard will disengage and make their way out of the area by stealth, so far as possible, to be picked up by light utility floaters well away from the insurgent camp. We'll be very interested in how the enemy responds, and how much difficulty the marauder squads have in disengaging and getting away."

Voker contemplated the two calm-seeming T'swa. Not calm-*seeming*, he told himself. These bastards *are* calm! "Frankly, gentlemen," he said, "I can visualize offhand about twenty things that could go wrong, resulting in your regiments being chopped up and your marauders wiped out."

"Of course," Biltong replied, "there is always that possibility. But the demands on your air crews should not be excessive, and our people are extremely competent. Your adjectives 'resourceful' and 'proficient' come to mind. And 'nimble-witted,' if I may coin a term using Standard roots. Each of our people has survived fourteen years of war."

High-elevation parachute jumps? Body planing! Voker had never heard of such things. *How nonstandard can they get?* he asked himself. Without noticing, he began to feel excited.

"Colonels," Voker said, "I suggest we all go to base headquarters. We can find there all the aerial holos you'll want, and a large-scale tank to project them in."

When they left Colonel Biltong's headquarters tent, Colonel Koda took with him the audio recorder that he'd transcribed the conference on. It might be useful to their new publicist to have a record.

Varlik quickly fell into a routine that combined his desire to live with and learn about the T'swa and his other responsibilities as a journalist/publicist. He would spend one day with the T'swa, the next at the main base, narrating his reports and editing his cubes. There was never any difficulty now with his coming and going, and he gave Bakkis and Konni access to his material.

Meanwhile, progress on the new T'swa camp was rapid, the sort of thing that can happen when an army puts its manpower resources to work on a project. The base construction battalion was turned loose on it, and on the seventh day the T'swa moved in. Now their tents had floors, there were showers and wash stands, and their jungle boots padded on boardwalks when they went to meals.

And with the new camp, the video team was allowed to visit the T'swa, shooting their own pictures. One afternoon they even rode along behind Company A on a training run, their cube showing Varlik running with the T'swa. He'd begged them to record some other outfit, but they'd have none of it.

The T'swa would have twelve full days to enjoy their new facility before their first action on Kettle, because when Lamons had been informed of their projected raids, he at once decided to follow them up promptly with a full-scale invasion and takeover of Beregesh. General preparations for the invasion had already been planned and were well underway, but even so, his staff had insisted that sixteen days, around the clock, was the minimum time needed to complete preparations.

With alternate days to recover in, those parts of the T'swa training regime that Varlik took part in were not too hard for the young correspondent. Not quite. The close combat drills he didn't even attempt. Parts of the bayonet drills he did attempt, though his muscles screamed obscenities at him. The speed marches he survived, sometimes taking a break in the hovercar that was always at hand. And the holo-briefings on the Beregesh mining site he found exciting. His bowels found them uncomfortably exciting.

Then one evening Colonel Koda sent him to the airfield with B Company, which had been selected to provide the Beregesh marauder squads. The T'swa strapped on their freefall chutes and loaded into several small utility floaters for a practice jump, Varlik with the First and Second Squads of the First Platoon.

He wore no chute; he was along for the ride.

When they took off, the troops were as bland and cheerful as always. Varlik was nervous, even though he wasn't going to jump. Shortly, they put on their oxygen masks. At what he'd been told was 30,000 feet, the troop doors were retracted; the air that swirled in was shockingly cold. This time their drop zone was their old camp site in the prairie, from which they would jog the twenty-six miles to the new one. The T'swa lined up as casually as if for breakfast, but wearing gloves and encumbered with chutes, weapons, and the heavy coveralls that would protect them from scrub vegetation when they jumped at Beregesh. Their protective mesh face masks were tilted up to make room for oxygen masks; they'd clip them into position at a lower altitude.

The blackness snarled and whipped about the door as they waited, and Varlik, camera busy, hoped desperately that he wouldn't be sick in his oxygen mask. The red light beside the door changed to yellow, and the floater slowed, stopped. Then it flashed green, and five T'swa trotted out the door into icy nothingness, Varlik dutifully recording the process.

The floater made three small circles then, simulating flight to another drop site, and at the end of each circle, five more men jumped. The greater moon was early in its first quarter, its light not enough to do an Iryalan much good, but by it the T'swa were supposed to see and body plane to the old campsite, where a target had been bulldozed that they could see from high in the night.

When the second stick of jumpers stood up, Varlik crouched beside the door, grateful now for coveralls and heated gloves. Camera in hand, he followed their drifting fall in his monitor until the floater's circling put them out of sight.

And when the last stick had gone, an exhausted Varlik, chilled and shivering, slumped down on a bucket seat while one of the air crew closed the troop door. He visualized the T'swa falling spread-eagled, planing through quiet darkness, eyes on the drop site and sometimes on the altimeters at their chests. To an Iryalan, the very concept was outrageous. Yet despite that, and despite the bone-numbing fear he'd felt when they'd jumped, he wished he was with them, though it seemed to him he'd surely have soiled himself before stepping out the door.

Eighteen

In a time which your people have long forgotten, when the many nations of man spoke each its separate language, it was well known that children up to a certain age—about seven of your years—could learn to speak foreign languages quickly and with ease. Then, over the course of a few more years, it became much more difficult, the degree of difficulty varying markedly among individuals.

In part the same is true of learning the T'sel. But in learning the T'sel, the effect of age seems more marked, for we have been able to teach some of your people to speak Tyspi—all of the few who wished sufficiently to learn it—but we have never succeeded in leading one of them to the T'sel. Of course, only perhaps a dozen before you have asked to be taught. But if you really wish your people to know the T'sel, it would be advisable to send small children among us and let them live as T'swa until they are well grown. Send children of five of your years. Then they would come to know T'sel without effort. They would know it as do those born to it, but with an additional viewpoint, for even as little children they would have an initial affinity with their own world and culture, and a greater personal, nonverbal knowledge of them than you might suspect.

And once trained, it is they who would be best suited to bring the T'sel to your world.

But even then, unless new techniques were developed, I suspect that most interested adults on Iryala would, in the main, only learn *about* the T'sel, and that is not having it. They would no doubt have pieces of it, which would not be without value to them and to Iryala, but it would be exceptional for one to gain the entirety. Therefore, it would be most effective if those children, once grown, returned to Iryala and formed a small community of their own, where more children could learn. If nothing else, that would save others from suffering the heat of Tyss.

Meanwhile, you do not yourself have that option for learning. But you are here, and much of value can be accomplished, so let us begin. Perhaps you will find your stay with us sufficiently rewarding that you will decide to see to the other when you have returned to Iryala.

And if you wish to propagate on Iryala an interest in the T'sel, let me suggest further that you not propound it, or expound on it, or talk much about it at all. Say only a little, to this one and that, and very casually, as if you found it mildly interesting but not important. Those who wish to know will no doubt hear of it, and of you, without effort on your part, and if any seek you out and question you, perhaps you will wish to speak with them about it at greater length.

—Master Fen Dys-Gwang to Dr. Barden Ostrak, by the waterfall at Tashi Dok (unedited from the recorded comments).

The two T'swa regiments stood in the late afternoon heat, heavily laden with weapons and gear, waiting to board the armored troop carriers, while Varlik, sweating copiously, walked nearby with busy camera.

Around them on three sides of the broad landing field were acres of ordnance, other equipment, supplies, minutely organized, with an armada of tarp-covered cargo movers parked and ready, waiting for the intensive activity of the morrow and days after, when the invasion proper would take place. Varlik wouldn't try to cover that; for better or for worse, he was committing his time and efforts to covering the T'swa. Even Bertol and Konni were giving the T'swa raid their full attention today. With their deluxe Revax camera, they would go with the Night Adders to Kelikut to film the raid there.

Lieutenant Trevelos and his own small staff of cameramen and copywriters would cover the actions of the Confederation Army, and their material would be available to Central News and Iryala Video.

The T'swa marauder groups had already left, on utility floaters like they'd jumped from in practice, and Varlik had recorded their departure. Now he moved to the assault floater that would carry the first and second platoons of Company A, and stood beside the ramp. An order was whistled—he knew the code well now—and he recorded the approach and loading of the T'swa. They loaded quietly, showing no sign of nerves, only a clear and quiet sense of controlled exhilaration.

Even as he recorded, their exhilaration troubled Varlik. Not that he begrudged them, but it seemed unreal, scarcely conceivable, that men who had known battle so intimately and for so long, had seen so many of their fellows killed or maimed, could feel that way. He himself felt nothing remotely like exhilaration; he was grateful that he had his work to do, to hold his attention and keep down the intensity of his fear. When all the T'swa were aboard, he followed; his seat was waiting for him at the end of First Squad, First Platoon.

The assault carriers were not large. With floaters, because they could take off and land vertically and had a long range, there was little advantage in larger craft for combat landings. These, which carried only two platoons each, could put down on rough ground, in small openings, and relatively few men would be lost if a ship was destroyed by heavy rockets.

A row of padded bench seats ran down each side of the craft, and two more rows extended back to back down the middle, divided by a padded back rest, neck high. The result was two wide aisles with facing seats. Now the aisles were partly filled with gear, notably large petards, and pole charges fitted with shoulder straps, their poles telescoped. If a rocket should penetrate the hull, the result could be spectacular.

With the state of his nerves, Varlik was grateful there'd been so little delay in boarding. Once closed, the carriers were cooled somewhat, and when they lifted, pressurized. Now there would be the long haul to Beregesh, 1,900 miles south, where the climate would make Aromanis seem balmy. He was glad the attack would be by night, that they'd be back in the air before dawn, and these thoughts he recorded.

Out by dawn. That was assuming everything worked out more or less as planned. Colonel Koda seemed confident, but Koda—Koda was *Homo tyssiensis*, not *Homo sapiens*. That also he murmured into the voice pickup at his throat; he could edit it out later if he wanted to.

Varlik used his camera again, recording the T'swa troopers who sat facing each other along the sides, seemingly relaxed, though only a few were talking. It would be hours before they landed, and he wondered how he, at least, could survive the trip, commenting to the cube that there weren't even windows available to look out of.

The T'swi beside him was a man named Bin, not much older than himself but whom he thought of, as he thought of all the regiment, as considerably older.

"Bin, how do you feel about the possibility of dying?" Varlik asked quietly. As usual, he spoke in Standard when recording, knowing that the T'swi would answer in kind.

Bin looked at him and smiled mildly. "How do *you* feel?" Bin countered, not bothering to keep his voice especially low. "We're in the same squad. It seems to me that you are at greater risk than I, because I have experience of battles and surviving them. How do *you* feel about the possibility of dying?"

"But you're T'swa," Varlik persisted, "and it's the T'swa that people on Iryala want to read about and see and hear on video."

Bin only grinned at Varlik, his T'swa eyes failing to look ingenuous despite their size and roundness.

"Well, tell me this, then," Varlik said. "How many of us do you suppose will be alive at this hour tomorrow?"

"Hmm." Bin appeared to calculate in his mind, frowning soberly. "I'd say . . . There are eighty-nine of us on this floater now, not including the crew. While tomorrow . . . tomorrow there will be approximately that number minus the number killed. That is as close as I can tell you."

For just a moment Varlik felt miffed, then the T'swi chuckled, and after a moment's lag, Varlik joined him. Somehow the throaty sound of the T'swi's laughter not only removed any sense of offense, but added a facet to T'swa humanity. It was the first time Varlik had been joked with by one of them.

And now Bin surprised him. "You asked," he said, "how many I suppose will be alive tomorrow. Most of us, I suspect; perhaps almost all. But ask me how many will be alive at the end of this contract."

Casually as it was delivered, the question seemed to paralyze heart and lungs. "How many?" Varlik managed to ask.

"Very few; possibly none." He looked at Varlik with an expression the newsman could only think of as kindly. "In war there are winners and losers. And who are they? The question is irrelevant. I've been told that your people tend to think of us as the supreme warriors, against whom none can stand except sometimes with a strong advantage of numbers or position. And that is not far from true. Yet we of the Red Scorpion Regiment are not much more than half our original number. Many of our brothers have lost their game pieces, their bodies, looking down at them bloody and lifeless in dust or mud or snow. Or have sat leaning against some wall or tree or rock, looking at a shattered limb, at some wound that takes away their warriorhood. The winner becomes a loser.

"Eventually the regiment will be so decimated that the lodge will deactivate it as too small for further contracts. Then the survivors will be finished as warriors. This war will do it for the Red Scorpions, I suspect: The conditions appear to be difficult, and the enemy reputedly quite competent." He peered quizzically at Varlik. "Wouldn't you say?"

Varlik didn't say anything. Despite the somber content of the T'swi's words, he still felt that the trooper was somehow playing with him. He was also aware now that the T'swa around them were listening and watching.

"Yes, the winner eventually becomes the loser," Bin continued, "in any activity in the real world. And if things don't balance out in this lifetime, there will always be other lifetimes to complete the equation."

The T'swi stopped there, but his eyes remained on Varlik's, as if he expected the journalist to reply. Varlik started tentatively.

"Then . . . It sounds as if you feel it's your *fate* to die. Or be maimed."

"Fate? I am aware of the term from my student days; we study something of your philosophy, you know. What you refer to here as 'fate,' we simply look at as one of the laws—a tertiary, not a primary or even secondary law—but one of the laws regulating the activities of man in this universe. One may sometimes win predominantly, or lose predominantly, through an entire lifetime or even a sequence of lifetimes, but the equation will eventually tend toward a balance. Or perhaps it is just then balancing from some earlier winning or losing sequence."

Varlik frowned. "But why do you fight then, if you feel doomed to lose eventually? Why would anyone go through the pain and exhaustion and danger, and see his friends killed or mangled, when he's only going to lose in the end?"

"Ah! But we have no doom, and it is not the end."

The T'swi looked at Varlik for several seconds without saying anything further, as if considering how to make his answer more meaningful. "Varlik, why do *you* live?" he asked at last.

"Why? Because I can't help myself. A person is born living, and with the instinct to survive. That's why I live."

"Um." The blue-black warrior nodded thoughtfully. "Yet if you stay with us, you will see us put ourselves repeatedly in great danger. How is it then that the instinct you speak of is inoperative in so many of us? Including you, it seems, for here you are, going to battle with us.

"What you call 'the instinct to survive' is simply an emotional attachment to a body, growing in part from the misapprehension that if it is destroyed, you cease to exist. But in fact, while bodies are notably destructible, you yourself cannot avoid survival.

"The challenge is to live with *interest*. Unless one's fear is too great, which seems to be rather common among the worlds of man, one normally prefers that that existence be interesting."

A hint of smile touched the wide mouth. "And even then, consider the possibility that the person who is fearful, who perhaps is even in hiding, may at some hidden level enjoy the experience.

"As warriors, we find our greatest interest and pleasure in battle, and our next greatest in preparing for battle. Winning is preferred, but the preference is slight. We are not allowed to—ah, 'graduate' is your nearest word to it. We would not be allowed to graduate if we did not know deeply and truly that the fullest joy and reward of the warrior is in being a warrior, and performing the actions of a warrior, with artistry! And that winning is something to favor only very slightly. We do prefer to win, but it is not *important* to us. We do not allow the matter of winning or losing, surviving or dying, to interfere with our pleasure. We go into battle ready to enjoy the experience, without anxiety over the outcome."

Varlik didn't answer, but after a moment looked away. He could see a certain logic in what the T'swi had said, but it wasn't what he felt in his guts.

After a moment he turned off his recorder, buckled his seat belt, and closed his eyes. Maybe, he thought, he could go to sleep; sleeping was the best way to kill time in a situation like this.

But instead he sat there, more or less slumped, thoughts drifting through his mind on no particular theme. There were questions, speculations, things that were or might have been. He was relaxed now, and it occurred to him that this was not much inferior to sleep itself as a way to kill time. Then, after an hour or so, he slept.

Varlik awoke gradually, nagged into consciousness by the discomfort of prolonged, unrelieved sitting. It was night; the four windows, two flanking each troop door, told him that. The lights had been dimmed, and almost all the T'swa seemed asleep, some propped against one another. Sergeant Kusu's eyes were open, though; they moved to Varlik, and the T'swi smiled, nodding acknowledgement of Varlik's notice. Varlik looked at his watch; he had almost two hours to wait.

It struck him then that among the more than eighty men, most of them apparently asleep, not one was snoring, and he wondered if they'd somehow been trained not to. Perhaps men who'd slept so often where a prowling enemy might hear, somehow subconsciously didn't allow themselves to snore.

He stood and stretched, twisted his trunk, rotated his shoulders, then sat and closed his eyes once more. It seemed to him he hadn't really gone to sleep again, and that no more than twenty minutes could have passed, when Platoon Sergeant Tok's voice barked out. "Ten minutes to Beregesh! By squads! First Platoon, stand and stretch!" Behind him on the other aisle, Varlik heard a similar command to the Second Platoon.

The first squad, with Varlik, stood and stretched, raised their knees, squatted and straightened, touched toes, twisted trunks, some with a quiet comment or chuckle, then sat back down, giving the aisle to the second. Varlik began to feel tension again, and it occurred to him to wonder what the tension would be like if they all felt it, if it fed back from man to man, building.

The two platoon leaders, with their sergeants, had gone to the two windows flanking the portside door. Varlik wondered what they could see. Then it occurred to him that he was not a trooper here, but a journalist with a journalist's functions, and he went over also. The windows were large, from deck level to above the head and forty inches wide, to let officers examine the scene before landing and unloading. From their elevation of perhaps 15,000 feet, Varlik could see low mountains, fairly rugged, silvered softly with moonlight. The four T'swa were gazing intently at a forward angle, as if they knew where to look, but Varlik could see nothing significant there. He decided they must be getting information over the radio speaker each wore in an ear. His camera alternated between landscape and men.

A minute later he saw a bright spark—an explosion, he realized—seemingly on the surface miles ahead, followed seconds later by two more. His muscles tightened. The four T'swa seemed as relaxed as before, strong black presences waiting for something more. The troop carrier was rapidly drawing up on the site, and Varlik could feel their craft descending, contributing to the weakness of his jellied knees. He could see in abun-

dance now the tiny flashes of what he assumed was
gunfire, or perhaps the hits of rockets. His colon felt
extremely nervous.

The sporadic firefights drew nearer as the floater lost
altitude, and Varlik lost himself in watching. Suddenly
he realized his fear was gone, replaced for the moment
by something like the exhilaration the T'swa seemed to
feel. Lieutenant Zimsu called the order to belt down
and be ready. Varlik moved back to his own place as
the troopers fastened buckles, his camera recording
T'swa faces, powerful forms, then he too buckled down.
Around them somewhere was an entire fleet of assault
floaters, with someone coordinating their movements,
and it occurred to him to hope that the someone was
competent.

Twice in the last half minute, Varlik flinched at the
loud frightening bangs of light rockets exploding against
the armored hull, and the carrier touched down harder
than he'd expected, as if the pilot had been caught
unaware by the ground, or felt hurried. The T'swa were
striking the instant-release buckles of their seat belts
and getting quickly to their feet, he scarcely slower.
The troop doors opened and the ranks of troopers double-
timed out, their weapons in their hands, Varlik carrying
his camera in front of him, recording what he could
from within the hurrying ranks. He'd lowered his monitor, but now he peered beneath it for wider vision, to
see where he was going, his camera continuing to record.

Then he was on the short ramp and into the night,
the T'swa dispersing to the sides, Varlik trying to stay
within a couple of steps of Bin as he'd been told to do.
The sound of gunfire was loud, sharp, immediate, and
Bin was shooting short bursts. It occurred to Varlik that
they ought to hit the ground, take cover, but they
didn't.

Then the T'swa almost stopped shooting, and he realized that the nearby gunfire had been theirs, that Bin
had not been answering it but adding to it. Still they

ran, not hard but steadily, a trot. The low dark humps ahead must be the bunkers they were to destroy. Suddenly they came to a shallow ditch, and there Bin hit the dirt, Varlik landing next to him, most of the others running on. Varlik lay panting, wondering what was happening, why they had stopped. It occurred to him that they'd been off the floater for no more than twenty seconds. He raised his camera above the ditch's shoulder, panning, using his monitor now, seeing what he was capturing on his cube.

Gunfire burst out ahead to their right, and the men who'd stopped at the ditch directed concentrated fire in that direction. Except for Bin and himself, the men who'd stopped in the ditch all seemed to carry blast hoses; their racket was terrific, shocking, stunning, and in seconds the enemy fire had stopped.

Then they simply lay there, waiting in what seemed like silence, although less intense gunfire continued, apparently directed elsewhere. He thought to question Bin; why had the two of them stayed here? But he knew without asking: Bin had been told to take care of him; keep him alive.

From somewhere well ahead a rocket rose, followed quickly by another, and another, and more. Varlik knew from night exercises in his army days that the enemy had lobbers. He followed their upward flight, realized they were aimed at this ditch and its hosemen. As they began to descend, he saw others arching overhead in answer from behind. He tucked his camera under an arm and pressed his body hard against the forward ditch slope, waiting, aware of increasing gunfire. Seconds later he heard and felt the exploding rockets, a string of five evenly spaced crashes that threw rocks and dirt on the men prone in the ditch, echoed by a series well ahead, a booming background to the racketing gunfire.

Opening his eyes, he raised to his knees on the hard stony dirt, camera ready again for whatever was offered. The enemy firing seemed directed mainly elsewhere now, but the T'swa in the ditch with him were triggering leisurely bursts in the direction the earlier enemy fire had come from, so he recorded that.

Then massive explosions sounded ahead, a series of them overlapping, and Bin jerked the shoulder of Varlik's shirt. They all leaped up and ran forward, apparently not coming under fire. There were more big explosions somewhere. The bunkers, when they got there, were collapsed. Varlik lay with the others on the sloping heaps that had been bunker walls, in a smell of explosions and settling dust, sweating hard. For the first time Varlik realized how hot it was.

The troops that had charged the bunkers were gone—he hadn't even seen a body—and it seemed for a while that he and the men he was with had been forgotten, overlooked, the gunfire unrelated to them. Bin's attention was to their original right; the T'swa had lined up facing that direction now. Varlik could see muzzle flashes ahead that must be enemy fire, and when this increased in intensity, the men he was with opened up with their blast hoses again, the sound shredding the night while still more heavy explosions sounded, preceded by big flashes that flared and were gone. When they paused, a minute later, Varlik wasn't sure whether it was truly that quiet or if perhaps he'd been deafened.

The next ten or fifteen minutes alternated between relatively quiet inaction, brief outbursts of firing, and sporadic heavy explosions. Twice they came under brief fire from lobbers, and several rounds landed very near. He could smell hot hose barrels. A number of times he wiped at the sweat pooling in his eyebrows, his wet hands gritty with the dirt he crouched on, converting the sweat of his face into mud. He was recorded constantly now—even when the lobber rockets arced downward and struck—commenting frequently for the audio pickup.

Then he heard T'swa bugles well behind them, and shrill whistling from several directions: somewhere troops were pulling back, but not those he was with. Instead, the hosemen opened fire again, shooting without benefit of seen targets, spraying covering fire ahead and to their left. From the general direction of the carrier, lobber rockets left bright thin trails that threaded the sky, then stitched the blackness ahead with flashes.

Nearby whistling commanded, and he stood up with the T'swa around him, trotting back in the direction of the carrier, not coming under fire again so far as Varlik knew. There was gunfire, but no sounds of blast slugs striking near or rockets landing. Like the others, he jumped the little ditch, pleased that he was able to, and after a minute could see their floater ahead of them, no lights showing. They slowed to a near-walk, jogging up the ramp past the two platoon lieutenants and their sergeants, who stood by the foot of it peering past them.

Most of the T'swa were already on board, had returned ahead of those who'd stopped at the ditch, and even in the darkness, Varlik was aware of gaps in their seated ranks. The door to the rear compartment—the aid station—stood open, a blackout curtain blocking the light within, and Varlik felt a lump in his stomach.

But the carrier did not lift; the platoons' four leaders were still outside by the ramp. Three troopers were helped in, wounded. They pushed the curtain aside and disappeared into the aid station.

Still the floater sat. Four more T'swa entered, each pair carrying a wounded man, and also went into the aid station. The lieutenants followed, with the platoon sergeants, and the troop doors finally hissed softly shut.

Seconds later the floater began lifting rapidly, pivoting as it rose, then Varlik felt horizontal acceleration as they headed north toward Aromanis. No rockets struck them. When the acceleration had stopped, the compartment lights came on low. Varlik looked around; the gaps were not large or numerous. Soberly, camera in hand, he got up and headed for the aid station.

It was daylight when they landed, but not by much; the daytime heat was only starting to build. Thick-witted from dozing, Varlik went straight to his old media quarters, showered, then went to the officers' mess for whatever he could get. They were still serving breakfast. When he'd finished, he returned to the air-conditioned comfort of his room to begin editing and narrating. He'd been at it only briefly when someone knocked.

"Come in," he said.

It was Konni. She was sweaty, dirty, and he could see she'd been crying. He got to his feet. She simply stood there, her face writhing with the effort not to cry again. Once more Varlik's stomach knotted.

"What?" he asked simply.

"Bertol," she said. It was all she got out before she broke down and began to cry like a little girl, utterly despondent. *Oh shit,* Varlik thought, and feeling wretched, went to her, wet-eyed himself now, to stand holding her till she'd cried herself out.

Nineteen

Bertol Bakkis's body would never again pickle in ethanol; Graves Registration personnel had treated it with something more permanent. At least, though, it had been spared the indignity of being torn up by blast slugs; a fragment of lobber rocket had ripped through his sternum and right ventricle, killing him instantly.

Not that Bertol and Konni had tried anything as strenuous as accompanying a platoon into action; they'd stayed near the carrier, shooting what cubeage they could from there. Several lobber rockets had hit nearby, and he'd been one of the casualties.

It took Varlik and Konni most of the day to edit their cubes and narrative reports. After they'd delivered them to the communications center for the next day's pod, they'd gotten maudlin drunk together in honor of Bertol. Then Varlik had jogged, sweating, through the prairie night to the T'swa camp.

He could have stayed in the air-conditioned media quarters at base camp. But if he had, he'd have ended up in the sack with Konni—she'd seemed to be inviting it—and he wouldn't allow himself that. Mauen, he felt, deserved better than an adulterous husband.

The first mile of jogging had taken him in uncertain wavers along the travelway, but by the time he arrived, he was pretty much sober from the exertion and sweating. And had begun to wonder and worry. Had the T'swa held a memorial of some sort for their killed and he missed it? At the tent of the First Squad, all of whom had returned unscathed, Sergeant Kusu raised his head for a moment as Varlik entered.

"Can I talk with you?" Varlik whispered.

In answer, the T'swi had swung his legs out of bed, and together the two of them went outside.

"I had to work all day, on my reports," Varlik said. "And one of the video team was killed at Kelikut, so the other one and I—got drunk this evening, in his memory. I hope I didn't miss anything you guys did, any memorial you held, for your dead."

"You didn't," Kusu said. "We make our farewells privately, personally."

Varlik nodded and turned on his belt recorder. "At the communications center they told me the regiment had lost twenty-nine killed and sixty-one wounded, but they said there weren't any missing. How could anyone tell the killed from the missing in the dark like that, pulling out the way we did?"

In the moonlight, the black face seemed to smile very slightly. "We have our method."

"Is it—all right to tell me about it?"

"Certainly. But you might prefer not to know."

The answer froze Varlik's mind for a moment. Then, "I see," he said, not seeing at all. "I would like to know."

"The dead come to us as spirits, thus we know who they are. All the rest returned physically. Thus no prisoners, no missing."

The dead tell them. Varlik had nothing to reply and nothing more to ask; he simply nodded. Kusu stood for a moment as if waiting for possible further questions.

When none were forthcoming, he said good night and went back to the tent.

Mind spinning in slow motion, Varlik got his towel and walked to the showers where, beneath the stars, he washed away the sweat of his run. Somewhere in the process his mind relaxed, and when he went to bed, he lay awake only briefly. *The dead came to them, and the farewells were personal and private.* The sort of things—superstitions—that you could expect from gooks. But these "gooks" weren't gooks. And if they said it, he would not gainsay them, even inwardly to himself. Even if he couldn't accept it as truth.

Then he slept, and dreamed, and when the whistles wakened him near dawn, he felt rested and revived, and surprised by it, ready for the day despite all he'd had to drink and his shortness of sleep.

That day he trained with the T'swa. The day after that he went to the base. There wasn't much to report, although he sent off a letter cube to Mauen, but he wanted to update himself on the Beregesh invasion. He ended up flying south again, in an armored staff floater with Information Office personnel, to see and record the battle site. He hadn't thought to get a cool-suit, and had had the choice of either going later or going without one. He was the only one on the plane who didn't have one bundled beside him.

At Beregesh, he found the battle over, with two full divisions, one Iryalan and one Romblit, securing the surrounding area. Cargo carriers were landing equipment and supplies in quantity, the area resembling some mad and disorderly quartermaster depot. Casualties had been moderate, and yes, a major told him, the T'swa had done a thorough job of neutralizing Bird fortifications.

Occasionally he heard distant firing; some of it couldn't have been much farther than a mile away.

He ran into Konni at the field HQ. She'd arrived the

afternoon before, when there'd still been sporadic hard fighting close by. She'd spent one night sleeping in a cool-suit, and was going back to Aromanis later; she'd share her cube with him if he'd like.

Next he caught a ride on a hover truck hauling digging equipment to the perimeter, where fortifications were being built. The driver was a Romblit reservist, a tall ex-farmhand corporal who looked rawboned even in his cool-suit.

"Mate," the Romblit said, "I don't see how you can live without a cool-suit. It's bad enough here with one. I tried to sleep without mine for a while last night and liked to have died. How d'you do it?"

"Not very comfortably. But I thought I'd better give it a try."

The driver steered around a caved-in bunker, then nursed the rig through a shortcut, angling down into a shallow rocky draw and up the other side, to hurry jouncing along a rough track bulldozed through open scrub growth. Mostly the way was slightly downhill. Varlik kept his camera busy.

"You're that news guy that lives with the T'swa, ain't you?" the man asked.

"Right."

"I figured, what with no cool-suit and that funny-lookin' spotty uniform. How come they make 'em like that?"

"They're harder to see in the woods. They call them camouflage suits."

"Huh! I've heard you train with the gooks—run all day through the hot sun like a herd of buck." The man's tone was not disparaging; he sounded impressed.

Varlik understood how things could get exaggerated. What puzzled him was how this man, and presumably therefore many others, had even heard of him. He decided it wasn't worth puzzling over; he'd relax and enjoy his new reputation.

"Yes," he answered, "I train with them."

"How come would anyone do that 'less they had to? I'm glad I'm in the Engineers, so's I don't have to even drill."

Varlik recorded a file of troops trudging along in cool-suits, rifles slung, headed the same direction as the truck.

"I thought I'd like to get an idea of what it's like to be a T'swi," Varlik answered. "Besides, if I'm to go with them in combat, I'd better be able to keep up or the Birds could get me."

The construction site was just ahead along the upper edge of a long declivity. Men with beam saws were felling the larger scrub trees and cutting them into short timbers. Reaction dozers pushed dirt and rock, gouging a broad trench, pushing the spoil into piles. Soldiers manhandled timbers into place, shoveled and tamped dirt, all in cool-suits. It occurred to Varlik that someone had manufactured a lot of cool-suits in the last year or so.

The driver spat brown fluid out the door. "I wish we had time," he said. "I'd like to hear more about them T'swa. They're supposed to be some tough gooks. You with them here night before last?"

"Right."

"Without no cool-suit."

"Right again."

The Romblit shook his head as he stopped the rig by a group of soldiers. "Maybe I'll see you again sometime," he called as they dismounted out opposite sides. "Maybe when we get this place civilized. I'll buy the beer and you can tell me about it."

Varlik poked around the area, keeping out of the way of equipment, visiting fortifications in different stages of construction. Half an hour was enough. Beregesh would take some getting used to; despite taking mineral tablets and drinking heavily at one of the huge water bags slung from tripods, he felt ready to head back to field

HQ, and caught a ride on another truck. Its driver was taciturn, repeatedly eyeing his lack of a cool-suit, or perhaps his T'swa uniform, but saying nothing. The officer in charge at the landing site chatted briefly, commenting on his lack of a cool-suit, then pointed out a staff floater he could board that would be northbound in minutes.

The floater soon was full, and when the last seat had been taken, took off. Excepting Varlik, all the passengers were officers. Most looked tired, and there wasn't much talk. He got some looks at first, or his sweat-soaked T'swa camouflage suit did, but he ignored them and napped much of the way back.

Twenty

The staff car pulled up in front of Colonel Biltong's headquarters tent and Carlis Voker got out. The new camp boasted duckboard sidewalks, and the tent a lumber frame. Although Voker had called ahead, no one was outside to meet him—his visits were frequent and he knew his way—but the two T'swa colonels were waiting when he stepped inside. And Varlik Lormagen was there, sitting back out of the way, recording; that was different.

"Colonels," Voker said, "I have a new mission for you."

"We've been expecting one," Biltong replied.

Voker looked at the two black men. Their invariable equanimity—it could be read as smugness—sparked a flash of irritation that quickly passed. The T'swa, he told himself as he took a seat, were the only troops who could do what the general wanted done.

"We know the Birds have radios," Voker said, "and we can assume they've notified their headquarters, wherever that is, that we've taken Beregesh back. The last time we took the place back, or the Rombili did, the Birds sent up troops and drove them out, and there's

163

no reason to believe they won't try to take it back again. If they were willing to let us have the place, they wouldn't have started this war to begin with."

Wouldn't have started the war. The statement offended Varlik, a reaction unexpected. It seemed to him that the Rombili had started the war when they'd started enslaving the Birds. It was just that the Birds had taken nearly three centuries to mount an offensive.

"We know they have floaters," Voker was saying, "but apparently only light gun floaters—for which, incidentally, we're prepared now. Every unit, even administrative and service outfits, has M-4 rocket launchers ready to hand. At any rate, the only way the Birds can bring up troops is overland on foot. And the only source of large numbers of them has got to be the equatorial forests. Farther north, our surveillance platforms would spot large encampments without fail.

"Likewise, the only routes they can move north on are through the mountain forests, and for the last three hundred miles or so even those aren't safe cover for large bodies of troops; they're too open to aerial observation and attack." Voker paused. "Do you see what I'm leading to?"

Biltong nodded. "You want us to interdict the trails—make it difficult for them to bring troops up."

"Exactly! And I'd like you to begin soon." Voker got to his feet. "Why don't you look the mission over and see me at base HQ tomorrow morning. We can start working out transportation and supply. Now, unless there's anything more we need to discuss at this time, gentlemen? Good."

He looked at Varlik. "Good to see you, Lormagen. I hear you were along on the Beregesh night raid and visited there again yesterday. I'm glad things are turning out well for you; I suspected they might when I saw how hard you worked preparing yourself."

Turning to the T'swa, he saluted. "Colonels!" he said,

then turned and left. When they heard his staff car's engine hum, Biltong grinned.

"Koda," he said in Tyspi, "by Confederation standards that is an unusually adaptable officer. At heart he's not as Standard as he's supposed to be."

Koda chuckled. "Perhaps we should have told him we'd already foreseen his need."

"We'll do it obliquely," Biltong said, and turning, called to the sergeant major. "Wuu-Sad, bring the file on the interdiction plan. And have Dzokan bring the car; Koda and I are going to army headquarters at once."

Koda laughed out loud, then turned to Varlik.

"Colonel Biltong and I have listened to and watched some of your cubes. They were copied by our communications chief when you turned them over to him. Do you object?"

"Would it make any difference if I did?"

"It would not prevent us from doing it again, if we thought it necessary; we do have an interest. We were very impressed with what you've done. I hope your editor appreciates you properly."

"I won't object to your looking," Varlik replied, "as long as I don't have to tailor my reports to fit anyone else's ideas about what I've seen.

"Not at all. You know the people you write for far more intimately than we do. And you do a good job of describing us objectively."

Koda changed the subject then. "Sergeant Kusu tells me you've done remarkably well on training runs here, but we are not sure it is physically feasible for you to accompany the troops on an extended subtropical assignment. You've spent a few hours at Beregesh now; do you think you could tolerate field conditions there without a cool-suit? Cool-suits won't be practical on interdiction patrol."

"I'm not sure whether I can or not. I'd like to give it

a try, though. At best, the cool-suits hamper a person's mobility, and all I heard at Beregesh were complaints about them."

They heard a hovercar pull up. "Good," Koda said as he and Biltong got to their feet. "We're leaving now. Do you want to go to army headquarters with us?"

Varlik shook his head. "I think I'd better spend the rest of the day with my squad, if I'm going to try the tropics without a cool-suit."

Voker had ridden out with the air conditioner off and the windows open, to the concealed unhappiness of his driver, who had dared, while Voker was in the T'swa tent, to close the windows and turn on the cooler. When the colonel appeared in the tent door, his attention still behind him, the corporal quickly lowered the windows and turned the cooler off.

Voker didn't even notice the residual coolness in the car. Something that had occurred to him before had captured his attention again: There was little question that the Birds had been manipulating them from their first offensive. They'd made their resources known gradually and profitably, with full use of surprise. Drawn Confederation forces into actions that optimized their own, still not fully known, strengths and advantages. The Birds couldn't have done those things without a thorough knowledge—a considerable knowledge, at least—of Confederation military resources, psychology, and practices.

Someone from off-planet had more than armed and trained them. Someone was undoubtedly also directing them. But who?

It was as if a clue was staring him in the face, but he couldn't see it. He'd have to ask himself the right question—whatever that was. The reason, maybe: why were they doing this? Or who'd be able to use the technite if the Birds controlled it?

He'd have to review the situation—program an analysis and see what he came up with. He wasn't well trained as a programmer, or very experienced, but he wanted to work on this by himself, for a while at least. And sometimes just playing with the factors, flow-charting, could give you the answer you were looking for.

Twenty-One

By the time the T'swa headquarters was relocated there, five days later, the army's Beregesh base was beginning to look as organized as it actually was, and a newer, more permanent defensive perimeter was rapidly being built a mile outside the original, complete with mine fields and cleared fields of fire.

The new perimeter was more than fifteen miles long, with as many bunkers built or under construction as the army was prepared to man at the time. As more divisions arrived, more bunkers would be built. Crews were out with beam saws, clearing the ground for 200 yards out, saving the more useful lengths of wood for use in bunker construction. The rest was pushed into piles by dozers, sprayed with a high flammable, and ignited, sending columns of smoke high into the dry, previously transparent air.

When the piles had burned themselves out, the dozers returned to level the field, leaving no cover, no depression or hump to hide in or behind. After the dozers moved on, a wirelayer floated out, laying down coils of accordion wire near the clearing's outer edge, and after that, mines of different descriptions—string mines, jumpers, compression mines, radio mines, mines that would trigger at the hover field of a vehicle no larger than a scooter, just in case the Birds showed up with any.

According to rumor, more wire was on its way from Iryala and other worlds, and still more was on order.

Bird attacks did not seriously hamper construction. Patrols in cool-suits operated constantly outside the construction zone. Other patrols worked the bush inside, hunting any Birds who might have infiltrated. Gun ships also patrolled, occasionally coming under rocket fire. Their armor was resistant to M-3H rockets. About a dozen, hit, had returned with little or no damage, but two had been shot down.

A new construction battalion had arrived from Rombil, and base support troops had been assigned on rotation to help. Timber and cement in quantities were being flown in on arch trucks and pallet trucks from the sawmill and cement plant west of Aromanis. Four power receivers had been installed and were receiving transmissions from the new orbiting power station. Prefab cool-huts for the troops were going up rapidly and being covered with timbers and earth for protection. Twelve-hour shifts, including the frequent rest breaks necessary when laboring in cool-suits, were standard for both officers and men, and work went on around the clock. The troops were too busy, and off duty too tired, to complain much, and besides, they felt they were accomplishing something.

The sporadic Bird attacks had been mainly against construction crews, although several patrols outside the perimeter had been wiped out or dealt nasty casualties.

Meanwhile, the T'swa troopers had been flown directly from the Aromanis Base to interdiction operations some two hundred miles south of Beregesh. All that the T'swa had at Beregesh was a joint regimental field headquarters and an office at the Beregesh communications center.

Colonel Koda had kept Varlik at Beregesh to see how he managed in the subequatorial climate. It was supposedly hotter than the equatorial zone, though much less humid. Also, he said, he was waiting until the danger level could be evaluated for the new T'swa operation. "We have almost eighteen hundred warriors," Koda replied to Varlik's impatience, "but only one accomplished publicist."

At least Varlik couldn't complain about lack of information or sweat. He was privy to all reports from T'swa troops in the field, and exposed to air conditioning only at the comm center or when he accompanied Colonel Koda to the army's Beregesh HQ. He even slept in a T'swa tent instead of a cool-hut, and never so much as tried on a cool-suit. His exercise regimen wasn't what it had been up north, but he accompanied Koda on the colonel's almost daily runs, each about an hour long.

He also spent an hour every other day trying to duplicate the unusual strength and flexibility exercises that most T'swa base personnel did in pairs in lieu of the more time-consuming workouts the combat troops had done up north. At first he was sore from them—belly, shoulders, hamstrings, arms—but he survived. Not comfortably as the T'swa did, but he survived, without heat prostration or total exhaustion—and with pride.

Confederation personnel reacted variously to Varlik: A few looked away in resentful irritation, and a few others glared: surely his behavior reflected disrespect for Standardness and his own people. But mostly his activities spawned good-natured exaggerations of his toughness and prowess, told as truth and even believed by the tellers. He was the only white man at Beregesh who went without a cool-suit—or who was allowed to, for that matter.

The Confederation troops were never briefed on what the T'swa were doing, but rumors flowed, a military tradition as old as armies. They started with the pilots who'd dropped the T'swa as numerous individual squads far back in Bird Land, or had flown in to evacuate casualties or drop supplies. Imagination took it from there, the T'swa reputation never suffering in the telling. Varlik, in a fey mood one evening, circulated among the army hutments, interviewing troops on what they thought of the T'swa. Selected interviews and excerpts went to Iryala and Rombil aboard pods, along with video recordings from the evacuation center showing wounded, both white and black.

Whenever a call of T'swa wounded was received, a small evac floater was sent out, but such calls were not abundant. Reportedly, casualties weren't heavy, and the T'swa didn't call for a floater unless (1) the wound was incapacitating, and (2) the wounded could be gotten alive to a place reasonably safe for the floater. The Birds were known to post lookouts, some with night scanners, in occasional tall ridgetop trees, so a floater landing could endanger an entire squad.

Every day after breakfast, Varlik reported to regimental headquarters, until one morning, when they'd been at Beregesh a week, Colonel Koda made his decision.

"Lormagen," he said, "I have a question. Are you quite sure you want to join your squad in the bush?"

Varlik's pulse quickened. "Absolutely, sir. When?"

"Late tonight. They have called in that they will withdraw from the contact zone for a supply drop. Have you ever parachuted?"

Varlik's bowel spasmed. "No, sir."

"Are you willing to?"

"If it's the only way, sir."

"It's the safest way. The floater flies a confusion course low over the forest—about three hundred feet above the trees—and drops supplies to a signal beacon. If Birds are watching, hopefully they will not know at what point the drop occurred, but if the floater stopped to lower you . . . You see."

"I'll jump, sir."

"Fine." Without turning to the door, Koda called his orderly. "Makaat!"

Makaat came in; he'd left half his left hand on Emor Gadny's World. "Yes, colonel?"

"Get Varlik equipped with forest jump gear. He's going south tonight. Drill him in landing rolls and letdown procedure; there must be some suitable trees around here. Then go over everything he needs to know about jumping over forest at night, and make sure he gets it all, thoroughly. When you're satisfied he can handle himself without excessive risk of injury, let me know. When he's ready, get him equipped with a lapse release chute, drill him in its use, and take him to the landing field. Major Svelkander, in charge of supply and evacuation, will have a floater for him. Take Varlik up and have him jump from, oh, 800 feet local the first time, over the marshalling field.

"The second jump should be from 400. We'll consider two jumps enough."

"Yes, sir."

"One other thing. You will go with him tonight and be his jumpmaster."

"Thank you, sir."

Koda's attention went to some papers again. They'd been dismissed. Numb, Varlik left with Makaat.

The forest jump gear was more cumbersome and awkward than Varlik had imagined. After drilling on landing rolls for a few minutes from a standing position on the ground, Makaat had him practice off the bed of a parked truck. After several jumps from there, he graduated to jumping off the cab roof, all to the attention of a small but very interested group of soldiers. Varlik was glad the Orlanthan gravity was lighter than Iryala's, even though the difference wasn't large. When he'd jumped from the roof three times, Makaat raised the truck to its maximum of thirty inches above the ground, then drove it at a speed of about five miles per hour and called out to jump. The landing roll worked so well that Varlik began to feel there was nothing to this.

Letting himself down from a tree proved simple and relatively easy, but Makaat had him do it half a dozen times, the last three blindfolded to simulate doing it in the forest night. And if the tree, the largest available, was only 35 feet tall, the procedure, he told himself, would be no different for a tree of 80 or 120 feet.

The preliminaries took them through lunch time. It was early afternoon when they reached the landing field, where a small group of airmen, apparently having heard of his impending jump, were on hand to watch.

Varlik didn't start to get really nervous until they took off. The light floater went straight up, faster than seemed necessary, leaving his stomach behind, then stopped at what Varlik assumed must be 800 feet. Makaat opened the door and looked back at him.

"Are you ready?"

Varlik nodded. He would *not* disgrace himself. He *would* step out that door into sunlit nothingness, and he would not soil himself.

"Ready," he answered.

His mouth felt dry; he was surprised that the word came out sounding so natural. Did the T'swa feel this way the first time they jumped?

"All right. Stand in the door as I showed you, with your hands on the sides. When I slap your shoulder, you step out. Agreed?"

"Of course." Varlik shuffled to the door, awkward in coveralls and harness, eyeing the lapse release Makaat wore on his belt. When he got fifty feet out, it was supposed to open his chute automatically—"explode" it, in a sense, from its pack. He wondered if they ever failed.

Better than having to pull a release handle himself, the way the T'swa marauders had done in their freefall jumps. His body felt too numb to pull a handle.

He stood in the door, hands on the edge, looking

out, his whole gut clenched. It didn't seem possible to . . .

The hand struck his shoulder and he jumped, plummeted, and felt the opening, without the jerk he'd expected. He swung, swooped beneath the flowering chute, then the oscillating stopped and he was floating suspended, with the most glorious sense of joy he could remember! He looked down past his feet, utterly without fear now, then to one side saw the cluster of troops pointing up at him.

Let's see now. Hands on guide lines. Pull right—that's the way. Hey! It works! Great! I'm heading right toward them. Let's make them scatter. Oops, going to overrun them. Pull right again and spiral. Wow! Look at that! Now! Right at them!

Then the ground seemed to accelerate, the airmen in their cool-suits scattering. At the last moment the ground jumped up at him and his feet struck, his knees striking the ground because his legs had been too relaxed. He rolled back to his feet, whooping. The airmen applauded. The floater was already halfway to the ground to pick him up.

The second jump was anticlimactic. As he addressed the door, his bowel felt the same as it had the first time, but now it was an objective phenomenon, belonging to the body, not to himself. This time as he stepped out, the floater had a forward speed of about seventy miles an hour, as it would that night.

He held a right spiral to the ground; it took only seconds to get there, and this time he kept proper tension in his legs. He could easily have kept his feet, but Makaat had told him not to.

As they rode back to the T'swa camp, he felt cockier than he'd ever felt before in his life.

Twenty-Two

This time there was no sun, just the scant pale light of the sickled major moon, and the second moon similarly slender, spread over the forest roof. For a long, beautiful moment the treetops appeared remote, then seemed to accelerate upward as he fell toward them, and for brief empty seconds, alarmed, he tried to withhold himself. One grabbed for him. Branches buffeted, submerging him in darkness; his descent half halted. Then suddenly nothing held him and he dropped precipitously, to be somehow stopped short, panting, disoriented.

He hung there in blackness, regathering his attention, wondering if his chute had lodged securely or would slip loose, wondering how far it was to the ground, wondering if it was safe to move.

He had no choice. Looking around, down, he could see nothing. His hands felt for the coil of slender rope clipped to his side, found an end, and with a minimum of body movement wove it through harness rings and made it fast. He then ran a bight below one foot, stirrup-like, gripped the line clamp in his right hand—harder than necessary—removed the snap, and struck the harness release with his left. For one sickening moment, as the harness let go, the chute gave slightly in the branches above, but only to lodge more firmly. Then he let himself down, never seeing the ground, finding it with his feet. He must have been, he decided, some twenty feet up.

On the ground he removed the heavy canvas coveralls, the masked crash helmet, and the steel-arched forest jump boots, then dug jungle boots from his pack and put them on, felt forth his holstered M-1 sidearm and attached it to grommets on his belt. Next he took out his video camera, its battery fresh, put it into a capacious breast pocket, and slipped the strap over his head. Then he donned his monitor visor, followed by a field cap. Finally, he closed the pack, put it on his shoulders, and lay back against it to wait for the T'swa.

He was beginning to sweat just sitting on the ground.

He couldn't see his hand inches in front of his face. He could have activated his monitor visor, of course, but it operated off his camera, and his camera cells were not inexhaustible. And he'd probably be there for a week or longer.

Somewhere, perhaps thirty or sixty or a hundred yards away, would be the supply bundle he'd followed out the door—a large, foam-padded box with a ribbon chute that should first have slowed it, then presumably slid from the branches to let the box fall to the ground. Like his dangling harness, it would emit a weak radio signal for about twenty minutes.

But they'd hardly come and get him right away; even a T'swi couldn't see in such darkness. They'd take a bearing, then wait till dawn, itself not much more than two hours away. They'd have picked up the two signals and be wondering what the second package was.

Briefly, he wondered if they'd be pleased to find it was him, or disappointed, or neutral, and then it occurred to him that he'd never seen a T'swi irritated! He wondered what an irritated T'swi would be like; or an angry T'swi! Would a T'swa warrior enraged be more dangerous in battle than one with the usual calm?

After a bit he allowed himself, there in the close hot dark, to play with the idea of a Bird patrol somewhere nearby, equipped with a directional instrument that could pick up the signal from his harness. But that was too farfetched. Next he played with a scenario in which he'd come down too far from the squad, their instrument failing to detect his signal. He imagined himself alone in the forest, waiting until it was obvious he'd been overlooked, then striking off northward to find his way back to Beregesh.

And which way was north?

The sound galvanized him, a low hard "s-s-st," repeated seconds later. It could be no farther than twenty feet away, probably less. He strained to hear, thought he detected a sound, very slight, from the same direction. Then, nearer, in Tyspi, a whispered "Khua?" (Who?)

With equal quiet he whispered: "Varlik."

The T'swa claimed the night vision of a cat, but he wouldn't have thought even a cat could see in such darkness.

The chuckle was even softer than usual, almost as soft as the whispers. "Good. Good. Are you all right?"

"I'm fine."

Then nothing more. Varlik lay back and let himself relax. There must be insects out here, he thought; the climate was wetter than at Beregesh or Aromanis. Makaat had given him a field-issue insect repeller, an inch and a half disk with a two-day battery—the same thing sportsmen sometimes used when fishing. It was attached to his field belt, and when the battery died he would throw the thing away, replace the whole unit from his pack.

He closed his eyes then, intending to sleep if he could. Could Birds see in the dark like the T'swa? It seemed to him that in such opaque darkness his eyes could come open without waking him up. The next thing he knew was the calling of forest birds, and his eyes opened to faint gray dawn. Quickly more birds joined in, building to a literal din of warbling, whistling, twittering, screeching—a chorus, a wild arboreal laud to encroaching day. The T'swi named Tisi-Kasi was kneeling near him, grinning. Varlik looked around: Six of the squad were in sight close by. Only six. His breath stuck in his chest for a moment; had they lost four? No, he told himself, they had lookouts posted. They must have.

Nothing happened though until, after three or four minutes, the dawn cacophony thinned to scattered cries and trills. Then Kusu stood, raised his face, and made a querulous cry not unlike some from the trees, repeating it three times. He was answered from a little distance. The answer seeming to come from higher, as if from a ridge.

Kusu looked at Varlik. "It's good to have you back with us, my friend. Now it's time to leave; we have Birds to find, and havoc to create."

They were not six, or ten either any longer, but eight—nine now, counting Varlik. They hiked through much of the morning, not jogging but moving hard and fast, pausing occasionally to drink from their canteens, lick salt, or snack on dried rations during breaks. Varlik recorded samples of it on video. They crossed several brooks, refilling their canteens at each, dropping in a tiny capsule and shaking briskly to kill possible parasites not protected against by their broad-spectrum immunization. The combination of heat and humidity was definitely worse than at Beregesh, yet it seemed to Varlik that he was going to handle it all right.

The forest wasn't as thick as he'd expected. On flats and benches and in the bottoms of ravines it could be almost jungle-like, like the place he'd landed, but on many sites the trees were scrubby, the canopy thin or broken, the forest floor patched and dappled with sun-

light, green with forbs and graminoids. Occasionally
there were old burns, not large, seemingly where lightning had struck dead snags, setting them afire to sew
the ground around with burning brands. Here and there,
storms had thinned or flattened the stand, and in some
such places thickets, large or small, had sprung up.
Birds called occasionally, and sometimes a furry arboreal animal swung or scampered, noisy or silent. Varlik
saw a large snakelike thing, thicker than his arm and a
dozen feet long, and slowed, pointing, but Bin, who
walked behind him, only grinned and nodded.

Three times he glimpsed large ungulates trotting away,
and twice, on muddy stream banks, he saw the prints of
some large animal, presumably predatory, with retracted
claws.

After three hours they encountered a tiny rivulet
flowing from a dense stand of saplings in the saddle of a
ridge. Kusu hissed a halt, and again they refilled their
canteens. Then he led them up through the thicket to
the saddle's crest. There the saplings stood less densely,
and there they stopped.

Four men disappeared to scout the vicinity. The
others watched and listened while Kusu explained briefly
to Varlik how the squad operated. Unless the scouts
decided it was too hazardous, this place would be the
rendezvous for the next two days. Kusu, along with
Shan, the squad medic, would stay here with the supplies and radio while the rest went out in two-man hit
teams, armed with M-1s and grenades, to find and
attack Birds.

The heart of the region was a narrow plateau, hundreds of miles long, dissected lengthwise by long narrow draws into longitudinal ridges. Near the edges of
the plateau, the ridges were less high but more rugged
and broken, the draws deeper, and the forest more
open. Thus the fringes were much less suited as lines of
march than the central ridges, and it was among the
fringe ridges that rendezvous were established.

The Birds were moving north in small columns of platoon size, following or sometimes making small trails. In the heavier central forest, this made it virtually impossible to spot them from a surveillance platform or gun floaters. A hit team would find a column, usually avoiding its scouts, ambush it—empty their rifles into it and perhaps throw grenades. Then they'd get out as rapidly as possible—not back to the rendezvous, but always away from the trail and the central ridges. Usually the Birds would not pursue them for long; apparently their orders were to continue north. When they did pursue more persistently, it was usually possible to ambush them.

The biggest hazard was occasional Bird hunter patrols.

Late the second day, the teams would return to the rendezvous, using utmost care not to be followed. There Kusu and Shan would be waiting, and they'd all move. Bird hunter patrols made it dangerous to stay long in one location.

When Kusu had finished the briefing, he sized Varlik up thoughtfully. "You kept up well this morning. What have you been doing since we left Aromanis?"

Varlik told him. Kusu nodded.

"Good. Very good. Now, what we do—what the hit teams do—is quite dangerous. The Birds move well; they are forest wise and very tough. We have succeeded as well as we have because we move freely while they feel constrained to move northward. But this advantage will diminish; the Birds will undoubtedly form more and more hunter patrols. We expect our activities to become increasingly hazardous."

So far, Kusu had spoken almost blandly. Now his gaze intensified, just a little, and he gestured at Varlik's camera.

"Which brings us to you. Your function here is presumably to show us not merely living in the field but also in action. And that is more dangerous for you than for us, because we can run faster and farther than you—and so can the Birds. Also, we observe more than you, move with greater stealth, and if necessary, we can find our way by night. The Birds, incidentally, seem to have no better night vision than you do, or not much.

"Frankly, I would keep you here with me, except that apparently it is of some importance to Koda that you record us in action."

Varlik nodded, feeling uncomfortable—not because of the danger he was in, but because he was a problem to this man he admired.

"So I will send you out with a team," Kusu continued, "but not into action at first. Bin and Tisi-Kasi will spend two days teaching you to move as silently as possible, disturbing the ground as little as possible. It is desirable that Bird hunter patrols not notice if they come near or cross your trail.

"Do you see the desirability of that?"

Again Varlik nodded, determined that this would work out. In two days he might not learn to move like a T'swi, he told himself, but he could come decently close. He'd always been a quick study, in things physical as well as mental.

"Of course," he answered. "I don't want to get killed, or to get anyone else killed."

"Fine. You have done well in all other respects; I'm sure you will do well in this also."

The burly T'swi gripped Varlik's hand on it, then they relaxed on the ground and waited for the scouts to return.

It was among the fringe ridges that Bin and Tisi-Kasi tutored and drilled their student. Three times that day they heard flurries of distant gunfire, near the edge of hearing—twice to the northwest, and once to the southwest. Other squads, the T'swa told him. Varlik had practiced into midafternoon, learning to recognize the ground conditions that showed tracks plainly, and those where tracks were least noticeable; how to move slowly without a sound; and how to run with the least possible noise. Then the two T'swa had lain with their eyes closed, and he'd crept up on them, had touched Bin's foot without being heard. They had also followed him at a little distance while he ran, critiquing his noise and the tracks he left. He'd never before thought of running "lightly"—running had simply been running. No longer.

It was then they heard the noise of nearer fighting, brief but furious, westward perhaps a mile—an eruption of automatic rifle fire followed by what had to be a blast hose. Then there was silence, interrupted moments later by two short bursts of rifle fire.

All three men had stopped as if frozen, listening, then drawn together. "Probably one of ours making a hit," Bin said to Varlik.

"Do you think they got away afterward?"

"If one of our people were killed, I would ordinarily sense it. If one was wounded . . ." His gaze went out of focus for a moment, then returned. "I believe they are all right. The danger now is that the Birds will chase them and get clear shots, or possibly run them down."

"Can they do that? Run them down?"

"Yes, in the sense of following them until they come up on them somewhere, unaware. The Birds, as Kusu said, are forest wise, perhaps as much as we are. But now we have things of our own to . . ."

There was more firing—long bursts from several rifles, overlapping. This time Bin disregarded it, gesturing to Varlik. "Begin."

Varlik began trotting again along the side slope, as soft-footed as possible, swerving uphill to avoid a steep stretch of bare, loose, ash-dry soil where tracks would be conspicuous, then along the contour just below a crest, where the forest was thin and the ground covered with a low thick growth of vines that would rebound when he had passed. More firing sounded, seemingly an exchange of short bursts—two rifles answered by one, then quickly again two. Varlik stopped, saw Bin grin before the T'swa waved him on.

Varlik angled downslope through undergrowth to the bottom of a draw, where a brooklet trickled from a seep. There the three of them stopped to refill canteens and take a break. In the soft mud, Varlik saw the prints of numerous clawed paws, as of a pack of large canids. Bin drew his bayonet, and from his pack a sharpening steel, and began to touch up the blade.

Tisi-Kasi knelt down a little apart, back erect, hands resting loosely on his thighs, and closed his eyes—one of the things they learned to do as children, Kusu had said. Varlik had never before seen a T'swi in that posture by daylight, and after a minute he questioned Bin quietly.

"What is Tisi-Kasi doing? He looks like he's in a trance."

"He is regaining *t'suss*."

"*T'suss?*"

The obsidian eyes moved from Tisi-Kasi to Varlik.

"*T'suss* is a condition similar to what your culture calls 'nonchalance,' and your scholars have so translated it. But translated as 'nonchalance,' *t'suss* is readily misunderstood, for often the term 'nonchalance' is applied to a state resulting from confidence in one's ability to prevail over whatever difficulty may exist in the situation at hand.

"Like nonchalance, *t'suss* is a casual calm, a lack of fear or worry, but the word does not apply to states growing out of either confidence or apathy. *T'suss* involves complete readiness to accept whatever outcome, regardless of the alignment of that outcome with, against, or across one's own intentions and efforts. Ability and prevailing are irrelevant to *t'suss*, and in a sense, confidence is subsumed in the higher attitude of *t'suss*."

"Well, how does kneeling like that help someone regain *t'suss?*"

"It is not the kneeling. Posture is a matter of prefer-ence and circumstance, although kneeling erect is most often used. Tisi-Kasi is creating images. He might be said to be dreaming, but as the knowing father of his dreams."

Varlik nodded. "I believe I understand," he said. "We do that too, some of us, though I've never prac-ticed it. It's called image rehearsal. A person sits down and pictures victory in his mind, over and over again. It's supposed to help him win . . . But you said—you said that winning isn't the purpose."

"Correct. The images that Tisi-Kasi is creating in-clude images of victory and also of defeat, of continuing to live and of being killed. Perhaps he found himself wishing too strongly for victory, or being partisan on the side of coming through alive, or of his friends doing so—which is all right, but it is not our way. It causes a reduction of pleasure in war, and also a reaction on the spirit—the being himself—in case his body is disrupted. And it commonly leads to an anxiety response in battle, which might result in inappropriate combat behavior."

Varlik contemplated Bin's words. "Our psychologists," he replied at last, "tell us that to rehearse defeat can cause defeat. The idea is that you get what you rehearse."

Bin smiled. "That would be a special case, depend-ing on certain predisposing conditions that may be com-mon among your people. But it is not the general case. If a person is oriented on a win-lose polarity, this image rehearsal of victory may help him win if he has experi-enced enough defeats that it is time for a reversal."

This meant little to Varlik. Meanwhile, the T'swi turned back to the bayonet's edge, and after peering as if at some faint vestige of a nick, stroked first one side and then the other with the sharpening steel.

"But in the long run," he said as if in afterthought, "the win/lose equation will tend to balance. And in the long run, pleasure of action is not controlled by out-come. Pleasure is increased by near neutrality of desire. One can enjoy battle more—or games or work or learning—if one is nearly indifferent toward the outcome.

"So the intention to win should not go beyond a slight preference. Tisi-Kasi is creating images to reattain that state, which is *t'suss*."

Bin examined the edge again, returned the sharpening steel to his pack, then got up and slid the weapon back into its scabbard. "And he will not only enjoy battle more—he will also perform war more perfectly." He grinned at Varlik. "We have sometimes been depicted as epitomal warriors, and that is not entirely inappropriate. But our ability does not result from some genetic difference; your own warriors would be comparable if they had the T'sel, of which *t'suss* is a part."

The next day Visto-Soka was wounded by a steel bullet. Otherwise, he'd have been killed. The Birds, like the T'swa, used steel bullets in the forest. Blast slugs had the disadvantage that they did not ricochet; at first strike they blew up. Thus in sapling thickets or brush they were likely to be exploded prematurely by striking a twig.

The bullet had hit Visto-Soka high in the chest. It had ripped through the left pectoralis major just inside the shoulder, holed the scapula without shattering it, and emerged. He continued to fire his rifle, however, and with his partner, Bik-Chan, killed or wounded their pursuers.

Varlik was not clear on what Bik-Chan, or perhaps Visto-Soka himself, did to control shock, but the two returned to the rendezvous together on foot. The wounded T'swi had what was left of that day, and the night that followed, to rest. At first light the next morning the squad moved again, about two hours south, a little slower than they might have, and established a new rendezvous in a grove of large old trees on a broad bench, in an area thick with saplings. There Shan became Bik-Chan's new partner, while the wounded Visto-Soka took over as medic!

And from there, Varlik went out with Bin and Tisi-Kasi on his first hit. As they set out, they again heard distant firing: Some other T'swa were in action.

It was midday when they made first contact, and not from a selected ambush. They were moving quietly along a bench through heavy timber when abruptly they glimpsed a Bird patrol not two hundred feet ahead. Each side saw the other simultaneously, and opened fire as they hit the ground behind trees. Between bursts, Tisi-Kasi, in the lead, barked a command that Varlik didn't catch. Bin, snapping an order for Varlik to follow him, began to crab rapidly backward. Varlik did the same, trying to keep a tree between himself and the Birds while bullets thudded, ricochets sang, grenades roared. Bin and Varlik rolled on their bellies over a large fallen trunk where the bench broke into the slope beneath, and doubling over, scuttled downhill away from the fight.

"Tisi-Kasi is back there!" Varlik gasped as they ran.

Bin didn't answer, simply careened through the trees. Varlik struggled to keep up. For a minute they almost sprinted, then Bin, looking back at Varlik's bulging eyes, slowed to a trot. They were in the draw by then, the trees thicker again. The firing had stopped. Varlik wanted to ask if that meant Tisi-Kasi was coming now, but he had too little breath for it, and besides, he knew that wasn't it. They'd abandoned Tisi-Kasi! Bin had abandoned his lifelong friend, left him badly outnumbered; Varlik was certain he'd seen at least half a dozen Birds! Now Tisi-Kasi was surely dead, and here they were, running like rabbits!

And he knew why. Bin was getting him away to safety, or trying to, by Tisi-Kasi's order.

The Birds were probably following them. Clearly Bin assumed it. After jogging long enough for Varlik to regain a little wind, the T'swi changed course, angling up the slope, the timber less dense here but still fairly heavy. After two hundred feet of running uphill, Varlik could run no more, but slowed to a driving uphill walk. Bin, seeing this, slowed, waving him on while he himself crouched behind a tree, looking backward with his rifle poised.

It occurred to Varlik that if Bin were killed, or stayed behind and lost him, he could never find the rendezvous. The T'swa always seemed to know where they were, relative to any other place, but he wasn't so gifted. So he slowed, preparing to stand with Bin to fight, but the T'swi, after a moment, turned and started up the slope again, suiting his own pace now to Varlik's.

"Is he . . . ?" Varlik asked between gulping breaths.

"Dead," Bin said. "He's with us."

Varlik's hair stiffened, even as his legs drove him up the ridgeside. Shortly they topped the ridge, put the crest behind them, then Bin turned north, running again, along the contour now.

"And the Birds . . . are following?"

"Right."

They kept running along the ridgeside for half a mile, sweat burning Varlik's eyes, then Bin crossed the crest again, slanting down the first side into the bottom, which here was a narrow strip of marshy meadow. It occurred to Varlik that the Birds would be slowed by having to follow their tracks. They'd be back there now, somewhere along their trail, eyes on the ground. Or probably just one or two would watch for tracks; the others would be watching ahead and to the sides.

Then it struck him: He hadn't gotten any of this on cube! He'd forgotten what he was there for. He glanced down at his left hip. At least the belt recorder was on; its tiny red light glowed.

Bin led him up the next ridge, and again they slowed to a driving uphill walk, through a dense young stand that gave excellent cover. Partway up was a bluff. They worked past it, then Bin stopped and crawled out on its top, Varlik close behind. From its brink they had a partial view of the wet meadow in the ravine, and Bin held his rifle ready to fire. Varlik peered downward, his camera raised.

He had only a minute to wait; two Birds came into view a few feet apart, rifles poised. Varlik watched them in his monitor, zooming the camera until he could see, besides lean limbs and loincloths, the pouches on their belts and harnesses, the bolos at their hips. A dozen feet behind the first two, two more appeared. Bin fired a long burst, and Varlik saw all four fall. Instantly Bin shoved back from the edge, rose to a crouch, and led him off again on a run, angling up the ridge in the direction of their first encounter. But not for long. Near the crest they leveled off again, along the contour, still trotting, Varlik gasping. A little farther and Bin slowed to a walk.

"Are there more of them?" Varlik asked. He prayed there weren't; he could hardly hope to run much longer.

"I caught sight of two more. They took cover when I fired."

"Only two? Do you think they'll follow us?"

"Only two that I saw. And yes, I think they will follow. But warily."

He didn't make Varlik run anymore right away. They passed by the next dense cover, but at the one after that, Bin led him running through it downslope, and through a tangle of blowdown in the bottom, then a little way up the other side. Varlik thought he saw Bin's plan: Shoot the Birds from above while they were climbing over blown-down trees. But instead of taking cover there, Bin doubled north along the contour a short distance, then into the bottom again, among trees not far from the blowdown.

It was there they took cover, Varlik wiping again at the sweat which threatened to blind him, trying to keep his gasping as quiet as possible. He saw now what Bin had in mind. The Birds would bypass the blowdown, foreseeing an ambush from above. If they bypassed it on this side, Bin would get another chance at them.

And they did. There were four of them, crouching and well separated. Bin let the first two pass nearly out of sight among the trees, then opened fire; the last two fell. Those ahead opened fire from cover, but Bin led Varlik scrambling backward, keeping trees in the line of sight, then turned and once more ran, Varlik behind.

But only two! Almost surely now only two of the Birds were left! Bin led him fleeing northward along the bottom a little distance, then angled up the east ridge again, until shortly they slowed to the hard-driving walk, almost as hard on the legs as running but easier on the wind. Varlik, puffing, rubber-kneed, sweat-blinded, had almost nothing left, and told Bin so.

"A little more," Bin answered. At the ridgetop they paused. Varlik dropped gasping to his knees. Bin looked him over, then looked northward where the crest sloped slightly up. "Can you hit anything with that sidearm?" he asked.

Varlik nodded.

"Good. Take cover up there, in that brush. I'll climb this tree. I should be able to kill them both from there, but if I can't, I will surely get one of them. The other one, if there is only one, will be up to you. Let them get close before you shoot; a sidearm is for short range only."

Then he pulled Varlik to his feet, clapped him on the shoulder, and began to climb a liana that partly hung, partly clung to the trunk. Varlik started along the crest but stopped well short of the thicket, to lie behind a buttress-rooted tree with his holster flap unsnapped and his camera in his hands, watching Bin crouched on a branch with the trunk between him and their backtrail.

It was several minutes before the Birds showed up at an easy half-trot, one looking at the ground, the other ahead and around. Varlik's eyes shifted to his monitor and he picked them up with his camera.

He recorded Bin in the tree. Obviously the T'swa couldn't see the Birds—he was keeping behind the trunk—but he seemed to hear them. Apparently he planned to let them pass and shoot them from behind.

They stopped at the tree's very foot, one examining the ground. They seemed to talk, then one moved around the tree, both scanning the area. Abruptly one spotted Varlik and hit the ground, firing a short burst that sent bark, splinters, and dirt flying around the newsman. There was the roar of a grenade, and the shooting stopped. Another grenade exploded. Varlik peered out again; both Birds sprawled dead, Bin was looking down at them. Then the T'swa grasped the liana and began to lower himself to the ground.

That was the moment when Varlik saw the third Bird. He'd come up the ridge about twenty yards north of the others, and now stood nearly forty yards from Varlik, raising his rifle in Bin's direction. Somehow Varlik's sidearm was in his right hand, and without taking time to aim, he squeezed the trigger. Four shots burst out before he could release it, and the Bird went down, his upper torso shredded by blast slugs. Bin let go of the liana and dropped the last ten feet, rolling, coming up with his rifle in his hands, but there was nothing left for him to shoot at. Still crouched, eyes downslope, he moved toward Varlik, who lay shaking on the ground.

"There are no more," Bin said. "I am sure of it."

You were sure before, when you killed the two with grenades, Varlik thought. But he didn't say it, because he too felt sure that was all, and because, except for him, Bin could easily have been well away from danger.

Then, reaching down a large blue-black hand, the T'swi helped him to his feet.

They didn't wait until the next day, but went cautiously back to the rendezvous, as if another patrol, attracted by the much repeated gunfire, might come checking and find them. Which could happen, Varlik told himself.

The next day Bik-Chan returned alone, Shan having been killed, while Jinto and Dzuk came back with Dzuk's right wrist bullet-broken. The squad was down to six T'swa, two of them wounded. Kusu moved them a few ridges farther east, where recent fire had swept away the undergrowth and killed the older trees. There, from an opening on the crest, he called on evac headquarters to pick up the wounded and Varlik.

Then they sat together in the ashes, waiting. It would be somewhat less than an hour before the floater could arrive. After the pickup, Kusu and his three effectives would move back toward the Bird trails, operating as a single hit team instead of by pairs.

The floater was actually in sight when Bin, one of the two lookouts, saw the Birds, and the shooting began at once, furiously. Varlik snatched up Dzuk's rifle and hit the ground with the T'swa. As he dropped, he felt the bullet slam his left hip, but somehow it didn't seem serious except that his vision was blurred. So he fired blind, a long burst and then another in the direction of the Birds; then the clip was empty. He tried to crawl to Dzuk, a few feet away, for another clip, but his leg wouldn't obey. And then there was heavy firing from overhead—surely a heavy caliber blaster—overriding the noise of rifles, its exploding slugs making a series of loud violent slaps farther along the crest, so closely spaced as to seem almost a single long sound.

It was followed by silence. Then a long burst from a Bird called forth another staccato roar from overhead, and the shooting was truly over. Apparently the Birds hadn't seen the floater until after the firefight started, and were caught exposed.

Dzuk and Visto-Soka were still alive; they'd been lying down to start with. Kusu's chin had been shot away and Jinto was both gutshot and lungshot; Bin was the only one unwounded. He and a profusely bleeding

Kusu helped the evac floater crew load the rest, and they all left together. Then the two Iryalan medics began work on the wounded.

Varlik had recorded none of the final fight on video, though its sounds were all on cube, but now, sitting weak and bleeding on the floater, he began to record the wounded and the busy medics. Then one of the medics knelt beside him with a syringe and shot him with it. That was the last thing Varlik recorded before he slept.

PART THREE

Tyss

Twenty-Three

When Varlik awoke from sedation, he was in a troop carrier fitted to move wounded from the Beregesh field hospital to the base hospital at Aromanis. He could remember nothing beyond the evac floater and the medic with the syringe. He'd known something was wrong with his hip, but now his guts hurt badly, too.

He moved his head, his eyes finding a doctor with a captain's collar lozenge. The doctor saw his movement and spoke to him.

"You're back with us, eh?"

"More or less," Varlik answered thickly.

Taking a syringe from a case, the doctor walked over. "The pilot tells me you're the famous white T'swi," he said. "You keep dangerous company. I'm going to give you a little sedative now. It's another hour to the base hospital, and it's best if you sleep your way there."

The way he hurt, it seemed a good idea, but he had a question first.

"Wait, doc."

The doctor paused.

"How are the guys in my squad?"

"I have no idea. I don't know who was in your squad."

Varlik looked at him blankly. Some of them were probably aboard this craft, and if he asked by name . . . But he was having trouble thinking.

"What happened to me? Something hit me in the hip, and then I couldn't move. Now my belly hurts."

"You were hit in the ilium—part of the pelvis, the hip bone—and the left end of it was broken off. Then the bullet went through the abdominal cavity and some of its contents emerged through the obliquus externus on the right side. They opened you up at the field hospital at Beregesh and did a nice repair job. Now all you have to do is lie quietly in a nice cool ward at Aromanis and heal. Just like your buddies."

The doctor pressed the syringe against Varlik's bare shoulder and fired it. Somehow it seemed to Varlik that he had more questions, but he couldn't remember what they were. Then the sedative took him.

It was one of the T'swa wards, a busy place well stocked with medical technicians and wounded. His Romblit doctor there told him with some amusement that reception had initially been unwilling to put him in a T'swa ward. True, he'd been brought in with T'swa wounded, and his tag said "Company A, T'swa Second Regiment," but clearly he was not T'swa. Then a big T'swa sergeant with his lower face heavily bandaged had gotten off his stretcher, backed the reception sergeant into a corner, gathered a fistful of shirt front, and in grunted, barely intelligible words, made it clear that all his squad went with him, Lormagen included.

Varlik wondered if this was another case of facts inflated and embroidered, but the story pleased him. And he was glad to be where he was, a feeling that increased with the days. T'swa wards had a reputation among hospital personnel as the most cheerful, and

T'swa the patients who were easiest to work with and recovered most rapidly.

Meanwhile Varlik enjoyed a rich dream life, though he could never recall more than bits and pieces of his dreams. Long afterward, he'd remember his days in the T'swa ward as among the more pleasant of his life, even though it was there he learned that only four of the First Squad had survived, besides himself. Bik-Chan had been killed on the ridge, and Jinto had died on the evac floater of multiple wounds.

On his first day they took him into surgery, where they welded his pelvis and did a mesh job on some ligaments. His visceral and major vascular damage had been handled at Beregesh.

By the end of the third day he'd talked the hospital into giving him temporary use of a small examination room, and there, after recording a long and reassuring cube to Mauen, he narrated his report on the T'swa raiders and the last days of the First Squad, then edited cubes both for newsfacs and broadcasting. This took him two days—his energy level was low—but when he was done, the cube was the best facs feature he'd ever seen or heard.

Three days later General Lamons came through the ward, pinning medals on the wounded. Varlik, who'd been sitting in bed reading, was deeply surprised, but not too surprised to slip on his visor and pick up his camera. Lamons saw him with it, scowled only briefly, then continued. When he got to Varlik's bed, he stepped in beside it and looked down at him. Varlik set the camera aside, though the audio recorder was still running.

"Your T'swa have been doing a good job," said Lamons.

"Yes, sir."

"Your Colonel Koda showed me a copy of your reports on the T'swa interdiction teams. That was good work you did. Took guts."

"Thank you, sir."

The general grunted, then bent and pinned a medal

on Varlik's pajama top. "Carry on," he said, then turned to the next bed.

By that time the hospital had begun to feed Varlik solid food—not whatever he wanted, but solid food. And he was allowed to wheel himself to the "library," where boxes of books had been spread unsorted on tables. Walking would have to wait a while.

It was in the library that he ran into Konni. Eight days earlier she'd been recording the hardening of perimeter defenses when a Bird lobber rocket had hit a hover truck less than twenty yards away. Pieces of truck had smashed her left humerus and cracked her left supraorbital ridge and four ribs, while small rocket fragments had struck her in the left arm and leg. The left side of her face was an interesting purplish-green.

"My Revax is all right, though," she said, "and I ought to be out of here in about three weeks. The home office is sure to be sending another team out, so I'll probably go back to Iryala then, although . . . it's a temptation to stay. How about you?"

How about him? He hadn't looked at that. And for the first time, it occurred to him that there was nothing here to report on the T'swa now except more of the same. Maybe later, if there was a later, if the T'swa were given a new assignment. But now . . .

"I'm going to Tyss," he said. The statement took him totally by surprise, but he continued from there. "To the world that produces the T'swa regiments. There are guys going there from my ward—guys disabled or requiring prolonged rehab and reconditioning. I should be able to talk my way into going with them."

Having said it, he felt a pang of guilt. He could, after all, go home to Mauen now if he wanted to, and they could start the family they'd been approved for. Central News wouldn't complain. After all, he'd almost been killed. Probably they'd treat him like a hero.

He kept the pang for about ten seconds, then his attention went to procedural matters. Legally, his status with the Red Scorpion Regiment didn't validate traveling to Tyss without a visa from the Iryalan Foreign Ministry. In fact, legally he'd probably had no right to work for a foreign military force. But he was sure that Colonel Koda would approve his request, and for practical purposes, that would settle that. As soon as he had approval from Koda, he'd send word to Fendel. He was supposed to be here covering the war of course, but his reports to date would have built up a lot of interest in Tyss, and he had to spend his rehabilitation somewhere.

Besides which, he'd be gone long before they could get any argument to him.

He and Konni talked a while longer, mostly about the T'swa and his experiences with them in Birdland. She told him how impressed both she and Bertol had been with the early cubes Varlik had let them copy, then Varlik let her borrow his cubes of the Birdland mission. After that she'd gone back to her own ward, and he'd called Lieutenant Shao, the one-armed officer who'd been left in charge of the T'swa's Aromanis camp. He explained that he wanted to be evacuated to Tyss so he could record something of the planet and its people.

It was marvelous, Varlik thought, how casual the T'swa were about so many things. Without a moment's hesitation, Shao promised to add him to the roster on the evac ship which would arrive, and leave, later that week. And no, the lieutenant assured him, there'd be no problem; he had all the authority necessary.

It was late the next day that Konni reappeared, just after Varlik had sent off letter cubes to Mauen and Fendel telling them what he was going to do. It was a lot harder to tell Mauen than Fendel.

"Well," said Konni casually, "how's your plan coming along to be evacuated to Tyss?"

"I leave day after tomorrow," he said. "No problem. Lieutenant Shao has even issued me the clothes and stuff I'll need there."

Her eyes lit up. "Good!" she said. "Look at this." She handed him a sheet of stiff paper.

TO WHOM IT MAY CONCERN:

KNOW YOU BY THIS CERTIFICATE THAT KONNI WEN-TER, BY VIRTUE OF HER PARTICIPATION IN THE 711. 10.01-02 NIGHT RAID ON KELIKUT, ORLANTHA, IS HERE-BY APPOINTED AND RECOGNIZED AS AN HONORARY MEMBER OF THE NIGHT ADDER REGIMENT, LODGE OF KOOTOSH-LAN, WITH ALL THE RIGHTS AND PREROGA-TIVES PERTAINING THERETO.
(SIGNED)
BILTONG, COL., COMMANDING

When he'd finished reading, Varlik stared at it for a moment longer and then at Konni. An extraneous, non sequitur thought drifted into his mind—that T'swa apparently only had one name each.

"In the name of Pertunis!" he said. "How did you get this?"

"When I left you the other day, the first thing I did was listen to your Birdland report and look at your video cubes. And decided I wanted to go to Tyss, too. Actually, I wanted to as soon as you talked about it; that just hardened it. So I called Colonel Voker and asked him if he could think of any way to do it without my having to go through the Foreign Ministry back home. That might take a year. He said he'd see what he could do. And this afternoon, this came from Beregesh. I know Colonel Voker's behind it. He had this made up in his office and sent it south for Colonel Biltong's signature, I'm sure of it."

She took the "certificate" back. "I'm going to call your T'swa lieutenant now and apply for evacuation."

"It's Lieutenant Shao," Varlik said, and she hurried from the ward.

She was right, Varlik thought—it must have been Voker. How nonstandard—perhaps even non-Standard—

they'd become, getting around regulations the way they were! And Voker most of all—that was flagrant! Konni's certificate was an even flimsier legal basis for bypassing the Foreign Ministry than his own position as regimental publicist. Back home, for something like that, a person could be charged with a misdemeanor, at the very least. For Voker, surely a felony.

But that didn't disturb Varlik at all, because the T'swa couldn't care less, and no one at the hospital was going to question it.

He realized he was grinning broadly.

Twenty-Four

K onni wiped sweat from her forehead. "Do you understand these people?" she asked. "The people themselves, I mean, not the language."

They were eight days out from Kettle, with thirteen more to go before they reached the Oven—Tyss. She had copied Colonel Voker's Tyspi cubes, and with Varlik's help had been doing a cram course on the language. The warship *Hedanik* was Iryalan but leased by the T'swa, and her operations crew as well as medical and housekeeping staffs, plus thirty-seven of her thirty-nine casualties, were T'swa. So the temperature was kept at a constant, and to T'swa pleasant, 95 degrees Fahrenheit. Not that the T'swa required high temperatures: They simply had an easy physiological and psychological tolerance of them. T'swa regiments had more than once fought in snow and ice.

"Understand the T'swa?" Varlik looked at her question; he'd never explicitly thought about it before. "I guess I don't. But I don't think I really understand Iryalans, either; I'm just used to them. And I suppose I'm getting pretty used to the T'swa now. Why do you ask?"

"I've listened to all the cubes you've loaned me of your conversations with T'swa. The ones where you were speaking Standard, that is. And some of their attitudes and responses—I don't believe I could ever understand them. I wondered if it's the same for you."

"I suppose it is. I just don't notice it so much anymore—I take it for granted.

"I'll tell you something, though. When the T'swa talk Tyspi to me, I usually understand everything they say. I'm a quick study, with excellent recall. But sometimes when two of them talk to each other, I hardly understand anything at all. Sometimes too many of the words are unfamiliar, but at other times I know the words and still don't know what they're talking about. So I guess I *don't* understand the T'swa all that well. But it's never seemed very important; it's as if I understand them well enough."

Varlik got up stiffly. "I'm hurting. Let's go to physical therapy for a bit."

"You go," Konni said. "What I need is a nap."

They left the small reading room, Konni turning right toward her room, Varlik hobbling left toward the therapy section. As he passed an open office door, he glanced in and saw a T'swa medic named Usu. On an impulse he stopped.

"Usu, may I interrupt you?"

The T'swi looked up from his papers and nodded, gesturing to a chair. "How can I help you?"

Varlik entered and sat, groping for an answer. "It's nothing really important, I guess, but . . . Well, there are a lot of things I don't understand about the T'swa."

"Oh?" The T'swi said nothing more then, waiting.

"For example, sometimes two T'swa will be talking and I don't understand at all what they're saying—even when I understand the words."

Usu nodded, eyeing Varlik thoughtfully. "I can see the difficulty. Let me make a few comments that may help. In the Confederation, not only most of your activities but also much of your reality are deeply constrained by the compulsion for and environment of Standardness. Both your Standard Technology and your Standard Management spill over onto beliefs and attitudes that, strictly speaking, are neither technological nor pertain to management. In fact, Standard Technology and Standard Management are, to quite a large degree, specialized codifications of broad, long-standing attitudes and beliefs. A codification which then reinforces those beliefs and attitudes by particularizing, institutionalizing, and enforcing them.

"Those attitudes, constraints, and prohibitions have severely inhibited seeing, and even looking . . ."

"My vision is better than most people's," Varlik interrupted. "I see really well."

"I do not doubt that. But I was not referring to your eyes. I referred to the inability of your culture to put its attention on, or even to notice, things that do not fit its conceptual framework." The bright T'swa eyes peered mildly at Varlik as if watching for some glimmer of comprehension; then Usu continued.

"Thus, you lack the concepts necessary to understand T'swa life and reality broadly, and where you have no concepts, your language has no words.

"Now in learning our language—those few of you who have undertaken to—you learn many of our words. But at least at first, the meanings attached to a Tyspi word—the meanings *you are able* to attach to a Tyspi word—are concepts you already have in your own culture. For many words in Tyspi, your concepts are quite adequate to our meanings, but for numerous other words, they allow only a partial and frequently crude understanding. Which means you understand the word, or approximate its meaning, in some contexts but not in others.

"While there are numerous other words that are not translatable at all into Standard because they apply entirely to concepts that you do not have."

Varlik sat frustrated. If that was true, then it seemed to him he would never understand the T'swa, and somehow just now it seemed important to.

"However," Usu went on, "it is certainly possible to begin gaining those concepts and thus share more of the realities of the T'swa. Indeed, perhaps you have already begun. If you would like, I can undertake to help you."

Varlik looked at the T'swi, this one a man smaller than himself, with artist's hands. "I'd appreciate it." He paused. "You're not a warrior, are you?"

A grin flashed. "No. While I am employed by a war lodge, the Lodge of Kootosh-Lan, my way is the Way of Service, not of War. Do you know the Matrix of T'sel?"

"I've seen a chart; in fact, I ran off a copy. It had headings like play and fight. And work."

"That is it. I have tasks to complete now, but if you wish, I can meet with you here at 15.50 and we can look into this matter further. And bring your chart; it will be useful."

Varlik got up. "Can I bring Konni Wenter with me? She's interested, too. In fact, I wouldn't have brought this up if it hadn't been for her questions."

"That will be fine. I will procure a third chair and expect you here at 15.50."

At half-past fifteen, Varlik and Konni were there. Usu had brought with him a T'swa woman, strongly built, whom he introduced as Dzo-Dek, the lab director and his wife. Her hair too was straight and short. Varlik had already been told that T'swa didn't cut their hair, that it seldom grew as long as an inch. Apparently that was true for both sexes. It behaved more like coarse fur, Varlik told himself, than like human hair.

He handed Usu a printout, creased from having been folded. "Here's the chart."

THE MATRIX OF T'SEL

	FUN	WISDOM/KNOWLEDGE	GAMES	JOBS	WAR
PLAY	Play just for fun	Study as play; learning unimportant	Games as play; winning unimportant	Job as play; reward unimportant	War as play; victory unimportant
STUDY	Study for fun; learning secondary	Study for wisdom &/or knowledge	Study for advantage	Study to enhance job accomplishment	Study for power
COMPETE	Compete for the fun of winning	Compete to be wisest or most learned	Compete to win	Job as a challenge	War as a contest
WORK	Work at playing	Work at learning	Work for advantage	Work for survival	Soldiering
FIGHT	Fight to control pleasure	Fight to control knowledge	Fight to subdue	Fight for monopoly	Fight to kill or destroy

Usu scanned it and smiled. "Ah, yes. And here, the heading 'Jobs'—the Tyspi word is *R'bun*, which I translated as 'Service,' but 'Jobs' is also a reasonable approximation. *R'bun* partakes of both concepts."

Usu had returned his gaze to Varlik as he spoke. "You have had experience with T'swa warriors. Where in this matrix does the T'swa warrior fit? At what action level, in what activity?"

"Why, at *Fight*, I suppose. At the action of *Fight*, in the activity of *War*."

"Ah. And where do the Iryalan troops fit?"

"Hmmm. Most of them—most of them fit at the action of Work, in the activity of War."

"Very good. And in the activity of War, which action level do you suppose would be most successful in terms of victory?"

"Why, it would have to be Fight. Here." His finger touched the chart's lower right-hand intersect.

"And what would you say if I told you that T'swa warriors fit here instead?" A long black finger touched down at the intersect of Play and War.

Varlik peered, then looked up at Usu. "I guess I'd have to ask how that could be. It's my understanding that your warriors almost always win, although I've had a lecture by a trooper named Bin on the win/lose equation always tending to balance at unity—one."

Usu grinned. "Then your education in T'sel began before today. But I must tell you that the activity of the T'swa warrior is not Fight, but Play. And I must take the lesson given by your warrior friend another step: The T'swa warrior *neither wins nor loses*, because it is all the same to him. What transpires in his career will be interpreted as winning and losing by those who do not have the T'sel; therefore, to discuss it with you, he spoke of it as he did. The T'swa warrior, in fact, has no victory nor defeat, no enemy nor any rival. He is an artist creating in the play form called War, and what another might regard as his enemy, the T'swa regards as a playmate. Almost always, their playmates regard the T'swa warrior as an enemy, but our warriors regard themselves as no one's enemy, and no one as theirs."

Varlik recalled Tisi-Kasi kneeling on the forest ridge, regaining *t'suss*, a neutral attitude toward win/lose, and wondered if he still had *t'suss* when he was killed. Somehow he hoped so.

"Each T'swa warrior," Usu continued, "becomes a master at the art of war before his regiment is ever commissioned, and performs his art as perfectly as he is able, without distracting himself with concerns of victory or defeat, survival or death. The warrior at Fight will usually fall to him. And for just those reasons, our regiments enjoy great success."

Briefly, Usu's eyes caught Varlik's with a glint that Varlik had seen in other T'swa eyes. "But let me tell you something else about this," Usu went on. "If you play at War without skill—if you are not an accomplished artist—then this fellow"—his finger moved to the Fight/War intersect—"*is very likely to kill you*. Even if he is not particularly skilled, his intention and energy make him dangerous." Usu chuckled. "Of course, if you are truly at Play, death will not matter to you. But the person at Play will seldom opt for War without the intention of becoming an artist at it."

Varlik nodded. Conceptually he could see and accept this, though as a reality . . . "Usu," he said, "I hope I don't offend you by asking, but how can you be so sure of the warrior's state of mind?"

Usu's grin was broad. "That is a very good question, my friend, and perhaps my answer will not entirely satisfy you. On Tyss, our *training*, to use your word, is in whatever activity we have chosen for our life. But before that, and beginning in infancy, all children and youth receive the same basic *education*, which is education in the T'sel.

"Now I have used your Standard word 'education' because you have no word closer to *tengsil*, our word which encompasses that concept. But the actions which constitute *tengsil* include those that allow a person to see, to experience, to verify for himself, the very basis of T'sel. And *tengsil* is the same for he who plays at any of these." His finger moved across the row at Play, from Fun to War.

"I am a—your people have translated it 'physician,' though 'healer' might be closer. Those to whom I administer may either live or die. I may help them recover numerous times, but sooner or later they *will* die, and I am agreeable to their doing it. Truly! If my patient dies, he departs with my full willingness and best wishes. I will perform my art to the utmost of my not inconsiderable skill, but if he dies, I am neither distressed nor offended. I do have a certain preference, only slight, that he survives and regains health and facility, and I intend that he shall. But that preference has nothing in it of desire, and I do not even remotely insist on it."

Varlik blew lightly through pursed lips, then nodded slightly, not in agreement so much as acknowledgment. "So then . . ." He paused, looking at the chart. "Are all T'swa at Play? And if they are, why do you show these lower levels? How do you even know about them?"

"May I answer that?" Dzo-Dek asked, looking at Varlik.

"Of course."

"Not all T'swa are at Play," she said. "About two percent are at one of the other levels, and we regard them as somewhat retarded, which they are. But our enlightenment about the other levels did not grow out of studying them. It grew out of the study of other cultures. And the lower levels are part of the Matrix because they belong there; they exist."

"And in the Confederation, what percent are below the Play level?" Varlik asked.

"Among adults, approximately ninety-seven percent. It varies a little from world to world."

Varlik's lips had thinned slightly. "And how do you know that?" he asked.

Dzo-Dek reached past her husband to touch the intersect of Play and Wisdom/Knowledge. "Those who play here"—she tapped the chart—"have direct access to an immense—let us say an immense data base. And their training provides tools your culture is not yet familiar with. The rest of us—those at War or Service or Games or Fun—we learn the easier of those procedures in order to have direct access to the T'sel, but only those who specialize become able across the full gamut of them. They are our educators and— You have lost the concept: our *scientists;* our *researchers*."

The last word meant nothing to Varlik; his head was beginning to hurt. "So apparently you lump us, the people of the Confederation, with your retarded." His voice and face were strained when he said it.

Dzo-Dek smiled slightly. "No, there are major differences. First, what you mean by 'retarded' is mentally retarded. What I referred to is emotionally handicapped, although that certainly hampers rational thinking. And secondly, the two percent on Tyss that I spoke of are the way they are *despite* being exposed to the T'sel from birth. The people of the Confederation have not had that opportunity."

Usu interposed, looking first at Varlik and then Konni, the largeness of his eyes accentuated by their lack of visible definition between pupil and iris. "I believe we have taxed your receptiveness on this subject," he said. "You are still patients, and it might be well if you went to your beds."

Varlik nodded. His brief antagonism had died but he did feel depressed, and a little groggy. Getting up, he left the room without a word, Konni following. He went to his ward and she to her tiny room, and both went to bed without taking time to shower. Varlik didn't even try to sort out what he'd been told, and sleep took him quickly.

* * *

Not for the first time among the T'swa, he dreamed richly, though ten seconds after waking in the morning he could recall none of it.

But it seemed to him that remembering the dreams was unimportant. They'd been enjoyable when they happened, and the new day felt great to him, even in this mole of a ship burrowing through space. Konni, too, when he met her at breakfast, looked relaxed and cheerful.

And neither of them approached Usu or Dzo-Dek for any further lectures on the T'swa or the T'sel.

Twenty-Five

Excerpt from "Tyss, the T'swa World," by Varlik Lormagen. *Central News Syndicate,* Landfall, Iryala, 712.09.05.

Tyss, with an equatorial diameter of 9,100 miles, is somewhat larger than Iryala, and its surface gravity is 22 percent greater. Its axial tilt is only 9 percent, which means that while it has a winter and summer, the two seasons are not as different as we are used to on much of Iryala.

While its gravity is higher than all but a very few inhabited planets, Tyss is most remarkable for two things. One, it is extremely hot. And two, it is extremely dry. How hot can be shown by looking at some representative temperatures for different latitudes at different seasons.

REPRESENTATIVE DAILY HIGH AND LOW TEMPERATURES ON TYSS [degrees Fahrenheit] AT DIFFERENT LATITUDES

	midsummer		midwinter	
Latitude	*high*	*low*	*high*	*low*
0 (Equator)	140	110	140	110
30	140	105	135	100
50	125	100	110	85
80	110	80	85	55

Oldu Tez-Boag, the principal city of Tyss, is at 48.7° south latitude.

As for dryness, only 32 percent of Tyss's surface is sea, compared to 78.8 percent on Iryala. This means there is much less free water surface giving off moisture into the air. The combination of heat and dry air has resulted in a planet that is mostly desert.

Unfortunately, the coolest parts of Tyss are absolute desert on which virtually nothing grows. In places these polar deserts extend toward the equator as far as 55° latitude. Because of extreme polar and subequatorial deserts and particularly intense equatorial heat, most of Tyss's estimated 30 million people live at between 40° and 55° latitude, in whatever regions and locales have enough moisture to grow crops without being too hot for the heat-tolerant T'swa.

For all is not desert on Tyss. Almost without exception, there are belts of forest and marsh on the downwind sides of the several seas, and the marshes are sometimes drained for farming. And where mountain ranges don't intervene to block the flow of moist sea air, back of the forest belts are belts of savannah and grassland.

The air is a little thinner on Tyss than we are used to on Iryala, but you probably wouldn't notice it unless you were doing something strenuous. The atmospheric pressure is about the same as at Eagle Lake. . . .

Mineral resources on Tyss have not been valuable enough to attract off-planet investment or development, nor have T'swa agriculture and fisheries been attractive to Confederation export interests. Until very recently, the only significant exports from Tyss have been her famous mercenary soldiers.

Most of the people on Tyss, however, are employed at growing and harvesting food. Transportation and manufacturing are quite primitive, and because there is no synthetics industry there, lumbering, quarrying, and mining play a much more prominent role in people's lives than on Confederation worlds. . . .

Twenty-Six

The city of Oldu Tez-Boag was a metropolis by T'swa standards, with an estimated 30,000 people. It sat on a coastal plain, mostly on an ancient river terrace above the Lok-Sanu River, out of reach of the infrequent floodwaters. Viewed from the hospital, Oldu Tez-Boag had little to recommend it aesthetically except the abundance of ancient shade trees, particularly the gray-green tozut trees standing broad-crowned and tall in yards and along streets; and the thick-walled adobe houses, stuccoed over in pastels and white, almost all their windows facing south—away from the sun in this southern hemisphere town.

Oldu Tez-Boag had taken shape some four miles upstream of the highly salty Toshi Sea, but even at that distance, when Varlik and Konni stepped onto the third-floor balcony, their noses could detect the sweltering beds of kelp on the tidal flats.

A T'swa on the hospital ship had told him that Tyss had not always been a desert world. Like Orlantha, it had had great oceans once, millions of years before man had come there. Varlik had been exposed to geology in school, so he hadn't wondered how the T'swa knew.

What he had wondered was what had happened to all that water.

The hospital, occupying a modest prominence just outside the city, was run by the Lodge of Kootosh-Lan for its own warriors and those of the other four war lodges. It was one of the few multi-storied buildings in Oldu Tez-Boag—at four stories the tallest except for grain elevators along the river.

Kogi-Ta, one of only a handful of administrative personnel at the hospital, nodded pleasantly to the two Iryalans when they came to his desk. His short, stiff hair was white, but he looked strong nonetheless. Apparently he'd been a warrior once. A deep seam, a product not of age but youth, creased the left side of his face from jaw to hairline, interrupted by an eye patch. The combination gave him a dangerous appearance with which his good-natured smile was inconsistent.

"Good morning," Varlik said. "Our doctors told us we could take leave if we'd like. We want to visit the town and some of the countryside."

Kogi-Ta leaned a large hand on the desk to help himself to his feet; more than his face had been damaged.

"If you want to visit the town, then you will want money," he said, and turned to an ancient file cabinet. There was no computer or terminal to be seen.

He pulled two folders and looked into them. "No pay record! Have either of you ever been paid?"

Both indicated they hadn't. "But I'm afraid I'm only an honorary member of my regiment," Konni asked, "not a paid member."

Kogi-Ta looked up. "A technicality," he answered cheerfully. "You have been lodged in lodge facilities, as an employee and an honorary member, and someone in authority signed an order sending you here, so you both have allowances due you. Are you familiar with the lodge's disbursement system? No? It is based on the Standard calendar because the regiments serve on so many worlds."

From another drawer he took a leather bag and grinned at them. "You are about to learn how little a warrior is paid. But you will be surprised at how little things cost on Tyss. Quickly, his nimble fingers counted out small piles of silver coins, then he made entries on two pages in a ledger, glancing up as he did so. "We T'swa do keep *some* records, you know," he said, chuckling, and handed the coins to the Iryalans.

Varlik looked at them. "This is Confederation money," he said.

"Indeed. It's what the lodges usually require for their services, and it's as acceptable here as any. On Tyss the service co-ops mint their own, but they have long since used Confederation denominations and weight standards."

They already had some Confederation money in their wallets, but if this was theirs, it seemed as good a time as any to get it. "Do we have to sign anything to show we received it?" Varlik asked. "And to show that we left the hospital?"

Kogi-Ta's eyes glinted as if in amusement. "Not unless you insist on it. The lodge is satisfied as it is on both matters."

"When do we have to be back?" Konni asked. "Is there a set time?"

"Not unless your physician gave you one. No? It is preferred that Mr. Lormagen not come in after his ward is dark. If he does, I trust he will be as quiet as he can. But as you have a room to yourself, that consideration does not apply." He chuckled. "Do not be surprised if you are invited to spend the night in some residence, however. You are sure to arouse the interest of townspeople. If you wish, feel free to accept."

They thanked him and left, cameras slung, audio recorders as usual on their belts. The hospital, like the ship, was air-conditioned to 95°—the only air-conditioned building in the district. Yet outside, the heat that swirled around them was oven-hot as they began to walk, even though the autumnal equinox was well past and the winter solstice little more than a dek away. From a tree, something Varlik supposed might be an insect made a long keening sound at the upper edge of hearing, and the dirt street, though well shaded, was dusty. "I can hardly believe that Kogi-Ta," Konni said. "Or the hospital in general. Either no one cheats here, or they just don't care."

"I'll bet it's the first," said Varlik. "No cheats."

"How can that be?"

"I have no idea. That's just the way it feels to me, after the T'swa I've known."

She thought about it as they walked. "All we've been around are warriors and other professionals. Mostly warriors. Do you suppose other T'swa are like them?"

"I wouldn't be surprised. From what Usu said, they all get the same education; only the training is different."

"At home," Konni pointed out, "or in the whole Confederation for that matter, practically everyone does the same curriculum until they're fourteen. Yet while most people are at least fairly honest, some turn into criminals."

Varlik shrugged. "Education's got to be a lot different here. The men in my squad, common soldiers, all seemed like—no, they all *talked* like—professors. The kind of professor that really knows and can teach."

They both were beginning to sweat freely with the mild exertion of walking, but neither paid attention to that.

"They were different from one another in various ways," Varlik went on. "Their wit, how much they talked—that kind of thing. Some laughed out loud at things that others just smiled at. Some seemed a lot more interested than others in things like that strange white man living with them. And some played cards while others read, although none of the card players seemed to take their gaming seriously; they didn't even bet.

"But all of them seemed bright and—stable, I guess is the word. I never saw one of them upset or behave badly, although I heard a rumor that one of them got a little truculent once," he added, remembering the story of Kusu and the base hospital reception sergeant.

"Anyway, whatever they do with them in school seems to work."

They were in the town now, the dusty road passing between rows of homes and yards. There were few gaps in the shade of roadside trees, and all about were gardens, some remarkably lovely, others simply utilitarian vegetable patches with fruited vines clinging to poles and frames. Several dogs investigated the two Iryalans, and while they definitely seemed to be genus *Canis* rather than some canoid look-alike, they were neither hostile nor noisy. They were what you'd expect T'swa dogs to be like, Varlik thought: civilized.

There were children, too, peering from yards and the roadside. Now two of them, seeming perhaps five and seven years old, trotted barefoot onto the powdery dirt to keep pace alongside. The girl was smallest. Konni stopped and turned to them, Revax at her chest, its tiny light glinting as it recorded. Her visor was tilted up; for close work she could see well enough in the horizontal view frame atop the camera.

"Hello," said Konni in Tyspi.

Both children had stopped, not staring so much as simply gazing.

"Are you Ertwa?" asked the little girl.

"I don't know what 'Ertwa' means," Konni said.

"She still gets times mixed up," the boy put in. He turned to his sister. "They are Splennwa. Ertwa were very long ago."

The little girl studied them. "Splennwa?" she said, cocking her head critically. "I think not. They are abroad unprotected in the heat of day."

Varlik would have contributed to the conversation but could think of nothing to say in the face of such seeming precocity. Then the children turned and trotted tough-footed to a nearby yard, saving him from the risk of saying something inane.

A little farther on was a small building, smaller than the residences, with a sign that read "cool drinks." On the roof was a solar converter, the first they'd encountered here except for the large battery of them at the hospital. Varlik paused. They'd walked half a mile or more by then, his longest walk since Birdland, and while he felt no pain, his legs were tiring in the T'swa gravity. It might be best, he thought, to take it easy.

"Shall we?" he asked, beckoning.

"I like the sign," Konni answered, wiping away sweat. "Especially the first word: *cool*."

Within the thick, insulating adobe walls it was some fifteen or twenty degrees cooler, and they closed the door behind them, shutting out the heat. The room was lit only by daylight, through three windows that penetrated the thick south wall. They stood for a minute, looking around while their eyes adjusted from the outside glare. Even then it seemed dim, reminding Varlik of the T'swa's catlike vision.

There were only two others present: a waitress—the slenderest T'swi they'd seen—and a man in a loose white shirt who sat alone with a drink, watching them interestedly. Konni and Varlik sat down by a window; the waitress was already coming over.

"What you would like?" Her voice was quiet, her school-Standard rusty, her manner poised.

"What do you have?" Varlik asked in Tyspi.

She recited a list, most of which meant nothing to either of them.

"We are not familiar with those," Konni said. "Bring us what you yourself like best. I'm sure we'll like it, too."

They did, even though "cool," in Tyss, was not "cold," as they'd expected. It seemed to be a fruit punch, rather thin and non-alcoholic. The glasses were about pint-size, and after sipping briefly, the two Iryalans carried them around the room, looking at the numerous pictures hung on the walls. The waitress, as if knowing the deficiencies of their twilight vision, turned on an electric ceiling lamp that added moderately to the light.

The walls were paneled with boards, varnished and burnished, and the paintings and drawings excellent. They seemed to be by numerous artists, and varied from landscapes to portraits, from work scenes to archaic battles, from families to children sitting in a circle on a nightbound hill. Most of the subjects seemed T'swa, but some clearly were not. The styles included realism and impressionism—the styles accepted in the Confederation—and several others, including one that particularly took Varlik's fancy: landscapes done seemingly in ink, with an economy of brush strokes, suggestive rather than explicit. Konni's camera and his own were busy.

The voice of the other customer interrupted them in easy Standard from half across the room. "My name is Ban-Shum," he said. "If you have questions, I would be happy to answer as far as I can."

So they sat with him, asking questions about the art and the city. The paintings were not by a number of artists at all, but by the proprietress and her husband, each having mastered a variety of techniques. No, there was no particular market for art here; there were many fine artists, most painting for pleasure.

Ban-Shum was a teacher, a teaching brother of the Order of Dys Jilgar, and he would enjoy being their guide to Oldu Tez-Boag. This was a holiday for the children—there were numerous school holidays. He took the two Iryalans to his nearby home, where he harnessed his ilkan and hitched it to a buggy, to take the two Iryalans around. The ilkan was an indigenous species—all T'swa livestock were, he said—an ungulate with long legs, long erect ears, and short, soft, mole-like fur.

They saw and recorded the small school at which

Ban-Shum taught; visited the wharves, some with barges, river boats, and small seagoing steamers tied to them, and others for fishing boats; racks where fish, split lengthwise, dried in the sun; the water-treatment plant. They saw people at work—mostly men but also numerous young women with no children yet to care for, and older women whose children had grown up. There were shops and markets where produce was sold, and others with meat or dairy products. Much was primitive, but where refrigeration was needed, there it was, powered by solar converters.

By the time they felt they'd seen and recorded enough, Konni was enervated from the 120° heat. Ban-Shum took them back to the place they'd met him, where they talked quietly over cool drinks again. This time the drinks were a light and fruity wine.

"So we have regiments on Orlantha," Ban-Shum said. "Interesting." Then he added something in what was definitely not Standard but didn't seem to be Tyspi either.

"I'm afraid I didn't understand that," Varlik said.

"It is Orlanthan. One of the principal dialects."

"Orlanthan?!" Varlik was startled—almost shocked. "How did you learn Orlanthan?"

"A T'swa regiment was on Orlantha more than two hundred and fifty standard years ago, to help put down a revolt by tribes from which mine slaves had been conscripted. It was there for two years, and each company had two Orlanthan scout/interpreters assigned to it. Naturally, T'swa being T'swa, some of the warriors learned the language and brought it home with them.

"Since then it has been of interest to some of us because, besides Tyspi, it is the only language in this sector entirely distinct from Standard. Even the other resource worlds have languages at least recognizably similar to yours."

"Huh! I never knew that a T'swa regiment had been

on Kettle before. I don't think the army knows, either. What was it again that you said in Orlanthan?"

"*Wisosuka seikomaril, sensumakono.*"

"What does it mean?"

"A straightforward translation is, 'If you understand me, tell me so, my friend.' The root *wiso* means 'to know,' *su* is the second person singular, and *ka* is the suffix for the conditional case, equivalent to the word 'if' . . ."

Ban-Shum stopped short, laughing. "Forgive me; you are not interested in a linguistic analysis."

"I'm surprised, somehow," Konni said. "It's such a lovely language; so musical."

"Yes. Certainly it is a more aesthetic speech than Tyspi—softer, and there is a scale of stresses that can be played to provide maximum beauty. The Orlanthans had—I trust still have—great bardic poets, and the use of meter and tones were their favorite techniques. Their most highly developed implement was not a weapon or tool, but a stringed instrument used by poets as accompaniment."

No one said anything for a long moment. If Varlik had examined his discomfort of the moment, he might have identified both grief and guilt. Ban-Shum sipped again at his wine before breaking the silence. "You said you'd like to see more of our planet. Right now you are within a mile of the greatest highway on this part of Tyss, the Lok-Sanu River. It can take you through a cross-section of landscapes from coastal plain to the Jubat Hills, then through the Kar-Suum basin, and finally to the Lok-Sanu Mountains—from forest, particularly in the Jubat Hills, to deadly desert in the west."

"How would we go about taking such a trip?" Konni asked.

"There are river boats that carry passengers. One leaves the wharf at the foot of Central Street every morning and makes numerous stops along the river. It takes five days to reach the end of navigable water, at

Karu Lok-Sanit, where there is a steel mill in the desert foothills. Both iron ore and coal are dug near there, in the Lok-Sanu Mountains. You could get off at any stop you liked, stay a while if you'd care to, and catch a boat on a later day. The boats are owned and operated by the Rivermen's Co-op."

"When does the boat leave here?" asked Varlik.

"At approximately six o'clock, I believe. That used to be the time, and I know of no reason it would have changed. Surely no earlier than five-fifty.*

"And they'd accept Confederation money?"

"I'm sure they would. Meanwhile, my wife and I would be pleased to have you as our guests tonight. That will allow me to drive you to the wharf before I must go to school."

Varlik looked doubtful. "We'd like to, but we have to walk back to the hospital to get a few things and tell them what we're going to do. We can probably arrange a ride from there in the morning and not impose on you."

"It would be no imposition. Let me make a proposal," Ban-Shum countered. "I will drive you to the hospital. You can go inside, get what you need, and I will wait for you. My wife and youngest daughter will soon be home, and will truly be disappointed if I do not have you there for supper and an evening with us."

Varlik looked at Konni; she nodded.

"That sounds good, then, Ban-Shum," Varlik said. "Let's finish our drinks and do it that way."

---

*Half past five by the hundred-minute clock.

Twenty-Seven

The ilkan's hoofs raised puffs of dust as it trotted down the riverfront street. On the wharves, smoking engines chuffed, powering cargo booms that loaded or unloaded nets of cargo from holds or decks. Voices called directions and warnings. And over and around it all, the morning's sea breeze brought the odor of kelp beds, adulterated here by a smell of sooty smoke from dock engines and deck engines and ships' funnels.

"That is the passenger boat," Ban-Shum said, pointing. "The one with the tall slender smokestack and the long deckhouse aft."

Smokestack? Varlik didn't realize for a moment what was meant, then following Ban-Shum's gesture saw a riverboat, with a thin plume of smoke rising lazily from an erect cylinder amidships. The vessel was some hundred or more feet long with a beam of perhaps twenty-five feet, built to carry both deck cargo and humans. The ilkan trotted even with it and stopped, then Varlik and Konni climbed out with their packs.

Ban-Shum reached down and shook their hands. "May your trip be all you wish," he said.

229

"Thank you for your hospitality," Varlik answered. "And for bringing us out this morning."

"And thank Ling-Sii and Gon for the meals and for their company," Konni added. "You were all very kind."

Ban-Shum grinned, his teeth still strong and white. "It was our pleasure to host you."

He clucked to the ilkan then, turned the buggy in the street, and drove off without a wave. It was like a dismissal by Zusu or Colonel Koda, Varlik thought, watching him go, then turned to the river boat. It occurred to him that he didn't know where to buy tickets, but considering how things were done on Tyss, one probably simply bought them from the man standing at the foot of the gangplank. The man wore a loose white shirt, like Ban-Shum's, only unbleached—they were common among civilian T'swa—but his cap was the only one in sight, suggesting an official function.

Picking up his own and Konni's packs by the straps, Varlik headed for the gangplank, then realized he didn't know the Tyspi word for "ticket." So he slowed his steps to allow a tall, high-shouldered T'swi to get there ahead of him. He'd listen and watch—see how it was done.

To his surprise, all the man with the cap said was, "Going back to Tiiku-Moks?"

"Right." The tall man then handed him a coin or coins and went aboard; apparently no ticket was involved.

The capped man looked curiously at Varlik and Konni as they stepped up to him. "Where to?" he asked in Tyspi.

"Up the river," Varlik said. "We've never been there before—never been on Tyss before—and we don't know just where we'll want to get off."

The man looked them over with unconcealed interest. "All right," he said, waving them up the gangplank, "go aboard. I'll collect from you when you get off. If you have any questions, you can ask me—I'm the mate—

and I'll answer them if I have time. But you might get answers quicker from other passengers."

Varlik grinned at Konni as they crossed the gangplank. "No tickets, pay when you leave . . . It may not be Standard, but I'll bet here it works just fine."

She nodded without speaking, camera busy. On Tyss, Varlik had been lax with his own; her big Revax was better and more versatile.

The tall T'swi who'd boarded just ahead of them was leaning against the rail in the shade of an awning, watching a fishing boat pull away downstream in the direction of the sea. Varlik walked over to him.

"Good morning," said Varlik in Tyspi.

"Good morning," the man answered, surprised. "Do you understand Tyspi?"

"Quite a bit; we both do. This is Konni and my name is Varlik." He reached out and they shook hands. Like Ban-Shum's, the man's palm, though somewhat hard, was not as callused as the warriors'.

"My name is Lin," the man replied. "I'd thought of speaking to you, but I hadn't anticipated your ability with our language."

He was a forester, employed on a forestry operation in the Jubat Hills, and had come to Oldu Tez-Boag to visit his parents and a sister. The Lok-Sanu River region had been his home all his life, and he enjoyed answering their questions about it.

They'd been aboard no more than a quarter hour when they felt the vibration of the ship's screw turning. Longshoremen cast the lines off, deckhands retrieved them, and slowly the riverboat pulled away from the wharf. The current pushed her nose as she angled into it, her screw biting water, and she shoved her way upstream.

There were more docks just above the city, where they could see wheeled engines, long and squat, attached to trains of wheeled wagons—the *railroad*, Lin told them. Cargos were transferred from ships and riverboats to the railroad trains, which then distributed the goods throughout this part of the coastal plain. There too were the grain elevators from which, in turn, ships and riverboats were loaded.

Soon, though, they left the dock area behind, and the shores became farmland, with frequent water uptake structures for irrigation. These too were powered by the chuffing, stationary, smoke-belching engines, or sometimes by solar converters, and in a few cases by livestock plodding around a capstan. There were rowboats with fisherman, and occasional downstream rafts with goods piled on them, guided by T'swa at long sweeps. Wooden barges with smokestacks also passed, some with lumber stacked on their decks, ricks of fuelwood, or piles of stony black soil mounded above hatch coamings. Once they passed a flatboat with a cargo of what seemed to be thick metal rods.

"Is that steel?" Varlik asked.

"Yes. The largest steel mill on Tyss is at the foot of the Lok-Sanu Mountains, up the river 480 miles."

Varlik remembered Ban-Shum mentioning the mill. "Where do they get technetium to make steel with?" he asked. He used the Standard word for technetium; he didn't know any other, and they'd probably borrowed it into Tyspi anyway.

"Technetium? I'm not familiar with that. But I know little about steel-making; actually nothing. If you go as far as Karu Lok-Sanit, the town where the mill is, I'm sure they can tell you."

Varlik nodded; he'd try to get his question answered before he left Tyss. There might be more technology here than he'd realized.

"Lin," he asked, "what powers these vessels? What makes them go?"

The forester's brows raised. "Come with me," he said, and led them to a broad door in the deckhouse. Inside, the room extended not only to the overhead but part of it well below the deck, seemingly to the bottom

of the ship's shallow-draft hull. It was filled with sound
and machinery, long piston shafts rising and falling
amid the smell of steam and hot oil, all ministered to by
a wiry engineer, the smallest adult male T'swi Varlik
had seen. He held an oil can whose long spout dipped
and pecked among moving parts like some depraved
giant hummingbird.

"Khito!" Lin shouted; obviously he knew the man.
The engineer paused amid the booming, turning to
look.

Lin pointed at the two Iryalans, gesticulated, bent
over and made motions with his arms. The engineer in
turn grinned and nodded, dismissing them with a wave.
They backed out onto the deck again.

"That is the engine room," said Lin. "The engines
are driven by steam under pressure. Come. I'll show
you where the steam is made."

They followed him a few yards farther aft, where a
narrow door stood open to the deck. From it flowed a
river of heat considerably hotter even than the outside
air. A short steep companionway led down into the
ship's bowels, from which came a ringing of steel striking steel. Lin paused only long enough to tell the
Iryalans that Khito had said it was all right, then he
started down the hellish companionway, Varlik and Konni
trailing hesitantly behind.

It led into a chamber like something from a night-
mare, weakly lit by two small tubes, one next to the
companionway, the other above a gauge of some kind.
The heat was terrific; outside was nothing by comparison. The ringing noises had stopped before they'd started
down, but the pounding of the engine could be felt and
heard, and somewhere a leaking steam valve hissed. A
grizzled T'swi, short and stocky and a virtual anatomical
chart in holo, stood stripped to the waist, amazingly
sinewy, all fat long since boiled away. The man's jeans
were so sweat-soggy they stuck to his thighs.

Shovel in hand, he was watching the gauge. To his

right was what seemed a metal wall with two small metal doors, behind him a bulkhead with a barred opening from which had slid a pile of the stony soil, shiny black, that Varlik had seen on passing barges.

Varlik and Konni stood transfixed, sweating extravagantly, their cameras recording the motionless tableau. Shortly the stoker turned to the metal wall and threw open one of the doors; inside was intense fire, glaring whitely. With a single easy bending stride, he slid his shovel crunching beneath the pile of stony dirt, half straightened, pivoted, and slung the shovelful into the fire, a smooth swinging movement, the heel of the shovel ringing on the baseplate of the door. Then he turned, dug again, and threw again, his movements as if choreographed, until he'd cast half a dozen scoops of soil into the fire. Then he closed the door, grinned at his visitors, and returned his attention to the gauge.

Lin nodded to the Iryalans and led them back out onto the deck, where briefly it seemed cool.

"That is where the steam is made for the engine," Lin said, leading them aftward. "And back here is where the force is applied to the water to propel the boat."

On the fantail he leaned over the rail, pointing downward. "Down there is the propeller. It works on the principle of the screw to push against the water."

Varlik didn't understand all the words, but he got the general idea. Only one thing demanded explanation.

"But Lin," he said, "why was the man throwing dirt and stones into the fire?"

"Dirt?" Suddenly Lin realized, and laughed out loud. "You are right; that's what it is," he said. "Dirt and stones! It's just that we don't think of it that way. We call it 'coal,' and it is flammable, burning hotter than wood and requiring considerably less storage space and handling for a given value of energy."

He laughed again as they picked their way among crates on the freight deck to the ship's bow, where the breeze of its movement was unbroken, there to watch the shore and the water traffic. *Incredible,* thought Varlik, *that the T'swa could have done these things. How could they have learned, have been so clever?*

Then he remembered something Voker had said: Every Standard practice had been an innovation once. An unheard-of concept, yet now that he looked at it, compelling; it *had* to have been that way once! Vaguely Varlik got the concept of innovation growing upon innovation over time, leading perhaps from this, or something like it, to the technology of the Confederation. In some remote, long-forgotten past, his own people must have been clever too, must have thought new thoughts and tried things for the first time.

The realization made him feel slightly ill rather than excited, as old and hidden psychoconditioning was activated, and he pushed the thought away. Within moments he didn't remember it—didn't even remember there'd been a thought.

Twenty-Eight

Tiiku-Moks, several hours upstream from Oldu Tez-Boag, was the biggest town they'd come to, with maybe three or four thousand people. Well before they got there, they'd left the coastal plain, the river flowing through a gap in a series of transverse ridges that got higher eastward.

The Lok-Sanu's current had continued smooth and unchanging, a third of a mile wide, and deep enough for shallow-draft traffic. No rivers of size had entered it, and it had occurred to Varlik to wonder where, on such a dry world, the Lok-Sanu got its water. The answer, Lin had explained, was the Lok-Sanu Mountains, Tyss's highest, with many ridge crests rising sixteen thousand feet above the basin at their feet, and peaks to more than twenty thousand. Precipitation was relatively abundant there—snow as well as rain; it was the wettest place on the planet.

On this particular mid-autumn day, Tiiku-Moks was hotter than Aromanis had usually been. For miles now the river's shores had mainly been forested, with here and there a hamlet fronted by its own wharf, and Tiiku-Moks had the feel of a lumbering town—one with shade trees. Except along the wharves, there were trees enough that the buildings seemed almost to have been fitted in among them.

As a river port, its principal function was clearly the shipping of lumber: There were long stacks of it piled along the wharves, as high as men could build them by hand, and numerous carloads were parked on railroad spurs. The Jubat Hills, Lin explained, were the major source of wood for this whole part of the planet— everything upstream as well as down, and the districts all around the Toshi Sea, especially the dry eastern side.

Lin led them to a low building with the welcome "cool drinks" sign. Like the one in Oldu Tez-Boag, it had wooden paneling inside a thick layer of stuccoed-over adobe bricks. This one, however, was near the docks, and much busier and noisier with conversation than the T'swa cantina the two Iryalans had experienced the day before. The forester told them he had to stay in town for a day of meetings. If they decided to visit the forestry operations, the railroad ran north from Tiiku-Moks through fifty miles of them, with a sawmill village every few miles. Lodging and meals could be found in any village by asking around.

When Lin had left them, Konni and Varlik discussed it and decided they'd go on up the river. They could take this side trip on the way back if they wanted to.

Meanwhile, they had another hour to wait before the boat left, so they wandered along the riverfront, slowly, so as not to soak their clothes with sweat. The railroad line, which headed away from the river, was flanked here by a side track with a long string of empty lumber cars waiting for return to the sawmills. But not all the cars were lumber cars, nor empty. There was a flatcar with machinery, perhaps for a sawmill, boxcars with goods, even refrigeration cars with small solar converters on top. Toward the head end were three passenger coaches.

There were also three gondola cars with long bundles of steel rods visible atop their loads. When Varlik saw them, he felt a momentary thrill of discomfort, went over and climbed the rungs of one to peer over the edge. There was raw steel in bars and bundled rods, on underlying sheets of rolled steel, obviously going away from the river.

Going away from the river. What would some sawmill village do with three carloads, or one carload, of untooled steel? All the peculiarities, the little incongruities associated with Kettle, the insurrection, the T'swa—the whole business—boiled up for a moment, and he dropped to the ground looking troubled.

"What's the matter?" Konni asked.

"I'm not sure. Maybe nothing. But I want to take the train after all. I want to see where these"—he indicated the three carloads of steel—"get left off, and if I can, see what they're used for. Come on. Let's find out when the train leaves."

"Now wait a minute!" Konni insisted as they walked. "Give! Something's bothering you, whether you're sure or not. What is it?"

He walked on a dozen paces before answering. "I'm really not sure. I haven't had time to think about it yet. But steel! Where do they get the technetium to make it with? Would the Rombili ship technetium to a gook world, considering the shortage of the past year?"

"What would following these cars tell you?" Konni asked.

Again he kept walking silently while thoughts formed. "Konni," he said at last, "what if the T'swa are making weapons? Suppose there's an arsenal off north here somewhere?"

"Who would they make weapons for?"

"For whoever is shipping them technetium. The T'swa export soldiers, why not weapons?"

She slowed him, holding his sleeve. "But that sounds like a lot of trouble for someone just to get weapons, when they could make them themselves or buy them from us. Especially if they got caught; then they'd really have trouble!"

"Exactly! Anyone who'd go to that much trouble and take that big a risk isn't only up to something illegal, but something big enough to make it seem worthwhile. Maybe they're trying to arm up secretly. Maybe it's a trade world that's buying them! Maybe the Splenn. Remember the little kids that talked to us in the street, back in Oldu Tez-Boag? They thought we were from Splenn. Why Splenn? Do quite a few Splenn come to Tyss? And besides being one of the few trade worlds with space ships, Splenn's supposedly a haven for smugglers."

They'd been approaching the railroad administrative office, not much more than an adobe shack near the head of the siding, and stopped talking as they went in. The cheerful T'swa manager told them they had almost an hour, and there would be someone at the coaches, probably himself, to receive fares.

So they returned to the cantina to wait, replenish their body fluids, and refill the water flasks they carried in their packs. Konni was thoughtful now; clearly Varlik's arguments had impressed her. Then they walked to the siding again, paid their fares, and boarded a coach.

The coach windows bore no glass. The presence of forest in such year-round heat attested that it rained here fairly often and fairly heavily, but apparently the T'swa didn't mind getting wet. Shortly the couplings jerked and the train began to move, picking up speed to about thirty miles an hour, clicking along a track that kept close to the contour. On left curves, Varlik could see the locomotive, even glimpse the fireman pitching long lengths of firewood into the furnace. The smoke-stack, topped by a large spark arrester, trailed a plume of white.

They stopped at every sawmill village to drop off flatcars and sometimes other cars, until only a few cars were left. By then the sun was low, and the cars with steel were still in the train, close behind the engine.

Then the train slowed again, finally stopping, but this time not at a village, only a short siding, where a spur track disappeared into the forest. On the siding was a gondola car, and a flat car with large crates strapped on it. The cars with the steel were uncoupled from the train, and a little switch engine shunted them onto the siding. Then the train recoupled and drew slowly away, leaving the steel cars behind. Varlik lowered his camera. When they rounded the next curve, they saw another sawmill village just ahead.

He nudged Konni. "Here's where we get off," he said in Standard. "We can visit the sawmill today, a logging operation tomorrow"—he paused—"and take a walk in the woods tonight."

Visit a sawmill they did, recording its yowling head-rig and squalling resaws, its snarling hogger and screeching planer. And above all, the energetic, sure, and strenuous activities of T'swa workers defying the heat. Afterward they found a home with two rooms they could rent for the night, and ate supper there. When they'd eaten, they walked the evening darkness of the village's main street, often pausing to use their cameras, planning their spying in quiet murmurs, finally stopping at the local watering place for the usual "cool drinks," avoiding anything alcoholic.

They talked little there; their attention was on what they were about to do, and they'd said all there was to say about it. By deliberately nursing their drinks, they took another half hour; then they left, to stroll along the unlit dirt street that paralleled the railroad track. At the edge of the village the street continued, became a forest lane, and they just kept strolling, accompanied on their right by the railroad and blessed by a moon that was, for all practical purposes, full. They rounded the curve, leaving the village out of sight behind them, the cars on the siding slowly taking form in the darkness ahead.

So far they could easily explain their presence as an evening walk. Now the question forced itself on them: Might the cars be guarded? Would some T'swi step out of the shadows when Varlik began to snoop?

When they got there, Varlik dug their monitor visors and cameras from his pack, and they put them on. Then he climbed onto the flatcar to examine the packing boxes, while Konni recorded. The boxes were nearly as tall as he was, and not only were they strapped to the car; each was also wrapped around with metal straps and strongly cross-spiked. They must, he muttered to Konni, be very heavy to require such strong packing.

Next they looked into the gondola cars. From the ground they looked empty, but actually they were decked with layers of flat wooden cases, each case as heavy as he cared to lift in the gravity of Tyss. He stood staring at them.

"What are you going to do?" whispered Konni, clinging to a rung and peering in. "Break one open?"

Varlik shook his head. "It would be too obvious. Someone would wonder what happened, and someone else would remember the two Confederatswa."

"We could take one back in the woods and break it open where no one would notice it. No one would ever know; it would be just one case less."

He thought about that, then shook his head. "Not yet, anyway. Let's follow the spur track back into the woods and see where it goes. This stuff must come from back there somewhere."

They climbed down.

"What if there's a guard?"

"I'm hoping there isn't. You know how trusting the T'swa are, and they probably don't get foreigners in this district once a decade."

How trusting the T'swa are, he repeated to himself. *As if they're so honest themselves that they overlook the*

possibility of criminality, at least at home. And how did
that fit his suspicions? He shook the question off; he'd
see where this track led him.

Back among the trees it was darker, much of the
moonlight being intercepted. But using camera and
visor to find the way would be a greater nuisance here,
so they set off down the spur-line track, stumbling
occasionally on the ties. When they'd gone half a mile
and found nothing, they almost gave up and turned
back, then saw moonlight ahead through the trees.

It turned out to be a clearing, roughly square and a
quarter mile across, and from beneath the eaves of the
forest they stopped to look. In the middle was a building like a very large, tall shed, of metal instead of
adobe, resembling the sawmill, and for a moment Varlik
wondered if that's all it was. But there were no log piles.
The sides were open for several feet above the ground,
and again below the eaves, presumably for free airflow.
The ground around it had been plowed and harrowed,
and at first he thought of a mine field. Then it occurred
to him it might be a fire break, to protect the building
in case of forest fire, or perhaps the opposite. At any
rate it would show footprints conspicuously.

There was no sign of a light in or around the building, but he reminded himself of the T'swa night vision.
A watchman might not use a light. He looked at Konni;
she was looking at him.

"C'mon," he murmured, and started across the clearing on the well-trod path that they now could see
accompanied the spur track, no doubt worn there by
workers going to work.

The little steam engine used to shunt freight cars
waited in solitary silence by a loading dock. No one and
nothing challenged them—nothing but the darkness of
inside. The place was full of heavy machinery, and their
cameras recorded all of it. There were conveyors, fur-
naces, drop forges, steam hammers, forging presses,
lathes. . . . He couldn't have named most of them, but

he could recognize or guess what they did. Then he examined some dies, and that left no doubt: Weapons were made here.

This place must be as loud as the sawmill, Varlik thought. Maybe that's why they built it so far back in the forest.

On the long loading dock they found rifles ready for packing, along with sidearms, blast hoses, rocket launchers, lobbers—every light infantry weapon. The rifles lacked stocks, as if those were added elsewhere. At destination apparently; the crates and cases on the cars seemed built and secured for the whole trip. Varlik turned to Konni.

"I've seen enough," he said. "They're arming someone, or helping arm them. I'll bet it's Splenn, or someone the Splenn smugglers contract with. And that's the source of the technetium used to make this steel."

"Not necessarily," Konni said.

"What do you mean?"

"Maybe the T'swa manufacture weapons for themselves here."

Varlik shook his head. "I doubt it. Could they make them cheaper than they can buy them? This place can't be as efficient as the Royal Armory on Iryala."

"Maybe they're stockpiling," she suggested. "Maybe they're training and arming a secret army to conquer someone."

"Who? They can't have more than a few leased troop transports. The Confederation fleet would stop any transstellar invasion in a hurry."

"Maybe they plan to conquer another resource planet. That might not bring the fleet down on them."

He shook it off; conquest didn't fit the T'swa he knew, either in the regiment or here. *Or do I really know any T'swa?* That thought, too, he tried to banish. "Conquest plans wouldn't explain how they get the technetium," he said.

"They don't have to. They could still get it through

smugglers, and maybe steel doesn't take very much. Maybe they even get it legally. Certainly the Confederation knows they make steel here."

"Maybe the Confederation *doesn't* know," he countered. "Remember how little there is in the library about Tyss and the T'swa? No one in the Confederation pays any attention to them except as a source of mercenaries. And with technetium as precious as it must be by now . . ."

Konni didn't respond at once, but her expression told him an idea was forming.

"Varlik?"

"Yes?"

"What if the T'swa have their own technite mine? It wouldn't have to be very big."

The T'swa with their own technite mine? How could you disprove something like that? After a moment he reached into a partly filled packing case and transferred a sidearm to his packsack. Konni watched soberly; to steal on Tyss seemed an enormity, despite their suspicions.

"Let's go," Varlik murmured. "Let's go back and sleep on this, or try to. I don't know what to think. Or what to do next."

But by the time they reached the village he knew: Their next step was to get back to Oldu Tez-Boag and off of Oven.

PART FOUR

Death of a Regiment

Twenty-Nine

Their return to Orlantha was less comfortable than the trip out, for it was a troopship they rode, the aged but well-maintained IWS *Davin*. She carried the Ice Tiger Regiment, a virgin regiment newly contracted for. Varlik had a shelf-like bunk in a troop compartment, while Konni enjoyed the privacy of a four- by eight-foot gear locker temporarily converted to her use.

The *Davin* was hotter than the hospital ship had been, too. The temperature was around 110° F during the wake period, Varlik guessed, though cooled during the sleep period by a dozen or fifteen degrees.

According to a lieutenant he'd talked with, the new regiment had been contracted for by the Department of Armed Forces, not the Crown, and requested by General Lamons. Varlik accepted this as truth; the T'swa were given to openly briefing officers and men of all ranks, and rumors seemed to have little or no place or function among them.

Apparently Lamon's medal-bestowing visit to the T'swa hospital wards had been more than politics.

Varlik and Konni talked together a great deal while killing time playing cards in her "room." They agreed

249

to say nothing about the arsenal or their suspicions until they'd both returned to Iryala, and then only jointly. To make it known on Orlantha could only upset operations there.

Also, together and separately, they talked with T'swa mercenaries. These troopers were eighteen and nineteen years old, but seemed scarcely less mature than the fourteen-year veterans Varlik had lived and served with. Varlik joined them in their exercises, which were restricted by lack of space but strenuous nonetheless, and by the time they raised Kettle, he felt strong again.

They landed at Aromanis, of course, and Varlik, per protocol, checked in with Trevelos—*Captain* Trevelos now. The information officer had been given a larger staff and office—the Kettle War was much bigger news at home than it had been. Inwardly, Trevelos credited Varlik with making it happen, or at least helping it happen, with his coverage of the T'swa.

In fact Trevelos, usually polite, now positively deferred to him. It made Varlik a bit uncomfortable, and he stayed for only a few minutes, making small talk about Tyss and the new regiment.

Then Varlik checked Voker's office, and to his surprise found the colonel there. Voker, grinning but sharp-eyed, got up and offered his hand when Varlik came in.

"Sit," said Voker, motioning to a chair, and Varlik sat. "How did you like Tyss?"

"Interesting. And friendly. Someday I'd like to go back and really explore. Visit a war lodge. Maybe a monastery." Varlik had surprised himself with the latter because he hadn't thought of it before. "There's a lot more to the T'swa than mercenaries," he added.

"So. And meanwhile, what next?"

"Next? First a shower in unrecycled water, then listen to my mail. Then I'm going to send off some letter cubes and a report on Tyss. And after that . . ." He shrugged. "I don't really know. I've been thinking of going straight home. But I'll probably go to the T'swa reconditioning camp, at least for a few days. Get a feel for what's going on now and see whether there's anything more I want to do here before I leave."

Voker leaned back, contemplating the younger man. "Just don't talk yourself into going south again. The T'swa aren't doing anything different, and you've already covered that. There's a good chance of getting yourself killed if you go back down there." He stroked the morning's regrowth on his chin. "You've done a damn fine job here and made a name for yourself on Iryala. Go home and enjoy it."

Somehow the colonel's pitch put Varlik off, just a little and for only a moment, but Voker's eyes didn't miss it.

"Maybe I will," Varlik said. "But right now I want to say something while I think of it. I want to thank you for working my ass off on the way out here. And for your tip that got me back with Colonel Koda." Varlik chuckled. "I thought I was going to die that first day out on the prairie with them."

"Just make sure you don't die on your last day with them," Voker said.

That killed the conversation, but neither had anything more to say anyway. They exchanged a few trivialities, then Varlik excused himself. The rest of the day, the question occupied at least the fringe of his mind while he did other things. Why *shouldn't* he go straight home? The wisdom in Voker's suggestion felt compelling, but somehow he couldn't decide to do it.

Voker, in turn, after Varlik left, still had him on his mind, if only briefly. He recognized a certain responsibility for Varlik's being with the T'swa, and for the young man's likely death if he continued with them.

But if Varlik decided to, that was his prerogative. He'd survived so far, and the ultimate responsibility belonged to the person himself. Voker sipped thoughtfully at his tepid joma, then dismissed Lormagen from his thoughts and turned back to the plan he'd been working on.

Thirty

The T'swa colonels, three of them now, arrived together at Lamons's weekly command meeting, each with his aide. The nineteen-year-old Colonel Jil-Zat seemed as poised, as relaxed and sure of himself, as Biltong and Koda.

Lamons had his staff with him, and a personal aide to the Crown—Lord Kristal. Introducing Kristal was the first order of business; when that was over, the work of the meeting began.

Currently, problems of logistics, coordination, and authority were minor, and could be handled at lower levels. These were reviewed briefly. Finally, there was nothing left but the major situation review and discussion.

"And now," said Lamons, "we come back to our purpose in being on Orlantha. We need to reestablish the reliable mining and refining of technite on a scale adequate for the continuance of Confederation industry. We have a time frame to work within, dictated by the need for steel. Lord Kristal has something to say to us about that." He turned to the dapper aristocrat in his precise and correct civilian garb. "Your Lordship?" said Lamons, and sat down.

Kristal stood. "I will be brief, and what I say here must not be repeated—in whole, in part, or in substance—by any of you to anyone not currently present. It would be regarded as treasonous, and no extenuating circumstance would be considered. Is that understood?"

Sober nods around the table assured him that it was.

"Good. I said that not from any concern that one of you might be loose-tongued. I simply wanted to stress the importance of silence on this subject." He scanned the table with its seated officers. "Now. Technetium shipments to trade planets have been embargoed for more than seven deks. This has had a very severe impact on the manufacturing and economy of those worlds, and as a result, on their ability to purchase goods from Confederation worlds. A side effect has been a growing depression in substantial sectors of the Confederation economy. Furthermore, the shipment of steel outside the Confederation, already tightened, was discontinued entirely almost three deks ago, and that is exacerbating matters seriously.

"And here are the most sensitive data: At the present reduced levels of use, existing stocks of technetium will last less than eleven deks. However, use restrictions will be put into effect at the end of this dek which, at the cost of increasing economic problems, will stretch the supply by approximately five deks to, say, fifteen deks. The capacity to ration supplies more severely than that is closely limited by what the economy can stand."

His hard grey eyes scanned the assembled military. "That establishes your time frame, gentlemen. And we can't wait the full fifteen deks; a certain lag time is involved in the economy. His Majesty wants significant new technite shipments underway from Orlantha no later than a year from now. Therefore, you have ten deks."

He nodded at Lamons then and took his seat. The general stood up. "Thank you, Your Lordship. For the purpose of establishing the operational situation, let me say first that the Orlanthan insurgency clearly has considerably greater resources of men and ordnance than we had thought as recently as two deks ago. And they are very effective fighting men." He turned to an aide. "Major Emeril, give us the current data on insurgent attacks and on our progress toward renewed technite production."

Emeril stood. "Thank you, general. Gentlemen, my lord, in the week ending last midnight, lobber rockets landing within our defensive perimeter numbered 387, up from 209 the week before and 117 the week before that. Apparently the insurgents are not only continuing to get reinforcements through; they are now bringing up munitions in greater bulk, on pack animals.

"We have stepped up our combat patrols outside the perimeter, and our ground contacts with the insurgents increased from 17 to 42; that's 247 percent. Again, this was for the week ending last midnight. Also, the intensity of those contacts has increased: Our patrol casualties rose from 61 to 239, with 81 killed. Yesterday alone we had 20 killed on patrols.

"Enemy were increasingly sighted by reconnaissance flights and platform surveillance, indicating either enemy carelessness or, more probably, increased activity. Gunship attacks on seen enemy troops increased from sixteen to twenty-seven. On the other hand, gunship losses to enemy fire increased from three to eleven. Apparently the enemy has now brought M-4 rockets into use, and may in fact be baiting our gunships into what we might call ambushes."

At that point, Lamons interrupted. "Let me add here that the Romblit engineering teams have completed renovation of the technite mines with heavy concrete mineheads. Given our existing defense perimeter, both the refinery sites and mineheads continue susceptible to enemy lobber fire. We hit such lobber positions quickly and hard as soon as they show themselves, but rebuilding the refinery goes slowly for now. We have to construct it like a fortress. But if it was ready now, bulk carriers landing for ore would be subject to rocket attacks, and they're not built to stand that sort of thing. Arrival of the four new divisions will permit us to man a larger defense perimeter, but establishing and building it will cost us." He turned to Emeril. "Major, please continue."

Nodding, Emeril went on, his eyes on Lord Kristal. "Equipment recently received has enabled us to begin expanding the Beregesh secured site. Our attempts the past week to establish six key strong points outside the defense perimeter were successful. Casualties in so doing were high but not quite exorbitant: 103 killed and 307 wounded, not including patrol casualties but including men killed and injured by ground-to-air attack on floaters being used to land them, again evincing enemy use of M-4 rockets. Casualties also include operator losses from rocket attacks on armored dozers clearing fields of fire around the strong points.

"Our success in strong-point construction has been encouraging, but of course they remain six isolated strong points—only a beginning in a defensive perimeter that will be"—he paused meaningfully—"over twenty-five miles long.

"Today we have begun the establishment of six new strongpoints." He turned to General Lamons. "Sir, that's the end of my presentation."

Emeril sat down and Lamons stood up. "Thank you, major." He looked around the table. "You will have noticed a second new face among us: Colonel Jil-Zat of the Ice Tiger Regiment. This is a virgin regiment with a full complement of men, and the contracting authority assures us that they are fully combat competent, albeit without combat experience. The latter will be remedied shortly. Colonel, will you stand, please."

The T'swi stood, tall and with shoulders big even for a T'swi, but almost shockingly young-looking. Jil-Zat nodded without speaking and sat down. The Confederation officers around the long table could not entirely conceal their misgivings.

Lamons continued. "I should add that the contracting authority tells me it is the only additional T'swa regiment likely to be available to us in the near future. Colonel Biltong, please brief us on T'swa combat activities during the last week."

Biltong stood, impassive as always at these meetings. "General, Lord Kristal, gentlemen. To our specific knowledge, T'swa raiders made 474 attacks last week on insurgents and their pack animals. Casualties inflicted are not known, but presumably are fewer per action than in previous weeks because of the increased insurgent tendency to move in small groups—now commonly in twos and threes—and to disperse their travel over a broader zone.

"This tells us something of the dedication and discipline of insurgent troops, and their ability to find their way in wilderness not personally familiar to them.

"Our own casualties have also been lower, partly because such small groups of insurgents have less opportunity and ability to return fire, partly because there are fewer of us for the insurgent hunter-killer patrols to find, and partly because of adjustments we have made in our tactics.

"And to echo General Lamons's comment, it seems abundantly clear that insurgent numbers are far greater than originally thought, while our two regiments have been shrinking. The two engaged regiments, as of yesterday, numbered only 396 men active behind enemy lines. Actually, some of those may be casualties not yet reported. We also have 80 men on rest rotation, 92 more in rehabilitation training following hospitalization, and 77 in the hospital with wounds that should not prevent their reassignment within a reasonably short time. That is a total of 645 men."

Biltong sat down then, and Lamons stood again. "We

are aware," Lamons said quietly, "that the T'swa have been operating under sustained, very hazardous conditions, and at heavy cost in blood. We also realize the extreme importance of what they've accomplished. Colonel Voker, you have a proposal to make with regard to the T'swa."

"Yes, sir." Voker got to his feet. "Not all the T'swa in insurgent territory have been raiding insurgent lines of reinforcement and supply. I've had several three-man teams on long-range reconnaissance, tracing insurgent trails farther south. The trails come from a particular region of jungle within which I strongly suspect the insurgent military command and supply centers can be found, and probably the insurgent government.

"A few weeks ago I also put down several small T'swa exploration teams in the equatorial jungle, to report on operating conditions there."

Voker looked around the table. "At the same time, we have analyzed aerial reconnaissance holos of the landforms in regions we thought might contain those centers. Considering that roofed supply depots are necessary in such a rainy climate, and that suitable buildings should be detectable from recon platforms but weren't, I assumed that caves are probably being used. These would have to be extensive, and because of drainage requirements would almost surely be found in hills with certain characteristics. I've made certain other assumptions as well, and come up with a limited number of candidate areas.

"What I propose doing next is to withdraw the existing T'swa hunter-killer squads to Aromanis for rest and refitting, replacing them with two battalions of the new regiment. I recommend that the other new battalion be used at Beregesh to disrupt and inhibit insurgent activities in the vicinity of our strongpoint construction.

"Meanwhile, veteran T'swa scout teams will be flown south to find, if possible, the central insurgent command area. Assuming they find it, the veteran T'swa regiments would be used to strike the area by surprise, with the sole purpose of capturing and bringing out insurgent headquarters officers who might be able to tell us who trained and supplied them, and how, as well as giving us locations of other strategic sites we can hit from the air."

Voker scanned the intent faces around the table, then continued. "For interrogation, incidentally, we have several psychiatric specialists being flown here from Iryala with their equipment.

"After withdrawing the T'swa and their prisoners, we can strike key coordinates from the air, and hopefully seriously impair the insurgent ability to continue, while turning over to the Crown any information on off-world supporters of the insurgency."

Again Voker looked the silent group over. "That is the outline of my proposal. It has the apparent potential to weaken seriously the insurgents' supply capacity and to end any future outside aid to them."

He sat down, and for a moment no one spoke. Lamons started to rise then, but before he said anything, Lord Kristal spoke. "General, I recommend that you recess this meeting, its members to remain available on short notice. I'd like to speak with Colonel Voker and yourself with regard to the colonel's proposal."

That evening, with the decisions made and detailed planning underway, and a coded message cube off to His Majesty, Lord Kristal let his thoughts wander. The standard military mind! Even Voker, easily the most imaginative of them all, wore a mental strait-jacket. With the proper innovative use of resources at hand or available in short order, ore could be shipped within a dek—two at most. *But of course, if they were up to that,* he said to himself, *this project wouldn't be necessary in the first place.*

Thirty-One

Rehab Section C came in from its two-hour speed march in the typical wild closing gallop, with Varlik, as usual, bringing up the rear. *If there was just some way to market sweat*, he thought as he stood in ranks again, chest heaving, waiting for dismissal while wiping his forehead.

It wasn't until after they'd been dismissed that he noticed the Red Scorpions' regimental area had been reoccupied; the regiment was back.

Or what was left of it. Walking between the rows of squad tents to the showers, he found about one in three occupied. Subconsciously he'd known it would be like this, would have said so if asked in advance, but seeing it was like being slugged in the gut.

The troopers seemed not to feel that way. The returnees and the men of the rehab sections greeted each other cheerily, some even exuberantly, and asked about others who might simply be elsewhere at the moment or dead. And as Varlik soaked this in, it so disjointed his sense of the appropriate that his initial depression became something different—a low grade, ill-defined resentment.

"Varlik!"

It was Kusu; the big sergeant stepped from a tent as Varlik was returning from the showers. The surgeons hadn't returned his chin to its old profile, had rebuilt it more roundly than before, but he was easily recognizable.

"So you are back from Tyss!" He stood back and looked the Iryalan over, reading Varlik's discomfort, and in response toned down his own high cheer. "Fit again, too," he added. "Apparently the physical differences between Iryalan and T'swi are more complexion than constitution."

Somehow Varlik wasn't able to reply.

"May I walk along with you?" asked Kusu.

"If you want." Varlik's tone was almost surly.

"There aren't many of us left, are there?" Kusu said calmly. "There's been a lot of recycling going on. Recycling tends to come a lot earlier among warriors than among others." His chuckle was barely audible. "Newsmen, for instance. I suspect most newsmen grow old and gray and watch their grandchildren grow up."

Varlik said nothing.

"What rehab section are you in?" Kusu asked.

"C."

"Then you are almost ready to join a unit, if that is what you plan. You told me once that you have a wife, and intended to have children."

Varlik answered without expression. "That's right."

"Fine." The T'swi slowed. "Maybe we'll talk sometime. I would enjoy hearing what you thought of Tyss." Then he turned back the way they'd come, and Varlik walked the last hundred feet alone to his tent.

What's the matter with you? he asked himself. *He's a friend. He was glad to see you. And you acted like a complete and utter ass.*

He wondered if Kusu had been offended, then rejected the idea. The man, the T'swa in general, seemed immune to that kind of emotion. But that didn't make it all right to act offensively toward him, to reject his friendliness.

Varlik hung his towel over the foot-frame of his cot, put on his off-duty uniform and fresh boots, then looked at his watch. They wouldn't serve supper for ten minutes, but he might as well do his waiting at the mess hall.

As he left, the rifle rack at the end of the tent caught his eye. He'd checked, and the rifles all had serial numbers, as rifles should; it was the only way to tell yours from the others. And he realized what was bothering him, had been bothering him since they'd been dismissed after training and he'd found the regiment back from the south. It was not just that the regiment—his regiment—was being shot to pieces bit by bit. It was that tied together with his suspicion that some T'swa faction was the source of this war, was supporting the other side—the Birds—and that the regiments were being sacrificed to duplicity.

But you don't know that, he argued. *All you have is circumstantial evidence. There could be various other explanations that haven't occurred to you.*

Yeah? Name one. Think of one.

He shook off the spiral of questions and, walking slowly, put his attention outward, on the visual: actually seeing the tents, duckboards, black bodies striding tentward from the showers, green-trousered troopers ambling toward the mess hall; blue sky, fluffy white cumulus, a high-soaring hawk riding an updraft.

In this way, by the time he'd walked the hundred yards to the mess hall he'd banished his upset—for the time being: The roots still were there. The regiment was decimated, on Tyss he'd seen what he'd seen, and all the anomalies, ambiguities, strangenesses in the situation remained.

On the mustering ground, something over five hundred veteran T'swa stood in ranks, at ease, in faint morning steam as the newly risen sun evaporated a thundershower of the night before. There were five hundred forty-six troopers—four under-strength companies—most of what was left of the two regiments. Their regimental commanders stood facing them, each flanked by his exec and his sergeant major. Somewhere out of sight of Varlik Lormagen, a bird trilled, some songster of the Orlanthan prairie, intruded upon but not far displaced by the black mercenaries. It or others like it, Varlik thought, would be here when the regiments, and the army, were long gone.

It was Biltong, as the "senior" colonel, who spoke, using only his big voice unamplified. His Tyspi was almost as easy for Varlik to follow now as Standard would have been.

"T'swa," said Biltong, "we have a new assignment: We are to strike the Orlanthan headquarters and take prisoners—assuming that we succeed in locating it. Several reconnaissance teams are in the candidate areas now, in the equatorial jungle, and we can presume they'll find it."

Biltong went on to describe the plans in some detail, and Varlik listened in near shock. It sounded suicidal. Finally, Biltong finished. "Ground-model briefings will be made when the area has been identified and the ground described. You all know the enemy and his fighting qualities, so you see the challenge we face. It will almost surely be a battle of highest quality, and may prove to be our final action. Colonel Koda and I will be there with you, of course."

He turned and said something quietly to Koda, who shook his head as he answered. Then Biltong turned again to the troopers.

"Regiments dismissed!"

The troopers broke ranks and began walking to breakfast, and it wasn't until then that Varlik became aware of a deep and powerful *something* that had risen in them.

They weren't saying much, but there was a sense of anticipation; he could almost hear their deep psychic chuckling, and it made his hair stand up.

In the mess hall at breakfast, a regimental clerk announced that Varlik Lormagen should report to Colonel Koda at 06.00. He was there minutes early—right after breakfast—and the sergeant major motioned him into the colonel's office. Varlik entered and, for some reason unknown to him, saluted.

"Sit down, Lormagen."

He sat. Koda looked at him, seemingly into him, through large black eyes.

"I want to thank you for the excellent job you've done as publicist. I believe you'll find, when you arrive back on Iryala, that you've succeeded equally well for your other employer." He smiled. "The one that pays well."

Varlik nodded without smiling back.

"You were in ranks this morning," Koda continued, "so you know what our next action will be. And it seems to me that for you, the risks this time outweigh the benefits. Perhaps it would enhance your reputation to die in the jungle, but I question whether death in battle was part of your purpose when you entered this lifetime.

"So I called you in this morning for two reasons. One, the army wants this action kept secret until it happens. I want your word that you'll say nothing till it's over."

Again Varlik nodded.

"I have your word, then?"

"Yes, sir."

"Good. And secondly, I'd like you to give me your resignation as T'swa publicist."

Varlik stared at the colonel from a viewpoint at which time seemed to have stopped, seeing the face more clearly than he ever had before—the strong bone structure; heavy jaw muscles; wide thin-lipped mouth that somehow was not in the least severe, seemed just now actually kind; the steady eyes that were neither shallow nor deep, their dimension being outward.

Time restarted when Koda spoke again. "I'm not insisting on your resignation, you understand. I do not know your deepest purpose."

It occurred to Varlik that he didn't know it either. "What are the odds of your actually getting the prisoners you're after?" he asked. "And the information?"

"Perhaps five to one that our search teams will find and report the Orlanthan headquarters. If they don't, of course, the action cannot take place. If they do, I would guess the odds to be roughly even that we bring out useful prisoners."

"And the odds of bringing out most of your troops alive?"

The eyes never withdrew. Most men, Varlik would think afterward, could scarcely have discussed the weather with such total equanimity.

"Call it one to two," Koda answered. "Understand though that in war, one cannot know the script; that is part of its charm."

Its charm. Varlik could only stare.

"You don't have to decide now," the colonel said. Then he turned away, picking up a folder, Varlik dismissed from his attention. The Iryalan got up and left.

That evening after supper, Varlik asked Kusu if they could talk somewhere privately. Kusu suggested one of the empty squad tents, but Varlik wanted more privacy than that, so they walked out of camp across darkening prairie. Insects buzzed and chirped, keened and stridulated, and overhead, like some feathered projectile, an insectivorous bird dove with a piercing and protracted "keeeeee" at the edge of human hearing. A veil of stars had crept up the sky from the east, over the vault of heaven, sending scouts after the departed sun to explore a silvery western horizon.

It occurred to Varlik that Kettle was a beautiful planet. Why had technite been found here? Why couldn't it have been on an uninhabited world? Why had the Rombili decided to use slave labor? Gooks! Gooks weren't really people; that had been the rationale. Gooks were a resource, like their worlds.

You'd think, he told himself almost bitterly, *you'd think the T'swa would refuse an assignment like this one. You'd think they'd sympathize with other gooks. Except the T'swa didn't think of themselves as gooks. Probably no one did. Gooks were always other people.*

Kusu interrupted Varlik's silent soliloquy. "What did you wish to talk about?" he asked.

"About the T'swa. And the regiment."

"All right."

"You're being killed. Inside a dek or two there'll hardly be any of you left." He peered at the T'swi through thickening dusk. "A lot of you will die just in this action alone."

"Quite probably."

"Is that the goal of a warrior? To die?"

"The goal of a T'swa warrior is to play at war, skillfully and with joy. Death is a common accompaniment."

"But . . . it's such an *empty* life!"

"Is it?"

Varlik stopped. "Isn't it?"

"It would be for someone who wanted to raise a family, or paint fine pictures, or"—Varlik could see the eyes turn to him in the near night—"create with words."

"And you kill people!"

"True again."

"Even if they have a new life afterward, the way you believe, you take away from them what they want desperately to keep."

"That too is true, more often than not. But ask yourself who it is we kill."

"What do you mean?"

"We kill those who, knowingly or not, choose to put themselves into battle with us."

"These Birds didn't choose to put themselves into battle with you!" Varlik snapped. "They're just trying to end the slavery they've been subjected to. I'm surprised you aren't helping them, instead of fighting them. That would be the ethical thing to do."

"Would it?"

"Wouldn't it?"

"That would not solve their problem, and it would worsen the problem the Confederation faces here while putting Tyss at war with the Confederation.

"Besides, we T'swa do not fight. For us, war is a form of play, and we play most skillfully at it. And true play does not have problems, but challenges and opportunities.

"Problems, you see, are a matter of attitude; one being's problem might be viewed by another in the same situation as an opportunity, perhaps for a game or a war. With the attitude of play, you may see a situation and decide you will create a different situation in its place, without any determination that you must succeed. What you think of as success has no part in play. You do it for the doing.

"Think of play as a journey in which the place you have chosen to travel to is far less important than the traveling."

Varlik groped for his indignation, and somehow couldn't find it. At one level he felt as if he'd been had, snowed by sophistries he couldn't get a grip on—as if someone had told him that solid wasn't solid, that the obvious was fallacy. Yet somehow—somehow, he felt distinctly better than he had minutes before. He let go of the matter, and smiled at Kusu, not widely.

"You're something," Varlik said. "You know that? All of you are."

"Thank you, Varlik. You are something, too."

For just a moment that stopped Varlik. Then a chuckle welled up in him that grew to a laugh, long and hard.

The powerful T'swi kept him company in a rumbling bass until they gripped hands and shook on it.

Varlik had been sitting at a table in the work room of the army's media quarters. Not that he had anything to send to Central News. After making another letter cube for Mauen, he waited for Konni, idly browsing, admiring old field cubes. After a bit it was lunch time, and Konni hadn't appeared. Iryala Video had sent two new teams to Kettle, both at Beregesh today, and she was scheduled to leave for home the next morning. Varlik wanted to talk to her before she left.

Surely she'd show for lunch, he told himself, and got up to leave for the officers' mess. He hadn't reached the door when it opened, and Konni came in.

"What's up?" she asked. "Did you finally make up your mind to go home?"

"Not home. Not yet. The T'swa, both veteran regiments, have a new assignment. The word came in this morning confirming it; we'll be going next Fourday."

She stared at him. "What kind of assignment?"

"They're going to hit the Birds down in the equatorial zone, then blast enough of a hole in the jungle that floaters can come in and take them out."

"And you're going along on *that?*" Her fists were on her hips. "Varlik, you had to be crazy to go out on the last operation. This sounds twice as bad."

"It's five times as important, and I want to be close to it."

"Important how? What's it about?"

"It's confidential. I've already said more than I should."

Her brows drew down angrily. "Are you saying you don't trust me? After the information we've both kept to ourselves?"

"I trust you. But I had to give my word," he added unhappily.

She looked at him, her anger dying.

"It shouldn't be as dangerous for me as the last one,"

he went on. "For one thing, it's a single quick raid—land, strike, and leave. And I'll be in the least dangerous part of the operation. But, of course, there's always that little chance. So I wanted to tell you that if I'm killed, you're free to do whatever you want with what we recorded on Tyss."

Briefly her eyes tried to pry him open. "You're going to get yourself killed," she said at last.

He didn't answer, just shook his head.

"I'd have propositioned you deks ago," she continued, "but you were married. The reason I didn't was my respect for your wife. But if you're not going to get back to her anyway . . ."

"No, I'll be back. I don't know why I feel so confident, but I'll be back here when it's over—not even wounded this time."

Konni backed off. "Maybe you're right. I hope so." She grinned then, unexpectedly. "Anything I *can* do for you?"

He grinned back. "Sure. You can have lunch with me."

"You've got a date," she said, and took his arm.

Thirty-Two

Only the least moon watched, low in the east, little more than a bright point of light and less vivid than a clouded planet.

The floaters settled slowly, dull black landers from the large troopship miles above, guiding vertically down lines of gravitic flux. Eyes could not have seen them, even if there had been sentries above the jungle's canopy—not even as occlusions against the star field overhead, because clouds moving up the bowl of sky were approaching the meridian, eclipsing more and more the view.

To the proper instruments, of course, the floaters would have been as visible as at midday. But such an instrument would have to stand above the forest roof, and would have been detected in advance by recon flights. It had been a radio antenna that brought special attention to the site—a slender steel structure rising inconspicuously a dozen yards above the layered jungle.

Seeing by instrument themselves, and holding formation by keeping each to its own gravitic ordinate, the stealthy floaters stopped their still descent half a hundred feet above the tallest trees, those shaggy giants emergent from the general canopy. Now would come the first real hazard: letting down the troops. If they alarmed the birds and arboreal animals, the general cacophony might draw the attention of unfeathered Birds.

Unlit hatches opened. Slender weighted cables slid out and down, into the foliage below. Only isolated brief complaints could be heard, no more than might happen in the random mini-dramas of an ordinary jungle night. Below some threshold of excitement, silence and concealment were favored over noisy alarm by the jungle galleries.

The creatures near the cables adjusted quickly to their dangling presence and, already alerted, less susceptible to being startled, made even fewer audible responses to the men who followed, despite the movements of cables as they descended, and the release of branches as heavy bodies first depressed and then slipped free of them.

After he'd passed through the dense crown of a canopy tree, Varlik squeezed the let-down control of the harness he rode, slightly speeding his descent. From there to the ground, he passed through the branches of only one frail, light-starved undertree. Then his feet touched down on a narrow twisting root a foot high, and his ankle turned, throwing him heavily to the ground.

At least he hadn't come down on an ant mound, he told himself. The scouts had radioed more than the locations of the military encampment and cave entrances; they'd described as well the ground conditions.

To Varlik it seemed too dark even for the T'swa to see. They'd anticipated that, and the T'swa had night goggles.

Varlik had rejected night goggles. Instead, he took off his battle helmet and put on his monitor visor, then scanned about with his camera. In such dense darkness, visibility was limited even so, and the quality of seeing was strange. Beyond fifty feet he saw only dimly, and beyond eighty nothing at all. Nor was there much undergrowth where he was; by day few plants could photosynthesize in such dense shade.

He could see four T'swa. Two of them were Kusu and Lieutenant Zimsu; he recognized their insignia. Kusu was the platoon sergeant now.

Varlik had been the last man down his cable. Now he heard it twitch, the prelude to its being drawn back up. Half a minute later he watched and recorded it snaking upward out of sight, heard faintly its dangling harnesses swish through branches, and with its passing felt a heavy finality.

Then, visor in place, he put his battle helmet back on his head and reached up to make sure his communicator was turned on.

This was a very different kind of operation from the earlier ones; high mobility wasn't needed here. They'd been put down in the position they were to hold, would make only small adjustments in their line till time to leave. Thus the T'swa here carried and wore equipment that would have been more burden than help up north—not only battle helmets and night goggles, but quantities of grenades, while every third man had a blast hose and a satchel of box magazines for it.

Every third man. They were the ones who would hold their positions if necessary to let the others get away. Abundant explosives had been lowered too, to clear a place for evac floaters when the time came.

Somewhere out in front of them, B Company of the Night Adders was less encumbered. Carrying only rifles, side arms, and a few grenades, they'd been put down by squads at coordinates where they could cover the trails away from the Bird cave and headquarters area. The scouts were to have met them there. When the air strike began, they were to pick up fleeing Bird officers, then move quickly with their prisoners toward the defensive circle formed by the rest of the force, dropping off men as they went—men who would fight any rearguard action necessary.

The defensive circle was nothing to fight a prolonged action from. There were too few T'swa for that, and too much cover for attackers, and there'd be little opportunity to clear fields of fire. They'd clear as much as time allowed after the bombing began and the need for silence ended. But ideally, the pickup squads would bring their prisoners while the Birds were still confused, and the evac floaters would take them out quickly, with little or no fighting necessary.

And it could happen that way. Or the Birds might respond quickly and in force.

According to Kusu, this wouldn't have been an exceptionally hazardous action against enemy they'd faced on other worlds, but the Birds were special. Even on trail interdiction, where the T'swa had been able to choose the time and place of their hit-and-run ambushes, they'd quickly learned the quality of the men they fought. Here, on the other hand, the T'swa were committed to fixed but unfortified positions. It was a question of speed—how quickly the Birds realized what was happening and responded. Time would tell. Or as the T'swa said, time would expose the script.

And they would revise it as the cast and stage and props allowed, ad libbing from moment to moment. That was how Kusu had described battle to him the day before—an odd concept.

The T'swa had been in a strange, almost joyous calm. Varlik had gotten used to this, adjusting to their reality, and had even found it rubbing off on him to the extent that, at times, he'd been almost cheerful.

But not now. Now he had a prime case of nervous gut, even hidden as he was by opaque and silent darkness. He didn't wonder if the T'swa were nervous, too; they weren't.

After a time a sound began, a distant susurrus, increasing quickly to an irregularly pulsing swash of heavy rain upon the jungle roof, rain that soon began to penetrate the canopy above. Some of the T'swa, taking advantage of the noise, moved out with their swordlike bayonets and chopped away what undergrowth and saplings there were. This scarcely provided a field of fire, but it would help. Somewhere behind them, in the middle of their ring, two platoons were setting explosives. Some of the men, with climbing irons, were setting charges well up the trunks so the trees would come down in sections. Otherwise, many would lodge crisscross, perhaps denying the floaters adequate landing space.

The men cutting undergrowth finished and returned to lie waiting with the others. Photography done for the time, Varlik curled on his side and dozed in semisleep, wakened now and then by water running in his ear or by infrequent thunder. Before long he became aware that the rain had stopped, though dripping continued from above. Now he could see more and farther than before; dawn was breaking. The morning bird chorus began, and when it ended he slept.

And awoke with a start to the first crash of bombs. He'd expected them louder—the target zone was only a mile away—but the jungle vegetation absorbed and deadened sounds. It was full daylight, and raising his head to look around, he saw the T'swa peering steadily outward. Somewhere out there, not far, lookouts had been posted. His hand touched the holster of his sidearm, then went to his audio recorder and camera.

There was little enough to record—the constant thudding of bombs, the T'swa lying ready with rifles and blast hoses—for about half an hour. No pickup squads arrived with prisoners, but he told himself it was too soon; there hadn't been time for that. Or they might have come through somewhere else. Then rifle fire erupted well up front, spreading, developing into a firefight that went on sporadically for minutes before dying. There'd been blast hoses, and the pickup squads hadn't carried any.

He spoke his thoughts for the record, mentally tuning out the sound of bombing. Without the firefight it seemed almost quiet—an almost-quiet ruptured suddenly by great roaring explosions, almost stopping his heart; the T'swa were blasting their evacuation clearing, a stupendous sound of high explosives and trees crashing. After a moment, pieces of branchwood fell through the canopy to patter on the ground. And when that was over, a matter of seconds, it was truly quiet, because the bombing had stopped.

The silence was brief, a minute or two. Nearby to his left a blast hose ripped a long burst of bullets, to be answered by hose fire from outside the circle, brief but shockingly violent. And close. Then all the T'swa were firing. Rockets hissed and slammed, and Varlik heard insistent Tyspi in his helmet radio, asking the pickup squads to report. None did.

The command came to move back. He did, crawling backward on knees and elbows, pausing frequently to record with his camera. The T'swa withdrew slowly, taking advantage of cover, maintaining fire. The shooting was intense. Lieutenant Zimsu exploded, literally, hit by a rocket. Varlik had seen it in his monitor while scanning with his camera.

After that for a time he didn't know what was happening or what he was doing, until he found himself behind a section of blasted tree trunk near the edge of the evac clearing, which he could see through the fringe of tattered trees behind him. Kusu was kneeling beside him, and a little way off, Captain Tarku crouched.

Kusu was gripping Varlik's shoulder. "Varlik," he was saying in Standard, "go to the clearing. That's an order. Floaters are taking people out. Sergeant Gis-Tor is in charge of loading, and he knows you're to have priority. I want you out of here."

Varlik nodded, numbly willing. "And keep low!" the T'swa reminded. "I don't want you killed." Kusu peered into Varlik's eyes as if looking for something, then grinned and thrust him on his way.

The Iryalan crawled through debris into the steamy sunlight of the clearing. It was perhaps three hundred feet across, littered with blasted trees. He could see three evac floaters loading personnel, half hidden by jumbled debris, and Varlik paused to use his camera. Another floater, settling in, was hit by a rocket as he watched, and pitched forward, downward, impacting heavily. A few Birds had obviously reached the edge and could see and shoot at the floaters.

The din of firing was continuous now. A floater raised under fire, its rate of lift like a leap, angling up and away. Still another came in, almost recklessly swift, braking abruptly only a few yards above the ground, then settling quickly among the debris to load.

Another popped upward, was hit by a rocket, circled momentarily out of control, was hit again, and fell sideways to the ground. Others, hanging or circling well above, were hidden by jungle and could only be glimpsed. One came in and landed unhit. It occurred to Varlik that the Birds might have let it land, to shoot it down later loaded with men. As if to verify that, another, popping swiftly up, was hit at least twice, to fall back slowly. Another raised. It too was hit, but continued upward and away, as if the round had failed to explode after penetrating. Still another landed, and another.

He realized he'd been crouching there with his camera in his hands, recording. He was supposed to load and leave; no one would ever see his cube if he died here. Cautiously he moved, crouching toward the floaters.

Another floater lifted, jumping as if on a spring, was hit some fifty feet above the ground and fell crashing on top of one still loading. Then Varlik heard a radioed command in Standard.

"Floaters, attention. Floaters, attention. This is Major Masu, acting commander on the ground. Move away. Repeat, move away. Evacuation is cancelled."

That they were to be left here was not what impacted Varlik's mind. Rather, it was that Major Masu was in charge. That meant Biltong and Koda were probably dead. He glimpsed floaters still circling; they hadn't left yet, and he felt a brief surge of pride, for their pilots were Iryalan, or maybe Rombili: Confederatswa.

Again the radio commanded; this time the voice wasn't Masu's. "T'swa, regroup," it said. "Take cover in the clearing."

Of course. The litter of fallen trees here gave better cover than they'd find elsewhere. But where was Kusu? Crouching, crawling over fallen trees, Varlik started back toward where he'd seen him last.

"Lormagen!"

He stopped, knelt. Captain Tarku was on his knees behind a massive fallen trunk, looking at him.

"Where are you going?" Tarku had shouted to be heard. Varlik realized he'd been heading out of the clearing.

"To find Kusu."

"Kusu is dead. Stay here by me."

Varlik scuttled toward the officer. Grief surged, and the thought came that that was silly. Kusu wasn't grieving. Kusu was alive somewhere, laughing at all this. And he . . . Varlik stared at his hands through brimming eyes. He'd lost his camera somewhere, or discarded it. His hands groped. No, it was on its strap, inside his shirt—he held his sidearm in its stead.

Then bullets struck a branch stub in front of him, throwing bark and wood, and he hit the dirt, clinging to it, heart pounding. Someone hurtled over the log to land beside him headlong, and Varlik found himself staring at a Bird, head bullet-shattered. Shoving his side arm back in its holster, he picked up the Bird's rifle and peered over the log. All he could see on the other side was debris and a T'swa body. Then bullets struck the log inches away, and again he hit the ground, not too shocked to wonder why he wasn't dead.

Off to the west, the bombing had begun again.

Tarku raised up and peered over the log, holding his head sideways, looking awkwardly across his nose to see, exposing almost none of himself. For the moment the shooting had slackened, as if the Birds were preparing something. After a few seconds the captain lowered his head again and spoke calm Tyspi into his mike.

"This is Captain Tarku," he said. "Major Masu is dead and I am in command now. Scorpion A Company, report if you receive me. Over."

The firing had almost died, and Varlik wondered what that meant. "This is Sergeant Gow, in command of A Company. We're at the west edge of the clearing and seem to have twenty or thirty effectives. Over."

The captain ran down the roster of companies of both regiments. Two didn't reply at all. *So few!* Varlik thought. *We're finished; done for.* And wondered that he felt so calm now. He rolled the Bird over and lifted two ammo clips from the man's belt. *I might as well go out like a T'swa,* he told himself.

Then he heard Tarku's voice, both directly and in his radio. "All right, T'swa, on my signal we will charge the enemy. Each of you has my admiration."

He folded the mike away from his mouth and looked at Varlik. "Lormagen," he said, "I want you to stay where you are until the fighting is over. Then call out your surrender in Standard. The Birds will probably come and take you prisoner; you should find that interesting. And it will be safer to have them come and get you than to try to make your way to them."

Varlik simply stared. Then, surprisingly, the captain winked before speaking to his radio again.

"Do I have trumpeters?"

Varlik heard the radio answer "yes." Two yeses.

"Good," said Tarku. "Sound the dirge, then the attack."

Not far away, surprisingly close, a trumpet spoke

clearly, its sound as precise as if at parade, joined in mid-phrase by another some distance off. Tarku gathered his legs beneath him, and Varlik noticed now that one trouser leg was soaked with blood. It had been out of sight till then.

The trumpet call was something Varlik had never heard before. Not mournful. Not even solemn. Not like any dirge he'd heard or imagined. More like a fanfare—a fanfare on two trumpets, an announcement of death without regret. Then abruptly it changed, became an exultant battlecry, quick-paced, and the T'swa nearby rose up, rifles in hand, bayonets fixed, the captain vaulting over the fallen tree. The trumpets were almost drowned out by the sudden shattering roar of gunfire.

Varlik clung to the ground. The roaring thinned, thinned, then after a couple of minutes stopped, leaving only sporadic shots and short bursts. It occurred to him that no T'swi was likely to be captured conscious; even down they'd fight to the death with grenades and sidearms.

The Regiment is dead, he thought. And felt no grief now despite the moisture that blurred his vision. With a grimy hand he wiped it clear. No grief, only numbness. He sensed—possibly heard—movement, and lay still, eyes slitted. Someone passed about seventy feet to his left, tall and slender, sinewy, wearing Bird loincloth and battle harness, and disappeared out of his small field of vision.

It occurred to Varlik to look at the Bird rifle in his hands, look for the serial number. There was none. As his camera recorded the absence, the unmarked receiver where the number should have been, he wondered if the army had noticed this, and what they'd made of it.

The shooting seemed to have stopped entirely.

And here I am alive. What I have to do now is get back to Iryala and find out why the regiment had to die.

At the moment he had no doubt he'd do it. And no doubt that Iryala was where the answer lay.

He rose to his knees, raised his head, and shouted in Standard as loudly as he could: "I surrender! I surrender to the Orlanthan Army!" Then he tossed the rifle away and his sidearm after it, sat back against the log, and waited for them to come get him.

PART FIVE

Finding the Trail

Thirty-Three

Sitting against the log waiting, Varlik sank into a mental and emotional fog. At some point he took off his battle helmet and left it on the ground. Later he roused enough to call out again, and later again, then wondered vaguely if they were interested or whether perhaps he'd be sitting there when it started to get dark.

He became aware that the sounds of bombing had stopped, though he wasn't sure how long before. Perhaps the army felt they'd destroyed everything worth destroying here. Maybe they had. He began to rouse himself mentally, took another of the mineral tablets he'd been issued for this tropical mission, and drank the last of his water. His watch told him it was after 06.40, and the day's heat was building. He began to consider hiking in the direction of Bird headquarters, then became aware of being watched. Slowly he raised both hands empty and open overhead.

"I surrender," he called.

There were three of the Birds. To him they said nothing, and among themselves spoke their own language. One of them took his bayonet, camera and belt recorder, and his light field pack. A second searched his person, not particularly roughly, while the third tied his hands behind his back. Then they took him to a broad, well-packed trail where they began to trot, though not so rapidly that he had trouble keeping up with his hands tied, and soon he could hear the sound of chopping. Before long they came to men working, cutting saplings and vines and carrying them westward—the same direction that Varlik was being taken.

He began to miss a major use of the hands on Kettle—wiping sweat from the eyebrows. By that time his mind had begun to function more normally, though emotionally he was still numb. The sight of dead T'swa didn't touch him.

Shortly his captors turned aside on a lesser trail, and here too were work parties, numerous now, carrying saplings, long poles, matting, and other material, at least some of which he supposed had been salvaged from the bombed area. They were, he decided, moving camp to a new location.

After perhaps a mile more, he could see concentrated activity ahead: the new campsite. Shortly one of the Birds said something, and they halted. One uncoiled a leather thong from his belt, looped it around Varlik's neck and knotted it, pulling hard on the knot. It would, Varlik thought, be difficult to remove without cutting. Not that that made any difference; he had no intention whatever of trying to escape.

The one who'd given orders looked him over, then drew a heavy-bladed knife and, stepping around Varlik, cut his hands free. After tying the other end of his neck tether to a liana, the man departed, leaving the other two with Varlik. Both the Birds sat down, eyes on their prisoner, and Varlik, after hesitating, also sat, wondering if they'd roust him to his feet again. It was encouraging that so far he hadn't been harmed or even directly threatened.

He looked the two over obliquely, not wanting to offend them, and could read nothing in their faces. But they talked calmly enough between themselves, with no indication that they might abuse him. Tall and slender, they were a little darker than himself. The Birds at Aromanis hadn't seemed like these; the physiques had been similar but the demeanors different. These people bore themselves with calm self-certainty. *Rather like T'swa*, he thought.

After a few minutes the third man returned, accompanied by a considerably older Bird whose breechclout was indigo, and who wore in addition an indigo headband. At their approach, the two guards got up, and Varlik also; the older man seemed clearly to be an officer.

He looked Varlik up and down from a distance of six feet, curious rather than hostile or gloating, then spoke in Standard. "Who are you?"

"My name is Varlik Lormagen."

"Why were you accompanying the T'swa?"

The man knows what the T'swa are called, Varlik told himself. *And he speaks Standard. He's no jungle savage. He knows; if he wanted to, he could tell me who's behind this insurrection.*

At that moment Varlik knew how he would get out of this place, and his mind cleared, became sharp and directed.

"I'm a news correspondent from the planet Iryala," Varlik answered. "I've been with the T'swa in order to tell the people of the Confederation how the T'swa train and fight."

While he spoke, he watched the man for any sign of confusion, blankness, irritation, which would suggest he hadn't understood; the words and concepts would be unfamiliar to a true gook. But instead the old Bird's face reflected thought, calculation.

"Perhaps," Varlik continued, "I could describe the life and training of your warriors for my people."

The Bird regarded him calmly. "I will discuss you with certain others. We will decide what to do with you. Meanwhile, if you have urgent needs and cannot make them understood, speak my name, Ramolu, to your guards. They will send for someone who knows your language. But do so only if the need is severe; do not presume upon our tolerance. You are, after all, our prisoner."

"Yes, sir. And General Ramolu, sir, I have a—what is called a camera. It captures pictures. And a recorder that captures sounds. Do you understand? They . . ."

"The corporal has shown me what he took from you."

Varlik nodded. "If you are interested in my suggestion, they will be helpful in letting my people know what your soldiers are like. I'd like to have them back."

Lips pursed, Ramolu studied Varlik for a long moment, then spoke rapid Orlanthan to the three guards. The corporal unslung the instruments and handed them to Varlik.

"And spare recorder cubes are in my field pack."

Ramolu took the pack, hunted through it, and finding nothing harmful, handed it also to Varlik. Then he turned and walked away, in a manner that reminded Varlik of a T'swa dismissal.

Apparently the Bird *was* a general. At least, Varlik told himself, he hadn't reacted visibly to being addressed as one. It was as if he was used to it.

Varlik recorded his surroundings and guards with his camera, then switched it off. Gradually his earlier detached, slow-motion feeling returned. One of his guards took the canteens, including Varlik's, and left, returning with them full. Then briefly it rained again, heavy and warm, steamy. Later a Bird arrived with gruel in a clay bowl, and meat wrapped in a leaf; they proved edible.

A notion occurred to Varlik, and he tried speaking Tyspi to his guards, to no avail.

Also he wondered about certain things: What had happened to queer the raid—it shouldn't have gone *that* badly. They'd been attacked almost as soon as the bombing began, as if the Birds had been expecting them. Of course, they could have been detected in the night, and the Birds could have found their positions by dawn light, but that seemed unlikely. It was more as if they'd known in advance.

And had Ramolu become as familiar with the Confederation, its language, its technology, as he seemed, without going off-planet? Varlik doubted it. He never wondered if Ramolu was an escaped slave, though; nothing about the man fitted that.

The guards were relieved by a new shift, and the new men understood no Tyspi either, nor Standard. Then a young officer came, who also spoke no Standard, and with the guards, took Varlik to a rude shelter, a roof without walls. Ramolu was there with five other Birds who, like Ramolu, wore indigo loincloths and headbands. They had no chairs, but waited squatting, not rising at Varlik's approach. That surprised Varlik. They should have moved to dominate him, stand over him. Instead they seemed content with the knowledge, on both sides, that they were the masters and he the prisoner.

When he entered, he too squatted. His guards remained standing. Once down, Varlik turned on his recorder. "I'd like to record this in both sound and pictures," he said. "With your approval."

Ramolu nodded, casually waving a hand. "You tolerate our heat," he said. "I am surprised."

"I've been living with the T'swa for months now, and training with them. One either comes to tolerate the heat or collapses from it. Only three weeks ago I returned to Orlantha from Tyss; it is very hot on Tyss, too."

Ramolu seemed to know what *Tyss* was, for again he showed no sign of blankness, confusion, or irritation. "And what were you doing on Tyss?"

"I'd been wounded, and spent part of my recovery

time there, to better understand and describe the T'swa to my people."

Ramolu smiled slightly. "And did you? Come to understand the T'swa?"

"Somewhat, I hope. Certainly I've gotten used to them, learned to feel comfortable with them."

Ramolu didn't react facially. "What would you tell the people of the Confederation about us," he asked, "if we allowed you to return to them?"

For a moment, with the sudden realization that his ploy might work, Varlik actually stopped breathing. "I would report what I saw. I would show them the battle, in the pictures I have taken. And I would tell them what the T'swa said of you: that you are the best fighting men they'd faced. And these T'swa were veteran troops. They'd fought on one world and another for fourteen years."

"Ah, but the T'swa are gooks, are they not? Like us. Great warriors, of course, but gooks. We are more interested in what the people of the Confederation think of us. What *do* they think of us?"

"To them you are a faceless enemy who prevents them from getting technite."

Steady hazel eyes held Varlik's during a brief silence. Finally Ramolu spoke again. "And what do *you* think of us?"

The question took Varlik by surprise. "I hadn't thought about it. The T'swa said you are not an enemy—that you are simply someone with whom they shared a war. I have been somewhat influenced by their viewpoint."

"But the Confederation thinks of us as the enemy."

"Oh, yes. Very much so."

"And you do not."

"*Enemy* is a consideration from a viewpoint. I learned that from the T'swa. From my viewpoint you are not my enemy. But from your viewpoint, you may be."

Ramolu eyed him as Koda might have. "Suppose you

ruled the Confederation. What would you do about us?"

"I would—I would ask to confer with your leader. I'd offer to buy the technite mines from you and pay you a duty on all technite removed. I would offer to hire your people to mine it, and if they didn't want to, I'd bring in miners of my own. There would be no more slavery."

"And what of Aromanis?"

"Aromanis would not be important to me."

"If you, as a teller of the war, made such a suggestion to your people, of what use would it be to us?"

"Some people would like the idea; maybe many would. I first heard it from a common soldier from Iryala— Corporal Duggan. What would you think of it as an Orlanthan?"

"I find it attractive." Ramolu eyed Varlik quizzically. "And what do you think of me, an Orlanthan who speaks your language with considerable facility and knows enough about other worlds to talk with you as I have? What does this mean to you?"

Varlik looked at the tallish, graying, loose-jointed Bird who squatted opposite him in a loincloth, speaking Standard more precisely than most Iryalans. Only a light, singsong tonality clearly marked his speech as foreign.

"A Confederation officer, Colonel Carlis Voker, has pointed out to me numerous anomalies regarding what is called the Orlanthan insurgency. He felt they pointed to some Confederation world or faction cooperating with you." Varlik was talking ahead of his thoughts, winging it. "So I'm not astonished to find someone like you here. Colonel Voker wouldn't be either, or General Lamons. Or His Majesty, the King. They'd expect it.

"Whoever equipped and trained your army has reasons of their own for doing it. It might be they wouldn't like the Confederation to make an offer like the one I mentioned. But it's an offer whose time has come, and I speak to many, many people via pictures and words that travel widely by something like radio. And even the rulers listen."

It had to be the T'swa, he told himself—*the T'swa, who obviously have their own technite. It not only looks as if they'd armed and trained the Birds; they'd educated their senior officers, at least. Who else could produce a man like Ramolu?*

And the T'swa had sacrificed their regiments as a cover!

The Orlanthan was eyeing Varlik with one brow raised. "You are not a man greatly burdened with modesty," said Ramolu, "but perhaps modesty would be inappropriate."

He turned and began to speak musical Orlanthan to the five others who wore indigo, as if summarizing the interrogation. Three of them seemed already to have understood, for they were looking at the other two instead of at the speaker. When he had finished, they conferred for several minutes, then Ramolu turned back to Varlik.

"We have decided to send you back to your people with some T'swa wounded—those fit to travel."

It was as simple as that.

After that he was tethered in a shelter not far off, still under guard. It seemed clear that the six whom Varlik now thought of as "the general staff" were the leaders here, perhaps even the leaders of the whole insurgency, for they'd made the decision themselves, without further consultation.

And repeatedly he found himself wondering if he really would be sent home with what he knew, what he'd seen. It was as if they considered it unimportant. He was certain they were too alert and intelligent to have overlooked it.

Thirty-Four

Varlik waited tethered in his small, open-sided shelter while one day passed and then another. Ramolu didn't appear again, but guards saw that their prisoner was fed and his canteen refilled as needed, all without visible animosity.

Not that it was a pleasant interlude. His sleep stirred ugly with nightmares. He'd waken gasping and desperate, or desolate, the dream content slipping away even as he opened his eyes, leaving him with no more than the sense that it had been about the regiment, or the Birds, Voker or Mauen or Konni. And sweatier than even the hot Kettle night accounted for.

His most restful sleep was in naps by day, and he slept about a dozen hours out of the twenty. To occupy his waking time, he undertook to learn Orlanthan from his guards—there were two at almost all times—and they were casually agreeable to cooperating. In part they taught him nouns by pointing and naming. Fingers walked and ran and jumped. He learned to count, name trees and body parts, insects and food items. And he recorded all of it, interjecting Standard equivalents.

Nor was there any sign that they were playing word jokes on him, and at any rate it passed the time.

Varlik realized that this decent treatment, this absence of abuse, was remarkable, given what he knew of the Birds' history. He did not appreciate, of course, how bad it might have been. He had no criteria for comparison, nor did his imagination stretch far in that direction.

Meanwhile, there was no further bombing.

He wondered how the Birds planned to return him north; by their long trails through the forest, no doubt. It had to be at least a thousand miles to Beregesh, and he didn't know how well he'd hold up, hiking day after day. He'd done well enough on the trail raids, but that had been only four days, and the humidity there hadn't been nearly as bad as here. The mineral tablets would help, as long as they lasted, but he only had about a week's worth. He stopped taking any while he waited; he'd save them for the trek. He was almost out of water-treatment capsules.

On the morning of the fourth day an elderly Bird appeared wearing a cross-slung rifle. He was unusually short, still sinewy beneath age-loosened skin; he leered almost toothlessly down at Varlik, who sat cross-legged on the ground.

"Me boss you fella," he said. "Me name Curly. Take you fella you people, give you back. Me talk good Standard, give orders, you and black fellas go along you."

Varlik doubted that the man was anybody's boss; he wore no armband or headband of rank. His function was probably to relay orders. Then the guard corporal spoke Orlanthan to the old man. "You stand up," the old man ordered Varlik. "Some fella sweat bird him cover you eyes."

Varlik stood up reluctantly. Did he have to walk a thousand miles blindfolded? What reason would they have for that? They tied his wrists in front of him, which at least would let him wipe away sweat. A hand grasped his arm, letting him know it was time to march, and blindly, hesitantly, he began walking. It wasn't as bad as he thought it might be. Once he relaxed and trusted his guide, it went almost without a stumble.

Curly! A Standard nickname. The man must be an actual escapee, an ex-slave from either Beregesh or Kelikut, probably born into slavery, Varlik decided. He seemed different from the other Birds here, at least those Varlik had seen much of, as if the jungle nation had evolved its own culture, different from that of the labor camps and no doubt from the original tribal cultures, too.

Varlik knew at once when they were joined by the T'swa. Not that they spoke. But they moved, walked, and already his ears were functioning more perceptively. And the wounded men slowed the pace markedly. At this rate, he told himself, it would take them two or three deks to walk to Beregesh. But the slower pace would be easier on the long, hot trail.

It would be ironic if they were killed by army gunfire when they got up there. And even more so if they were killed by T'swa hunter/killer teams, though that was less likely; T'swa raiders were much likelier to see who they were shooting at than the soldiers were.

The trail changed. The new one seemed to be the hovertruck trail the scouts had reported, that led beneath the trees from a small river to the storage caves. It seemed fairly smooth, and wide enough that some of their guards were several feet to each side. Here and there it went through shallow water, once halfway to his knees, the bottom soft and mucky but not treacherous.

After a while he smelled something besides jungle, recognized it as a river in high summer—everlasting high summer here. Shortly they slowed, stopped, and he could hear thumps—the sound of activity on small boats. Then someone led him out onto a mudbank, and uncertainly, with a bumped shin, he got into a narrow, unsteady boat, to be led along it crouching, then seated on the bottom by someone wading alongside. His legs were somewhat bent, his feet against someone ahead of him—a T'swi, he supposed.

From the sounds and delay, they were loading several boats, and perhaps some wounded T'swa were having to be manhandled in. Finally his boat was pushed free of the shore, and he heard the bump and scrape of paddles on gunwales, helping the current move them. They were headed *down*stream. And from what he remembered of maps he'd seen, downstream here meant south, not north. He wondered what that might mean; it worried him.

It was tiresome and eventually painful, sitting on the boat's uncushioned bottom with nothing to lean back against and his hands bound in front of him. He wondered how long it would be like this, and whether he'd become comfortable with it after a while. There were almost no distractions, only the smooth rhythmic sounds of paddling, and now and then a few words of musical Bird, unintelligible to him. Once there was a low tense call from another boat, a break in the paddling, a short burst of rifle shots. Then there came a few rapid syllables, more shooting, a brief spate of rapid Bird again, with laughter, the tension gone. Some animal, Varlik thought, something dangerous, perhaps a river creature, and they'd killed it. The blindfold and bonds exasperated him more than ever now: He'd like to have seen and recorded the event on video.

The river was narrow, he knew, because on the recon photos much of it was completely overhung with trees, showing only as discontinuous interruptions in the jungle roof. Of course, the giants along the banks would lean out over the water and reach with branches farther still, to take better advantage of the sunlight, but still the river could hardly be much wider than seventy or eighty feet. And the occasional cries of birds and tree animals were sometimes close at hand, even overhead.

Once he got thirsty and spoke the Orlanthan word for water. He couldn't understand the reply, but after a bit someone handed him a canteen cup and he drank, probably river water, he decided.

Thunder rumbled distantly, then nearer, then boomed not far away, and rain began to pelt, then pour. Quickly he was sitting in water, but he had no complaint because, warm though the rain was, it cooled. When it stopped, however, after perhaps half an hour, the air was steamier than ever.

His physical discomfort, which had become acute in the second hour, deadened, along with his mental functioning. Once they stopped to eat, but he was not untied nor his blindfold removed. A Bird held the food in what seemed to be a large leaf, and at Curly's instruction, Varlik ate by putting his face to the food.

It was late in the day when they stopped and the bow was pulled up on a shore. Someone took Varlik's blindfold off, and he blinked in the daylight, looking around. The sun was low, and the river had widened or, more likely, was a different stream, some hundred yards across.

He counted seventeen T'swa distributed in six canoes. Two other canoes seemed to have carried an escort of guards. On the shore by the boats, guards and paddlers sat or squatted or walked around. Varlik decided that the guards were those who carried their rifles in their hands, the paddlers those who wore theirs cross-slung.

The canoes had been carefully hewed and hollowed from single logs, their sides no thicker than a board. Clearly the Birds had been supplied primarily with military necessities; beyond those, they apparently made do with primitive resources.

Just ahead was a river greater yet, a quarter mile wide or more, into which this river flowed. The shore they were on was the angle between rivers. Varlik looked around and found the old ex-slave, who now sat by a tree. "Curly," Varlik called, "what happens next?"

"You people they come sky, take away you. When little dark come. Me people got far talker, they tell you people what place."

"Can we get out and walk around?"

The old man looked at him a long moment. "You anyway got to be in *riilmo*. You people come down on water, take you out *riilmo*. No place here"—he patted the shore beside him with one hand—"no place here they come down. Not nuf room."

Riilmo must be Orlanthan for canoe, Varlik decided. A Beregesh slave would never have been exposed to the Standard for it. And the old man was right—there wasn't room on the shore for a floater.

"Can we get out and walk around now? Until 'little dark' comes?"

Curly's old eyes glittered but he only shrugged. Then a sergeant asked him something in Orlanthan, and the old man answered. The sergeant spoke again, again the ex-slave shrugged, then the sergeant called an order. Several Birds came down to the boats and began helping the prisoners to their feet, and over the gunwales into the shallow water.

For the next hour or so they lay around on the shore, the T'swa saying little. It was as if there was nothing to say, for they didn't seem depressed. Perhaps, Varlik decided, they were adjusting to their new condition as survivors being set free. Only one of them was anyone Varlik recognized, though in his own uniqueness he'd be known by all of them. It didn't seem appropriate yet to question them—ask how it had felt to see their lifelong friends killed around them, or what it was like to be without a regiment. There'd be time enough for interviews at Aromanis.

Then, in the fleeting equatorial twilight, a floater appeared. Three floaters actually: a large evac floater accompanied by two gunships that stood off a hundred yards or so. The prisoners were loaded into the canoes again, and stolid paddlers took them to midriver. Gently the evac floater settled almost to the water, nearly touching Varlik's canoe, and two paddlers grasped the edges of the wide door to steady their dugout. Cautiously Varlik half-stood and climbed in, helped by med techs and followed by the two T'swa.

Then the floater raised slightly and moved to the next canoe.

Inside was dark, and somehow unreal. A quiet medic asked if he was hurt or ill, and Varlik answered no, he was fine. The T'swa were helped to cotlike stretchers while Varlik walked forward to clear the door. When all seventeen T'swa had been loaded, a handful of Birds— exchange captives—were transferred to the canoes. Finally the doors were closed, and the floater rose smoothly and swung away. Through a window, Varlik watched the dugouts disappear in the thickening dusk, and with a dreamlike objectivity noted that he felt no jubilation.

Then the cabin lights came on and the medics began to examine the wounded.

Thirty-five

It was little short of dawn when the evac floater landed at the base hospital at Aromanis. Because he'd eaten native food and drunk untreated water, Varlik too was entered, to be checked for parasites. The first thing he did was get a letter cube off to Mauen telling her that he was safe.

As usual, the T'swa wards were well occupied, mostly with young troopers of the Ice Tiger Regiment. From the veteran regiments there'd been fewer than thirty until the seventeen arrived, and the word was that only some forty had been evacuated unwounded, or too slightly wounded to remain hospitalized. Along with a couple of hundred disabled or undergoing rehabilitation from earlier actions, they were all that remained alive of more than eighteen hundred who'd landed on Kettle scant deks ago—they and a handful still among the Birds, too badly injured to be moved.

The forty able-bodied, informed of the exchange, had been at the hospital to greet them. The greeting had been neither exuberant nor somber. There were wide grins, handshakes, soft laughter, and an incredible sense of spiritual togetherness that left Varlik feeling left out.

Not that he was ignored or slighted; he simply could not share in the feeling that was part of it, and that depressed him. He kept busy through it with his camera.

The new media people had not been informed of their pending arrival, and none of them were there.

There'd been a letter cube waiting for him from Mauen—long and warm and carefully devoid of worries or problems. He hoped she wouldn't hear of his brief "missing" status before she got his letter.

His nights in the hospital weren't as bad as some in the jungle, but the days were worse; around him were bandaged reminders of the regiment and what had happened to it. After two days of tests, shots, and observation, he was discharged from the hospital. He went straight to army headquarters, where he was accosted by a newly arrived young man from Central News and a team from Iryala Video. They seemed ridiculously impressed with him—the "white T'swa," they said he was called back home.

Somehow they angered him, though he knew the feeling was unreasonable—a matter of his own condition, not theirs. He shook loose from them as quickly as he decently could and went hopefully to Voker's office. Voker was the only one at Aromanis that he wanted to see. But the colonel was at Beregesh, expected back that day. Finally, Varlik arranged to leave Kettle on the next ship to Iryala, the *Quaranth* again, two days hence.

Then he arranged with Trevelos for a place of his own to work; he wanted privacy from the new media people. Trevelos was friendlier than ever, eager to help; the brief barrier between them had left no scars. Varlik spent most of the day editing his material and preparing his report. He didn't show Ramolu, though, only talked about him, as if the man had refused to be recorded. His recordings of Ramolu weren't news; they were *evidence*.

When he was done, he found Voker in and played it for him—the battle in the jungle and what he'd been able to record of the Birds. Voker, in turn, told him of fierce firefights between Birds and T'swa around Beregesh. The Birds had also mounted more concentrated hunt-and-kill sweeps to cut down T'swa trail harassment, resulting in increased casualties on both sides. But meanwhile, progress on rebuilding the refinery had improved markedly.

It had been necessary, Voker said, to keep revising upward the estimated size of insurgent forces. The figure now was thirty to fifty thousand, with no confidence that further upward revisions wouldn't be necessary.

Over Voker's good Crodelan whiskey, they speculated on why the Birds had blindfolded him and the T'swa while taking them out for evacuation—what was it they didn't want them to see?—and came up with nothing compelling. Perhaps nothing was the answer. Again Varlik didn't mention the arsenal on Tyss, and withheld his belief in T'swa complicity. He agreed to play his report again for Lamons at the next day's staff meeting.

After supper Varlik went to the T'swa camp. The men of the two veteran regiments shared a single company area, with only a few men to a tent. The Ice Tiger Regiment had moved into the rest of the camp, but most of them were south now, fighting.

Varlik didn't feel right with the T'swa anymore. He felt an urgency, a compulsion, to get home to Iryala. There, he told himself, was the answer to the Kettle mystery. Not its roots, perhaps, but on Iryala he would learn what those roots were.

The general's staff meeting wasn't particularly interesting, what Varlik saw and heard of it. After a little, he was asked courteously to leave; what would follow was confidential. He seriously doubted that the confidential session would be very interesting either. *You people think you have secrets!* he said to himself as he left. Afterward, he talked to the other media people. The new man from Central News talked a good job, but that he was still at Aromanis instead of Beregesh suggested otherwise to Varlik.

Most of the rest of the day, Varlik hung around the T'swa wards where the wounded from the Red Scorpion and Night Adder Regiments were. He got their views on what the future held for them: Some would marry, have families. For a few there would be lodge-related jobs—scouting children who seemed to have the warrior purpose, or training recruits, or administrative jobs, or maintenance or other duties. Others would take outside jobs. Several would join a monastery and become masters of wisdom; some of the best-known masters had earlier been warriors.

For him there was Central News. It hit him then for the first time that he didn't want to work for Central News anymore. He told himself that maybe he'd feel different about it by the time he got back. Fendel would give him an interesting assignment and he'd be ready to go again. But he didn't really believe it.

That evening he bought a bottle of decent whiskey and got drunk by himself. The next day, hung over, he boarded his old friend, the IWS *Quaranth*, for the trip home.

Thirty-six

On the trip home, Varlik was effectively a recluse. At first various ship's officers tried to strike up conversations, for he'd become more a celebrity than he'd realized, and they were eager to question him about the war. But Varlik's answers were brief and evasive, though by intrinsic courtesy he avoided rudeness. He took to finding an unoccupied table at meals, and after a few days only Mikal Brusin gave him any attention at all.

Brusin was an exception, of course—an old friend— and Varlik had accepted the mate's invitation to a drink and a visit the first day. But after half an hour of avoiding the enigmas that had trapped so much of his attention, it seemed to Varlik that he was repeating himself. Brusin was too perceptive to be offended when Varlik excused himself. He could see the man was troubled, and connected it with the death of so many friends. So he didn't push—merely repeated occasionally his offer of a drink, usually declined and never leading to much talk.

To pass the long trip, Varlik again borrowed a firefighter's suit, and worked out long and hard in the gym. It helped him sleep, which he did a lot of, although here too he was often beset by bad dreams. Unintentionally, it also added to his mystique as "the white T'swa."

On the first day he'd checked the computer for instructional material on the Orlanthan language, and found nothing. So he played and replayed the cube he'd made in the Bird camp, finding in Bird conversations many of the words they'd taught him the meanings of—these numbered more than forty. Then, with these to start with, he'd analyzed the possible meanings of words he'd recorded but hadn't been taught. In this way, and because the language was agglutinative, he increased his vocabulary to about sixty words whose meanings he felt fairly confident of, with about fifty more whose meanings he could reasonably guess at. Then, although he knew almost nothing of Orlanthan grammar, he used his small vocabulary—including words with guessed-at meanings—in every combination he could think of, giving him mastery of what he knew. Probably, he told himself, his skill with Bird resembled Curly's skill with Standard, though Curly's vocabulary was no doubt larger and more functional. But if he was ever again in Kettle's equatorial jungle, he'd have a basis for communicating.

Not that he ever expected or intended to be. His language studies and drills served briefly as a pastime—something to do besides work out, sleep, and sit reading in the ship's library.

Eventually, the day of landfall arrived. And conscious of his aloofness on the trip, Varlik made a point at breakfast of going around the officers' mess shaking the hand of every man there, thanking them for the voyage. The thank-you didn't make a great deal of sense, and had he delivered it coolly, might have been taken as hauteur. But it came across with a tinge of regret, almost as apology, which in a sense it was, and when they left the messroom, in almost every case it was with the opinion that the white T'swa was a good guy, if not very social.

At 07.77, ship's time, the *Quaranth* came out of warp, and Varlik went to the observation room to watch intently the brilliantly glinting point that was Iryala grow to a beautiful cobalt and white orb, then to a looming planetary ball that moved in on them until it blocked out the sky. Soon a planetscape formed beneath him and Landfall appeared, spreading to cover the view.

He could see the spaceport, watched it grow and spread until it was the ground. Service trucks stood or moved; workers watched upward or went about their work. The *Quaranth* settled, touched down almost imperceptibly. He was back on Iryala.

Thirty-seven

It was 09.63, nearly midday, in Landfall and by ship's time, too. With a long layover planned, ship's time had been gradually adjusted until it agreed with destination time, helping circadian rhythms into sync.

In the terminal, Mauen had come into the reception area from the glassed viewing deck. She'd been waiting for almost three hours, had been there early, not wanting to miss him if the *Quaranth* should arrive ahead of schedule. Space flights seldom missed schedule by more than minutes, but she was taking no chances.

She wore her prettiest—a new sheer yellow dress with white underlining, of party quality but wearabout cut that showed quite a bit of pretty leg. Her hair was newly coifed, and she'd taken more than usual care with her makeup.

The first man in the door was Varlik—from his eagerness to see her, she was sure. But preoccupied, he almost didn't notice as she started toward him; he had other things on his mind, and somehow it hadn't occurred to him that she'd have gotten off work to meet him. He'd planned to take a cab to the office and report in, then ring Konni. But Mauen called his name as she ran, jerking his eyes to her. Then, after the merest lag, he was running too, to set down his bags and gather her in his arms, hugging her too tightly, his mission suddenly forgotten. They kissed avidly until they became aware that people were staring.

"I can't believe how much I missed you," he breathed.

She noticed neither the underlying profundity of his words nor their surface absurdity, hearing only the love they expressed. "It seemed like forever!" she murmured back. "Half a year."

He signaled a luggageman and, with his bags being carried, walked hand in hand with her through the building and out to the cab area, where the first cabbie in line stowed Varlik's bags, then held the door for them.

"Where to, sir?" he asked.

The sight of Mauen had banished office, report, and phone call from Varlik's mind. "Media Apartments Three," he said.

Varlik came out of the bathroom belting on his robe, poured a drink, then went out onto the canopied balcony where he sat down on a chair. The afternoon sun was warm, though the season was late. Many trees were already bare; on the rest the foliage had turned—yellow, bronze, red. He sipped his drink reflectively, and a minute later Mauen joined him. When she sat, a knee peeked out at him from her robe.

"Do you feel properly welcomed?" she asked.

"That was maximum welcome. More welcome than that I could hardly handle."

"You've always had a nice body," she said. "Now you're so hard and muscular it's almost unbelievable. But I like you this way." She touched his hand. "And I'll like you just as much if you gain weight again."

They touched glasses and drank. Then he held his up to the sun, eyeing thoughtfully the gleam through amber brandy. "I'd like to make a phone call," he said.

"Invite a colleague to dinner with us, to talk business. My business and hers. Yours now." He saw Mauen's smile slip at the pronoun *hers*. "Her name is Konni Wenter. She was on Kettle for Iryala Video," he went on, "and we ran into some strange things—evidence of a criminal conspiracy against the Confederation. We agreed to hold back what we found out until we learned more."

Mauen said nothing, asked no questions, simply waited soberly for Varlik to continue.

He got up. "Come back in," he said. "I'll show you some pictures that I haven't made available for newsfacs or videocasts. We can talk about what they mean, or seem to mean."

She followed him in and closed the doors behind them, feeling chilly now, and dialed the heat control while he activated the wall viewer and inserted a cube. Then they sat down together, and he played first his talk with Ramolu, pointing out the anomalies not only of the man's fluency in Standard but his obvious knowledge of the Confederation and technology and his general sophistication.

"So how did he get like that?" Varlik asked. "Who trained the Birds? Or probably the more correct question is who trained and educated the leaders like Ramolu, because the common Bird soldier doesn't speak Standard—or Tyspi, the language of Tyss. Probably the people who trained them are the people who armed them. Here's one of their rifles." He moved the halted sequence to the image of the rifle he'd picked up in the jungle, and pointed out its lack of serial number.

"Konni and I, after being wounded, went to Tyss for rehabilitation, and walked into town from the hospital there. We recorded this." He sat quietly, letting Mauen watch and listen to the two children who'd talked with Konnie and him. Varlik stopped the sequence after each line of dialog, to translate from the Tyspi. "Are you Ertwa?" asked the little girl, and from the audio,

Konni's voice answered, "I don't know what 'Ertwa' means."

"They are Splennwa," the little boy corrected his sister. "Ertwa were very long ago."

Mauen interrupted, and Varlik touched the *pause* key again. "What are 'Ertwa?' " she asked.

"I have no idea. The point is that he responded as if he assumed we were from Splenn. That suggests that Splennites visit Tyss often enough that people are aware of them as frequent visitors—even little children."

Then he played the audio recording of the teaching brother, Ban-Shum, their host and guide in Oldu Tez-Boag, who could speak Orlanthan. Why would a teacher on Tyss know Orlanthan?

And finally, he showed his video recording of the arsenal in the Jubat Forest and the weapons without serial numbers, then removed from a bag the T'swa-made side arm he'd taken, also without serial number.

"How does all of this seem to you?" he asked. And realized that his body was tense, trembling slightly at some undefined stress.

"It looks . . . it looks as if it might be the T'swa who armed and trained the Orlanthans. But . . . where does Splenn fit in?"

"Splennites could have smuggled the weapons from Tyss to Kettle. Splenn has space ships, and at least in adventure fiction the Splennites are supposed to be smugglers. But I haven't told you all of it yet." He explained his theory—Konni's actually—that the T'swa had a technite mine of their own.

"And—why do you want to ask Miss Wenter over?"

"To show her what I recorded in the jungle. And she'd planned to see what she could learn here; I want to know what she's found out."

Mauen nodded. "All right. Ask her." She paused. "Why do you think there's anything to learn about this, here on Iryala?"

"The T'swa colonels wanted their regiments publicized here. Why? And more than the colonels wanted it; they'd already arranged for publicity to be channeled through the T'swa ambassador here. Besides that, apparently someone had expected both Central News and Iryala Video to have the T'swa featured." *And got the king to contract personally for the regiments,* Varlik added to himself; he'd never looked at that angle before. "It's as if someone here, someone in a very high place, is involved."

Mauen got up and went to her desk in their activities room, then returned with an address book. "Perhaps I have something helpful," she said. Varlik looked at her, puzzled. "I got interested in the T'swa from your reports," she went on. "Lots of people did, but especially me because I'm your wife. So I called the Royal Library for anything they might have on them. I didn't find much. But I thought there might be material that I didn't know how to access, so I called the library's consulting office. When the supervisory consultant realized I was your wife, she gave me the name and number of an expert on Tyss and the T'swa philosophy—Melsa Ostrak Gouer."

Mauen handed him the address book, open to the Gs. The name Gouer didn't mean anything specific to him, though he recognized it vaguely as belonging to an aristocratic family. But Ostrak—the Ostraks were one of the better known aristocratic families, holding certain interstellar trading rights in fief from the crown.

"Have you called this Melsa Gouer?"

"No. I hesitated to bother someone of a family like that."

"I think I will," he said. "Tomorrow. It could be that you do have something helpful here."

At least it could provide a lead to highly placed families with a prewar interest in the T'swa. He made his call to Konni and she accepted the dinner invitation. Then Varlik got dressed to report to the office. When he was ready to leave, he stopped to kiss Mauen.

"Varlik?"

"Yes?"

"Did you sleep with this Konni Wenter?"

The question startled him. "Sleep with her? No. Or anyone else since I met you. Not ever." He stepped back to arm's length. "I hope you haven't been worrying about that."

"Not until you asked to call her. And then said you'd traveled to Tyss together. Is she pretty?"

"No, she's fairly plain. Not homely, but . . ." He grinned. "She's nothing like you. Except that she's nice, too. I think you'll like her. And she'll like you. Have you ever wondered about things like that before when I've been gone?"

"Not really." She smiled a little. "A time or two, maybe. I know that women must put themselves in your way sometimes. But while you were talking, it occurred to me that you shared something with her out there that was important to you both, and that I had no part in—a mystery, a war, and friends killed."

His eyes rested on hers. "True. But now the mystery is yours, too. You've even given me a lead."

Varlik checked in with Fendel, who told him to take a week off; then he'd have a new assignment for him. Varlik told him he wasn't done with the T'swa assignment yet, that there were odds and ends of it to look into here, and that when he was finished he was going to take two weeks off.

When he left Fendel's office, Fendel stared after him. The young man had certainly changed. Independent! But he was worth a little temperament. Subscriptions had soared with his coverage of the T'swa.

Varlik stopped at his own desk before he left, to place a call to the T'swa embassy. He got an appointment with the ambassador for the next morning at 07.75.

* * *

Varlik had been right. As different as they were, Mauen and Konni hit if off.

Konni hadn't learned much of value. A week after returning to Iryala, she'd been back at work and busy. She'd read or scanned everything the library had on Splenn, though, giving special attention to Splenn's politics and interstellar trade. It had been interesting but not very helpful. But clearly the Splennites—the Splennwa, Varlik and Konnie called them, using the Tyspi—had a penchant for intrigues, at least at home.

And there had been several smuggling convictions by the Confederation Tax Commission, though the Splennite reputation was worse than a few convictions would account for. Also, T'swa regiments had been hired more than once to help in power disputes on Splenn; the current dynasty of the leading state on Splenn owed its position to T'swa regiments.

Varlik in turn told them about his appointment with the T'swa ambassador. He'd call Konni afterward, he promised, and tell her what happened.

Konni left by midevening—at 17.20. It didn't seem to her like an evening to keep Varlik and Mauen up late.

Thirty-eight

It had not been a good night for Varlik, though it started exceedingly well. Near dawn he'd wakened from a seemingly unending dream in which he and his platoon had been walking through a landscape that sometimes was like the Jubat Hills, looking for—whatever. Perhaps the source of the war, of their deaths. For they were dead; Varlik, too. And their bodies had been decaying. Their biggest difficulty was that body parts kept sloughing off as they hiked. The T'swa had been in high spirits nonetheless, as if it were a holiday outing, but for Varlik it had been constant and desperate struggle.

When finally it had wakened him, he'd gotten up quietly, not to disturb Mauen, had had a drink and read a bit before going back to bed.

Nor was morning a success. Overnight a front had moved in with dirty gray clouds. Strong raw wind clawed the last leaves from the trees, sending them hurling and swirling through the parklike city, leaving skeletons behind to greet the coming winter. Varlik, waiting at the transit shelter, was glad to get aboard the hover bus, and gladder yet to get inside the government office

317

building where the tiny T'swa embassy was tucked away.

Like all government buildings, this one was aesthetic, a fact he took for granted, not consciously appreciating it. The register in the lobby informed him that the T'swa Embassy was on the ninth floor. The silent lift, rising smoothly on its AG unit, gave a broadening view of the bleak morning, and Varlik turned his back on it to face the door. The trip was quick; the government work day had already begun, and he had the lift to himself. Its doors opened to floor nine, and another register faced him as he stepped out.

The door to Suite 912 bore a simple sign that read, appropriately, "T'swa Embassy." It was open, and he walked in. A white-haired T'swa woman sat behind a desk, and smiled at him when he entered.

"Mr. Lormagen!" she said. "It's so nice to see you in person. Just a moment. I'll tell the ambassador you're here."

She's the ambassador's wife, Varlik thought, *I'll bet anything.* How T'swa that felt! *We'll see how nice they think it is when I'm finished here.* Varlik himself felt ugly and somehow perverse, but neither analyzed nor resisted it. He merely nodded acknowledgement as she touched a key on her communicator.

"Mr. Lormagen to see you," she said. Varlik couldn't hear the ambassador's reply—it came through the ear-piece she wore—but the woman smiled and beckoned as she stood up. He followed her to a door which she opened for him, and he went in.

The ambassador was standing, looking somewhat older than his secretary and a little hunched, the hunch seeming somehow the result of old injury instead of age. Yet hunched though he was, he was scarcely shorter than Varlik, and considerably heavier. His body looked solid, although his stubbly hair was white, his face wrinkled, and deeply creased knuckles gave his thick fingers a telescoped look.

His eyes still showed large, not hidden by folds of aged skin.

He reached a beefy right hand to Varlik and Varlik shook it, not surprised at its hard strength, then the old T'swi waved him to a chair. Varlik sat, putting his open shoulder bag on the floor beside him and surreptitiously pushing the "on" switch of the audio recorder it held.

"Mr. Lormagen," the ambassador said, "it is a pleasure to meet you personally. My name is Tar-Kliss. Before we address your business, let me say how very much I enjoyed your reports. I hadn't been prepared for someone of your unusual ability and dedication, with the willingness to learn our language. To train with a regiment and accompany it in combat—especially in the Orlanthan climate! And your professionalism was the highest, your affinity with your regiment remarkable."

My affinity with my regiment! Varlik's expression sharpened, his emotion hardening, focusing, targeting. What did this old diplomat, this player at intrigues, know about affinity with regiment!

"You think so!"

"Oh, yes. I am confident of it. You gave your readers, your listeners and viewers, a remarkably accurate feel of the Red Scorpions—of any regiment. I know. I was a battalion commander—for a time the regimental commander—of the Rimla-Dok Regiment, which was also of the Lodge of Kootosh-Lan. With it to the end, or within hours of the end. Deactivated forty-six years ago."

Varlik's hostility fractured and dissolved. "You were a T'swa mercenary?"

The old head nodded. "And later a monk-scholar and master of wisdom, for the last twenty-seven years ambassador to the Royal Court of Iryala."

He smiled, showing strong square teeth.

"And—how did *your* regiment die?" Varlik asked.

Tar-Kliss's smile became reminiscent, almost beatific.

"In a war between pretenders to a throne, on the planet Grovald. Two princes, both quite corrupt. It was a lovely war. Each had very presentable fighting men, in quantities, and some nicely unpredictable allies. Qualities highly contributive."

Though the smile remained, the old man's expression became shrewd now, yet kindly, the eyes penetrating but not aggressive, and he shifted the conversation into Tyspi. "But you didn't come to hear about me," he went on, "nor to hear me appreciate you. You have something to tell me, or something to ask."

"Something to *show* you." With Tar-Kliss's invitation, Varliks' mouth had gone dry. It occurred to him that he could never have given his presentation—his accusation, for that's what it was—without visible hostility, even open anger, had not the old T'swi set the scene for him with his personal history, his little comments. Another T'swa colonel! Or major, in this case. How Biltong had handled the truculent Lamons that first meeting! In Lamons's own headquarters, surrounded by his staff, in the midst of his divisions! Using just the right words, the right tone, all spur of the moment. And Lamons, as arrogant and stiff-necked as any general, perhaps more than most, had backed down without apoplexy, in time coming to respect, even admire, the T'swa.

Varlik took the player from his shoulder bag and inserted the "case" cube he'd prepared for this meeting. "If you'll turn on your wall screen," he said.

As the old man did so, Varlik switched on the player, and they listened to his recorded résumé of the war according to Colonel Voker, then continued with his recorded talk with Ramolu. Next they listened to the children in Oldu Tez-Boag. Occasionally he halted it for comment, continuing through Ban-Shum speaking Orlanthan; barges on the Lok-Sanu River with their cargoes of steel; the three carloads of steel on the siding at Tiiku-Moks; the siding and arsenal in the Jubat Forest, its products without serial numbers; and finally, the unnumbered rifle he'd taken from the dead Bird.

Once the pictures had begun to move on the screen, a relative calm came over Varlik. He felt less tense than when he'd presented his "short cube" to Mauen the day before. And when his little show was over, he asked a seemingly non sequitur question, not what he'd planned at all.

"So you knew that Central News was going to send someone to report on the T'swa regiments."

"Oh yes. In fact, I suggested it to your Foreign Ministry. They in turn suggested it to your employer, and to Iryala Video."

Varlik nodded, saying nothing for a long moment, gathering himself. Now was the moment of truth, and again his mouth was flannel-dry. "It seems to me that the T'swa are behind the Kettle War; that they armed and trained the Orlanthans."

Tar-Kliss nodded gravely. "The evidence, such as it is, seems to point that way—at least as regards arming and training. But of course someone further would be required—some smuggler, as you pointed out, and also someone who provided the Orlanthans with the floaters they've used."

He paused while Varlik reacted to the last comment. He'd overlooked the Bird floaters. "The question that comes to me now," Tar-Kliss added mildly, "is why we T'swa would do that."

Varlik's mind shifted. The old man was playing a game with him, agreeing on details while preparing to throw up barriers. They'd see how well, or how poorly, it worked. "The Splennwa could smuggle the arms in for you," Varlik replied, "and provide the floaters, too. As for a motive—Tyss has a technite deposit. It must have, to make steel. The Confederation wouldn't ship technetium to Tyss—not now, anyway."

The obsidian eyes neither flinched nor hardened. "I can assure you," said Tar-Kliss, "that Tyss has no technite.

All the technite worlds lie within a two-parsec-wide corridor, and Tyss is nowhere near it."

"Then where do you get your technetium? You make steel!"

"There is a very simple answer to that question. An answer very accessible, very open to you. Figuratively speaking, it is staring you in the face. I will let you recognize it for yourself, which you will when you are ready."

It seemed to Varlik that the conversation was slipping away from the real issue: T'swa responsibility for the insurrection, and the apparent involvement of some highly placed faction on Iryala, with their motives, whatever those might be. "Suppose I publicize what I found on Tyss, and on Kettle," he said slowly. "Or suppose one of the people I left cubes with does. People would pay attention. They're interested in the T'swa now, and the war, and they respect what I say."

The old T'swi didn't seem to change, but what he next said flustered Varlik. "How familiar are you," Tar-Kliss asked, "with the policies of Standard Management?"

"What do you mean? We learn Standard Management throughout our education, at whatever point the individual policies are pertinent. And in the fifth level we have a whole year's course on the principles. We have to. Standard Management isn't only relevant to government and business, it's relevant to the individual's management of his life! Especially the policies dealing with principles!"

Varlik realized he was tense again. Tar-Kliss by contrast was as relaxed, as casual, as—as a T'swi.

"And who," Tar-Kliss asked, "who in the Confederation is responsible for foreign affairs? Per Standard Management?"

"Why, ultimately the Administrator General, His Majesty, Marcus XXVII." Varlik began to recite from "General Principles of Responsibility": "Narrower responsibilities for specific areas and duties belong . . ."

Tar-Kliss interrupted. "That's right. And to simply publicize, indiscriminately, what you've found, with your suspicions therefrom, would be to ignore, to depart Standard Management by bypassing the proper posts. Let me quote from the same source, even if needlessly: 'To bypass any proper post is to degrade the authority and function of that post and endanger the area of its responsibility.' In this instance your king, His Foreign Ministry, and the Office of Intelligence within that ministry. Again to quote, or very nearly: 'Therefore, to bypass any official government post—whether local, district, regional, planetary, or Confederation, when that post is functioning viably, is a crime. It may be a misdemeanor or a felony, depending on the consequences. Within a business or family or in ordinary interpersonal relations, bypassing has no formal statutory standing, but has common law standing in civil suits dealing with those areas.'

"You see, of course, the point I'm making. What you were suggesting is not only seriously illegal; it is very basic."

Varlik sat chagrined.

"I am not trying to stonewall you," Tar-Kliss continued. "You simply need to take your story to the proper person in the Foreign Ministry, which for you would be the Filter Section in the Office of Incoming Communication, via commfac."

The lined black face was sympathetic. "I realize that you distrust me, but I'm quite interested in seeing where your investigation leads you. And I can help you get your information directly to a decision-making level at the Foreign Ministry without the danger of its being dismissed or backlogged by a lower-level functionary. If you will resume for a day or two the position of publicist for the T'swa, I can properly refer you as my agent directly to the Deputy Foreign Minister for Intelligence, Lord Beniker. I'm sure he will find your discov-

eries very interesting, and quite possibly he will have
information of his own that this will fit with."

Varlik was staring, not knowing what to answer. Could
Lord Beniker be an Iryalan conspirator? When he didn't
answer the ambassador, Tar-Kliss reached to his communicator, his thick fingers tapping keys. After a short
delay, a secretary appeared on the screen. "Lord Beniker's
office," she said. "Oh! Good morning, ambassador."

"Good morning to you, Jaren. I'd appreciate speaking
with the Deputy Foreign Minister, if you please."

"Just a moment. I'll see if he's available."

The comm screen went black. Varlik sat silent. If
Beniker *was* a conspirator, seeing him was dangerous.
But it was also an opening. In seconds the screen came
to life again, and from some telecast Varlik recognized
the long, strong face of Vikun Dor, Lord Beniker.

"Good morning, Tar," the image said. "What can I
do for you?"

"Good morning, Vikun. I have a young man in my
office, an agent of mine, whom I feel you'll want to see.
At any rate, I'd like to send him over to talk with you
personally. He has information that could prove considerably important to Iryala and the Confederation, and
he can present it better than I." Tar-Kliss paused meaningfully. "His name is Varlik Lormagen."

"Varlik Lormagen! Excellent! I'd like to meet the
young man, in any event." Lord Beniker turned away
as if looking at something, probably a clock. "Send him
over now. It's 08.15. He should be able to get here by
08.65 with no trouble at all; I'll inform the Routing
Desk and they'll have someone waiting to escort him.
Is that it for this time?"

"Yes, Vikun, that's all. Thank you. I appreciate your
attention in this."

"I'm happy to oblige. Let me know if there's anything more."

The screen went blank and Tar-Kliss switched off the
communicator. Varlik got to his feet.

"Why?" he asked. "Why are you doing this?"

"So that hopefully you can learn what lies behind your mystery."

For a moment longer Varlik looked at him, then turned and left. Tar-Kliss watched him out the door. When it had closed, the elderly T'swi reached to his communicator and again keyed Beniker's office code.

Lord Beniker watched and listened to the same cube that Varlik had played for the T'swa ambassador, and Varlik's comments were essentially the same. When he'd finished, the Deputy Foreign Minister, tall and rawboned, sat slouched, introspectively frowning. After a few moments he shook his head, as if to disperse like hovering flies whatever unfinished thoughts were buzzing there.

Beniker was a highly accomplished actor.

"Mr. Lormagen, that is the most intriguing, and may turn out to be the most important set of information I've had brought to my attention since I've been Deputy Foreign Minister. Admittedly, it is far from conclusive, but it certainly deserves investigation."

He stroked his jawline, one side, then the other. "The most interesting leads are on Tyss and in the Orlanthan jungle. In the latter case we have no effective access, while in the former, we have no jurisdiction—unless, of course, we decide it's essential to Confederation security. But there are things I can have looked into here on Iryala, and I'll ask friend Tar to see what can be learned on Tyss. I'll be surprised if he can't turn up something there."

Varlik frowned. "The ambassador? But if the T'swa government is part of the conspiracy . . ."

Beniker looked at Varlik as if surprised, then the surprise faded. "I see your difficulty," he said. "Few Iryalans are aware that the T'swa have no government."

"No government?"

"That's right. Tyss has no government, nor any nations in the sense of tribes or states like other resource worlds do. No other world I know of could get by that way. The various lodges, orders, and cooperatives are each to themselves a government without geographical boundaries, but without authority over anyone who chooses to stand outside them or remove himself from them. Remarkable place. The closest thing they have to an authority is the religious/philosophical order of Ka-Shok, and Ka-Shok exercises no power over anyone. It's the acknowledged parent order of the several religious/ philosophical orders on Tyss, each of them independent, but so far as I know not differing significantly from the others, or worrying about it. They seem to have split off in some far past as geographic or administrative conveniences.

"So it's the Ka-Shok we deal with, in lieu of any government. You've heard of the T'sel? The Order of Ka-Shok originated the T'sel—discovered it, if you prefer—and the T'sel is the basis of human beliefs and custom for the entire planet. So we've accepted the Ka-Shok as the de facto representative of all Tyss, and old Tar-Kliss is actually the Ka-Shok's ambassador. He's also an emeritus member of the largest T'swa war lodge, incidentally, the Kootosh-Lan—biggest of five—although that means nothing compared to his membership in the Ka-Shok. At any rate, if he decides to initiate an investigation on Tyss, he'll get cooperation, I'm sure. Not through any Ka-Shok coercion, but simply from the attitude of respect."

The deputy minister straightened. "Meanwhile, there is something *you* can do." He tapped keys on his desk console; within the desk a silent printer pushed out paper which Beniker tore off and handed to Varlik. "The address and call number of Lord Durslan, an expert on Tyss, including T'swa psychology, and occasional consultant to the Foreign Ministry. He's actually spent considerable time on Tyss. Try your presentation on him and see if he comes up with anything. Agreed? You'll do a better job of it than I."

Varlik looked at the printout and nodded. He wasn't sure, but he thought it was the same address and number Mauen had gotten from the Royal Library.

"Good," said Beniker, and tapped out a code on his communicator. From his vantage, Varlik couldn't see the screen, but audio was from a desk speaker, not a privacy receiver. And obviously, Beniker was answered by a secretary. No, Lord Durslan was away just then, but she could set up an appointment; actually, his calendar was quite open. Mr. Varlik Lormagen? Lord Durslan would be delighted to meet the young man, she was sure. Would Mr. Lormagen consent to be Lord Durslan's house guest?

Beniker turned to Varlik, eyebrows raised. "Would you?"

Varlik was flabbergasted. "I—guess so," he said.

"He would indeed," Beniker answered.

"Would tomorrow noon be satisfactory to him?" the voice asked.

Varlik nodded, and Beniker forwarded this too, as if amused at his function of go-between. The secretary said a car would be waiting for Mr. Lormagen at the airport—that he should notify them of his expected arrival time—and gave the same comm number Varlik had already been given by Beniker. The two exchanged courtesies then, and Beniker disconnected.

"A relative of Durslan's," he commented. "Sister, as I recall. Obviously not hesitant to commit him to house guests.

"So. Is there anything more, Lormagen?"

"I don't believe so, sir."

"Fine."

Beniker turned to his papers in dismissal, just as Koda would have. Varlik got up and left, gooseflesh prickling.

*   *   *

And Beniker, too, when Varlik had left, reached again for his communicator.

Beniker wasn't the only one who had a call to make. On the ground floor, central corridor, were enclosed comm booths. Varlik called Konni's desk at Iryala Video. To his surprise she was in. He summarized for her what had happened that morning, without mentioning the feeling he'd gotten when Beniker had dismissed him. It bothered him, but it also seemed paranoid to make anything of it. Konni might think he was losing his grip.

Konni's desk being one of several in a common work room, her communicator, of course, had a handheld privacy receiver. When she'd hung up, she sat for a moment, assimilating the information Varlik had given her. He'd seemed confident enough, but she was worried. He was looking for the key person in what seemed a major conspiracy, a person almost surely in some high or at least highly influential position. If that person learned what Varlik was doing, Varlik would unquestionably be in danger.

Government crime, and organized crime in general, were little experienced on Iryala, or on most Confederation worlds, but everyone was well aware of the concepts from histories, and from news, novels, and holoplays about trade worlds. She could imagine Varlik dying in some carefully staged "accident."

It also occurred to her that she was not immune. If someone should do something to Varlik—it really did seem rather unreal to her—they might suspect that she too had dangerous information. She decided to put together a report from the cubes she had plus additional recorded comments, and leave them with someone—a friend who wasn't a close friend and wouldn't be suspect. She thought she knew who—Felsi Nisben. Felsi was imaginative, a romantic, who'd take her seriously and follow through if necessary. If something happened

to Varlik, and then to her, Felsi was to turn the package
over to—who?

The Justice Ministry, obviously. But what if . . . ?
There ought to be a second person to send one to. She
thought then of Colonel Voker, who'd helped her get to
Tyss, and whom Varlik thought so highly of. Voker had
recognized that something was wrong before either she
or Varlik had. So she'd make two copies, one for Justice
and one for Voker.

I'll go home and make them right now, she decided,
and talk to Felsi tonight.

Thirty-nine

When he'd finished his call to Konni, Varlik went to the Planetary Media Center, to Central News and his desk console, and called first the Royal Library, then the Central News files, finding everything he could on the current Lord Durslan and the current Lord Beniker. There was quite a bit on Lord Beniker, rather little about Durslan, and in both cases nothing that seemed significant. All they had in common was their nobility and their attendance at the same private school. And at school they'd hardly overlapped, probably hadn't even known one another, for Durslan was nine years younger than Beniker—about ten years older than Varlik. After the national university, Beniker had gone into government service while Durslan had stayed at home to assist with the family enterprises.

Varlik turned off his terminal and called Mauen. "Hello, sweetheart," he murmured. "I'll be home in half an hour; seventy minutes at most. How'd you like to go to the conservatory? Shouldn't be crowded on a work day."

"I'd love to. And I have some exciting news for you when you get here."

"Tell me over the phone?"

"No, you'll have to wait. It's worth it, though; you'll love it."

"Hmm. If it's a disappointment, do I get to set reparations of my own choice?"

"On one condition," she answered playfully. "If it's as good as I know it is, you'll have to pay me any bonus I name."

"Bonus? All right, you're on. I'll see you."

The clouds had broken, forming fast-moving islands of cold sunshine that coursed like the raw and cutting wind through Landfall's pattern of subcommunities. Yet Varlik found himself humming as he strode toward Media Apartments Three. For the moment he had set tomorrow aside, and Lord Durslan, and the way Beniker had dismissed him.

She was waiting for him, grinning, wearing a housedress in which she somehow managed to be extremely enticing. "What's your exciting news?" Varlik asked after kissing her.

"What's yours?" she countered.

"Mine? That I'm home again with you. Ready for anything."

"That's not news," she said with a mock pout. "I already knew that."

He stepped back, eyeing her. "Not fair," he said. "I asked first. Tell me, so that one of us can collect reparations. Or a bonus, as the case may be."

"All right. We're taking a trip together!"

His enthusiasm blinked out, replaced by guardedness. "A trip?"

"A trip. I phoned Melsa Ostrak Gouer, the expert on the T'swa. When I gave the secretary my name, she asked if I was related to you, and when I told her I was your wife, she connected me with Mrs. Gouer. We had a three-way conference and—I got an invitation, too!"

Mauen beamed expectantly; Varlik only stood puzzled. "Too?"

"Mrs. Gouer," Mauen nudged. "Mrs. Garlan Gouer . . . Lady Durslan!"

Varlik stepped backward and sat down. This wasn't at all all right, but he didn't know what to say, how to handle it. He'd felt at least somewhat endangered at the prospect of going there, to some large private estate out in the forested Lake District, putting himself in the hands of people who might wish to silence him. And now Mauen intended to go with him.

She was laughing delightedly. "I thought you'd be surprised, but not that surprised," she said. "After I told them what I wanted—to learn more about the T'swa, and Tyss—the secretary told Lady Durslan she'd just made an appointment for you to see Lord Durslan tomorrow. That you'd be flying in to Lake Loreen in the morning, and someone would pick you up there. Then Lady Durslan—she told me to call her Melsa; isn't that marvelous?—Melsa asked if I was free tomorrow, and when I told her I was, she invited me to come with you. They even have their own conservatory. And a heated, glass-enclosed natatorium, so we're to bring swimsuits! Isn't that incredible!" Mauen spun in delight, a movement learned in dance. "She said she'd love to have us both for two days, even if your business with Garlan—that's Lord Durslan—only takes an hour. She said she hoped you'd talk with her about your experiences with the mercenaries; they're a part of the T'swa culture she hadn't had direct contact with. And she'd be happy to give you background on the war lodges that you might find interesting."

Mauen sat down across from Varlik. "We must have talked for fifteen minutes! And Varlik, she's such a lovely person. In appearance, too. I've already started to pack."

She paused then, for the first time perceiving that Varlik's reaction might be more than surprise. "Is anything the matter?" she asked.

"The matter?" From somewhere he mustered a smile.

"Yes. I'm worried about what that bonus is you're going to ask for."

Later, when Mauen decided to go out and buy some things for the trip, Varlik begged off, claiming need for recovery time and a nap. She laughed, then left. Tying his robe, he poured himself a cup of joma and called Konni, catching her at her desk. He told her what had developed.

"It really does sound all right," he said. "Lady Durslan made a big hit with Mauen, and Mauen's pretty sensitive to people. We're invited for two days. But if you don't hear from me by Oneday, maybe you'd better pass our information on to someone."

"Such as?"

"Whoever you think best. The authorities. And it might be a good idea to send a copy to Colonel Voker, on Kettle. You could send it by way of Captain Brusin, the mate on the *Quaranth*. Remember him? Tell him it's from me; I'm sure he'll do it. The *Quaranth* is being refitted; he mentioned it would take about ten days. And put it in a sealed package; that way he won't be tempted to snoop. It's slower than a pod, but somehow I'd feel better about it."

"Why?"

"Hmm. I don't know. Uncertified pod contents *are* subject to inspection, but it probably seldom happens."

Varlik paused. *I'm rehearsing trouble,* he told himself. "Not that it'll be necessary," he went on. "I'll be awfully surprised if it is. But it seems worth it to cover the possibility."

Konni told him then what she had done the day before, including arranging with Felsi Nisben as a backup. She hadn't told Felsi the nature of the information or that Varlik was involved.

Then she paused, hesitating. Varlik waited, sensing that she wasn't finished.

"Varlik," she said after a moment, "I've got a

question—a serious one. I like Mauen, I really like her a lot. And obviously you love her . . ."

"Yes?"

"So—why in the name of Pertunis are you letting her go with you!? Probably nothing will happen, but why take a chance?"

He looked at it. "I guess," he said slowly— "Okay. It's because she's so enthused about it. So pleased and delighted. If I tell her, she's not going to accept it. She's going to argue, and there'll be a big upset. And I'd have to make it really strong to support my refusal, make it seem really dangerous. Then she wouldn't want me to go, and if I insisted, then she'd insist on going with me. I know Mauen. She's little, and pretty, and sweet—and she just doesn't push around worth a darn.

"Like I said, the odds are good that everything there will be fine—that we'll have two of the nicest days of our lives."

Konni didn't answer at once. "Lormagen," she said at last, "I hate to say it, but I agree with you again. Have a nice trip. And tell Mauen I love her, okay?"

"I'll tell her. And thanks. Thanks a lot."

When they disconnected, a broody Varlik sipped his joma. He wondered if he'd just talked himself into something he'd regret.

PART SIX

The School

Forty

The T'swa ambassador looked up at the white-jacketed serving man. "I will have bacon, crisp, with four large poached eggs," he said, "and muffins with butter and norbal. The bacon and muffins should be in quantities appropriate to four eggs."

He poured cream in his joma then, followed by three heaping spoons of sugar, while Lord Beniker ordered. Beniker, when he'd finished ordering, put a hand on the serving man's sleeve. "And Kirt," he added, "the ambassador and I will need privacy; we have confidential business to discuss. We'll call if we need anything."

"Yes, my lord." The man left for the kitchen of Beniker's large and comfortable apartment.

"So," said Tar-Kliss, "what have you arranged? Assuming that Garlan and Wellem cannot defuse the situation."

"Well, it isn't the sort of thing I care for, but . . . First of all, we've had an interesting piece of serendipity, and you know what serendipity indicates about the dynamics of the situation. Lormagen is a professional newsperson, and his discoveries were of a delicate nature. And of course he is very newly arrived back on

339

Iryala. So it may well be that he hasn't shared his information and analysis with others than ourselves. The likeliest for him to have talked with is his wife. Nonetheless, Garlan considered it unwise to call Lormagen and suggest he bring her along; he's already suspicious, and that could easily cause him to do something unfortunate.

"*And then she, Lormagen's wife, called Melsa!* It seems she'd gotten Melsa's name from a librarian several days ago, as an expert on the T'swa, and the young lady wanted references she could read. It provided a marvelous opportunity for Melsa to establish a personal relationship and then invite her, which she did."

Beniker paused to sip his joma, which he drank black and unsweetened.

"Now, I have dispatched a team of four agents in my intelligence branch, men I can trust not to be impetuous or become needlessly physical. They'll be standing by near Garlan's, and if Garlan isn't satisfied with Lormagen's progress, he'll let them know. Then he'll have the Lormagens drugged and my men will pick them up with a light floater. They'll take them to the office of a psychiatrist in Loreen, who'll psychocondition them. He's been alerted, although of course he doesn't know yet who his subjects might be. It will take only a few hours, and when he's done, Lormagen won't remember ever having been suspicious, and he'll see nothing untoward in the information that right now has him so upset. He'll even have the idea that he spent the night asleep at Garlan's.

"I'd prefer, naturally, that none of that becomes necessary."

"Quite probably it won't," said Tar-Kliss. "I have great confidence in Wellem. But there remains the young woman journalist who was with him on Tyss. Presumably she knows at least some of what he knows. And there remains the possibility that he related his suspicions to someone else."

"Of course. I'm prepared to have the young woman abducted, if necessary. And regarding a hypothetical further person: in the process of conditioning, I'll have that looked into. If there actually is such a person, the odds are decent that we can have him picked up the following day or evening, certainly before he sees Lormagen and realizes something's amiss with him. We'll condition him and have him back at his job the next day, none the wiser."

"It would be preferable to have Wellem and Garlan work on them first," Tar-Kliss said. "Psychoconditioning is not, after all, beneficial to the mind, as witness the billions who've experienced the Sacrament."

Beniker nodded. "Agreed. But it may not be feasible for Garlan and Wellem to work on them."

As a commercial floatercraft it was small, seating thirty-two. But the season was late, and today it carried only eleven passengers besides Varlik and Mauen.

Varlik's dreams had been bad again; he'd wakened troubled and introverted, and was not a good traveling companion. He had not, of course, mentioned his worries to Mauen. She assumed that his mood simply reflected preoccupation with his mystery.

So they spoke little, watching the landscape over which they passed, an undulating countryside of farms and small towns. There were rectangular fields and pastured hills, with woods on steeper slopes, along the larger streams, and around some of the lakes. The lakes were marvelous—blue with reflected sky—for the day, if cold, had dawned clear and bright.

After a bit the land became rougher, though its hills were not high. Lakes were increasingly numerous; woods spread, became forest that held most of the ground, trees bare except where enclaves of evergreens stood, notably on lakeshores.

The panorama dispelled Varlik's grimness and left him merely grave.

The resort town of Loreen stood beside the large and vivid lake which had given its name. Or perhaps they'd been named independently for the same lady; the details lay lost in antiquity. The floater settled on the airfield at town's edge, where a chauffeur met them at the small terminal. He introduced himself as Bren.

Bren's good-mannered cheerfulness further lightened Varlik's mood. He picked up both their bags before Varlik could put hand to them, then, commenting on the welcome sunshine, led them outside to a limousine that was luxurious without ostentation, and held the doors for them. Neither Varlik nor Mauen had ridden in a vehicle like it before.

The travelway he took them on was three lanes wide, smooth and green, its grass mown short for hay. They followed it through forest broken only infrequently by small farms, past lakes whose blue they might glimpse through trees or across an occasional meadowed glade. There were numerous fine homes here, Varlik knew, but they were not visible from the road, or seldom and barely. Here and there lanes disappeared into the forest, unidentified by signs. Most, Varlik assumed, were for removing the logs of trees afflicted or well past their prime. Other lanes neatly mowed, almost certainly led—privately, unobtrusively—to the leisure homes of titled and untitled rich.

It was, to Varlik, very beautiful, though he had no least desire to live here. His glance moved to Mauen; she seemed entranced.

Before long they turned off on one of the manicured lanes. It wound through forest and down a gentle hill to a crescent of lake shore, to grounds half groves, half sunny lawn, where a home stood—a literal mansion. It probably was not Lord Durslan's ancestral home, not out here, but it was a mansion nonetheless, with two wings that seemed much too large to be accounted for by family use and servants' apartments.

He got just a glimpse of an island close offshore, with

a little stone causeway leading to it like a footbridge. There was a building on the island—a building too large, it seemed, to be merely for ornament or parties. Its architecture was something Varlik had not seen before. It was out of sight before he could sort out the curves of its graceful roof, the carved posts of its veranda, the sculpted trees and shrubs that framed and partly screened it. Then the hovercar pulled up before the house.

Bren let them out, and as he did, the large front door opened, a woman stepping onto the entry porch. By her bearing, Varlik decided, she was either Lady Durslan or Lord Durslan's sister. She met them smiling.

"Mauen!" she said, taking the young woman's hand, "I'm so pleased to meet you! I told Garlan—Lord Durslan, that is—that you were lovely, but you're lovelier still in person." She turned then to Varlik, and the hand she gave him was strong. "And you are Varlik, of course. I'm delighted to be your hostess." She examined his face. "Your picture has graced the cover of several newszines. Did you know that?"

Varlik's last misgiving expired in the light of her charm, while her uninhibited and seemingly genuine pleasure left him somehow surprisingly unembarrassed.

"My name is Melsa," she told him as she led them into the house, "and I hope you will call me that. I'm sure we all have a great deal to talk about. Right now Lord Durslan will want to meet you both. He's in his study, preparing a market analysis that he looks forward to laying aside."

A man waited just inside. He didn't fit Varlik's concept of a butler, but he took their jackets and disappeared with them into a side hall. "That's Elgen," said Lady Durslan, "a man who wears several hats here, all of them extremely well."

Varlik and Mauen walked behind her down a main hall, pausing at a well-appointed office. "This is where Rennore works, Lord Durslan's sister. She talked with you yesterday, Mauen, but she's left with her husband on holiday. Bren delivered them to the airport when he went in to get you."

A few doors farther brought them to a small, intimate parlor. Lady Durslan seated them, then went to tell her husband of their arrival. Mauen beamed at Varlik, then, remembering his earlier concern—his mission—tuned down her smile, keeping only a little of it. "I was right, wasn't I," she murmured. "She's a beautiful lady."

He smiled at her. "Not as beautiful as another one I know." They reached to each other, touching hands for a moment, and he wished they could have an hour of privacy then. *I haven't been as horny for years as I've been these past two days,* he told himself, and thought then, unbidden, of plants that produce large seed crops when dying—an impulse to reproduce before death. The thought irritated him: There'd been no threat here, nothing but the warmest welcome. Still, the notion of danger had resurfaced and would not go away by command. And interestingly, with it his ardor died.

Then he heard someone in the hall just outside, and got to his feet as Lord and Lady Durslan came in. Lord Durslan strode toward him, hand outstretched— a small-boned, slender man of less than middle height who nonetheless failed to seem small or delicate.

"Mr. Lormagen! A pleasure to meet you! And Mrs. Lormagen!" He half bowed, smiling. It struck Mauen then that these people actually were nobility, and for a moment she felt ill at ease. Not knowing quite what to do, she moved her hand to the chair arm as if to stand. Durslan raised one hand. "Please don't get up," he said to her. "We seldom stand on formality here."

He seated Lady Durslan opposite the Lormagens, and Varlik sat back down. Lord Durslan moved to a small desk with console at one side of the room. "I can turn the video screen on and off from here," he explained, "and access my own files if need be.

"I understand from Lord Beniker that you have something important to tell me, Varlik, and a video cube he'd like me to see, to do with the T'swa. I must tell you that he left me quite in mystery. But I'm always interested in anything new or unusual about the T'swa; they're a marvelous people, as you obviously know quite well."

"Yes sir, I do, and they are. The most traumatic experience I've ever had, the worst by far, was the death of the Red Scorpion Regiment. I've had nightmares ever since. But that's not what I'm here about. I do have a cube with me—partly about the T'swa, but also about other things."

"Do you mind if I record this," Durslan asked, "so I'll have copies of my own?"

"Not at all, sir; I hope you will."

Then Varlik played his cube for Durslan, commenting as appropriate. When he was done, all four of them sat soberly.

"Thank you," Durslan said. "I can see that this would trouble you." He got to his feet. "And I believe I can shed some light on it, but I'll need a little time to seek out data and prepare. I'll have cook fix an early lunch while we show you around. That will give me a chance to sort the data in my subconscious, so to speak, or my superconscious, if you prefer."

He gave instructions to the kitchen via intercom, took his guests to get their jackets, then led them through a patio door onto the grounds between building and lakeshore. The place was an utter surprise to both Varlik and Mauen. Not only was there a bathing beach and boathouse, but there was a stack of boat dock sections piled by the boathouse, and what appeared to be two conservatories. There was also playground equipment—a tall spiral tubular slide, swings, horizontal and parallel bars. . . . Varlik stopped for a moment, looking.

"There are young people here much of the time,"

Lord Durslan commented. "About forty of them currently. It's quite a lively place at times."

From there Varlik could see the islet again, a hundred feet offshore, with its causeway and intriguing building, and again Durslan, following his gaze, commented. "A T'sel *ghao*," he said, "a place where students can counsel with a T'sel master, initiates can begin advanced procedures, and adepts can pursue advanced studies under supervision, in preparation for their elevation to master. There is, of course, a master in residence here. Would you like to talk with him after lunch?"

"Oh, yes!" said Mauen.

Lord Durslan looked calmly at Varlik. "And you, Varlik?"

"Why, yes."

"Good. I'll let him know that you'll be out. He stays quite busy, actually, with several projects, and I like to warn him of impending visitors. Not that he minds, you understand; he enjoys people. We have a lot of them here much of the time, but they're gone just now, for the coming harvest festival."

As they'd talked, they'd strolled. "Would you like to visit our conservatory?" Durslan asked.

They did, spending half an hour in its fragrant, glass-enclosed galleries. The groundskeeper had just finished watering, and the air was as damp as the Orlanthan jungle, though much less hot. Some of the plants were from off world, and one tall chamber had several extraplanetary birds flying about among small trees and draped vines. The conservatory served several purposes; it was a place to walk among flowers in any season and to grow plants of many kinds. It was a source of flowers for the house, and in season, one wing produced flowering plants for transplanting around the grounds. Mauen was agog. She loved the public conservatories at Landfall, and it had never occurred to her that a household might have such a large one to itself.

They looked into the other glasshouse too—the natatorium, with its 100-foot pool and its passageway to the manor.

Like everything else, lunch was an experience. The food was light and the selection modest, but for Varlik and Mauen the quality was beyond any earlier experience. When that was done, Lady Durslan excused herself, and Lord Durslan took his guests to the *ghao*.

Both Varlik and Mauen were surprised and disappointed to find the master not a black man but white—a sinewy, middle-aged Iryalan in white duck shorts and a tee shirt, his brown hair cut army short, his blue eyes calm and direct, his smile friendly.

"Wellem," said Lord Durslan, "I'd like you to meet two friends of mine—Varlik and Mauen Lormagen. You know of Varlik, of course. Varlik, Mauen, this is our resident T'sel master, Wellem Bosler. He is one in a line of Iryalan masters originating from Master Dao of the Dys Hualuun monastery on Tyss."

Durslan stepped back. "I'll leave you to get acquainted. Varlik has brought a very interesting and seemingly drastic situation to my attention, and I need to spend some time at the computer, make a few calls—that sort of thing."

Durslan withdrew then. The T'sel master motioned to a settee, little more than a cushioned bench with back. "Have a seat," he said, and himself took a matching chair opposite.

"You'd expected a T'swi," he told Varlik in Tyspi. "I hope you aren't too disappointed." Then he turned to Mauen and repeated it in Standard. "I spoke Tyspi to let your husband know there's been continuity since Master Dao trained the first Iryalan children at Dys Hualuun more than four centuries ago. One of them was my grandmother, fifteen generations removed."

He paused, smiling, regarding the two. "So you see,

this family's interest in Tyss and the T'swa is of very long standing."

Neither guest had adjusted yet to the unexpected situation. And neither thought to wonder what he meant by "this family," which could mean his, or Durslan's, or that he was kin to Durslan. Mauen had wanted to see and talk with a T'swi of whatever kind, though she'd have preferred a warrior like those Varlik had lived and fought beside. Varlik, as Wellem Bosler had perceived, had been anticipating a T'sel master from Tyss. To Varlik, somehow, Tar-Kliss didn't count; he was an ambassador.

"Have you ever been on Tyss?" Mauen asked; it was all she could come up with.

"Oh, yes. All adepts on Iryala, when they are ready for their master's recognition, go to Tyss for their. . . ." He used a T'swa term, then saw that Varlik no more understood it than Mauen did. "It means something like 'dialog while operating in the reality of bodies.' It's more or less equivalent to the oral examination a graduate student has to pass before a committee of professors."

"And you did that?" Varlik said. "Who taught you?"

"My master was Melsa's great uncle, Tamos Ostrak."

Varlik was beginning to put things together now. "And the children who are away on vacation—they're studying the T'sel, hoping to become masters."

Wellem Bosler laughed, a pleasant laugh. "Yes and no. Only eight of our present students have Wisdom and Knowledge as their chosen area and will become T'sel masters. Of the eight, three are currently initiates and three are adepts. They serve as lectors and do much of the instruction and supervision of others. Most of our forty-two students are at Games, that being the area most satisfyingly playable in the Confederation. The games of business, government, money. . . ." It was apparent from the way he ended that his list was not all-inclusive.

"But talking alone won't enlighten you appreciably

on the subject. A touch of experience will be much
more informative, and make the words more meaningful." He got up, went to a bookshelf, and took down a
folio-sized volume. "A book of photographs from Tyss,
annotated," he said, handing it to Mauen. "They're
quite beautiful. Mauen, with your permission, and his,
of course"—he glanced at Varlik—"I'll take your husband to another room for a bit; the experience works
best in seclusion. Meanwhile, you can enjoy yourself
with this."

Mauen nodded cheerfully. "If I can have a turn later,"
she said. Varlik's response was uncertainty, tinged with
that low-intensity fear called *worry*.

"Varlik?" said Bosler.

Varlik nodded. "All right," he replied.

"Good."

They left her there with the book already open.

The T'sel master led Varlik down a hall to the opposite end of the *ghao*, where he opened a door, holding
it for his guest. Varlik didn't notice the door's thickness
or its insulated core. When Bosler closed it, the bottom
scraped dense carpet; there'd been no carpet, no floor
covering at all, in the waiting room or the corridor. The
walls inside were figured wood, unpainted and un-
stained, hung with simple paintings that were aesthetic
but most unstandard. That the walls were also effectively sound insulated was not visually apparent.

A person could howl in there without being heard
outside; even the windows were double-paned, of material responding poorly to sound vibrations.

All Varlik knew was that the place felt very relaxing.
As he looked around, taking in the pictures, his tension
drained away. They reminded him a bit of the art he'd
admired in the cantina in Oldu Tez-Boag.

There were two chairs, one a recliner. The other, by
a small desk, was a kneeling chair, like those used at

desks. Wellem Bosler waved Varlik to the recliner, then perched erect and straight on the other.

Their eyes met, and Varlik found nothing in the other man's to challenge, to flinch from, to avoid in any way. Bosler's gaze was comfortable—direct and comfortable. Varlik wondered whether a T'sel master, when he looked at someone, saw anything that others didn't—wondered and failed to notice how non-Standard the notion was.

Then Bosler spoke. "A T'sel master's functions include helping others to command their own lives more easily, and that's always a good place to start. So let me ask you a question: If there was one thing you could change in your life, what would it be?"

"Umm. I don't know. I guess—" He looked at the enigma of the Kettle insurrection, but when he opened his mouth again to answer, what came out was: "I've never been very able to laugh easily and feel really light about things. All my life I've known occasional people who seemed really cheerful and happy, as if they really enjoyed life. It's always seemed to me they had something important that I didn't; that I was missing something valuable."

Beneath his words were thoughts of those others. Mike Brusin was one. Brusin seemed to notice so much, enjoy others so much.

"All right," said Bosler. "What feeling goes with that inability?"

"Oh . . . seriousness, I guess. It's a feeling of seriousness."

"Fine. Give me an example, an incident, of something feeling serious to you as a child."

"Well . . . Once, when I was in the third level at school, we were assigned to make a little book. They passed out these little books of blank pages, and we were supposed to fill them up—draw a picture of an animal on the left-hand page and write about the species on the right. Only I did it the opposite, and didn't realize I had it backward till it was too late to do anything about it. When I did realize it, it really upset me."

"All right. Was there any emotion connected with that?"

Varlik looked back, feeling for it. "Yes. Fear. I was afraid."

"Okay. What were you afraid of?"

"I was afraid . . . I don't know. I was afraid the teacher would be angry. Or scornful. Maybe think I was stupid or something."

"Okay. So imagine, just imagine now, something that might have been done to you for getting the pages reversed. Something severe."

"Well, I could have been given a low grade—a failing grade." He blushed slightly. "Although I was only marked down one grade for it."

"Fine." All right, give me another thing that might have been done to you for getting the pages reversed. Some punishment."

"Uh, well—I could have been made to stay after school in the disciplinary office and do the whole book over."

"All right. Give me another."

"Huh! Those are about the only ones I can think of."

"Okay. Imagine a punishment. Make one up."

"Um . . . Well, the disciplinary officer could have caned me in his office, on the buttocks. That's done sometimes, you know, for flagrant misbehavior."

"Right. Remember now, we're imagining. It doesn't necessarily have to be something Standard, something actually done to children at school. Give me another thing you can imagine being done to you."

"Okay, I'll try. I could have been . . . I . . ." Varlik shook his head, looking apologetically at the master. "I can't think of anything else."

"All right. Imagine that this was on a world where they didn't know about Standard Management or Standard Technology, and people had to make up things as they went along. Imagine what might have been done to you for getting the pages reversed. Some severe punishment."

"Well, they could have . . . they could have . . . *they could have taken my recess privileges away for the rest of the dek!*" He said the last with distinct pride for having come up with it.

"Good! All right, another one."

Lag. "They could have . . . caned me in front of the class!"

"Very good! Another one."

"Uh . . . They could have caned me in front of the whole school, on a world like that!"

"All right! Another."

"They could have . . . They could have hung me, like they do on some resource worlds. They punish people by hanging them up by the neck so they can't breathe. After a few minutes they die."

"Excellent! You're doing great! Give me another."

"They could have tied me to a stake," he answered promptly, "and piled flammables around me—dry wood—and set fire to it."

"Barbaric! Another."

"They could have thrown me in the tiger yard at the zoo, after not feeding the tigers for five days!"

"Fantastic! Another."

Varlik was grinning now. "Thrown me into a pit of scorpions!"

"Horrible! Another."

"Put me in a kettle of water and brought it slowly to a boil!"

"Ghastly! Another."

Varlik's grin was ear to ear. "Cut xes on the ends of my toes and peeled my skin off them and right up my feet and on up my legs and body and off over my head!" Varlik laughed at that one.

"Good grief! Gruesome!" Bosler paused. "How do

you feel about having reversed the pages on that third-level assignment?"

Varlik laughed again. "Not very serious, I'll tell you that." Actually, serious seemed a remote condition to him just then.

"Good." Wellem Bosler smiled broadly at Varlik. "All right, close your eyes. Now, with your eyes closed— *turn around and look at yourself!*"

Varlik's hair stood on end. He didn't know what was happening; all he saw with his eyes was the inside of his lids, unfocused, dark purplish, overlaid with vague afterimages. But something was happening, something within that he couldn't describe even for himself. Externally, it felt as if his skin had drawn tight, the goosebumps pointed and electric.

"Fine." Bosler's voice sounded casual and far away, though easily heard and understood, as if it spoke directly into his mind. "Now, *erase your on-site personal history.*"

The words were like a trigger. The electric feeling discharged in waves, Varlik's body twitching and jerking like a faint version of that unrememberable but always present time as a little boy when technicians had carried out the Sacrament on him, the conditioning ritual, with their strap-equipped table, their drugs and electrodes and chant. But this time, that and much else were being erased from mind and psyche. He cried out once, hoarsely, not so much in pain as in surprise and release. It was something like a series of electric shocks, though not severe, and somewhat like an immense, too intense, whole-body orgasm. The phenomenon continued for a long half minute as he twisted and jerked, then gradually it tapered off. When it was over, he opened his eyes.

"That," said Varlik, "was the most incredible thing that ever happened to me—whatever it was."

The T'sel master was smiling at him. "Congratulations!" Bosler said. "Your handled it admirably." He got up, opened a small refrigerator in a corner, took out a tumbler and a jar of fruit juice, and poured some for Varlik. As Varlik drank, the T'sel master took paper and a pen from the desk. "I'm going to draw you a little diagram, and when you're done we'll continue."

When they entered the waiting room, Varlik was looking bemused but happy, his mind aswirl with strange unsorted experiences and concepts.

"Hello, Mauen," said Bosler. "I'm returning your husband, not too much the worse for wear." She had looked up, interested. "Varlik," he continued, "why don't you lie down on the couch for a bit. Let yourself sleep, and give old equations a chance to balance."

"A nap?" Varlik grinned. "Great idea."

"And Mauen, if you'll come with me . . ."

When she was settled on the recliner, Wellem Bosler addressed her. What, he wanted to know, was the principal barrier to satisfaction in her life. What would she most like changed?

"Lack of talent," she told him without hesitation. "I'd love to be a real artist, but I don't have much talent at all."

"All right. Tell me something bad that might happen if you had a great amount of talent. . . ."

Forty-One

Melsa Ostrak Gouer, Lady Durslan, led Varlik and Mauen to Lord Durslan's study and ushered them in. As they entered, Durslan stood and seated his guests, then sat down across from them, crossing his legs comfortably.

"Varlik, Mauen," he said, "you came here with evidence of a conspiracy. I can tell you that indeed there is one."

Varlik did not tense as he might have earlier, but he straightened slightly, alert. Durslan paused, seemed to change directions. "Tell me, what do you think of the Confederation as it now stands?"

"Well," Varlik said, "they taught us in school that we're in a 'golden age,' and when you compare recent centuries to history, I'd agree with that."

Durslan nodded. "A fair evaluation, speaking comparatively. Comparatively little strife or corruption, comparatively high living standards, government that is stable and, as governments go, rather efficient. To what would you attribute that?"

Varlik shrugged. "Standard Management, I suppose. As far as I know, Standard Technology was around

355

during the crazy days before history, and during the Empire."

"And looking at history, when would you say this golden age began? Or at least approached its present level?"

"Hmm. I don't know. Probably during the last two or three hundred years. Since the abdication of Fenwis IV in—the Year of Pertunis 371, I think it was."

Durslan nodded. "More than three hundred years after Wilman IX declared Standard Management into law. Right?"

Varlik nodded, eyes intent on his host.

"Standard Management was a definite and major factor in our present stability and prosperity, true enough," Durslan went on, "but by itself it was by no means sufficient. Among the Confederated Worlds we have hereditary monarchies with a great deal of power vested in the sovereign, as here on Iryala. There are meritocracies, in which the ruling echelon rises from the bureaucracy; and electoral democracies, in which the leaders are chosen by popular vote—all using Standard Management. Standard Management simply defines, regulates, channels *the administrative activities of the management machinery*. In a sense, that computer tank of seemingly immutable policy directives that constitutes Standard Management, those long shelves of sacred books—they are the management machine.

"But the topmost level in government—king or premier or president or first council—that authority which sets goals and aims the machine—arrives at his or her or their position in a variety of ways. Some of those people have been highly corrupt and self-seeking, and others highly ethical; some have been wise and some foolish; but most have been somewhere in between. And Standard Management has served them all, providing each with relatively efficient service.

"As you may be aware, some Confederate Worlds are better places to live than others. Their people enjoy

cleaner and more aesthetic environments, better econo-
mies, greater justice and social stability. Some of this,
of course, is due to planetary resources, but some of the
most prosperous worlds are rather poor in physical
resources. In fact, much of the difference reflects the
goals and decisions of rulers. And much of the rest
depends on how well their governmental machinery
operates: Standard Management is more efficiently applied, its policies better understood and more honestly
followed, on some worlds."

Durslan paused, regarding his guests calmly, as if
setting them up for what would follow. "Do you suppose the Confederation would be enjoying this 'golden
age' if Rombil was at its hub, and Rombil's First Council its administrator general?"

Both Varlik and Mauen shook their heads.

"Exactly. The golden age derives from Iryala, and on
Iryala it derives from an association of people who call
themselves 'the Alumni'—persons who shared certain
special training that goes beyond Standard Management."

And this is their school, Varlik thought. *That has to
be the connection.*

Durslan continued. "By ability which reflects their
training and experience, some of its members rose to
levels immediately below the Sovereign and were able
to see to it that the administrative machinery ran more
efficiently, more ethically. And in time, beginning with
Consar II, they recruited and trained the king. Every
prince since then has been educated and trained by the
Alumni in one of their schools."

"Some of them right here, I suppose?" Mauen asked.

Surprised, Varlik glanced at her. She never before
would have interjected something like that into a conversation with a man of rank. The experience of the day
was changing her as well as him.

Durslan smiled. "Actually, no. There is a less vener-
able school more suitably located. But both teach the

T'sel. There are eight such schools on Iryala now, and several on other Confederation worlds."

Varlik's eyebrows rose.

Durslan unfolded his legs and steepled his fingers. "There is a flaw in this 'golden age,' however. If our environment was as unchanging and self-contained as is generally assumed, it might not be a major flaw. But our environment is neither unchanging nor self-contained. You see, we, the humankind of this region of the galaxy, are not all the humankind there is. Nor is humankind the only intelligent life form."

"I've read about the concept," Varlik put in. "Generally, it's ridiculed. Do you have actual evidence for it?"

"You can read the evidence for yourself when we're done talking here. I believe you'll find it interesting. Basically, though, there *is* history which predates what the Confederation knows about—a great deal of such history.

"Now, about this matter of not being alone in the galaxy: It poses a danger, one which the Confederation as it presently stands is seriously unsuited to deal with, should it present itself—as it surely will. The conspiracy you detected, and the insurrection on Kettle, are the beginnings of a program to correct that deficiency."

The hands steepled again. "That is only some background to what I'll tell you about the conspiracy. But the rest must wait until you've read the outline of that 'prehistoric' history, and talked with friend Wellem again. How does that seem to you?"

Varlik grinned. "I'll let you know when I've read the history and talked with Wellem."

"Good enough," said Durslan grinning back, and they all got up.

Varlik's changing, thought Mauen, *just like I am. He'd never have said anything like that to a nobleman before. It'll be interesting, getting used to each other again.* But she had no qualms.

*   *   *

For supper, Konni Wenter commonly used the meal service in her building, even though it was somewhat more expensive than preparing meals herself. She seldom felt much like cooking after a day's work anymore. Being a team leader was more demanding than being Bertol's assistant, especially with the green assistant they'd assigned her. Also, it paid somewhat more, making the meal service more affordable.

She was eating in front of the video—braised beef cooked with gondel pods, over steamed barley with a side dish of steamed vegetables. There was a pint of ice cream in her locker for dessert. But tonight she was out of sorts, wasn't enjoying the meal. She should have invited someone for supper, she told herself—either a chum or the new guy in the sports department who'd taken her to lunch yesterday.

Her communicator buzzed and she got up to answer it. The face on the screen was a grinning Varlik, with Mauen beaming over one shoulder.

"Are you free tomorrow?" Varlik asked.

Tomorrow was Sixday, and B-crew had the weekend duty. "Yes," Konni said, "I'm free."

"Great! We're calling from Lord Durslan's. And look, things have sorted out beautifully up here. Can you come up? You have an invitation from Lord and Lady Durslan to get a rundown on things. We both really hope you'll come."

Their faces seemed to peer out at her as if, she thought, the screen were a window. "Why, I suppose I can." Somehow she felt muzzy-headed, as if she'd just wakened from a nap.

"Good. Look, *Lakes Air Transit* flies up here. I'm not sure what their weekend schedule is, but call and make a reservation. I'll call you back in an hour and you can tell me your arrival time. There'll be a car waiting for you at the terminal." He paused. "You okay?"

"Yes, I'm okay. This is just kind of sudden."

He looked back over his shoulder, as if someone was saying something to him.

"Konni, Lady Durslan says forget calling for reservations. The flight is on her and Lord Durslan; she'll arrange your reservations from here, against her credit print. I'll call you back and tell you the flight and time. How's that?"

"Uh, fine. That's fine. I'll be here."

"Good. I'll talk to you again in a few minutes. Oh, and pack your swimsuit. They have a big natatorium here," he added, then switched off.

She stared at the blank receiver, then went back to her meal. *Something's strange about that,* she told herself. *That was Varlik, no doubt about it. And Mauen. And they both looked all right. But there was something different about them. Not as if they were being forced to call; there was no one off to the side pointing a gun at their heads.* She tried to consider possibilities. *Maybe they've been drugged.* She didn't find the notion convincing, though. Things like that only happened in novels or holo dramas.

She returned to her meal. They were all right, she told herself. They'd just taken her by surprise. Getting all that stuff explained and straightened out could easily affect Varlik like that, considering how it had troubled him all these deks.

She finished eating and had just disposed of the debris when the communicator buzzed again. It was Varlik, and he gave her the flight number. He seemed just fine, but his grin was still not entirely real to her. She supposed she'd seen him grin before—she was sure she had, she could think of instances—but not like that.

After he'd hung up, she tapped in Felsi's number. It took a moment; Felsi answered with tooth cleaner on her lips.

"Oh, it's you," Felsi said.

"Who'd you think it was going to be—Reev Stoner?"

"I should wish. What's going on? Anything about . . . ?" she asked suggestively.

"Sort of. Look, Varlik Lormagen and his wife are up

in the Lake District, guests at the home of Lord Durslan. Lord and Lady Durslan are very interested in the Kettle insurrection, and the T'swa. And I'm invited to go up there; I'll fly up in the morning.

"Now, I have no reason to think anything will happen to me while I'm gone, but it's possible. So look. I expect to be back Sevenday evening; I'm supposed to be at work on Oneday. If I don't call you by Oneday night, something will be wrong, and you know what to do. Okay?"

Felsi nodded, big dark eyes staring out at Konni.

"Fine. Like I said, I'm about ninety-nine percent sure that nothing's going to happen to me while I'm gone. I just don't want to take any chances. And thanks."

When she'd hung up, Konni stared worriedly at the wall. She'd deliberately tried to put Felsi at ease. It seemed to her that in reality, the odds that nothing would happen to her while she was gone were more like sixty-nine percent than ninety-nine.

After "visiting" again with Wellem and talking with Konni, Varlik and Mauen retired to their room, but not yet to sleep. Lord Durslan had given them books from a classroom—books the children studied there—on the history of the Confederation, of the T'swa, and of T'sel. Hours passed before they went to bed, and the world changed even more for them.

In his sleep, Varlik was once more with the regiment—the platoon, actually—and they were in the sawmill in the Jubat Hills. But it was too noisy there, almost impossible to talk (although afterward, remembering, Varlik could not recall any actual audio sensation; it was the concept of noise). So they were somewhere else—not *went* somewhere else but *were* somewhere else—in a beautiful, quiet landscape of neat lawns among wooded, storybook mountains. And the platoon—led now by Colonel Koda—examined him with questions. It was an incredibly warm and beautiful experience. And for every question they asked, he had the answer, an ideal answer, lucid and brilliant.

He awoke at last, sat up in the darkness of the room with tears running down his cheeks. There was no grief, though, only a joy of reunion which seemed no less real for having been experienced in dream.

Of the dream, he could remember nearly all, with images of the world where they had tested him, a world not Tyss or Iryala or anywhere he knew of. He could remember how good it had felt to be there with them. He remembered everything except the questions and the answers, and their absence didn't seem important at all.

Because somewhere, he told himself, he knew. Smiling, he lay back down, rolled over, and went to sleep again, this time dreamless.

Forty-two

The night had brought hard frost, and a thin ring of ice along the lake edge, not at all like a night on Kettle or Tyss. But by a little past midmorning, when Bren drove up in front, the sun had raised the air temperature to over fifty, and in the virtual absence of breeze it felt even warmer.

Mauen had ridden in to meet Konni at the landing field. By the time they arrived at the estate, Konni was feeling relaxed; it was obvious that Mauen was all right, so Varlik must be, too. Mauen had smoothly avoided saying anything of substance about what had happened, slipping questions, letting Konni think she hadn't been privy to Varlik's conversations with Lord Durslan.

Melsa and Varlik greeted them on the porch. And no, Konni admitted to Lady Durslan, she hadn't eaten. She'd slept too late for breakfast. So she had a late breakfast at the manor while Varlik, Mauen, Lady Durslan, and belatedly Lord Durslan, kept her company over joma. They'd already breakfasted.

Konni, of course, was unwilling to question Varlik while the Durslans were present.

When she'd finished eating, Lord Durslan suggested

she get acquainted with the situation in the same order that Varlik and Mauen had, and they all trooped over the causeway to the *ghao*, where she met Wellem Bosler.

She'd taken Bosler a bit longer to open up than had Varlik or Mauen; her distrust had reactivated, a distrust more deeply rooted in personality than Varlik's had been, but a half hour later she'd emerged in much the same state that Varlik and Mauen had.

Then Melsa had shown her to her room and left her for a short nap. All three guests had spent the afternoon with books. Briefly, *The Story of the Confederation* had upset Konni, and Wellem had guided her into and through a brief, gentle procedure that had taken care of her problem with it. That evening, Lord Durslan had given her approximately the same rundown he'd given Varlik and Mauen the day before, with the others sitting in. Like Varlik, Konni came out defused.

The next morning, Durslan promised, he'd give them the full story of the conspiracy.

Felsi Nisben had had a date for that evening, but he'd called to say he had to work. So she'd had a solitary supper followed by a solitary drink. Then she thought about the mysterious package Konni had left with her, and the strange, danger-spiced instructions.

It seemed to Felsi that if Konni expected her to do something like that, she'd owed it to her to tell her what it was all about.

Actually, Felsi resisted temptation for more than an hour—until drought hit the video and she'd had another drink. Then swiftly, not to argue herself out of it, she unwrapped one of the two packages, fitted the cube into her player, and turned it on. A quarter hour later she told herself she wished she'd never thought of it, wished Konni had given it to someone else. Actually she was thrilled; Konni and her friends obviously were in very real danger. Why Konni hadn't taken it directly to the authorities was more than she could understand.

She took Konni's folded instructions out of her handbag. The business of taking a package to the spaceport and getting in touch with some Captain Brusin sounded altogether too difficult and complicated. And this Colonel Voker, deks away on the planet Kettle, wouldn't be able to do anything in time anyway. But the Director of Enforcement in the Ministry of Justice—he was only minutes away.

Then she reminded herself that Konni had said to do nothing before Oneday night. If she hadn't heard by Oneday night, then she could do something. She also reminded herself that she'd broken faith with Konni by opening the package.

Again swiftly, not to change her mind, Felsi rewrapped the package and returned it to her closet shelf. Then she had a double drink and went to bed.

The sign said "Cool Drinks." It was in Bird, and that surprised Varlik, even if it was in the middle of the Orlanthan jungle. Sergeant Kusu, wearing camouflage fatigues and his original chin, stood in the cantina door beckoning to him, and Varlik went over.

The cantina was much bigger inside than out, not very wide, but long. And hazy. Lord and Lady Durslan were there, wearing only breechclouts. For a moment Varlik tried not to look at Lady Durslan's breasts, and realizing this, she laughed. They were much bigger than Varlik would have thought, jutting roundly. The sling on her rifle passed between them, and it seemed to Varlik that she'd have real trouble unslinging it in an emergency.

All six of them then—Mauen and Konni were with him too now—walked along inside the cantina looking at the artwork. One of the pictures was of the arsenal in the Jubat Forest, and in it he could see Konni and himself looking out of the picture at him from behind door posts; both were waving to him from the picture, which seemed to Varlik very unusual. Kusu also saw them waving and, winking, nudged Varlik. Kusu was wearing a breechclout too now. Varlik took a rifle from one of the cases and looked for the serial number. Instead of a number, the words *Made on Tyss* were engraved on it.

As they walked, it was no longer the cantina, but a long, greenly lit aisle through the jungle. Varlik was impressed because, as he reminded himself, he didn't usually dream in color. All along the aisle were small stone steles marking the places where men of the regiment had died. Kusu named them off as they passed. At each one, Lord Durslan saluted and laughed, and as he did, a holograph of the T'swi who'd died there rose out of the ground and laughed good-naturedly back. But they were only holographs, Varlik knew. He asked Tar-Kliss, who was with them now, why holographs? Tar-Kliss told him the bodies had decayed, so the T'swa were using holographs to greet visitors with.

At the end of the aisle were the lake and the causeway, but the lake looked like the Lok-Sanu River and the causeway was a bridge. A bargeload of steel was passing beneath it, and Varlik looked down at it. Then Wellem Bosler called from the *ghao*, and they all hurried across and went inside. The whole regiment was there waiting, their new bodies looking just like the old ones, and General Ramolu was with them.

Ramolu came up to Varlik, shook his hand, then told him good-naturedly that he'd screwed the whole thing up. No, Varlik answered, it will all work out. Wait and see. It will all work out. Kusu laughed. It always does, Kusu said. Either way, it always works out.

With that, Varlik awoke and sat up. The moon had risen, and the curtains glowed with it. Very briefly he remembered the whole dream as a panorama, then most of it slipped away. All that was left, beyond some general impressions, was himself telling Ramolu that it would all work out, and a laughing Kusu saying it always did; either way, it always worked out. Varlik chuckled and shook his head. He didn't know what it was all about, but it felt right. He went back to sleep hoping to dream some more, but if he did, he didn't remember it afterward.

PART SEVEN

Resolution

Forty-three

Felsi Nisben woke up knowing what she had to do. Hurriedly, she got ready and left for the transfer stop with one of the packages Konni had given her, not taking time for breakfast. She often skipped breakfast on Sevenday anyway, and besides, she might think as she ate, and she couldn't afford to think. Right was right, and it was not okay to sit around rationalizing the way she'd done last night.

It was a matter of withholding evidence, and delay could endanger Konni's life—if she wasn't already dead. The thought sent delicious shivers through Felsi.

She'd gotten off the bus outside the Tower of Justice before it occurred to her that there might be no one available to see her. This was Sevenday, after all; that's why she was here instead of at work. *Though this takes priority over work anyway*, she reminded herself. *It's a matter of—Planetary? Confederation?—Planetary security at least.* The concept was so exciting she had another rush of shivers. They'd *better* be open here on Sevenday—this Sevenday, at least.

The lobby was different from any she'd seen before: there was no receptionist, though a solitary security officer eyed her thoroughly and impersonally as she passed him. There was no place to sit, just a long hall with a row of elevator doors down each side, each door marked with a single floor number.

There was a register; the *Office of Enforcement* was on the sixth floor. She went to one of the elevators marked sixth floor and touched the decal. The door opened at once. The elevator had been waiting for her, she told herself. A good sign; she was doing the right thing. She hadn't had to wait for a bus, either. It had come within fifteen seconds, a minor miracle; usually it took at least a couple of minutes—as many as ten on a weekend.

She wasn't aware of the electronic units that scanned her for various materials as she rode up. Had one of them detected contraband, the elevator would have taken her not to the sixth floor but to building security in the basement. And had she known that—duty be damned: Clean though she was, she'd never have gotten on the elevator.

But she didn't know, and psychologically fortified by good omens, she exited the elevator confidently into a reception area. Here security, though not a dominating presence, could clearly be seen—three officers sitting in little corner booths. The receptionist wore civvies, and watched politely as Felsi came up to her.

"How can I help you?" the receptionist asked.

"I have a package I need to give to the Director of Enforcement."

"Fine. May I have your name and registry number?"

"Felsi, F,E,L,S,I, 686 Nisben, N,I,S,B,E,N, 2546–3129–3217 Iryala."

As Felsi spoke, fingers moved on a keyboard, then the woman looked up and reached out a hand. "I'll see that the director gets it."

Felsi's expression hardened with unwillingness. "I'm supposed to give it to him myself. It's very important."

"I'm sure it is, Miz Nisben. But there are Standard

policies we have to follow. Otherwise, this place would be a madhouse and nothing would get done." She kept her hand out, expectantly.

Felsi shook her head stubbornly. "It's an emergency. And important."

The receptionist nodded. "Are you reporting a crime in progress? If so, we need to inform the local or district enforcement authorities."

"No, it's nothing like that. It's—special. Different."

"I see." The woman made a decision. "Let me show you something on my screen. I'm going to write something into the computer, and I want you to see the read-out."

She swiveled her screen enough that Felsi could see, then her fingers ran over the keyboard again. Suspiciously, Felsi watched words form on the screen:

SITUATION: IMPORTANT EMERGENCY, NOT A CRIME IN PROGRESS. PERSON REPORTING SITUATION WISHES TO REPORT IT TO THE HIGHEST PERMISSIBLE POST. WANTED: IDENTITY OF HIGHEST PERMISSIBLE POST.

The receptionist touched a final key and the words vanished, replaced by a short block of text. Her fingers moved again, isolating a line and enlarging it:

THE REPORTING PERSON MAY BE ALLOWED TO SEE THE EMERGENCY ALERT OFFICER ON DUTY.

"That's as far up as I can send you," the receptionist said with finality.

Felsi stared at the line. At least this would get her closer to the top, and she still wouldn't give up the package if she didn't want to. "All right," said Felsi, "I'll see the emergency alert officer."

The receptionist pressed a button. A moment later a young man arrived and led Felsi to an office door. He made no move to knock, only stood there by Felsi until a buzzer sounded. Then he opened the door and ushered her in without following her; the door closed. A sturdy, pleasant-looking woman was seated at a desk.

"Miz Nisben," she said, "how can I help you?"

Felsi repeated her request.

"Felsi—may I call you Felsi?"

Felsi nodded.

"Felsi, I'm not unsympathetic toward your feelings about this, but I'm required to follow policy; it's a matter of Standard Management. I'm simply not allowed to let you see the director except under very special circumstances. And at any rate, he's not in today. On weekends one of the assistant directors serves as acting director."

For a moment Felsi froze, didn't know what to do. "Will he be in tomorrow?" she asked.

"Almost certainly."

"Then I'll come back tomorrow."

"Wait a moment." The emergency alert officer regarded Felsi thoughtfully. "How important is this?"

"Extremely important. It could even mean life or death for a friend of mine."

For a moment the woman's eyes withdrew in thought, then returned to Felsi. "If your information is that important—for example, if someone dies because you withheld it, or if any major felony results—the act of withholding could constitute a felony on your part."

Her fingers too moved over a keyboard, and when she was done she swiveled her screen so Felsi could see the law she'd called up on it. The language was straightforward; Felsi read it.

"That's not a threat, dear," the woman went on kindly. "It's simply something that, under the circumstances, you need to know. Let me ask you another question: What is the nature of your information?"

"It's about—a conspiracy against the Confederation."

The emergency alert officer's expression didn't change.

She doesn't believe me, Felsi thought. *If she did, she'd look shocked or something.*

After a moment the woman asked, "Where did you get the information?"

"It's from a friend of mine with Iryala Video, who worked with Varlik Lormagen on Kettle. Both of them were wounded there. He gave it to her because he thought something bad might happen to him, and she gave it to me because she thought something might happen to her; it's all on the cube."

This time the woman's lips pursed for a thoughtful moment, and she drummed her fingers. Then she reached to her communicator and held a privacy receiver to her ear. "Monti," she said, "I'm bringing a young lady down to see the assistant director. . . . Right now. Yes. . . . I'll let her tell you that."

She hung up then and stood. "Felsi," she said, "this had better be good, because I'm sticking my neck out for you. The assistant director for internal operations has the duty this weekend—he's the highest ranking person here today. I'm taking you to see his secretary."

Hand on Felsi's arm, the woman led her out the door. "I'm allowed to deviate from protocol if I consider a situation sufficiently urgent. Standard Management allows for it. But if this is bullshit, I could be busted down to the secretarial pool."

The woman's words numbed Felsi for a moment, but she regathered her certainty. On another hall they stopped before a door, and the emergency alert officer opened it without hesitation. A lean, dark, youngish man sat waiting, hard-eyed and skeptical.

"This is Felsi Nisben," the woman said.

"All right, Felsi," the man said, "what have you got for us that's too important for normal routing?"

Felsi repeated what she'd said before. The man glanced at the emergency alert officer, frowning, then back at Felsi.

"So I repeat: what is there about all this that can't go

through normal routing? Why does the assistant director have to handle it?"

At that moment she got an inspiration. Of course! she thought. She'd known there was an important reason why Konni had addressed it to the director.

"Because it involves a foreign government and an Iryalan nobleman."

The man's eyes sharpened. After a moment he reached to the privacy receiver on his communicator. "Sir," he said, "the emergency alert officer has brought a young lady in. I think it best you see her."

Fifteen minutes later the assistant director, another lean and humorless man, was on his own communicator to the director, Lord Ponsamen, at his home. "And involving as it does a lord of the realm," he said, "perhaps two of them, I felt it best that you be informed. Personally? I see your reasoning, sir. . . . Within the hour, sir; I'll bring a squad."

Twenty minutes after that, with Felsi in tow, the assistant director was on the roof of the tower with a squad of armed marshals, loading into an unmarked, armored hover van.

"To Lord Ponsamen's residence," he ordered, then said nothing more.

Lord Ponsamen was waiting, not willing to fly away without first seeing some evidence. So while the squad lounged on an enclosed veranda with the driver, Ponsamen, in his study, viewed and heard the cube with the assistant director and Felsi. Lord Ponsamen watched the screen while Felsi covertly watched Lord Ponsamen. Tallish, he verged on portly, a man blond and pink, with pink, beefy hands. He was immaculately manicured, Felsi noted; she'd been a manicurist once. She had no idea what he was thinking; he looked as if he found the cube fairly interesting but not very exciting.

Yet when it was over and he went to his study closet,

she saw him don a shoulder holster before putting on a casual jacket. He paused briefly to draw the weapon and examine it, as if making sure it was ready for use, ejecting the clip to see if it was loaded. "Haven't carried this for, hmm, more than six years," he commented, holstering it, then redrew it three times more, swiftly, as if reinstalling old trained reflexes.

He looked at the assistant director and Felsi. "All right," he said, "let's go see what Lord Durslan has to say about all this."

To Felsi, he sounded as blasé as if he were going out to walk the dog.

Forty-four

The pool was cooler than Konni had expected, not something for lolling in. In middle and upper school she'd been on the swimming team, and now began to swim laps, smoothly, powerfully, enjoying the unaccustomed feel of her muscles pulling and stretching. But she tired rather quickly, and hands on curbing, hoisted herself out of the pool without using the ladder. Varlik and Mauen were splashing each other while Wellem Bosler swam strong easy laps along the opposite side.

That Varlik's got almost a gymnast's physique, Konni thought, *and Mauen looks like a dancer*. She'd have to get her own weight down, she decided.

The one that surprised her was the T'sel master. His face said forty-five but his body suggested a vigorous thirty-five. She wondered which was closer. The face, she supposed. *Konni*, she told herself cheerfully, *you need to get yourself a boyfriend and stop this secret ogling. Too bad Wellem doesn't live in Landfall*.

Bosler too climbed out of the pool, and walked around to sit down by her. "How do you like it here?" he asked.

"So far so good," she answered. "I know for sure I like

what's happened to me so far; I expect I'll like it even better when it's had a chance to settle in more. It feels as if things are changing in me that I don't even know about."

"That's the way it works," he said with a chuckle. "It's especially noticeable with adults. I had one call me up to tell me he'd just realized he hadn't felt regret for at least a year."

The concept startled Konni. Regrets were part of her standard repertory of feelings, or had been. She wondered if she'd regretted for the last time.

They were interrupted by Melsa, who announced that if they'd had enough of the pool, Garlan was in his study, ready to give them a rundown on "the conspiracy." She said the last two words with an emphasis after a pause, then waited. Varlik and Mauen swam to the ladder and got out, too.

"I'm ready," Varlik said. "How about the rest of you?"

Konni had already gotten up. "Me, too," she said, and looked at Bosler, who grinned back at her.

"I'll sit in," he answered, "although I'm probably familiar with most of it."

They separated to the two dressing rooms, dried, groomed briefly, and dressed, then regathered in Durslan's study. They'd just sat down when Elgen, in his role as butler, looked in without knocking.

"Excuse me, sir, but a hover van has just landed in the yard and armed men have gotten out."

"Thank you, Elgen. I presume they'll be coming to the door. Let them into the entry hall and then call me. I'll pretend surprise."

Elgen departed. "Well," said Durslan, "something unexpected to spice the day. Why don't we postpone my little seminar until we see what this is about."

They waited. Varlik wondered if the armed men had anything to do with the conspiracy. It occurred to him that for most of his life, a situation like this would have made him tense, guts tight, perhaps feeling half suffocated. Now he simply felt alert.

Konni wondered accurately if it had anything to do with Felsi Nisben and the packages.

Distant door chimes sounded. A minute later Durslan's intercom buzzed, and he pressed the receiver switch. "What is it?"

Elgen's voice answered; Durslan was taking it on the speaker so his guests could hear. "A group of gentlemen from the Justice Ministry, sir," said Elgen. "Lord Ponsamen, a Mr. Jomsley, a Miz Nisben, and eight armed personnel."

Shit! thought Konni. *I blew it! How in the galaxy do we handle this?*

"Armed personnel? Indeed! I'm with guests just now, but I suppose— Make the armed personnel comfortable in the front sitting room. They're no doubt on duty and can't drink alcohol, but have edibles brought out for them, and joma. Is Lady Durslan at hand?"

"She just came into the entry hall, sir."

"Good. Ask her if she'd kindly bring Lord Ponsamen and the two other persons you named to my study. A Mr. somebody and a Miz somebody."

"Yes, sir."

They could hear Elgen talking briefly to someone. More faintly others spoke. "Madam will bring Lord Ponsamen, Mr. Jomsley, and Miz Nisben down at once, sir," Elgen reported.

The comm went still then. "Armed men," said Durslan. "Curious." He sounded utterly unperturbed. Again no one spoke, and in a minute Lady Durslan opened the door. At that point, the three men present stood up—Durslan, Varlik, and Bosler.

"My dear," Lady Durslan announced, "Lord Ponsamen, Miz Nisben, and Mr. Jomsley." She ushered them in, then left. Jomsley was dour and Ponsamen genially businesslike. Felsi looked at Konni and almost cringed;

clearly, Konni was perfectly well after all, and so were her friends.

"Good morning, Durslan," said Ponsamen, and looked around. "Seems we're interrupting something. Can't be helped, though; I'm here in an official capacity, and I need to speak with you."

He eyed Varlik. "You're Varlik Lormagen, aren't you? And one of you must be Konni Wenter," he added, looking at the two young women.

"I'm Konni Wenter," Konni answered. "I'm afraid I don't know what your official capacity is, Lord Ponsamen."

"As well you might not; I'm not exactly renowned. Lord Durslan knows me; I'm the Director of Enforcement, in the Department of Justice."

He turned his attention to Durslan again. "I'd like Lormagen and Miz Wenter to stay. Feel free to dismiss the others if you'd like, though if they leave, I'll require that they join my men in your sitting room until we're done and I approve their further departure."

"Perhaps you'd care to tell me first what this concerns," Durslan answered.

"It concerns information on a certain cube made in part by Miz Wenter and in part, I believe, by Mr. Lormagen."

Durslan nodded. "I see. In that case I suggest they all stay. I believe they're familiar with the information you're referring to. There's no use their sitting in my parlor wondering what's being said about it in here."

So dreams can be prophetic, Varlik thought to himself. He remembered what Ramolu had said in his dream last night: "Lormagen, you screwed the whole thing up." *Funny that I picked Ramolu to say that in my dream. And Kusu said it would all work out.*

Varlik's chuckle was soft, yet every eye in the room turned to him.

"You've something to tell us, Mr. Lormagen?" asked Ponsamen.

"Not really. I was just looking at how this all came about."

One eyebrow raised, Ponsamen's gaze stayed on him for a moment, without any hostility that Varlik could sense. Then the director looked back to Durslan. "Please turn on your wall screen," he said, and Durslan complied. "Mr. Jomsley, prepare to play the cube."

Jomsley had brought a player from his office, a quality machine. For the next ten minutes or so they all viewed the by-now-familiar scenes, heard familiar words, with Konni's paraphrased summary of Varlik's suspicions and conclusions, and her concern about Varlik's safety here. When it was over, Ponsamen cleared his throat quietly.

"Now I believe you understand the presence of armed marshals. And while it appears that Mr. Lormagen and Miz Wenter are in fact quite well, that leaves unanswered the implications of the material recorded offplanet. Tell me, Lord Durslan, how do you account for what appears to be criminal conspiracy?"

Durslan leaned back in his chair, arms folded. "Let me begin," he said, "by stating that I serve as a consultant to the Foreign Ministry. And as we just heard, Lord Beniker referred Mr. Lormagen to me—not because Lord Beniker is unfamiliar with the facts, but because I am more fully conversant with the details. The Foreign Ministry has been aware of the enigmas described for some time now, as also in part the army has been. And you can see why the Ministry has given them a top-secret rating.

He gestured casually at Varlik. "Mr. Lormagen encountered certain peculiarities and, being particularly energetic, thorough, and persistent, took them to Lord Beniker, who found himself confronted with the distinct danger of someone knocking over the soup, so to speak.

"So Beniker arranged for Varlik to visit me here. I was to explain matters to him, and make him privy to whatever data and work in progress I saw fit—which is a good deal more than I am free to do for you, I might add. From me you'll have to settle for a summary.

"At any rate, as it occurred to me that Mr. Lormagen might have shared his information and suspicions with his wife, she too was invited. And when he learned the facts, he called Miz Wenter, who had shared both his investigations and suspicions. She arrived yesterday.

"And now here you are! Without your swimsuits, I'm afraid, though well equipped in other respects." Durslan smiled perfunctorily.

"The Foreign Ministry has activities in progress on several worlds, directed toward the solution of the enigmas pointed out. And as I've indicated, I'm not at liberty to discuss them. Perhaps Lord Beniker will be willing; certainly the authority is his. You might wish to ask him . . ."

"As I will," Ponsamen put in.

"One thing I am free to tell you about," Durslan continued, "is the matter of the T'swa arsenal, which is not, I hasten to add, to be talked about. It is, however, less sensitive information than the rest, being rather peripheral. Some centuries ago the Sovereign, in his role as Administrator General of the Confederation, agreed that the T'swa could manufacture steel for their domestic use, and allowed them to import small quantities of technetium for the purpose. Then, several years ago, our present Sovereign licensed them to manufacture their own light weapons—indeed, the only kinds of weapons they use—for their own use. Existing regiments, of course, still carried weapons of Iryalan manufacture, but new regiments were to be equipped with T'swa-made arms as available."

"About three years ago, the T'swa requested a rush shipment of Iryalan-made arms to Frey Marzanik's World. It seems that a supply of T'swa-made weapons had been shipped there for a T'swa regiment en route—a virgin regiment on contract to one of the warring states there.

Unfortunately, the supply base was overrun before the T'swa arrived, and the weapons were lost—weapons which the T'swa themselves weren't prepared to replace quickly. Thus their urgent request for replacement arms."

Durslan shrugged slightly. "From there the T'swa-made arms obviously found their way into some as-yet-unidentified smuggling channel, and thence to Orlantha, a fact of which we were well aware prior to Mr. Lormagen's independent discovery in the jungle. Our own intelligence branch is sorting out possible trails, which quite conceivably may provide us the identity of whoever made possible the Orlanthan insurrection."

Durslan straightened. "And that, Lord Ponsamen, is the story in a nutshell. Meanwhile, let me point out that even had there been some details in this mishandled by our government, I, as a consultant, would scarcely be liable. And as you can see, the Lormagens and Miz Wenter are quite well, so I believe your business with me here is at an end. I regret that your weekend was disrupted by this misunderstanding, but as we know, this sort of thing happens in government service."

Durslan stood then, signaling the end of their audience. He'd completely taken charge. "I trust you will keep all of this scrupulously confidential. To leak it could seriously compromise our investigations, and your positions as well, no doubt. I'll also trust you not to copy the cube you played here; I recommend you give it personally to Lord Beniker."

Ponsamen raised his large body from the chair more easily than might have been expected. A sour-looking Jomsley and an embarrassed Felsi got up, too.

"Indeed!" Ponsamen spoke a little stiffly now. "I shall personally take these matters up with Lord Beniker this coming week." He turned and followed Durslan from the room, accompanied by Jomsley and Felsi Nisben.

When the study door had closed behind them, the

Lormagens and Konni looked at each other, while Wellem Bosler sat back smiling. After a minute, Konni spoke quietly. "I told Felsi to do nothing before One-day night. She must have gotten curious, opened a package, and played the cube. And got all excited and worried. She may also have delivered a package to Captain Brusin."

"The *Quaranth* won't leave before Threeday, at the soonest," Varlik replied. "You'll have time to get it back if she gave it to him."

Lord Durslan returned several minutes later. "Well," he said, "they're off the ground. Now. Where were we?"

"You were going to tell us about the conspiracy," said Mauen. "Or was that it? What you told Lord Ponsamen?"

Varlik grinned. "I thought I detected some fictions in your story, sir. For example, in my experience, admit-tedly limited, a T'swa regiment travels with its weap-ons. They're not shipped ahead."

Durslan nodded. "No doubt. I thought I did rather well for spur of the moment fabrication, though." He held up an audio recorder. "I have it all on here, incidentally. When one lies, it's well to have a record of what one said."

"Maybe you'd better get a copy to Lord Beniker," Konni commented. "It sounds as if Lord Ponsamen is going to question him."

"I will get a copy to Beniker. But Ponsamen won't question him—not in any official sense, certainly. What Ponsamen and I said here was to mislead Jomsley, let him think that all of this was being handled and that Ponsamen was going to verify it himself. So that Jomsley could dismiss it all from his mind as a good Standard bureaucrat should.

"Incidentally, Ponsamen's an excellent actor, wouldn't you say? He needs to be. You see, he's an alumnus of our school here, as I am, of course. A classmate of Beniker's, matter of fact, and knows a good deal more about the conspiracy than you do. Which, if you will all sit and listen, I will now remedy."

He looked them over, smiled, and began.

"First of all, let me say that the conspiracy grew out of the T'sel, the Way, but began here on Iryala, not on Tyss. The T'sel is the T'sel anywhere, but persons who know the T'sel will create different activities in different environments.

"Until 630 years ago, interest in the T'swa was simply in their value as mercenaries. Then a son of the Ostrak family, Barden, decided to travel to Tyss and see how T'swa mercenaries were trained; it seemed to him that something of value might be learned there. He'd heard about the T'swa climate, and had planned to stay only two or three weeks—less, if it was too oppressive. He ended up staying four deks, though it was summer, retreating to his lander for sleep, some of his meals, and at any other time when the heat threatened to overcome him.

"On his return, to his wife's dismay, he arranged to send their second son, age five, to Tyss to learn the T'sel. They supplied him with an air-conditioned sleeping chamber, which, incidentally, the lad outgrew the need for. Within three years there were three Iryalan children on Tyss, and by the time the eldest was ready to come home there were seven. They returned wiser than their parents, by criteria Iryalan or T'swa, had already recognized the need for thoroughgoing change in the Confederation, and had begun to develop the basic features of a plan.

"Of course, they mentioned none of this to their families. Instead, with the backing of Barden Ostrak, they established a school on the Ostrak estate, which was later moved to this more secluded and aesthetic location.

"The alumni of the school, and of other schools which were established later, came to refer to themselves collectively as 'the Alumni,' as I mentioned to you yesterday. We do not have a formal organization, but we collaborate and keep one another informed.

"Incidentally, it's extremely unlikely that any other such illegal, conspiratorial society could have existed unknown in the Confederation for six centuries, or even six decades. Perhaps not for six years. There'd be dissension, group suppression of dissenters, desertions, and dissident splinter groups, and secrecy would be lost. And of course we are very non-Standard, and therefore susceptible to psychiatric imprisonment.

"The keys to our continuation have been the effectiveness of the T'sel in unlocking human potential, and the fact that its truths are sufficiently basic and self-discoverable that we act with a very large degree of agreement, to which are added mutual trust and respect.

"We impose no truths, incidentally, require no Beliefs or Standard behavior, preach no Basic Premises. Each of us discovers his own truth for himself or herself, but these have a high commonality from one person to another, and at the least are compatible. The T'sel drills simply make it possible and more or less inevitable that we do discover them. One person may come up with a talent or cognition that most others do not—to each his own, we say—and there are different levels of attainment, especially for those who play in the field of Wisdom and Knowledge. But there does exist that large area of commonality, of mutual experience and wisdom."

Varlik interrupted. "You said drills. What about guidance by questions, the sort of thing Wellem did with us?"

"What Wellem used with you are mostly techniques developed by Iryalan masters to help non-T'swa adults or older children. When children grow up in the T'sel, few such procedures are necessary. Mostly they grow up open and knowing, with few barriers to be removed."

Durslan drew his thoughts back to his dissertation. "At any rate, the early Alumni soon began to assume prominent positions in government. Firstly, they were very largely of wealthy, or at least well-to-do families, well connected, as is commonly still the case today. Secondly, their T'sel education and training allowed them to excel both in learning and decision making, and of course they were emotionally very stable. So when they left our school for college or the universities, they invariably did exceedingly well. And thirdly, their understanding of human behavior and their ability to deal with human emotions allowed them to manage human activities with unusual skill."

He grinned then at his audience. "There's a fourthly, too, but I'll leave you to discover it for yourselves.

"Unfortunately, though, because of the Sacrament and the social strictures and laws that grew out of it, the Alumni have been unable to break Standard Technology, despite the various high posts held—including the Crown for these many years."

"You talk about breaking Standard Technology," Varlik said. "What about Standard Management?"

"Standard Management is remarkably viable; it needs relatively little change. The limitations lie in Standard Technology and the psychconditioning that underlies it."

Durslan paused, as if shifting gears.

"You've read now that humankind exists elsewhere, in the home sector from which our ancestors came, and you've also read about the garthid. There are other races, too, some of them wanderers, which our seers and those of the T'swa have perceived. Some of those cultures, human and nonhuman, are predatory, with the ability to conquer or ravage worlds and peoples no better prepared than ours to cope with them. There is physical evidence, as well as observations one can make while in advanced T'sel states, that certain of them visited this sector of the galaxy before our ancestors came here, with power that dwarfs anything the Confederation has."

"Can you give us an example?" Mauen asked.

"Certainly. There once were much more extensive seas on Tyss. Millions of years ago they were removed, drawn off to about the present level, by a race which for some reason wanted and was able to take that remarkable quantity of water." He scanned the others. "Consider, if you please, the technology required to accomplish that!

"So far as we know, however, none of them has the T'sel. While we, having it, have the apparent potential to grow beyond their force and to raise a civilization like no other we know of. Yet as it stands now, we're cemented into technical and cultural immobility. So our first challenge has been to break the grip of Standard Technology on the Confederation.

"The conspiracy is the second step in that; the first was to quietly gain widespread positions of influence and power in the Confederation.

"It has been necessary to move carefully, which in this case has also meant slowly. Nearly three centuries ago, Orlantha became the new technite planet. Rombil was given it in fief, and decided to use slave labor, which was their legal right per policies on the exploitation of resource worlds. Foreign affairs, as you may not know, is a field rather largely outside the purview of Standard Management. The administrative *machinery* is Standard with a capital S, but the purposes of interplanetary relationships, and in part how they are carried out, are not covered by Standard Management.

"Early, there had been a trickle of slave escapes which the Rombili didn't take seriously because replacements were easily gotten, and the Rombili correctly considered the condition of the fugitives so desperate as to render them no threat.

"But the Alumni saw opportunity there. Standard Technology has it that steel cannot be made without technetium. We already knew this was false, but dared not say it. The falsity was attested by the tiny steel industry of the T'swa, which the Alumni knew of early and which for millennia had made steel without technetium.

"If this had become known in the Confederation two centuries earlier, it might have brought down aerial attacks on the T'swa, and the destruction of the material progress they had made, setting them back into primitivism and hunger—depending on who was sovereign here, and who his advisors. At the least, Tyss would have been embargoed—quarantined as unfit for human contact. While here, the knowledge of steel without technetium would have been encysted, walled off as a singularity, an unimportance not allowed to influence Standard Technology. Steel made without technetium would have been described falsely as very inferior, not fit for civilized use.

"But if the Confederation's supply of technetium were cut off, and the need for steel became serious enough, non-technetium steel might be accepted if properly introduced. The people who provided it would have to be considered as somehow outside of Standard Technology, and thus free of the stigma of apostasy. And if somehow they were already admired, they might even be regarded rather as *wizards*, a concept from antiquity meaning, loosely, those who operate beyond understood reality."

Durslan scanned his guests, noting their lack of conviction. "At any rate, that is the basis we've operated on—and with promising results. For example, Varlik, because of your very effective help, the T'swa are already admired in the Confederation, most particularly on Iryala and Rombil.

"As for acceptance of non-technetium steel, and of whatever other non-Standard introductions and innovations we may undertake, who do you suppose has controlled the Sacraments on Iryala the last twenty-three years? Indirectly, of course. Twenty-three years ago last Sixmonth we obtained a Crown decision, written but of course not publicized, that Standard Technology did not require the hypnotic drug to be prepared at the individual Sacrament Station by the station's High Technician. The rationale was that absolute Standardness was better served by preparation at a central laboratory—run by Alumni, as it happens. So a generation of children on Iryala, and increasingly on other worlds, has been treated not with the hypnotic drug but with a strong soporific that puts the person into a sleep too profound for hypnosis."

Durslan scanned his guests for any sign of difficulty with that knowledge. There was none.

"That small alteration of Standard Technology," he continued, "in its guise as a bolstering of it, seems to have been the first since at least the Amberian erasure.

"As a result, there are billions of young people in the Confederation today whose attitude toward Standard Technology is social only, not enforced by the Sacrament. The attitudes of most of them toward Standard Technology are presently pretty much like everyone else's, but they are much more susceptible to change.

"Incidentally, the Sacrament and other psychoconditioning is not irreversible. You lost yours, and a great deal of other burdensom mental baggage, in your first session with Wellem.

"But that is only groundwork. We also instigated the insurrection and its step-by-step escalation. Recently, technite production began again on a small scale at Beregesh; a pod arrived with the news late yesterday, and the jubilation has begun. In four or five days another pod will bring news that the refinery there has been destroyed again, along with the mine head, *by intense bombardment with superior lobber rockets of a design not known to Standard Technology*, launched from well outside the new Beregesh defense perimeter by Standard infantry lobbers whose range is supposedly somewhat too short.

"You can imagine what the effect of that reversal will be. The technetium shortage has already become desperate. Steel mills have shut down entirely on several worlds. Then, by a major and highly publicized effort, the situation seemed to have been brought under control. And suddenly the primitive gooks come up with an unexpected resource, this one beyond Standard, and the situation suddenly looks hopeless."

"One of the weaknesses of Standard Management, let alone of Standard Technology, is its severely limited ability to adjust to the needs of large-scale emergencies. Take my word for it, throughout much of prehistory in humanity's home sector, an insurrection like that would have been suppressed in far less time. Normal procedures would have been suspended and all necessary ingenuity and resources concentrated on handling it."

Durslan grinned wryly. "Consider. The resources of all twenty-seven member worlds could have been mobilized to handle the Orlanthan insurrection, and no doubt would have been if Standard Management allowed. While in the absence of Standard Technology, the resources of either Rombil or Iryala alone would have been enough, although in that case the situation would never have come up in the first place.

"But getting back to reality. A few days after public announcement that the refinery has been destroyed again, a T'swa metallurgist will arrive from Tyss, imported by the Crown. He'll bring with him the T'swa formula for making steel without technetium. And under the circumstances, he and his gift to the Confederation will be gratefully accepted and abundantly praised.

"Beyond that, our program is mostly rather loose and conditional, depending on events. But we Alumni are serendipitous, and accordingly optimistic. There will be an offer of autonomy to the Orlanthans—their technite will still be valuable, just not essential—and much rewriting of law concerning the rights of resource worlds in general. We'll continue to publicize the T'swa, expand our T'sel schools, and further defuse the Sacrament network. And we'll begin to introduce, little by little, the concept of *science*, which you encountered in your reading here and which will come to mean more to you, I'm sure."

Durslan spread his hands in front of him. "And that's about all there is to that, unless you have questions."

"You haven't told us how the weapons were smuggled to the Birds," Konni said.

"Ah! Of course! Sorry I overlooked that. Even on most trade worlds we have Alumni in at least a few positions of power or influence. On Splenn, for example, there is the large and wealthy Movrik family, which owns the planet's only interstellar merchant fleet—eleven ships. The other Splennite interstellar carriers are one- or two-ship operations, and it's those small carriers who've earned the Splennites their reputation as smugglers.

"But it's the honest and highly reputable Movrik family who hauled arms to Orlantha. Before the insurrection began, Rombil had no surveillance or security system on Orlantha. None was considered necessary. So smuggling was simple, and precautions rudimentary. The smugglers needed only to avoid encounters with the ore barges, which was easy because the barges followed very regular approach routines.

"Since the insurrection began, of course, smuggling has required extraordinary procedures and been restricted increasingly to ammunition and medical supplies. It has involved landings on an island safely outside the area monitored by surveillance platforms, and uses modified harvester submarines protected from detection by the high turbidity of the larger jungle rivers. On the lesser rivers they operate on the surface, under cover of bank forest."

Varlik nodded; the picture was developing for him. "And the T'swa trained the Birds?" he asked.

"Centuries ago the T'swa educated an Orlanthan cadre—educated them as children, on Tyss, in the T'sel.

That cadre then went home and trained a larger cadre, the foundation for the new Orlanthan culture, the jungle culture. Much later, when the time came, a new Orlanthan cadre, a military cadre, was trained on Tyss."

"How did the Orlanthans become so numerous?" Varlik asked. "Our military command on Kettle was continually having to raise their enemy manpower estimates."

"That was a matter of smuggling, too. We've been working on this for a long time, you understand. It was T'swa who found early escapees and led them south to the jungle. Later, T'swa-trained recruiters from the tropics were flown north to recruit additional Orlanthans. On some coastal islands, far to the north, lived tribes driven there from the mainland by rival tribes. Island resources are limited, and population pressures can develop which can't be successfully alleviated by emigration because the neighboring shores and fisheries are occupied by stronger tribes. Some entire island tribes were transferred south two centuries ago—several thousand people. Most of the insurgents are descended from them."

"It sounds to me," Varlik said slowly, "as if a lot of people have been manipulated."

Durslan's calm eyes met Varlik's without challenging. "Oh, definitely. Since the first Sacrament was delivered on the refugee fleet, hundreds of billions have been manipulated by coercion of the most extreme sort, and in early childhood at that."

"Touché," Varlik answered. "But I'm talking about Orlanthans."

"Ah. Of course. Since the first slave roundup by the Rombili . . ." He grinned abruptly. "Yes, we've manipulated them, too, in a manner of speaking, but never coercively. It is axiomatic in the T'sel that persons be given the broadest self-determinism appropriate to their ethical level. The island tribes were given an alternative to oppression and chronic hunger, and accepting it, were brought south to serve our purposes. By other Orlanthans, let me add, acting on their own determinism. For by that time the Orlanthans had made the idea of insurrection their own.

"You see, you cannot successfully manipulate people, once they learn the T'sel, but you can collaborate with them on the basis of overlapping interests and mutually held reality."

Varlik didn't respond for a long moment. His attention was elsewhere. When he spoke again, it was slowly. "All right. I can see that." Again he focused on Durslan. "There's another question that bothers me though."

"What's that?"

"The regiment, or regiments—sacrifice of. Why?"

"From our point of view and the viewpoint of our program, the use of T'swa mercenaries permitted strong and favorable publicity of the T'swa. From the mercenaries' point of view, it provided a good war."

Durslan leaned toward Varlik, forearms on knees, a pose unexpected of a nobleman. "Tell me, Varlik, are you familiar with a chart known as *the Matrix of T'sel?*"

"In a general way. It's been explained to me, but I forget the details. I probably have a copy somewhere."

"Good." Durslan got up and stepped to his desk, where his slender fingers tapped keys on his keyboard. The wall screen lit up, and a moment later a chart appeared on it, the now-familiar Standard translation, with an arrow. The arrow moved to the top row, the right-hand column. "Does this entry fit your impression of the Way of the T'swa warrior?" Durslan asked.

Varlik nodded. "Right. 'War as play,' " he read aloud, " 'victory unimportant.' " Then the words of Usu, the T'swa medic on the hospital ship, came back to him, clearly, almost as if he were hearing them again. " 'If you are truly at Play,' " Varlik quoted, " 'death will not matter to you.' A T'swa told me that on the ship to Tyss. And I accepted it as a concept, but it wasn't really real to me. It still isn't."

It struck Varlik then what made it unreal. "How can the T'swa," he asked, "how can *anyone*, find satisfaction in a war without purpose? Without a purpose meaningful to them? On Kettle, did the T'swa know what was going on—that they were being used?" *Or would they have cared if they'd known?* he added to himself.

"They may have known," Durslan said, "but I rather doubt it."

He stroked his chin contemplatively. "You asked how they could find satisfaction in a war without a purpose meaningful to them. Recognize first that you asked that from a particular point of view. Now let me ask you a question—a very personal question. Do you have children?"

The seeming non sequitur stopped Varlik. "Not yet. We hope to, though. We've recently gotten clearance."

"Fine. What was the purpose of your sex life before you got clearance? Was it a source of joy and happiness? A form of pleasure without regard to production of offspring? Sex as play?" Durslan paused to smile. "And now that you have clearance for children, do you go to bed with the attitude of a worker going to his job?"

Varlik smiled back ruefully, then unexpectedly laughed. "Okay, I see what you're getting at. I've had several T'swa, two at least, talk about the matrix to me. But you're the first one to find an approach that worked. Or maybe I was just ready this time."

Durslan grinned. "Maybe you were. Now, one more thing while I have it on the screen: Where do you fit on this chart?"

"Huh! Well, when I first went to work I was at 'Work for Survival'—payday, the weekly credit transfer. Then I moved to 'Work for Advantage'—promotions and raises."

"Fine. And very valid, both of them. But right now, does it seem to you— Can you imagine yourself operating at the level of, say, Job as Play, with reward unimportant? Not 'no reward,' but 'reward unimportant.' "

"I can imagine it, but it's not entirely real to me."

He turned from the screen to look at Durslan again. "Where are you on the chart?"

Durslan moved the arrow. "Games as Play. So is Beniker. So are Tar-Kliss and Wellem, even though, as Masters of Wisdom, they were at Study as Play for years. They moved to Games as Play when they agreed to take part in the game of overhaul the Confederation. At any lower level—say, at Compete or Fight—they couldn't hope to succeed in a game like this one."

Varlik contemplated the chart, and the things that had been said to him by Durslan, Usu, Kusu, Bin. To T'swa mercenaries, war was an activity as pure as healthy sex, and apparently as satisfying. Eventually, through death or wounds, they lost the ability to play at war any longer. That would happen to him with sex someday, through death or age or whatever.

And the people that the T'swa fought and killed? They were people at War, too, participating in it at levels of Fight or Work, most of them, though apparently not the Birds. That's why the T'swa warred as they did—very personally, knowing who they shot at, not killing indiscriminately, but so far as feasible shooting or striking only those who'd chosen war or allowed themselves to be coerced into warring.

"Okay, I can see it intellectually," Varlik said, "and I'm beginning to feel it at a gut level."

Durslan reached and the screen went blank. "Fine," he said. "Can I interest you in employment?"

Varlik's brows rose. "What do you have in mind?"

"Formally, you'd be self-employed as a free-lance writer. But the Foreign Ministry would contract with you confidentially to write certain types of articles, scripts, and books that would help prepare the people of the Confederation for changes to come. And it would be best if you stayed here; you could have an apartment in our guest house. Information and consulting would be more readily available to you, and Wellem could work on your education. Mauen could be your secretary." He laughed again. " 'Reward unimportant' wouldn't mean you couldn't afford to pay a secretary. You'd be well paid."

Varlik looked at Mauen; her eyes were bright and on his, expectantly.

"Garlan," Varlik said, "consider me your free-lance writer." *Job as Play! By Pertunis!* It was beginning to feel real to him.

Durslan turned to Konni. "And as for you, Miz Wenter, in the new phase the program is entering, we have need of a video photographer, director, and producer. I'm sure that we—you and Wellem and I—can develop some attractive projects."

She laughed. "If you hadn't offered, I'd have refused to budge until you did. This sounds like the best game around."

"Good. Then let's talk about terms and timetables. I'll want you available as soon as possible."

Forty-five

He was in a little two-seat floater, flying over steep, forest-covered, storybook mountains, and remembered seeing them before in a dream. *And I'm dreaming again*, he thought. *Even if this is in color*.

Below was a large fjordlike lake, richly blue, the mountains rising directly from its mostly beachless shores. Ahead, around the shoulder of a mountain, a broad park appeared, open and grassy, its green as rich as the lake's blue, Here and there were small colonnaded marble buildings with rounded roofs, and marble walks and benches. Not a typical dream setting—not a stage with props, so to speak. It was rich with detail.

The floater bent its course toward the lawn, where a large number of children were playing. *Some of them are T'swa*, Varlik told himself. *Some are black and some white*. The children stopped as the floater approached, watching calmly, not quite motionless. It seemed to Varlik that somehow they'd expected him.

Strange dream, he told himself. *But what dream isn't?* He knew who the children were, too. The regiment. Black or white, they were the regiment.

The floater was on the ground, on the lawn, and he

got out. There was no sense of his feet impacting the ground, and he told himself that proved it was a dream, if proof was needed, or made any difference.

The place was holding remarkably stable for a dreamscape, though. As detailed and stable as reality.

Then the children began to play again. He got the impression of voices laughing and chattering, but without the normal playground shrieking. *Of course not. They're the regiment,* he reminded himself. Several came walking up to him—his old squad, with Kusu. "We've been waiting for you," Kusu said, looking up at him.

A marvelous dream, Varlik thought again: *The impression of sound is almost real, almost sonic.*

And Kusu's face was Kusu's face, though he appeared to be perhaps nine years old. "Are these your new bodies?" Varlik asked. "You look half grown already, but you've been dead less than two deks."

Kusu grinned Kusu's grin. "Rules like those don't apply here," he said. "Time here is different. But that has nothing to do with how we look to you. We look like this *for* you."

A recollection came to Varlik then, of something he'd read as an adolescent in a book of myths from prehistory. *Is this heaven, then?* he wondered. He didn't want it to be. He wanted Kusu and the others to have recycled, to live again in bodies, back in the universe of reality.

But they were here and they were dead. And if *they* were dead . . . "Am I really here?" he wondered aloud.

Kusu laughed happily. "Of course. You're always here."

"Then—I'm dead," said Varlik slowly. The thought didn't upset him at all.

"No, you're dreaming."

That's right. This is a dream. It's not supposed to make sense. This is my superconscious playing.

"It doesn't feel like an ordinary dream. It's so detailed. And it doesn't shift around." Varlik tapped his foot on the ground, and this time felt the impacts. "Why am I dreaming this?"

"It's the clearest way for us to communicate with you. Look!"

He pointed, and Varlik turned around. Another child had walked up behind him, and Varlik stared, recognizing him at once: Himself, also about age nine.

Himself grinned at him. "We wanted you to know we're here," Himself said cheerfully. "You've—you and I have—taken on an interesting game, but don't expect everything to go smoothly."

"Know consciously," Varlik echoed. "Does that mean I'll remember this dream?"

It was Kusu who answered. "The parts you decide to. When you're ready for them."

"Will I come here again?"

"Probably. But like I said: Yourself is always here."

Of course! Turn around and look at yourself! Varlik nodded and changed the subject. "Some of the regiment is white now, but you're still blue-black. Are you going to be a mercenary again?"

"No. I'm going to play at Wisdom and Knowledge next time." Kusu laughed. "More knowledge than wisdom: I'm going to be a scientist. It'll be lots of fun, and open the doors to all kinds of neat games and jobs. Science is going to be the big thing to do in thirty or forty years, and I want to be in on the ground floor."

Science. Varlik recalled the term from some reading Lord Durslan had given him, but the meaning was vague yet.

"And will you remember after you recycle? Remember being a mercenary? Being Sergeant Kusu?"

"Possibly. But that isn't important. On this side I'll never forget. On the other—it depends on several factors."

"Will I ever see you again?" Varlik asked. He found he didn't want to lose touch with Kusu now that he'd found him again.

"Oh, yes. We'll see a lot of each other. I'm going to be Iryalan my next cycle. In about eight deks."

"Will we recognize each other?"

"On one level, certainly. But the life one is living is always the important one.

"I hope you get good parents."

"I will. I will. I've got my penalty slate quite clean; that allows me to choose."

The blue-black face grinned up at Varlik, the eyes friendly and touched with playfulness. Then the story-book world began to fade, the face fading with it, and as they disappeared, child Kusu's voice was saying, "Parents? I've picked the best, my friend, I've picked the best."

Then Varlik awoke. He knew he'd been dreaming, though he didn't remember what. Something good. Maybe it would come back to him.

He sat up in the dimness and looked at Mauen asleep beside him. She stirred restlessly; perhaps she was dreaming, too. He leaned over and softly kissed her, and her eyes opened. She smiled and reached for him.

ROBERT A. HEINLEIN

"Heinlein knows more about blending provocative scientific thinking with strong human stories than any dozen other contemporary science fiction writers."
—*Chicago Sun-Times*

"Robert A. Heinlein wears imagination as though it were his private suit of clothes. What makes his work so rich is that he combines his lively, creative sense with an approach that is at once literate, informed, and exciting."
—*New York Times*

Seven of Robert A. Heinlein's best-loved titles are now available in superbly packaged new Baen editions, with embossed series-look covers by artist John Melo. Collect them all by sending in the order form below:

REVOLT IN 2100, 65589-2, $3.50 ☐

METHUSELAH'S CHILDREN, 65597-3, $3.50 ☐

THE GREEN HILLS OF EARTH, 65608-2, $3.50 ☐

THE MAN WHO SOLD THE MOON, 65623-6, $3.50 ☐

THE MENACE FROM EARTH*, 65636-8, $3.50 ☐

ASSIGNMENT IN ETERNITY**, 65637-6, $3.50 ☐

SIXTH COLUMN***, 65638-4, $3.50 ☐

JOHN DALMAS

John Dalmas has just about done it all—parachute infantryman, army medic, stevedore, merchant seaman, logger, smokejumper, administrative forester, farm worker, creamery worker, technical writer, free-lance editor—and his experience is reflected in his writing. His marvelous sense of nature and wilderness combined with his high-tech world view involves the reader with his very real characters. For lovers of fast-paced action-adventures!

THE REGIMENT
The planet Kettle is so poor that it has only one resource: its fighting men. Each year three regiments are sent forth into the galaxy. And once a regiment is constituted, it never recruits again; as casualties mount the regiment becomes a battalion . . . a company . . . a platoon . . . a squad . . . and then there are none. But after the last man of *this* regiment has flung himself into battle, the Federation of Worlds will never be the same.

THE GENERAL'S PRESIDENT
The stock market crash of 1994 made the black Monday of 1929 look like a minor market adjustment . . . the rioters of the '90s made the Wobblies of the '30s look like country-club Republicans . . . Soon the fabric of society will be torn beyond repair. The Vice President resigns under a cloud of scandal— and when the military hints that they may let the lynch mobs through anyway, the President resigns as well. So the Generals get to pick a President. But the man they choose turns out to be more of a leader than they bargained for . . .

FANGLITH
Fanglith was a near-mythical world to which criminals and misfits had been exiled long ago. The planet becomes all too real to Larn and Deneen when they track their parents there, and find themselves in the middle of the Age of Chivalry on a world that will one day be known as Earth.

RETURN TO FANGLITH

The oppressive Empire of Human Worlds, temporarily foiled in *Fanglith*, has struck back and resubjugated its colony planets. Larn and Deneen must again flee their home. Their final object is to reach a rebel base—but first stop is Fanglith, the Empire's name for medieval Earth.

THE REALITY MATRIX

Is the existence we call life on Earth for real, or is it a game? Might Earth be an artificial construct designed by a group of higher beings—a group of which we are all members, and of which we are unaware, until death? Forget the crackpot theories, the psychics, the religions of the world—*everything* is an illusion, everything, that is, except the Reality Matrix! But self-appointed "Lords of Chaos" have placed a "chaos generator" in the matrix, and it is slowly destroying our world.

PLAYMASTERS (with Rod Martin)

The aliens want to use Earth as a playing field for their hobby and passion: war. But they are prohibited from using any technology not developed on the planet, and 20th-century armaments are too primitive for good sport. As a means of accelerating Earth to an appropriately sporting level, Cha, a galactic con artist, flimflams the Air Force Chief of Staff into founding a think-tank for the development of 22nd-century weapons.

You can order all of John Dalmas's books with this order form. Check your choices below and send the combined cover price/s to: Baen Books, Dept. BA, 260 Fifth Avenue, New York, New York 10001.*